BITTERSWEET

When Desiree focused on Gerard again, he was walking toward the stands with a ball in his hand.

His well-conditioned body looked magnificent in his uniform, Desiree thought. He was strong, with every muscle outlined against the fabric. He tossed the ball toward Desiree and surprisingly she caught it. "Thank you," she called out. By the way her pulse raced, she would have thought she was available. She had to glance at her engagement ring to remember she was marrying Paul.

Desiree shivered. She felt as if a change was in the air.

Bittersweet

Candice Poarch

Kensington Publishing Corp.
http://www.kensingtonbooks.com

DAFINA BOOKS are published by

Kensington Publishing Corp.
850 Third Avenue
New York, NY 10022

All Kensington Titles, Imprints, and Distributed Lines are available at special quantity discounts for bulk purchases for sales promotions, premiums, fund-raising, and educational or institutional use. Special book excerpts or customized printings can also be created to fit specific needs. For details, write or phone the office of the Kensington special sales manager: Kensington Publishing Corp., 850 Third Avenue, New York, NY 10022, attn: Special Sales Department, Phone: 1-800-221-2647.

Dafina and the Dafina logo Reg. U.S. Pat. & TM Off.

First Dafina mass market printing: July 2006
10 9 8 7 6 5 4 3 2 1

Printed in the United States of America

To my son, Gerard,
for his love of the game.
Thank you for answering so
many questions about baseball.

Acknowledgements

My sincere thanks to readers, book clubs, booksellers, and librarians for their continued support. A special thanks to the radio stations that promoted *Discarded Promises*.

As always, profound thanks to my parents, sister, and critique partner, Sandy Rangel, for their unswerving help. Thank you, Ferdinand and Betty Thomas, for supplying helpful information about PTSD and the military. Thank you, Gwen, for information on Atlanta. Please try her delicious recipe for lemon pepper chicken wings in back of the book. I am deeply grateful for my husband's continued support for my writing. And last but not least, thanks to my writer friends for keeping me sane.

Desiree Prescott heard the phone ringing even as she tried to twist the key in the lock of her sixth-floor apartment on Manhattan's West Side. Dropping her purse on the foyer table, she sprinted to the kitchen and caught the phone on the fifth ring. It must be Paul, her fiancé, making sure she'd cleared her schedule that weekend for his mother's visit.

She didn't believe that every mother-in-law was the devil incarnate, but Paul's mother was the exception to the rule. Mrs. Tremain wanted her stamp on every part of the wedding, as if it were her wedding, and that just didn't sit well with Desiree.

"I've been dialing this phone all night trying to reach you. It's a work night. What you doing out so late?" It was her aunt Nadine Smith from Macon, and dreaded anguish soared through Desiree.

"Had a late dinner meeting, and then I stopped by Paul's place." Aunt Nadine didn't call unless there was a problem.

"It's nearly about midnight."

"I know. The city never sleeps, Aunt Nadine." There was no need to check the answering machine. Her aunt never left messages.

"Well, we got trouble."

"Daddy's off his medication?"

"Stopped that couple of weeks ago. But he got this call today. At least I took the call. He won't talk on the phone when he's in one of his moods."

"What call?" Desiree asked. Her aunt could go off on a tangent for an hour of complaints before she got to the subject.

"This lawyer fellow in Atlanta called. Said your daddy had a son by some woman when he was in Vietnam. Name's Jordan Payne."

Desiree stumbled into a chair. "What?"

"Yeah. Your daddy's name is on the birth certificate. Can you believe it? He grew up no more than an hour and a half drive from here."

"Is it true? Is Daddy his father?"

"Levi said it could be true. He met the woman while he was there. Timing's right. Got pictures and stuff stored in his trunk. He pulled that stuff out. Every five minutes he came running over here to show me a picture of the woman or something from that time. You know how sentimental he gets."

"I know." His sentimental outbreaks had been commonplace when she was growing up. Especially when he wasn't on his meds. He liked to talk about the good days, before the war.

"Problem is, the boy and his wife died four months back. Bless their souls."

"Oh no. . . . "

"Yes, Lord. What a crying shame. They left three youngins behind. The wife was an orphan, so she's got no family except for some distant relative who took the kids in. But they were strung out on something. The baby was crying one night and the wife went crazy and hurt him."

"Oh my gosh. How bad?"

"Broken arm. Can you believe someone would hurt a defenseless baby? I don't know what this world is coming to. Social Services took 'em away, and a good thing, too. But I don't know about having ballplayers keeping them."

"Ballplayers?"

"They're looking after 'em till the lawyer hunted up family."

It was too late at night for Desiree to absorb all this. "How is the baby?"

"Out of the hospital, thank the Lord. I guess he isn't in any worse shape than he was before, but I don't like it. I tell you, folks need to get into the church. That's where your salvation is. All this mess in the streets isn't good."

Desiree's head swam with the information thrust at her. Maybe the sports players were married. She cut into her aunt's sermon.

"What's the lawyer's name? Did he leave a phone number where I can reach him?" Desiree searched for a pen and pad.

"Honey, since your daddy's been off his medicine, he can't go. And you know he can't keep those children anyway. I got my hands full with keeping an eye on him."

"I know."

"Let me get my glasses so I can read the number to you. Be right back."

Desiree heard her aunt mumbling in the background while she searched for the eyeglasses. She imagined her in her gown and housecoat, a satin cap covering little pink rollers in her hair.

"They were right on top of my head," she said when she finally returned. "If it had been a snake it would've bit me." She read off the information, including the address of the lawyer's office.

"How is Daddy taking the news?" Just one more thing to send him into depression.

"He's holding on. Clammed up. Never know what he's thinking. Especially since he's off his medicine. I tried to get him to take a pill, even got the pastor to come out and talk to him, but he wouldn't listen. He pushed the man right out of his house and shut the door in our faces. Told us not to come back. I'm his sister. How could he say such a thing to me? I told him he had the pure devil riding in him. Embarrassed me so bad I can barely hold my head up in church."

"I don't know why you did that." Aunt Nadine should have known better. Desiree had been embarrassed plenty of times when her father was off his meds.

"He won't do a thing till he's good and ready. You know how he is. Stubborn. But I pray for him anyway."

Desiree's heart sank. Her father had fought in Vietnam. He came home with PTSD. After more than thirty years, her father was still going through his episodes. Post-traumatic stress disorder wasn't something you got over. As a child she'd wished for miracles. Every time her father had an episode—and it seemed she'd lived through a million of them—she wished there was something she could do to fix him, and she prayed that he would improve, that he would be made whole again. As an adult she learned there weren't little magic formulas that fixed the ailments of the world.

Yes, Desiree knew. She'd lived a lifetime with her father's illness. But Aunt Nadine would deal with him. He would recover. Eventually, he'd apologize and get on her right side. Right now she focused on the children.

An aunt. Desiree was an aunt. She didn't know how she felt about that. As an only child, she'd never even considered it.

"Does Mama know?" she asked quietly. Her mother had suffered most of all. Years of being both father and mother to Desiree. While she lived with her husband, she never knew what each day would bring. Until finally one morning, he just walked out. A few days later, he turned up in Macon. Aunt Nadine called to let them know. He carved out a place in the shabby home, a house a stiff wind could blow down. Room by room, board by board, he began to fix it up.

A month later a lawyer contacted her mother telling her Levi Prescott had filed for a divorce.

Although her father had never completely dissociated himself from her mother's life, he left no room for her to seek a relationship with another man. Every couple of months he came back for a week or two.

Jacqueline Prescott's love story had been brief, but she'd loved someone who'd loved her for a lifetime. Yet after the war, he returned home a changed man. And as much as he loved her, he couldn't live *with* her. And now, Desiree wondered how her mother was going to digest this news—another kick in the teeth.

"I was going to let you call her," her aunt was saying. "She's out of town at a convention anyway."

Desiree's mother still kept in contact with Aunt Nadine and Levi.

"The last thing she needs is more pain," Desiree said.

"She's sacrificed her life for you and your dad. She deserves some good now. At least he didn't betray her. The boy was born before they met. He was thirty-seven when he died. Well, I don't usually stay up this late. I've got to get up early to try to get Levi to take his medicine." They both knew he wasn't.

"Get some sleep, Aunt Nadine. Thanks for calling."

"You take care of that mess in Atlanta and I'll hold the fort here."

As soon as Desiree hung up, she made a to-do list. By rote, she made reservations to Atlanta, called a car service to take her to the airport, and reserved a car at the airport in Atlanta. She got directions to the lawyer's office off the Internet and left a message on her supervisor's answering machine. Then she called the lawyer's office and left him a message, giving him the flight information and approximate time she'd make it to his office.

A thought suddenly struck her. How old were the children? She forgot to ask. They could all be under five.

They could be two-year-old *triplets* for all she knew. She shuddered at the thought.

In the bedroom she tossed clothes into a suitcase and thought of three frightened children struggling to deal with their grief for the only two people who loved them and with what must be unbearable fear for their future.

Moving quickly between the bed and the dresser, she bumped her toe on the dresser and hopped around like a rabbit, rubbing it until the throbbing lessened.

She could barely move in her closet-sized bedroom. Her *only* bedroom. The bed took up most of the available space. To accommodate three children, she'd have to find another apartment or buy a house farther out.

But first she had to get to Atlanta.

"You're never going to marry me, are you, Gerard Kingsley?" Andrea Warner, his girlfriend of the moment, asked with her hands on her hips. She was dressed in jeans and a pretty green top. Her short black hair was done in a feathery do. And she was steaming.

Gerard stifled a sigh. "Give me a minute," he said, easing up from the couch, careful not to jostle the baby.

Andrea had hunted him down at the Paynes' residence. Gerard had collected Christopher Payne from the hospital that morning, and the eight-month-old had clung to him like a tick ever since. The boy was irritable and probably in pain with the broken arm, and Gerard had the devil of a time getting him to sleep. Dogged if he was going to let Andrea's snit wake the boy.

Although Gerard's grandmother had moved in with the children until other arrangements could be made, she'd gone to bed hours ago, leaving Gerard to settle the child. Chris finally fell asleep on Gerard's chest. He eased the child to his shoulder, careful not to disturb the injured arm, and caught a whiff of baby powder and lotion. He was a soft little bundle, and if Gerard had kids of his own, he'd want one exactly like Chris.

Gerard pressed a hand against the boy's back for support and carried him upstairs. Gently he laid him in the crib, praying he wouldn't awaken. The little tyke continued to sleep when he spread a light blanket over him.

Gerard made sure the baby monitor was on before he tiptoed out of the room.

The doors to the other bedrooms were closed, and darkness emerged from beneath. It had taken some time getting the kids to settle in for the night. There was homework to be done and the boys wanted to play catch.

Gerard made it back to the family room to confront Andrea. He already felt like he'd pitched eight innings. Andrea made him feel like he had yet to field a press interview.

Andrea straightened up as he came into the room. Gerard sat on the couch across from her as she glared at him.

"I'm not ready for marriage, Andrea. Why would you want to marry a man who's away ninety percent of the time? My first game is tomorrow night. I won't get more than a few days off until late October. Why would you want to be tied to that kind of life?"

The stubborn tilt to her chin was certain indication she wasn't going to settle for his explanation. "Because I want some stability. I want children. I want to know this relationship is going somewhere."

Gerard scrubbed a hand down his face. "Children need a father who's going to be around, not one who's away nine months of the year."

"They need a father, period. You aren't going to play ball forever."

"I'm playing now. And if my health holds up I'll be playing for the next five years. What kind of life is that for you or kids?"

She crossed her arms beneath her pert breasts. They

could be snuggling on the couch. But no. She had to debate a subject that should already be clear.

"Tony's married. He and Pat are doing great," she said. Anthony Parker was Gerard's best friend and catcher for the Atlanta Eclipses baseball team. Anthony was a lovesick fool. A newlywed, the man still had stars in his eyes.

"They don't have children and Pat isn't trying to get pregnant right away."

"I'm not waiting five years to get married. We've been dating for two years now. And I don't see a future down the road. I know you're wealthy and women are waiting on the sidelines for you."

"I'm not looking at them." But he didn't love Andrea either.

"You're giving me excuses and I'm sick of them," she said. "The bottom line is you don't love me."

Gerard saw right then and there she wasn't going to give up. "I'm not seeing anyone else."

"And that's supposed to make me feel better?"

"Why are you trying to back me into a corner?" He'd had enough. She knew the score. "I've always been up front with you."

"I've played the cards you've dealt so far. You treat me as if you're the only important one in this relationship. As if my needs don't count."

"That's not true. You have a great career. I don't stand in the way of your success."

"All I'm saying is I always have to bend to your will. You're unwilling to make sacrifices for me."

Gerard spread out his hands. "I give you what I can. What more do you want me to do?" he asked. He'd made it clear when they started dating that he wasn't going to marry anyone as long as he played baseball. She assured him she wasn't ready to settle down, either. With three years of residency to get through, she had little spare time. She still had another year to go. So why was she coming out of left field with this marriage business now?

A sad expression crossed her beautifully made up face. "If you don't know by now," she said quietly, "we're doomed. Maybe it's time we called it quits. Perhaps we need time apart."

"Just like that?" He gave her a sidelong glance of utter disbelief. A certain chill hung on the edge of her words. Anger and something Gerard couldn't identify ripped through him.

"I think this is best for both of us. We need time . . . *I* need time to revaluate what I really want." She offered a self-deprecating smile. "Would you even care if one of my coworkers likes me? He's been asking me out for a while."

"A physician, I'm sure." Gerard sneered. Of course he was a physician just like she was. "You didn't have to go through this song and dance. You could have come right out and said you preferred someone else from the beginning."

She shook her head. "I can't believe you said that to me. I want to marry you, but since you want to stay single and *free,* what option do I have?"

"How long have you been seeing him?" Gerard asked with a calmness that belied his inner rage.

"Aren't you listening to me? I haven't been seeing him. But you aren't giving me a reason not to, are you?"

"You know what? If he's the one you want, I won't stand in your way." Regaining some of his composure, he stood, marched to the door, and opened it wide.

"You're deliberately being obtuse. But I have my answer, don't I?" In a moment Andrea followed him. He watched her as she got into her car and drove off into the night. Not once did she look back to see him glaring after her.

He shut the door with finality.

In the downstairs bedroom, Gerard stripped down, turned on the hot water, and stood under the spray, letting it fall on his head for several minutes. He couldn't believe she'd ended things in a matter of moments. He should have known better than to hook up with a woman he'd met at one of his mother's barbecues. Amanda Kingsley had wanted him to be a doctor, had pleaded for him to attend med school. But baseball was in his system. She never understood what it meant to throw a strike across home plate. She never understood what it felt like to want something so desperately his heart ached without it. To her it was just a game. To him it was more, so much more. It wasn't as if he chose the profession. It was more that the profession chose him.

Even though he wasn't looking for marriage, he was at a point in his life where playing the field, going to bed with a different woman each night, each week, each month was as unappealing as it was dangerous. He remembered Andrea's words as if she'd repeated them tonight. Theirs was a match made in heaven.

He should have known there was no such thing.

People either loved New York or hated it. Desiree loved it. She loved the anonymity. She loved the noise that swallowed up thoughts. She could be anyone she wanted to be. People didn't care whether she paraded as a corporate executive or a chimney sweep. They were too busy carving their own path to be overly concerned about their neighbors.

In the bars where loud music blasted, where drinks were passed from hand to hand like dizzying batons, where wall-to-wall people stood trying to outtalk each other, you could forget. Forget embarrassing moments.

It was the defining reason she chose New York in the first place. She yearned for anonymity.

The more the distance between New York and Atlanta diminished, the tighter the fist squeezed Desiree's churning stomach. The club soda sitting on her tiny tray table didn't begin to settle her stomach.

Most of the passengers on the early morning flight were sleeping, the lights turned down low. Desiree was uncomfortably squeezed in the center seat between two men.

Although she closed her eyes, she couldn't so much as doze.

She kept worrying about the children. What terrors they'd experienced, and wondering if they were staring into darkness and filled with worry. It was enough that their parents had died. To have been mistreated on top of that . . . Desiree shook her head and closed her eyes. But sleep still eluded her.

The bumpy plane ride was much too short. Now that she'd disembarked and was hunting her way through an airport larger than a city, she had decisions to make, the world to face.

On her way to the rental car counter, she dialed the lawyer's number and identified herself.

"He's at the airport waiting for you," his secretary said, so she canceled her rental car and rode the monorail to the luggage carousel. A man was holding a sign with Desiree's name printed on it. He was a trim five nine with a nut-brown complexion, and his bald head shone in the artificial light.

"I'm Desiree Prescott," she said, extending her hand.

"Robert Myers," he said. His handshake was quick and firm. "I'll carry your luggage. Just point me to the proper pieces."

"I didn't bring much. Just a couple of bags."

They made quick work of getting the luggage and making their way to a waiting town car. The driver hopped out and stored the luggage in the trunk.

"How was your flight in?" Robert asked.

"Peaceful."

As they drove from the airport in a snarl of traffic, Desiree was glad she didn't have to navigate.

"Where are the children?" she asked.

"They're in their home. Gerard Kingsley, a neighbor, and Scott Hayes, your brother's partner, are with them now, but both of them travel constantly. Gerard's grandmother is staying with them temporarily. As a matter of fact, both men will be leaving in a few days."

"How old are the children?"

"Fourteen, ten, and eight months."

They weren't all babies, Desiree thought. She could handle that.

"How long will you stay?" Robert asked.

"I'm not sure."

"Social Services want to make a thorough background check and make sure the kids are in good hands before they relinquish control of them."

"I'm debating staying at least until the kids are out of school. I should be able to take off from work that long, and that should give us enough time to work everything out."

"I've cleared the way temporarily with Social Services. I had a background check done on you, but they will do their own." Before she could respond, he continued. "I had to. Jordan asked me to start looking for his family the week before he died. I had to make sure who I was dealing with before I called. The children's welfare is my first priority."

Desiree nodded. "Of course."

"Jordan's chosen guardian for the children also died in the accident, which is the reason we have a problem. I'm telling you this because the other couple had a son and he's temporarily staying with Jordan's children. He's ten, Justin's age. Justin is Jordan's son. Is that going to be a problem?"

What was one more? "No." Her legs were so weak she was glad she was sitting. *Four children,* she thought, breaking out in a cold sweat. What she knew about kids would fit on the tip of her thumbnail. She hadn't babysat in high school like most teenage girls. God, they were going to run circles around her. She was going to wind up as one of those batty aunts at thirty.

Robert pointed out Turner Field and the State Capitol Building, the top of which was solid gold.

"Sorry about the traffic," he said. "It's hell times five."

Desiree chuckled. "I'm used to it."

* * *

When Desiree rode into a development, passing lavish estates and heading down the stately tree-lined drives, her eyes widened. "What was Jordan's occupation?" she asked.

"He was a sports agent."

"It obviously paid well."

"I would think so with the multimillion-dollar contracts he negotiated for his clients, not to mention product promotions," he said with pride. "We attended college together, so he was more than a client. He was always on the news here. Obviously you haven't heard of him."

"I haven't. Although I like sports." Desiree was an avid sports fan, but she followed the games, not the agents.

The driver pulled up into the driveway of a huge stately house and parked behind a black Porsche. They walked up the steps to the double front doors and Robert rang the doorbell.

The door was thrust open by a man carrying a child with a cast on one tiny arm. Desiree focused on the baby. He had what looked like mashed banana on his mouth and on one hand.

Two events occurred at once. The baby was smiling, one fist tugging on the man's collar, but when he saw two strange adults, he wrapped his arm around the man's neck and held on. Desiree felt as if she'd been punched in the stomach, because she finally noticed the man and he was the most drop-dead gorgeous male she'd encountered in a very long time. The odor of woodsy soap mixed with the fruity banana aroma reached her. She took a short shallow breath and her heart skipped a beat. It should be a crime to be that male and that potent.

Suddenly he was staring at her, a question on his brow.

"This is Jordan's sister, Desiree Prescott," she finally heard Robert say. She summoned her composure.

The man extended a hand. "Pleasure to meet you. I was trying to get Slugger to eat. He doesn't have much of an appetite. Come in. I'm getting ready to take the other kids to school. We're late. I let them sleep in."

His hair was cut short. He stood about six two, had amazing shoulders and a smile to die for.

"Gerard is the lead pitcher for the Atlanta Eclipses," Robert said. "Biggest mistake Milwaukee made was trading you. Last year wasn't a good year for them."

"I always wanted to come back home. It was a good move for me."

"Your preseason games were encouraging."

"We have a good team this year."

"Can we talk about the kids? The things I'll need to know? I'll be staying with them. To tell you the truth, I almost don't know where to start," Desiree interjected. They had much more important concerns than baseball.

"My grandmother's in the kitchen," Gerard said around a sly smile, the devil. "She can fill you in on whatever you need to know. Then Slugger and I will take you on a tour through the house when I get back."

"Don't you have a game tonight?" Robert asked.

"Yeah, but I don't have to be at the ballpark until after four. I try to chill out before the game."

And then three kids rounded the corner and stopped at the door with their backpacks.

"Meet your aunt," he said. "Desiree, this is Sherrice, Justin, and Steven."

"So nice to meet you," Desiree said.

The children spoke, but they were guarded as they sized her up. What should she expect after their treatment at the last relative's home?

"Okay, we've got to hit the road," Gerard said.

"Can I back the car out of the garage?" Sherrice asked.

"Heck no." They all piled out and Desiree found herself holding the baby, who took one look at her and screamed the house down.

* * *

Levi Prescott was holding his own. Hearing he had a son and that the boy was dead had sent a raging storm through his system. But he controlled it. He could do this, he told himself. He wasn't ready to face anyone, but he got up that morning. He dressed. He'd come to work because he wasn't ready to confront his grandkids.

Levi wasn't ready to look at picture albums of the son he'd never meet. A man was supposed to be there for his kids. He hadn't been much of a father to Desiree, but at least she knew he loved her. At least he saw her a few times a year and talked to her every blessed week when his mind was functioning okay.

He needed time before he faced his grandchildren. How would he ever explain why he hadn't been there?

So he'd made the only sane decision he could think of. He'd come to work. Most of his coworkers sensed when he needed space. They were sensible enough to leave him alone while he did his job, and he was okay—until the foolish new department manager shipped to Macon from Philly started screaming in his face like he was crazy. He was always hyped up. Adrenaline overstimulated with caffeine. Kept things stirring at work. Didn't he know this was the South, where the pace was slow?

The man's shirtsleeves were rolled up. His silly tie was so tight it was bulging at his neck. Levi stifled a laugh. Visions of stringing him up by the necktie danced in Levi's head, but he wouldn't look at him. He hunched his shoulders and continued to type on his computer.

"I'm talking to you. You hear me?" the man said, getting in his face.

"Leave me alone," Levi told him.

"I need the report like yesterday."

Levi had asked for the work a week ago and he'd kept sending him out of the office, telling him he'd get the data to him when he was ready. *You don't need to keep reminding me. I'll give it to you.* Then Levi had e-mailed him. He'd shot a missive back saying by now he knew

Levi needed the data. So why was he taking up room in Levi's tiny cubicle wanting him to work like hell to get a week's worth of work done in a day? Wasn't going to happen.

"You get it when it's done. I'm going to lunch." Needing breathing room, Levi slid his chair back.

"Lunch! Are you crazy?"

That's when Levi closed his fist and popped him, and before Levi could register his actions, the young up-and-coming pup was lying flat on the floor with his eyes rolling back and forth, his face as red as a lobster's.

"Yeah," Levi said, calmly looking down on him. The man had that dazed look, as if he'd been shot with a stun gun. His eyes didn't blink.

Several heads had popped above the cubicle dividers to see what had hit the floor. Their eyes moved from the fallen man to Levi.

Levi grabbed his jacket from the coat tree. "See y'all later," he said pleasantly as he marched down a corridor of cubicles. The action had released the tightness in Levi's chest. He felt marginally better.

The room had grown still and quiet. He liked the silence. Now and then he heard rustling like that of a slight breeze flowing through the trees and rippling over the water.

Nobody stirred to help the fallen man. Nobody spoke to Levi. He felt several pairs of eyes on his back as he shut the office door behind him.

Coming in to work had been a mistake.

His fists were still bunched at his sides. He couldn't be around people. Once he made it to the parking lot, he stood motionless, contemplated his directions. He should go to Atlanta to his grandkids. But he knew Nadine had called Desiree. He knew his daughter would take over, like she always did in a crisis. In his frame of mind, he would be no good around his grandkids.

He should call Veronica, his significant other. Told him

she was too old to be referred to as a girlfriend. But she got scared when his moods hit. He nixed that idea.

His sister would tell him to grow up and take one of his pills, but he got sick of taking pills all the time, every damn day of his life and feeling like he was swimming through cotton. He wanted a clear head, to feel normal sometimes. He deserved a break. Besides, this mess wasn't his fault. If his supervisor had left him the heck alone to do his job, everything would have been okay. He should go back to the office and tell him so, too, but he wasn't going back in there because he'd end up punching the fool again.

He arrived at the decision he should have made last night. The woods and wide-open spaces drew him. The heck with lunch. He was taking a vacation.

He got in his new red Ford Ranger and drove toward his cabin in the woods, a two-hundred-acre piece of property that had been in his family since the early nineteen hundreds. It had been passed down to his sisters, and brothers, and him. Over time, his siblings had sold out to him, all except Nadine's fifty-acre piece.

When he left the interstate, the fist clenching his chest loosened. The closer he got to freedom, a semblance of peace began to spread through his body.

The property was a forest of live oak and pine now. From time to time, his sister nagged at him to have the wood cut and sold, but he wouldn't let her do it. When her friends told her about all the money they made from selling their wood, she'd start adding up what she could do with all that money. Fear or no fear, she'd start nagging on and on until he gave her the look. Then she'd leave him alone. She was scared of him. She didn't realize how much at times like these he needed the cover of the trees. There was safety in the woods.

A son. Dead at thirty-seven, he thought as he navigated down a narrow path to the lake where the trees stood like canyons on either side of him. Levi had fought a war and

lived to have nightmares about it. A man shouldn't out-
live his children.

Levi didn't measure up in many ways, being messed
up like he was from his tours in Vietnam, but he had
always taken care of his responsibilities, and that gave
him some small sense of accomplishment.

Sometimes, his sojourn in Hong Kong seemed like yesterday, yet at times it seemed a lifetime away. Now and
then, he pulled out the memory like a faded photograph.

Levi parked his truck by the cabin, but stayed outside.
He sat on a stump and gazed at the rippling waters. Two
summers ago the lightning had struck the tree and split
it. Eventually—during one of his spells—he'd taken a
saw to it, and piled the wood for his nephew, who liked
to build things. It was a pretty piece of wood.

He'd left enough of a stump to sit on. It had been an old
tree. By the size and circles of darkened lines, he esti-
mated it to be several hundred years old, so his seat was
nice and wide.

He inhaled a deep breath, smelled the sap from the
pine trees, observed squirrels scampering in the light
spring breeze, listened to the birds singing above, thought
about his grandchildren . . .

And waited for his mind to settle.

She wore an engagement ring, Gerard thought as he
navigated the heavily trafficked streets. And she was
downright sexy without even trying to be.

Plenty of guys picked up groupies waiting in hotel lob-
bies, each waiting for the one player to pick her out of a
sea of willing women. One-night stands were good
enough for some guys, something many young women
were willing to accept just to say they went to bed with a
star, or if she was lucky, if she turned up pregnant by him,
she'd own a piece of his paycheck for the rest of his life.

He prided himself on the fact that he wasn't attracted

to any of that craziness. But after meeting Desiree, he wondered if she was one of those women, if he'd be able to walk away from her so easily.

Sherrice's sigh tore his attention away from Desiree, and he glanced over at her. Rightfully, she was leery of her aunt, and who could blame her after what they had experienced with their cousin? She sighed again. Her hair was straight, just touching her shoulders. His grandmother had taken her to the hairdresser for a touch-up and she'd dragged him one evening to a mall to replenish her wardrobe.

He'd never go shopping with a teenager again. Not if he could help it. She'd dragged him from one store to the next. She'd grab a handful of clothes and try on every last piece and not select one. Shopping was worse than pitching against Barry Bonds. After the fourth store, he'd told her to make a selection or do without.

"What's wrong, Sherrice?" Gerard asked.

She glanced at him out of wide imploring eyes. "I don't like the looks of her. Why can't you take care of us?"

"Honey, I'm not a blood relative and I travel too much."

"We don't care about that."

"You need a real family and stability. You can't have a neurotic sports agent and a ballplayer taking care of you."

"My dad was an agent. And most ballplayers are married and have families."

"Your mother was here to plug up the holes."

"You can hire a nanny. Please? We can afford it. Our cousins are always talking about how rich we are."

She broke Gerard's heart. Their cousins had only wanted them for the money they got. Hardly a dime of it was spent on the children. The older kids managed because they hadn't outgrown their clothes, but poor Chris had outgrown all his clothes. Gerard's grandmother had had to go shopping yesterday for outfits that fit the boy.

"I'm not abandoning you, Sherrice. You'll see me as

much as you always have." Stopping at a red light, he chucked her under the chin and smiled. "Just you try to get rid of me. Seriously, give your aunt a chance, okay? The moment she heard about you, she got on a plane and flew here. She cares. That goes for all three of you."

He got a grudging agreement before he dropped them off at school. Then he drove back to the house, where he saw Desiree again. The truth was, he was stunned and be-mused by his reaction to her.

She'd already unpacked her bags in one of the bed-rooms and he gave her a cursory tour of the house, very aware of the scent of the subtle perfume she wore. Gerard loved the physical pleasure women offered, but he'd yet to meet the one he couldn't walk away from, including Andrea.

A man didn't easily walk away from a woman like De-siree unscathed. Bless one foolish enough to get caught up with her.

He was stunned at how much he wanted to be around her. She seemed to wake up dormant desires he hadn't experienced in many years, if ever.

Gerard's grandmother prepared a hearty lunch and Gerard ate in the Payne household before he left.

"I promised the kids I'd take them to the game," he said. "I have enough tickets for all of you. I hope you don't mind. They don't have school tomorrow."

"I'm sure the kids will be disappointed if they don't go. I don't mind," Desiree said.

"I've arranged it so that Jordan's partner, Scott Hayes, will take you, but you'll return with me."

"Sounds like a winner. I noticed cars in the garage, so with directions I can drive."

"You don't want to negotiate highways in this area on game day, especially when you don't know your way around."

"The kids should be here soon," Mrs. Kingsley said

from the doorway. "They only have half a day because of spring break. Good thing, too. Gives them a chance to get to know you."

Desiree nodded. She was apprehensive after her cool reception earlier. Christopher was just beginning to let her near him, although he still wasn't completely comfortable.

"I hate to leave you so soon, Desiree, but I'll be leaving today," Mrs. Kingsley said. "I had planned to visit my cousin. She had knee surgery yesterday. In a few days she'll be home and I want to be there to help out."

"I'll be fine. Thank you so much for taking care of the children."

"They're fine kids. You'll be okay with them. You look like you're plain tuckered out."

"I didn't get much sleep last night," Desiree said.

"Well, the little one's going down for his nap soon. I usually take a short nap when he takes his. You should do the same."

"Sounds like a great idea."

But Desiree didn't get to sleep for another two hours because by the time Christopher fell asleep, the other children had arrived from school. They looked at her as if a demon from hell had descended on them.

On game day Gerard usually stayed in bed until nine thirty because of the long day before him. He ate breakfast and played with Christopher to give his grandmother some time for other things. He spent some time with the older children, got them settled in with their aunt before he left. He was worried about Sherrice most of all.

Desiree Prescott's eyes were as clear as glass. She wasn't on dope. He didn't have to worry about a straitlaced woman being strung out and slinging Chris against the wall. He wouldn't have to worry about the boy going hungry.

Gerard was used to beautiful women. They made a play for him like men were going out of style, but rarely did a woman turn him on like Desiree. He wanted to kiss the stiffness right out of her.

He didn't have time to think of her now. He had to get his head straight for the game. He was the starting pitcher.

He arrived at the stadium around four, after most of his teammates were already dressed and making preparations, stretching and having batting practice. After he spoke to the staff, the massage therapist gave him a complete work over—arms, legs, back.

"So tell me about your new lady," Gerard said. His therapist had been going on about her for a couple of weeks now. His relationships rarely lasted longer than three or four months before they were hitting the door.

"She's pretty straight up, you know. Her folks live in Virginia. When I get a day off, I'm going there to meet them."

"It's that serious?"

"Man, when it hits you, it hits you."

Gerard flashed back to Desiree. But she was engaged. "It can happen that way."

After the work over, Gerard sat in the hot tub for a few minutes and began his stretches. He talked to teammates who passed through the room. When he was starting, he was off-limits to the press.

Tony was today's catcher, and while Gerard was getting taped up he and Tony went through the batting lineup of the opposing team, hitter by hitter. They discussed how they wanted to pitch to each man.

With a knock on her door, Desiree awoke from a sound sleep and bolted up in bed. It took a moment for her to get her bearings.

"It's only me," Mrs. Kingsley said, peeping in the doorway. "I wanted to let you know I'm leaving. Sherrice has little Chris. He's being a lamb right now."

"I'll get up," Desiree said.

"I fixed a stew with my homemade biscuits for supper, so you won't have to cook dinner. The kids have eaten and I dressed Chris. You better eat fast and get ready for the game. Scott will be by soon."

"Thank you."

Desiree stood by the closet and picked out a casual outfit to wear. The night before she'd quickly tossed a few things in the suitcase. She had very little to choose from. After a shower, she went in search of the kids to make sure they were ready.

When she passed the great room, she noticed a family photo on a table. She walked through a room decorated in French Country, but she took none of that in as she focused on her target. Gerard had raced them through the house so quickly she barely had time to scan the opulently decorated rooms. Desiree's hand trembled as she gathered the frame in her hand. The bottom dropped out of her stomach as she gazed at her brother and his wife for the first time.

There was no question that Jordan Payne was Levi Prescott's son. From what seemed an impressive height to the broad width of his shoulders. From his serious expression to his medium brown complexion. From his full lips to his high forehead, and even his nose.

He was the spitting image of his father. How would her father respond?

Desiree had almost sunk into her own depression when she heard a noise. Christopher, the little scamp, had crawled around the corner, and her heart lightened. He stopped when he saw her. She smiled and said, "Hi."

Indecisive, he used the wall to stand. He seemed to contemplate whether he should flee or continue into the room.

Gingerly, Desiree set the picture back on the table. She still couldn't get over how small he was. There were still fresh bruises on him. She wanted to hold him and make all the pain vanish.

Speaking to him softly, she slowly approached him.

Suddenly his face scrunched up and he turned and fled, tripping over his feet.

When he howled, he sounded as if she'd attacked him. The other kids come running toward them.

"What did you do to him?" Sherrice asked.

"He fell." She was rocking him in her arms, but he didn't want a stranger. He wanted someone familiar. He reached toward Sherrice. Cutting her eyes at Desiree, she gathered the boy in her arms.

At the same time, the door opened and a handsome older man flew in like a whirlwind with a cell phone glued to his ear. After a moment he flipped it closed.

"Sounds like World War Three in here. What's going on?"

"She let Chris get hurt."

"He just fell," Justin said. "She didn't do anything to him."

The man extended a hand. "Scott Hayes."

"I'm Desiree Prescott."

"So are you ready?"

"Let me get the baby's things."

"Mrs. Kingsley packed the diaper bag," Justin said.

"Good." Before Desiree could move, Scott gathered the bag and hustled them to the car.

Desiree sat in the front seat beside Scott, catching her breath. She had not fared well on her first day in Atlanta.

2

Desiree and the kids arrived at the field a half hour before the game began. Excitement was in the air. The aroma from the concession stands made her mouth water. Huge food courts supplied everything from barbeque ribs and pulled pork sandwiches, to chicken sandwiches, burritos, pizzas, chili cheese fries, grilled Cuban sandwiches, and every type of hot dog and sausage sandwich under the sun. For drinks, they served lemonade, beer, wine, sodas, and coffees. Desiree chose lemonade. A glass of wine might settle her nerves, but the last thing she wanted the children to think was they were passing from a drugged-out cousin to an aunt who was a lush. The kids made a beeline to the stands. Surprisingly, Christopher let her hold him while Sherrice and a friend talked and ate their snack.

Desiree was introduced to some of the players' wives. Spirits were high. Animated conversations bubbled over about the success of last season and the hope for this season. Desiree couldn't help riding on the joy.

When Gerard walked out onto the field for practice throws, Desiree's breath caught in her throat. He looked toward the stands where she was sitting. Of course he was looking for the children, not at her, but it seemed his eyes met hers for a second before he approached the pitcher's mound.

With Gerard's sure expertise, the ball flew toward home plate with a power that took her breath away. He was amazing, Desiree thought. Not that she had any business thinking of Gerard that way. She had a nice reliable fiancé back home and she was looking forward to a lifetime of happiness with him.

Gerard's family arrived and sat nearby.

"Desiree, meet Nolan and Amanda Kingsley," Scott said.

"You're the aunt." Amanda Kingsley wore a neat pair of black slacks with a black and beige sweater. Gerard's eyes were the same shade of brown as hers.

"That's right."

"I hope you enjoy Atlanta. If there's anything I can do for you, please don't hesitate to call me or my husband."

"Thank you."

"What did you do in New York?" Nolan asked. Nolan was clean-cut in slacks and polo shirt. Gerard was built like him, except with the excessive exercise, his shoulders were broader. Their facial features were similar as was their medium brown coloring.

"I'm part of a retirement fund investment team," Desiree responded.

"Interesting," Scott said just as a man sat in the seat on the other side of Desiree.

"This is our son, Chad," Amanda said with a smile. "He's a resident at Atlanta General."

Chad smiled. Christopher reached for him and the older man slid the child into his arms.

"How are you, sport?" he asked. Chad was a couple of inches shorter than Gerard and not as broad about the shoulders.

"I thought you were scheduled to work," Nolan said.

"I switched with another resident. Guess I won't get another day off this week."

When Desiree focused on Gerard again, he was walking toward the stands with a ball in his hand.

His well-conditioned body looked magnificent in his uniform, Desiree thought. He was strong, with every muscle outlined against the fabric. He tossed the ball toward Desiree and surprisingly she caught it. "Thank you," she called out. By the way her pulse raced, she would have thought she was available. She had to glance at her engagement ring to remember she was marrying Paul.

Desiree shivered. She felt as if a change was in the air.

As Gerard walked away, she noticed a woman who sat on the other side of Chad.

"Desiree, meet Andrea, Gerard's friend."

The bubble inside Desiree burst and it seemed a cloud had covered the sunlight.

Gerard left the field wondering what was happening to him. When Desiree smiled at him, he didn't have a clue why his heart turned over. It was several heartbeats later before he put her out of his mind and entered the bull pen.

The last time Desiree went to a ball game where she actually knew the players had been in high school. Even though she'd just met Gerard, her throat tightened every time he went to the pitcher's mound. He was so obviously on display. It seemed it was him against the world. A lonely spot if there ever was one.

The first seven innings he pitched, Desiree couldn't eat. She could barely swallow her lemonade. She could always tell when the wives' husbands or friends were at bat, made a play, or fumbled. There was always that little catch that kept them on edge.

It was the eighth inning when the relief pitcher finally took Gerard's place. There were ovations for a job well done as Gerard made the lonely trek to the bull pen.

This was work, not just for the players but for families and friends too.

Desiree finally took a full breath and glanced at

Andrea. She was the perfect trophy girlfriend. A beautiful ornament on his arm.

Stop it. You're being catty, Desiree admonished herself. A woman's beauty was no reflection on her brain. Besides, it was none of her business. So why did she feel this horrible catch in her throat?

By the time the Atlanta Eclipses won the game three to one, Desiree was whipped. She clapped and screamed louder than anyone. Wives and friends were in good cheer.

"Desiree, we're having a cookout soon. I hope you can attend," Amanda said. "And bring the children."

"I'd love to, thank you."

Desiree didn't have a clue where she should meet Gerard.

"Chad, show Desiree to the clubhouse," Scott said. He was up and running.

"Well, I have to go."

"You're not going to wait for Gerard?" Chad asked Andrea.

"No. I have to get to the hospital." She hugged Amanda and then she was gone.

"Andrea is also a resident. She and Chad attended college together."

"How wonderful." Brains and beauty. *So much for first impressions.* Desiree felt like a fool.

On the late-night news Desiree watched Gerard's muscled frame fill the TV screen in an after-game interview. He wore a dark suit that appeared tailored specifically for him. His answers were intelligent and his composure unwavering as question after question was fired at him like volleyballs across the net.

As soon as Gerard's face left the screen, Desiree flicked the TV off and wandered to the patio outside her bedroom. Suburban Atlanta was so different from New York and

Washington, D.C., where she'd lived before she moved to New York. She'd lived in the city her entire life. Sirens and horns screaming were lullabies lulling her to sleep.

The intense quiet, the sounds of crickets chirping, were as foreign as the windmills of Holland.

The kids were in bed. Desiree had showered and donned sweatpants and a short-sleeved cotton top. She could almost fit her tiny apartment in her bedroom suite. An ocean-green spread covered the four-poster bed. The room was decorated in a mixture of midnight blue with turquoise, seaweed, lettuce, and bottle green. The walls were so pale, she had to strain to pick out the hints of green.

The love seat and chairs were covered with silk velvet fabric. Colorful Wedgewood candleholders held several ivory candles prominently displayed on the fireplace mantel. The television was hidden in a heavy armoire. And she still had an ocean of space to spare. She didn't have to worry about bumping her toes on the furniture there.

Paul had been in a conference all day and she had yet to contact him. After the conference, he and some of the senior members of his firm were entertaining a group of businessmen with dinner and drinks. She knew it would be late before he arrived home. When she finally settled down to call him, it was almost midnight.

"You're where?" he asked, astonished. She imagined him pacing the floor and pinching the bridge of his broad nose or running a hand over his short-cropped hair.

"I have a half brother." She gave him some of the details.

"What a shock."

"That's the understatement of the century. Can you believe I'm in Atlanta? Staying in my brother's luxury estate. He was a sports agent."

"Wow."

"I'm staying until the kids are out of school at least," she said.

The silence was loud. "You can do that?"

"Their lives have been turned upside down, Paul. They

need me. I can't yank them out of school and bring them back to New York. It'll be more than they can handle right now. Anyway, can you imagine five people living in my one-bedroom apartment? A closet-sized bedroom at that. This is the most logical solution."

"Have you talked to your supervisor at work?"

"He's okay with it. We're taking on the retirement account in September. I'll be back in the Big Apple long before then."

"But you're due for a promotion. This could stop it."

"I hope not. I should still get it when I return. I've earned it."

"It's a cutthroat world, Desiree. Out of sight could easily mean out of mind."

"I have to do what's right by the kids, Paul. I miss you."

"Miss you too," he said absently. "What about our plans for the wedding? My mother is looking forward to lunch with you tomorrow."

"Give her my regrets. We'll only have to delay the date a couple of months. I can start making plans from down here, but I can finalize things once I return."

"But you're talking about starting a new project at the same time you're planning for the wedding."

"I'm very organized. It's one of the things you love most about me, remember? I'll take care of everything. Don't worry so."

"What will eventually happen with the kids?"

"That's something you and I have to discuss, since we're getting married. But I'm too tired to think clearly right now. There's no one else, Paul," she said softly. "You should see the baby. Poor thing. Not even a year old and he has a cast on his tiny arm. It just breaks my heart. He wouldn't stop crying because he was hungry, poor darling. The cousin he was staying with hadn't fed him that day, so of course he was crying." She blew out a long breath to ease the ache in her heart. "One moment I want to knock that woman's lights out. The next second I just want to cry for Christopher's suffering. He's the sweetest little thing. So small."

"Don't get sentimental on me."

"I'm not the sentimental type. So tell me, is your mother still calling you every five minutes about the wedding plans?"

"She has a list of four hundred guests so far," Paul said.

"I was hoping for a small wedding with just close friends and family. No more than fifty people."

He chuckled. "Mother will never forgive you. She wants the society wedding of the year. My brother eloped, robbing her of the opportunity. So it all falls on me."

Desiree groaned. "I thought this was our wedding. What do you want?"

"We have to invite business associates as well as family. It's expected."

"If it's important to you, I guess I'll have to resign myself to planning the society wedding of the year." Desiree felt little enthusiasm for working with his mother, but if he could accept the children, the least she could do was work with his mother on the wedding. The woman always tried to lord it over Desiree because of their wealth—a result of marrying Paul's wealthy father. You'd think she came from centuries-old money the way she behaved, instead of marrying into it. Desiree knew exactly where she got the idea that every woman wanted her son for his family's largess and not for himself. She acted as if it was okay for her but not for anyone else.

Desiree wasn't marrying Paul for his money. She worked hard to take care of herself. As much as the woman got on her nerves, Desiree wouldn't hold Paul responsible for his mother's attitude.

She wished he was with her now. She wanted some affirmation that their future would hold all her dreams. She wasn't looking for the stars to explode as much as she wanted a companion who would hold true through all the trials life would throw them, in the era of explosive divorce rates. At some point, life had to settle into something that lasted more than a few years. Out there somewhere there had to be that one person who believed in trying to make it work.

Comet-exploding passions didn't last. But a man who appreciated her, respected her, a man who had the same hard-core values that she possessed would last. Someone who'd starve away the bitter loneliness of the dark and lonely hours.

Her mind flashed to Gerard and she didn't understand why.

"Long day tomorrow," Paul was saying. "I'm turning in."

"I'm about to fall asleep on this phone. I'll call you tomorrow."

"Unfortunately, I'm meeting friends."

"Okay. Call me when you can." She gave him the house number before they disconnected. As she was nodding off, she remembered to call her friend Deana.

She gave an abridged version of the situation. Deana had a key to her apartment. She'd locked herself out a couple of times and Deana shared a two-bedroom apartment with someone down the hall from Desiree. "I need you to pack up some of my clothes and things and ship them to me." She gave her a list of what she needed.

"Have you checked out the brothers there?"

"Girl, please. Men are as scarce here as in New York, if not more so," she said. "I'm not even thinking of that. Once they see me with four kids, their libido will freeze. It's a good thing I already have Paul."

"Hmmph."

"I don't know why you don't like him."

"He's okay."

"Well, he's my sweetheart."

"I don't know about that. You could do so much better than Paul."

"I'm too tired to argue with you. Thanks for packing my things."

"What are friends for? Get to sleep, girl. You're going to need it."

After Gerard dropped Desiree and her family off, he was too keyed up to go home. Instead he drove to a bar that wasn't the usual sports players' hangout. As he sat at the bar, he spotted a Braves player at a table talking to a beautiful woman.

"Scotch and soda," he told the bartender.

"Coming right up. Hell of a game tonight. Y'all kicked some butt. Starting off with another dynamite year."

Gerard smiled as the man set the drink in front of him. He'd spotted Andrea after he threw the ball to Desiree. Why did she even come?

He was nursing his drink while he thought of Desiree. Although he was used to gorgeous women, it took all he had to remain calm when he'd met her that morning. Still couldn't get her out of his mind. And he saw hot groupies all the time hanging around the ballpark and hotels. None of them ever hit him the way cool Desiree had.

Somebody slid onto the stool beside him, but he didn't pay any attention.

"Virgin piña colada, please," the melodious voice said. Calm and serene as a waterfall, Gerard thought as he glanced in the woman's direction.

Their gazes met and she smiled slightly before she turned away. Unfortunately she didn't kick him in the gut the way Desiree had that morning. But the woman was very pretty with shoulder-length straight brown hair that suited her café au lait complexion.

"Excuse me. Could you pass the nuts please?" she asked after a moment.

"Sure." Gerard slid the freshly filled bowl of nuts and pretzels to her and she smiled her thanks.

"Thank God it's Friday. It's been a heck of a day," she said.

"Tell me about it." She didn't recognize him. He should be insulted, as much as his face was splattered over print and TV. On the other hand, it was refreshing to meet a woman who didn't have her phone number written on her navel or who was oohing and aahing over him.

She perused him closely. Still no recognition, and he liked that. "Literally or are you humoring me?"

"I'm a great listener."

She regarded him a moment. "I'm a dancer."

"No kidding." He looked her over again. She was thin and shapely. She sat ramrod straight. She moved her hands in a graceful manner.

"I work at a ballet school part-time."

"Interesting. So what's your day job?" It was nice not having to be on guard. Of course he never completely relaxed when he was in public. He never knew when someone was setting him up.

"A nutritionist. I spend my days helping people rearrange their diets when they have health problems or just want to change their eating habits."

"What's your success rate?"

"Change is hard, but some people get with the program after several sessions. Others never change."

"So what was so hard about your day?"

"Well, a man who I set up a diet plan for came into my office absolutely livid. He was red in the face because I convinced him to switch to a pure vegetable spray for his bread instead of actual butter. Well, he gained weight on the spray and became indignant. Raving and punching the air. Needless to say his physician wasn't pleased. He was eating low-fat, high-fiber breads. He cut butter completely from his diet, he said. He was eating carrots and greens using the spray. He was supposed to *lose* weight, not gain, he emphasized by pounding on my desk. I was ready to jack him up. Finally I asked him which spray he used. Of course he asked me, why did it matter? Come to find out he was using margaine."

Gerard chuckled. She was very expressive, moving her hands gracefully with her story. She must be a great dancer, he thought, but he flashed back to Desiree's hand and the engagement ring. For a moment he tuned the woman out, then refocused on her.

"He was quite indignant when I told him he was using the wrong kind."

"I can empathize with him. This is the South, where butter is king. And you've taken it away."

"It's time for him to come into the twenty-first century. The South has to change along with everything else. Besides, that was just one of several incidents. And after I finally got him out of my office, I had to rush to dance practice with kids who normally dance as if I'd taught them something, but today danced like they had two left feet. I was demonstrating steps for a recital in June. And if they aren't in tune by then, we'll have some very disappointed parents."

"I can imagine."

She frowned and watched him closely. "You know, you look familiar," she said.

"Really?" He'd thought better of her. *Here it comes,* he thought, disgusted and tired of the games.

"Of course he's familiar," the bartender said. "Don't you watch baseball?"

Her frown deepened. "I don't think it's connected with baseball."

So much for my popularity.

"I know if I'd met you I would have remembered," Gerard said.

"I know I've seen you before." She sipped her drink and munched on peanuts as they continued to talk mostly about her.

"I knew I'd eventually remember where I met you," she suddenly said, eyes sparking, but then dimming.

"Where?"

"You know Jordan and Beverly Payne?"

He nodded.

"I'm their daughter's dance teacher. Sherrice is a wonderful dancer, but unfortunately she hasn't been back since . . . well . . ."

"Since the kids are home now with their aunt, she might return to class."

"I hope so. If she returns soon, she can still participate in the recital. She's been with us for years. It's a shame to stop an activity she loved so much."

"I'll talk to her aunt. See what we can do."

"I have an early day tomorrow. I'm Emily Boyd."

"Gerard. Gerard Kingsley." He didn't ask for her number and she didn't offer. How refreshing.

Gerard wanted to see Desiree again to measure if the reaction that had blindsided him that morning was still as strong or if it had been a passing thing. He wondered if she and her fiancé had set the date. And what reaction the fiancé would have to starting out as newlyweds with four children in his life.

The key turned in the lock. Chad dragged himself into the house. He was two inches shorter than Gerard, a point they had battled over as kids.

"Got anything to eat?" he asked.

"In the fridge."

"I'm dog tired. Good thing the mutts are next door. Where has the aunt been all this time? Everybody was whispering about it after the game. Great game, by the way."

"They didn't know Jordan was her brother. Long story and I don't know all of it."

Chad opened the refrigerator door, pulled out lasagna, and ate it cold.

Gerard forced himself to look away. He knew what tired was, but he never could stomach cold pizza or lasagna.

"I'm glad somebody showed up. I wasn't up for a

steady diet of a houseful of kids." The kids had started to hang out between Gerard's place and their own.

"You're all heart."

"Hey, I'm single and loving it. Mom's having a cook-out your next day off. Says to make sure you don't make plans. You can bring your crazy friends too."

"Can you take off?"

"I'm not scheduled to work. You skipped the last dinner. She wants you there this time."

"I don't know why."

"She's celebrating the beginning of your season. And she's happy you finally got rid of your house in Chicago."

"I'll be there." To wade his way through another tedious family gathering.

Wearily, Gerard climbed the stairs to his bedroom. It faced the Paynes'. The light was now off.

So here he was, unattached. Finding an interesting woman who clicked and who wasn't looking for a husband wasn't easy.

As he ran the water in the shower and quickly undressed, he wished he had that go-to person whom he could pick up the phone and call. To ask her about her day, to tell her about his. Desiree flashed in his mind again. He wanted to ask if she'd had any problems with the kids.

Damn, he was thinking of Desiree, again. She was engaged and out of his league.

A light was on in one of the guest bedrooms. Must be the room Desiree chose. Then he saw her open the balcony door and walk outside with a glass in her hand. She sat in the chaise and leaned her head against the back as she took a sip. She was talking on a cell phone—probably to her fiancé.

Christopher roused Desiree at six A.M. Didn't that kid know he was supposed to let her sleep in on Saturday mornings?

"And good morning to you," she said as she changed

his diaper, cleaned his face and hands, and carried him downstairs. She set him in a corner with his toys while she prepared his cereal, but he was uncooperative. So in one hand she held him and with the other she prepared his oatmeal.

When she tried to feed him, he was cranky and kept pushing her hand away. Desiree debated waking Sherrice. The poor darling had to eat something so he could take his medicine. She got the medicine bottle and read the instructions. It said he could take it with or without food, thank God. By the time she finished fighting with him to get him to swallow the allotted amount, she was his number-one enemy. Gerard walked in on the scene and she gladly relinquished the child into his arms.

"What's wrong with Slugger this morning?" he asked, planting a kiss on his cheek.

"If you could get him to eat while I dress, I'd be forever grateful," she said. "I just gave him his medication. It might take a little while for it to work."

Desiree just took long enough to wash her face and brush her teeth. By the time she returned to the kitchen, Christopher had calmed down and Gerard was feeding him.

"How was your night?" he asked, then glanced at Desiree. "Did he sleep through the night?"

"Thankfully, yes. I think the medication helped." She felt his gaze following her as she moved around the kitchen.

After he fed Christopher, he pitched in helping to prepare a huge country breakfast. Cheese grits, eggs, bacon, and flaky biscuits slathered with butter and jam. Since the morning was cool, she made hot cocoa. By the time the table was heaping with platters, the aroma brought the other kids downstairs.

"You put marshmallows in the hot chocolate?" Justin asked.

"Something better. Whipped cream."

He slid into his chair and dug in.

Gerard said grace. Then asked, "So what are you going to do today?"

"Maybe some sightseeing or visit a museum or something."

The kids moaned.

"The aquarium is always fun," Gerard offered.

Sherrice moaned again.

"Can we have a puppy?" Justin asked.

"I don't think so," Desiree said. "We won't have enough room in the city."

"We have plenty of room here," Sherrice said.

"We'll see," Desiree countered.

Sherrice looked at Gerard. "Gerard?"

"It's your aunt's decision."

Gerard held Christopher in one arm and ate with the other. The child munched on a piece of bread, little bits falling on Gerard's shoulder until he set the child on the floor and he scooted to a corner for a toy.

Sherrice glared at Desiree before she grabbed her little brother and went upstairs. The boys continued to eat in silence.

Well, that went well, Gerard thought.

"Are you pitching tonight?" Desiree asked.

He shook his head. "Normally I don't start more than once a week. The team has several starting pitchers." She wasn't wearing her ring, he noticed. He wished he could linger, but duty called.

"Justin, why don't you and Steven pack the dishwasher? I hate to eat and leave, but I have to work." The room cleared out immediately.

"I ran into Sherrice's dance teacher last night," Gerard said. "She said Sherrice is a good dancer. She might want to get back into it."

"I'll talk to her, thanks. And thanks for coming by."

"Any time." Gerard's gaze flashed on Desiree one last time. Her hair was pulled back in a ragged ponytail. She was still suffering from the lack of sleep, and she still looked like a woman he wanted to take upstairs to bed, but not to sleep.

He retrieved a business card from his pocket and wrote his cell phone and home numbers on the back before handing it to her.

"Call me if you need me." As much as he wanted to linger at the homey scene, he headed to the ballpark for his workout.

Desiree helped the boys clean up, then called Sherrice downstairs. Sherrice dragged herself downstairs with Christopher in her arms.

She ushered everyone to the family room. Favoring his left arm, Christopher crawled to his toys.

"We need to have a family meeting." There was so much to tell she didn't know where to start. When she had everyone's attention, she continued. "My home is in New York. I have an apartment on Manhattan's West Side."

"Do you live near the World Trade Center?"

"That's another section of Manhattan. You have a grandfather, Levi Prescott, and great-aunts and uncles. Many second cousins. You'll get to meet them all. Your grandfather will visit as soon as he can." When he was fully medicated, Desiree hoped.

"How come we never met you?" Justin said.

"We didn't know your father existed. Your grandmother and my father met during the Vietnam War."

"That was way before we were born," Justin said as if they'd met as far back as World War II.

"He'll tell you about all that. I don't know very much about that time. I know he has lots of pictures. And he loves to show them."

"What's going to happen to me?" The frightened look Steven tried to fight broke Desiree's heart.

At that moment, Desiree knew she had to keep him. "I'm hoping Social Services will let me adopt you."

"You're going to keep me?"

"I'm going to try."

His smile was like a ray of sunshine.

Desiree continued to talk. The kids asked questions. Even Sherrice stopped sulking and joined in the conversation until it dwindled down to what they were going to do the week of spring break.

"I have a book report to finish," Sherrice said.

"If you need help, I'm here. We aren't leaving town, so I think we should entertain ourselves with activities here."

"We've seen everything there is to see," Sherrice said.

"It doesn't hurt to see them again. We could bowl, you have a pool, but it's too cool to swim in it. Perhaps we can go to the rec center. You'll have to tell me where the closest ones are. This is your city," Desiree pointed out.

"Steven and I like to skateboard," Justin added.

"So do I."

Steven laughed in surprise. "You can't skateboard."

"You're too old," Justin said around a sly smile.

Desiree took up the challenge. "We'll see. Loser has to wash dishes for a week."

"You're on." They high-fived, already assured of their success.

"You can invite friends over, too," Desiree assured them.

For a space of time, the gloom lifted. Christopher crawled over to Desiree and handed her a white bear. She picked up both boy and toy. Suddenly, she had a snapshot of what his life must have been like before.

No human sounds. Only the noise of nature. Levi thought he heard the chirping of a million crickets. It was a cloudless night and the stars shone brilliant above. He picked out the Big and Little Dippers. Later he caught a glimpse of Mars, and a shooting star. On a night like this when he was alone, he could pretend there were no wars.

That there was peace in the world. Until he thought of the trouble he'd left behind.

That asshole would press charges against him. He might even get fired this time. Probably end up in court. He should never have gone in to work, he thought, as he soaked in the atmosphere of the evening and his mind drifted back more than thirty years.

He was finally given a week's R and R. He chose Hong Kong. Other soldiers had talked about merchandise you could buy for next to nothing. Women were theirs for the asking.

As he debarked from the plane, two Americans from the USO met him. They took him into the city and told him about the places to go, what to do, and where not to go. At the American hotel he changed his money to the local currency. He was free to do what he wanted to as long as he was ready to leave at the allotted time.

Feelings of relief from worry about flying bullets made him buoyant. Many soldiers went a little wild when they hit Hong Kong, and he was one of them. He wanted two things—drink and women.

He wanted to have fun.

His deepest desires were available—for a price.

He was half drunk when she walked in a few hours later.

She was beautiful and she was black. He had to blink to make sure. Few black women resided in Hong Kong.

When she neared him, he hopped up, nearly fell. "Here's an empty seat," he said, pushing off the soldier beside him. The man stumbled off to find another seat.

She shook her head, tried to keep from laughing, but she took the seat.

"So what's a girl like you doing in a place like this?" He was too out of it for cool, so he stayed with the tried and true.

"A drink."

"It's dangerous to drink alone," Levi assured her.

"From the looks of you, it's dangerous drinking with company."

"Me?" He patted himself on the chest and nearly fell off the stool. She caught him before he toppled over. "I'm as innocent as a lamb."

"Sure. A grasshopper please."

When she started to pay the man, he said, "Let me."

"I—"

"No, no. I'm a southern boy. Can't let a lady pay."

"It's a good thing I'm a southern lady, then."

"Where in the South?" he asked.

"My parents finally settled in Atlanta and I never left until I went to college. I'm an army brat."

"Atlanta. I'm a Macon boy. Close enough. You never picked up the accent." Her jet-black hair was twisted up in a French roll. Long dangling earrings hung from delicate lobes, and her face was dark and classically beautiful. She would always stand out in a crowd, Levi thought. He wanted her. Had to have her.

"I teach English to businessmen. I can't speak with a regional accent."

He frowned, remembering how the "Heat for the Seat" paddle on his elementary teacher's desk had cooled his libido. "Are you a mean teacher?"

"Of course not."

"You look like you've whacked a hand or two with a ruler."

Smiling, she drew back. "Never."

"Interesting."

"So did you arrive today?" she asked.

He tilted his glass to his lips. "Fresh off the plane."

"It shows." She sipped her drink.

He grinned. "You might not speak southern, but you remind me of home. You're my Georgia girl."

"I'm not your anything."

"I can pretend, can't I?"

"Well, it's been nice. Enjoy your R and R." She got up to leave, and Levi convinced her to stay a little longer and talk to him. Eventually they moved to a table. Although she drank little, he continued to talk. The bar was supposed to close at two, but rarely were the rules followed. It was four when he fell into bed in a drunken stupor that lasted until noon the next day. Over breakfast he made a bet with himself for how long it would take to get Rebecca Payne into his bed.

Christopher finally fell asleep. He had fought it for so long. Desiree put him in the crib and waited until she was certain he wasn't going to awaken before she left the room.

When she passed Sherrice's room, the light was on. With two quick knocks, Desiree entered the room.

"What are you reading?" Desiree asked.

"*To Kill a Mockingbird.*"

Desiree sat on the side of the bed. "I wanted to talk about the activities you were involved in. Gerard mentioned you used to dance. Did you take piano lessons or participate in sports?"

"Ballet and soccer."

"Would you like to continue with your classes?"

She shrugged.

"Do you have a number for the dance school?" Desiree asked.

"I have a brochure." She dug into the depths of her drawer for it.

"What about your brother?"

"He and Steven play baseball and soccer. It's baseball season now, but they aren't signed up."

"Do you have the information for that?"

"It should be in Mom's things."

"Why don't you get it for me?" Desiree said. "And I'll sign the boys up, too."

She bit her bottom lip. "I don't think I should do anything right now."

"Why not?"

"I need to help you with Chris."

Desiree weighted her words carefully. "I know how you feel. As the oldest you feel responsible for him. But I'm here now. And I promise to take excellent care of him. I won't hurt him."

Sherrice looked down at her book.

"Why don't we check these out tomorrow? In the meantime, I'll make phone calls."

She nodded.

"We're touring the Coca-Cola factory tomorrow," Desiree said before she left the room.

Before she went downstairs, Desiree looked in on the boys, who were in Justin's room on the computer. She finally made it to her room and called her aunt for an update on her father.

"Have you heard from him?" she asked.

"Not a word." Aunt Nadine told Desiree about the altercation in the office. "He goes off like this sometimes when he's upset. He should be back in a week or so. I called his lawyer. If the owner of the factory wasn't a Vietnam vet, Levi would have been fired a long time ago."

"Doesn't he have a cell phone?"

"Yeah. But he turns it off when he doesn't want to be bothered."

"And he left his medicine home, I take it."

"Of course he did. He'd be okay if he took it."

"The kids will be in school next week. I'm coming out there one day and will go to the land where he usually camps out."

"Just wait until he's ready," Aunt Nadine advised. "'Cause he won't come out until he wants to. If he doesn't want to see anybody, he stays hidden in the woods and you'll never find him."

"I have to try."

"Be good to see you again."

"You too, Aunt Nadine. I don't know what we'd do without you."

"Think nothing of it. He's my brother. You don't get over a war easily. My husband was in that war. He didn't suffer like Levi, though, so we got through it."

3

When Gerard came out of his house Wednesday afternoon, prepared to go to the ballpark, he nearly crashed into a woman on a skateboard. Fully geared with helmet, elbow and knee pads, and gracefully zipping down a hill, she was a sight to be seen. Bending low, she spun up a hill. Gerard's heart climbed from his chest to his throat when she tipped the board on one end and flipped. Before he could exhale she reversed directions and shot back toward him.

"What the heck?" It was a good thing he'd remained in his driveway watching her, else he would have crashed. He inhaled and exhaled slowly until his heartbeat decreased.

As she approached him, moving in graceful form, her face came into view. She was seriously concentrating on her moves. As her head angled thirty degrees he got a clear view.

Desiree.

She wore a one-piece stretch outfit that fit her like a second skin, showing every curve of her delightful body. Her hips tapered into long straight legs. When she faced him, he got a view of her lovely rounded breasts and narrow waist. She might as well have left the short jacket at home. It only reached her waist and did nothing to conceal her curves. The sight of her had him rooted to the spot.

Unbelievable.

He couldn't tear his eyes away.

His gaze followed her as she negotiated a curve, turned once again, and disappeared. Seconds later she materialized with Steven and Justin on either side of her. They were mimicking her routine. It was a dramatic if not heart-stopping show.

The boys were fully geared and resembled a group from Venice Beach more than from suburban Atlanta. With smiles on their faces, they were in a world of their own.

Gerard's impression of Desiree took a 180-degree turn. The first day they'd met he sensed she was definitely the straitlaced accountant type. Studious, serious, lacking in imagination—in other words, dull. And now she was ripping up and down the street with the kids, acting much like one herself. This woman knew how to have fun.

There were untapped layers to her. And observing her like this got his juices flowing in a way they had no business doing. She was engaged but he wasn't, and he was wishing more and more that she wasn't either.

When the trio reversed directions and coasted past him, Justin waved with both hands. Then Desiree glanced up. She smiled and threw up a hand. Steven spoke to her.

Desiree demonstrated a move. The boys tried to mimic her, and fell flat on their backsides. Picking themselves up, they practiced several times before they were comfortable with the move, and then the three of them skated in sync, as if they were executing the steps in a tedious dance.

Instead of behaving like strangers who'd met mere days ago, they gave the impression of a mother and sons who'd spent a lifetime creating memories together. This was the first time since their parents died that he'd seen the boys carefree and happy. Desiree was good for them.

He wished he had more time to watch them, but work beckoned. When they passed in the opposite direction, he accelerated. From his rearview mirror he watched them skate out of sight.

He wanted Desiree, she had that sexy, innocent beauty that made heads turn.

Andrea still hadn't told his parents about their breakup. If she had, his mother would have read him the riot act. He didn't know what Andrea's game was, but as far as he was concerned they were through. He was trying to be the gentleman by letting her spread the word. But gentlemanly behavior only went so far.

Retrieving his cell phone, he dialed her number. Sometimes he couldn't reach her when she was with patients. But this time she answered.

"So why haven't you said anything about our breakup?"

"I don't know," she said. He heard background noises from the hospital. "I'm still considering."

"You said it was over."

"That doesn't mean I don't have feelings for you."

"It's over, Andrea. I have to tell my parents. We're having a cookout tomorrow afternoon. It wouldn't be fair to give them false impressions."

"Just give it a little time, okay? Your parents mean a lot to me."

"I don't see the point."

She sighed. "You're leaving the day after. Just wait another week, okay?"

"I thought you'd be happy to start a new relationship with your doctor. I don't know why you want to play games." Gerard hung up. What was her game?

Gerard's team won five out of the six home games, and he was off the next day. His mother called early that morning to remind him to bring Desiree and the kids.

"I had the most disturbing conversation with Andrea. She said she has to work and the two of you are going through some problems. I hope you can work them out."

"Don't count on it."

"It's normal for couples to . . . Well, I have a million things to do before the cookout. I trust you to do the right thing."

So Andrea had finally told them. She also had them believing it was merely a spat. Not a permanent separation. His mother loved Andrea, so the right thing from her perspective was to patch the relationship.

Gerard gathered Desiree's crew into the SUV. Desiree felt like she was riding in a Mack truck it was so huge. The boys sat in the backseat, pleased to be farthest from the adults. Sherrice sat in the middle seat with Christopher, leaving Desiree up front with Gerard.

When they were almost at his parents' house, Gerard asked, "When's the big day?"

"What?" she asked.

He touched her ring.

"It was November, before Thanksgiving, but we're going to reschedule it after I return to New York." She twisted the ring on her finger.

Although Gerard lived in Alpharetta, his parents lived in the heart of Atlanta, in an old and quaint neighborhood. Gerard pulled to a stop on a tree-lined street of old graceful homes. The trees were tall and broad. The lawns were well maintained, the hedges thick and neat.

"Chris is asleep," Sherrice said.

"You kids go ahead. We'll be along," Gerard said. In seconds they cleared the car. He didn't have to repeat himself.

It was evident the kids had been to the Kingsleys' before. A few neighborhood children were playing on the street, and the boys joined them. Gerard told Sherrice her friend Casey was waiting for her in the backyard.

He lowered the window and turned the music on low. An intimate feeling enveloped the car.

"How does the fiancé feel about beginning a marriage with four children?"

Desiree was uncomfortable with the questions. But he

knew the children. He'd pitched in when they needed him most. He had a vested interest.

"I'm sure he's fine with it. It's unexpected, but so are a lot of things in life."

He raised an eyebrow. "You mean you haven't discussed it?"

"Everything happened so fast, you know? We just carry on snatches of conversations. He's really busy with his job right now." Desiree was rambling. She knew she wasn't making much sense. But she was an engaged woman. She and Paul should be burning up the connection between New York and Atlanta, yet they rarely talked.

"What will happen with the children?"

"I plan to adopt them."

"All four?" he asked, keeping his voice neutral.

"Yes. What's one more when you have three already? Steven's adjusting better now that he knows he has a home."

"All men wouldn't necessarily step up to the plate with that kind of responsibility. Raising four children is a huge undertaking."

Desiree raised an eyebrow. After seeing him with the children she could picture him as a father. "Is this a personal reflection?"

"I mean your fiancé. What if he decides he doesn't immediately want the responsibility of four children? What happens then? You're in love with him. What choice would you make?"

It never crossed her mind that Paul wouldn't accept the children, because she knew if it had happened to him, she'd step up to the plate.

"Paul understands. If the tables were turned, I'd welcome his nieces and nephews. I appreciate your concern, but things will work out." She stared at the Tudor house, wanting to rip her thoughts from the future.

"Ever consider staying here?"

"And not return to New York, you mean?"

"Exactly. What will your fiancé do?"

"That's not an option," Desiree said.

"The kids are used to the open spaces. You'd have to move out of the city, which will make your commute to work longer."

"Everyone will have to adjust. I know it's not perfect, but we'll work it out. For a confirmed bachelor, you certainly worry a lot."

He shrugged. "Can't help it. I'll miss them. Hate to see them go."

"They'll miss you, too. Thank you again for pitching in until I arrived."

Gerard smiled. "Other than that, everything's okay?"

"Of course not. Sherrice tests me at every turn. I'm not prepared to be a parent. I'm scared to death."

"Hey." He took her hand and rubbed it between both of his. "They don't expect you to be perfect, you know."

"Of course they do. I don't do anything like their parents. I'm not nearly as good as they were."

"They had years of practice and time to prepare. You don't have to treat them the same way. Just love them and work things out your own way."

"Easier said than done."

"Nobody said raising kids is easy."

Desiree closed her eyes and leaned her head against the headrest. "I feel like my life has changed so much in one week."

"It has. So has theirs—since their parents' death."

Desiree nodded "You're right. I'm being selfish, aren't I?"

"You're one of the least selfish people I've ever met."

"Why are you so understanding?"

"It's easy standing on the outside looking in."

"You don't have to spend so much time with us but you do. Why?"

"Your brother was a very good friend. I think I moved into the neighborhood because of him. He told me when the house was available. He was a great agent. He was a great man."

"I want to get to know him. There's this person who should have been an important part of my life. I know nothing about him."

"Then I'll tell you about him when we have time, at least as much as I know. But not tonight."

Desiree nodded.

Gerard was silent then, just gazing at her. He didn't understand why he was needling her this way. It wasn't as if *he* wanted the responsibility of four children, either. Although he loved the kids, he enjoyed his single status. He was at liberty to come and go as he pleased, without the worry of a wife and kids nagging at him about what time he was coming home or what he was doing.

Which was the reason his affair with Andrea had worked so well. She worked long hours. She never nagged. Until recently, that is. Now she wanted to get married. Gerard knew he'd want a family one day, but he had several playing years left. The life of an athlete wasn't conducive to family life. He had plenty of time to settle down.

But Andrea had a solution to that. She'd found herself a doctor.

"Hey." Somebody tapped the side of the car, waking Christopher. He screamed out.

"Y'all gonna stay in there all day?"

"We'll be right in. Go ahead," Gerard said.

Desiree was out the door in a flash, plucking Christopher from the seat and holding him close until he calmed down. What an idiot, waking the baby that way.

"Didn't mean to wake the little fellow," the man said.

"He's okay, aren't you, sweetheart?" Desiree kissed his warm cheek.

Christopher snuggled close and Desiree inhaled the sweet baby scent, patting his back.

A man and a beautiful woman stood next to her. Desiree remembered meeting the woman the night of the first game. Gerard came around the car.

"Desiree, this is Tony Parker, the best catcher on the field. This is Desiree Prescott, Jordan's sister."

"You're only saying that so I'll keep saving your hide." He gathered Desiree in his arms and kissed her cheek. "Pleased to meet you, ma'am."

A woman wearing a short skirt and sneakers stood to the side. "This is my wife, Pat."

Pat smiled a greeting, but she was clearly angry.

Gerard took the baby from Desiree. Surprisingly, Christopher went willingly into his arms, but he was rubbing his eyes, poor thing hadn't slept through his nap.

Desiree smoothed her slacks and walked with Gerard through the gate to the back of the house. It was a huge backyard, about half the size of her brother's. Tony and his wife were stopped by the kids.

Wearing a blue apron, Gerard's father was manning the grill. He wiped a hand on the apron and extended the hand to Desiree. "Pleased to see you again, Desiree."

"Something smells delicious. May I help?"

"It's all under control. Just enjoy yourself."

Gerard's mother came outside carrying a pan covered in foil. "I'm pleased you could join us."

"Thank you for inviting us."

"You must miss all the activities in New York. There's so much to do there. Such a fast-moving city. Of course Atlanta has grown tremendously over the years. Not as laid-back as it used to be." Amanda wore dark slacks and a knit top.

"Give me the baby, Gerard. You can get the playpen so you two can enjoy your dinner."

"I'll take him." Desiree gathered Christopher in her arms. When Gerard left, his mother smiled brightly at someone behind Desiree. Desiree turned to see Chad.

"You're here." Her greeting for Chad was warm and her smile wide.

"You look exhausted. Do you have the weekend off at least?" she asked.

He shook his head. "I have to be at the hospital early tomorrow morning."

"I can remember nights like that. We'll get you out in time to get plenty of rest. Chad has another year in residency before he can join us."

"How wonderful," Desiree said. It was easily apparent the parents doted on him.

"What would you like to drink? We have everything from water to wine and soft drinks," Nolan said.

"Water please."

"A twist of lemon?"

"Please."

Gerard arrived with the playpen.

Desiree divided her gaze between the brothers. Gerard favored his mother, his gaze sharp, his manner deliberate and reflective. Chad favored his father's more easygoing demeanor.

"It would be interesting if Chris actually likes the playpen," Gerard said.

"I don't use the one at home."

"That's because you spoil him."

"I give him what he needs. There's a difference," she defended. Desiree figured Christopher needed all the loving he could get to make up for his cousin's treatment the past four months. A child's sense of self was developed within the first few years of his life. Half of Christopher's life had already been crap. She had a lot to make up for.

"He's being good for a change," she said. Having been wakened out of his nap, he shied away from people. "I fed him before we left and he took his medicine. It seems to be working."

"He's a good little tyke." Gerard tickled him in the tummy and the child smiled and burrowed deeper into Desiree's neck.

"How are you adjusting to Hotlanta?" Chad asked.

She shrugged. "It's different. I'm sure I won't feel as

isolated once the kids return to school and I get out and meet more people. Now my conversations are mostly with the kids."

"You'll be with the in crowd in no time. Some of the players and their wives will be here tonight." He glanced toward the gate. Tony and Pat finally made it inside.

Pat was still angry. Desiree hoped it wasn't because the man had kissed her. Slowly the men drew together and left the women alone.

"I could just strangle him," Pat said.

"Oh." Desiree didn't really know the woman. She was clueless.

"He gives money to every sad story that comes his way. I could see sometimes, but . . . well, you'll soon see enough if you stick around Gerard."

"I'm just a friend. I'm not dating a sports figure."

"You be careful because some of these men want a plaything. Can't have that when you have children."

Desiree wiggled her finger. "I'm engaged, and Andrea's ring is bigger than mine."

"Doesn't mean a thing. Trust me. It's a friendship ring. Gerard's dating her but everyone knows he isn't going to marry her—any time soon anyway, if ever." She looked at Desiree critically. "Gerard hasn't taken his eyes off you since you arrived. Not once. And these men are used to getting what they want. You be careful, else you'll be slipping into Andrea's place."

Desiree frowned toward Gerard. She couldn't get used to the way she felt about him. There was safety behind her engagement ring. "I'm going back to New York the beginning of the summer." And not a moment too soon. "Besides, he's not pursuing me."

"Andrea's always working. Now, Tony says he's faithful on the road, but these men are healthy. They don't like doing without. And with you conveniently next door . . ."

"I'm not a convenient anything."

"I'm just warning you. I like you, Desiree. Oh, do you

think Chris will come to me? He's so precious." Her smile lit up.

She tried to take him from Desiree, but he clung even harder. "He just woke up. He'll probably go to you later."

"Not many wives live in Atlanta. Maybe we can get together for lunch sometime?"

"Sounds wonderful." Desiree sensed Pat was a gossiper. She was going to have to tread lightly with this woman. She didn't like the idea of her business in the streets.

"I just moved here a few months ago. So I'm still feeling my way. Gets pretty lonely when Tony's away."

"I can imagine."

"Gerard's parents are really nice, though. Amanda got me involved in working on a hospital charity. At least it takes up some of my spare time. Do you work?"

"In New York."

Gerard came and took Christopher from Desiree. Her arms felt empty without him.

Tony's cell phone rang. While he answered, Gerard put Chris in the playpen. Desiree was overprotective. He suspected if Chris even whimpered she'd have him out of there in a flash. Even now she was frowning at him. The boy couldn't be in her arms every waking moment. At any rate, the toys should keep his attention for a few minutes.

"Look, man, I gave you a couple of grand last month. You said it would be the last time," Tony was saying. Gerard stepped away a few paces to keep from eavesdropping, but Tony wasn't lowering his voice.

The person on the other end must have wheedled, because Tony responded, "Pat's giving me hell about all the money I'm doling out. I'm not a bank. This has got to stop at some point."

The conversation went on another couple of minutes before Tony finally, said, "All right. All right. But let this be the last time. I mean it. You hear me?" He closed his phone and turned it off before he slid it into his pocket with jerky motions.

"Man, people think money grows on trees. I got folks gunning for me I haven't seen since kindergarten. I'm tired of it."

"Tell me about it."

"Pat's mad as hell about all the money going out. I spent thousands last month. Thousands. Back home I go to the bar. They drink up a couple grand worth of stuff, expensive stuff they wouldn't think of buying with their own money, and expect me to pay the bill. And if I don't, they act like I'm being cheap. I'm tired of this crap."

"Got to draw the line somewhere. You work hard for your money. You're not getting a handout." Gerard gave to charities. Most players did, but they weren't banks.

"I know, but they think every athlete makes ten mil a year. I don't make that kind of money. I can't spend like there's no end."

"Tell them that."

"It's not that easy, man. I got the family, their friends. My own friends. You know how it is when you come from nothing." He looked around. The neighborhood was old but upscale. With both parents physicians, Gerard hadn't grown up in poverty. "I guess you don't know."

"It shouldn't matter."

"But it does. It does. You're the one who made it, you know. It's like everyone made it with you."

The boys had played hard and were finally winding down. Desiree was getting ready to gather them up so they could go home. "I'm going to be a baseball player when I grow up. A pitcher," Justin was saying to someone.

"We're almost ready to go home, boys," Desiree said.

"I'm going to get another cookie," Steven said.

"Get me one, too," Justin called out and started walking with Desiree.

If baseball was really his goal, she didn't want to squash his dreams. She was aware that sports figures seemed larger than life, especially Gerard. She didn't want Justin to be snowed by that, so she chose her words carefully.

"Justin, there are lots of wonderful careers out there. Not just sports. I know it seems exciting. Especially when you know the players. But try to leave your options open. There are many things you're capable of doing. You could become a scientist. Your grades are very good in math and science. You don't have to limit your goals to sports."

"But I love playing sports."

"Sweetheart, most children love playing sports. It's fun entertainment. You should enjoy it. It's also good exercise when you're older. That doesn't mean you make a career out of it. It's an extracurricular activity."

"What's that?"

"Something you participate in for fun. That's why I signed you up for baseball. You need the exercise. You can still play, but there are so many options open to you."

"But I like baseball," he said stubbornly. Of course he would. He was surrounded by larger-than-life sports players.

"You like math too, don't you?"

"Yeah, but . . ."

She rubbed his head. "You don't have to make a decision today. I just want you to think about what I've said. Mr. and Mrs. Kingsley are doctors. Your father was a sports agent. He was a lawyer."

"He was, wasn't he?"

Desiree started to say something else, but Steven joined them with the cookies and she noticed Gerard listening to them. He was holding Christopher again. This gazes met. His eyes were as cold as ice. She'd insulted him without meaning to. She had to say something, but what?

She took a deep breath and approached him. "Gerard, I didn't mean that sports isn't a worthy goal . . ."

His posture stiff, Gerard handed the baby to Desiree. "I know exactly what you meant. I'm going to find Sherrice so we can leave." A sudden thin chill hung on the edge of his words.

A cold knot formed in Desiree's stomach. He was truly insulted. And he'd been nothing but decent to her family and her. He didn't deserve that. But she had a right to explain the truth to her nephew. Only a few athletes actually made it. Most of those who tried did so for the glamour and a way out of poverty. Most needed someone to explain to them that there were other ways to make a decent living. Maybe they wouldn't make twenty million, but they'd live comfortable lives nevertheless.

Her temper rose. Gerard of all people should know that. He encouraged children to pursue other goals on his public service announcements. How could he expect her to do less for her children?

Scott came outside like a rocket with the phone glued to his ear. Didn't that man ever go without the phone attached to him? "Good to see you again, Desiree. I'm just getting back to town. So how is it going?"

"Very good."

"Tell me about yourself."

"Let's see. In fifth grade I won the lead in the school play."

He chuckled. "You've got jokes. Are you going to work while you're in Atlanta?" he asked, nodding to a player and his wife. "I'll catch you in a minute," he said.

"I'd like to find something temporarily, but I don't know about leaving Christopher right now. He's adjusting so well."

"Have you ever worked with budgeting? I mean with teaching clients how to budget."

"Yes. Both adults and children. And I've done some volunteer work before I moved to New York."

"Would you consider taking on a few sports clients? I have some that are in dire need of budgeting skills. Think about it over the next week. I'll be in and out of town. Let's meet next Monday to discuss it more in detail. In the meantime, if you're interested call my office for details and you can work out how you intend to set things up. You can use your brother's office."

"I'll do that, thank you."

He handed her a card. Then he was gone.

Gerard returned and Desiree thanked his parents before she joined him and the kids in the car.

Her comment had raised an invisible shield between them that screamed into the silence as Gerard drove them home. He was still courteous to a fault. Desiree wanted to clear the air, but anything she said at this point would make it worse. He wasn't open to her explanation, and although the children weren't asleep, they were listening.

The music was turned to an easy listening station.

"If you're thinking of going back to work, you might want to contact the old housekeeper," Gerard said. "She might be willing to return. I heard someone say she doesn't like where she's currently employed."

"Do you have her number?"

"I'll get it for you." He stopped at a red light but gazed straight ahead. They were unusually quiet. Conversation was never a problem, and she felt an acute sense of loss.

"Gerard?"

He turned to her, his gaze sharp and piercing.

"I want to apologize for my comment earlier. Not for what I said, but for how it was construed."

He faced forward. His hands tightened around the steering wheel. "No need."

"Yes, there is." She could see the tension in his jaw. "I know how hard you work."

"No, you don't. You don't have a clue."

"I know you're good at what you do. I watched you play. I know it's not easy being on display the way you are on the

mound when all eyes are on you. I know it's much more
than meets the eye. It's just that to kids, sports are so glam-
orous. They don't have a clue of what's involved. I want
Justin to keep an open mind. I want him to know he's going
to college. I want him apprised of the other options."

The light changed and Gerard accelerated. "You're his
guardian. I'm sure you'll point him in the right direction."

Desiree sighed. She only made it worse. She wouldn't
question why it was so important for her to make amends.
Just that she wasn't comfortable with insulting him. But
he didn't have to be such an ass about it either. He, most
of all, should understand.

And although she had insulted him, he was still helpful. The housekeeper would be a godsend. Christopher
knew her. Desiree wouldn't have to worry about him if he
was with someone he knew and who cared. Especially a
woman his mother chose.

Desiree glanced at Gerard again. How in the world did
she start spending more time thinking of Gerard than she
did her own fiancé? Something was definitely wrong
with that scenario.

"I'm leaving early in the morning. Chad will be in and
out, although he has long hours at the hospital. If you
need help for anything, call him or Scott."

"Thanks. But we'll be fine."

Gerard drove straight home, undressed, and showered.
Within a half hour he was in bed. But he couldn't sleep.

Desiree's comment about sports players stabbed him
and left him open and bleeding. It was bad enough his
choice of career wasn't good enough for his parents. For
her to prejudge him without knowing a thing about him
was worse.

No matter how successful his career or that his parents
only made a tiny fraction of his earnings, he was still just

a jock in a sea of physicians. His character, his finances, nothing else mattered.

Had it not been for his grandfather, he'd never have been able to play baseball. His grandfather signed him up for little league when he was only a scrap of a kid. He'd moved on to Babe Ruth, then to high school and legion baseball. Granddad attended every game. He'd encouraged him, and played catch with him on the front lawn while Grandma prepared dinner.

His grandfather was also a physician, but his first love was baseball. He was Gerard's champion, but he was no longer there to encourage him.

His grandfather's father had been a physician and had forced his grandfather to follow in his footsteps. It was probably because of that that his grandfather encouraged Gerard to follow his dreams. If he wanted to be a doctor, be one, he'd said. But if he wanted to play ball, then play. It was a new day. The doors were wide open. He could be anything he wanted to be.

His parents had married while they were in residency, and his mother had gotten pregnant before she finished. As an infant, he spent more time with his grandparents than with his parents. When they finished residency, they began their practices, and that left him with his grandparents again. Gerard didn't mind. His grandparents had loved him and doted on him.

But it would still mean the world to him if his parents accepted him for who he was. He did his best on the field. He made sure he didn't act like an ass in public. He always put his best foot forward. And that should count for something.

Gerard cleared his mind. He needed a good night's rest.

It wasn't enough. It was never enough.

4

On the kids' first school day after spring break, Desiree felt as if she were tossing in the middle of a storm-tossed sea. She never had to worry about getting anyone out in the mornings other than herself. Now she had three children to prepare breakfast for. Christopher was in his high chair munching on a banana. And her head was swimming.

She went to the foot of the stairs and called up. "Come on, guys. Breakfast is ready and we have to leave soon."

Justin was the first one down.

"Oatmeal or eggs?" Desiree asked.

"Oatmeal," he said, sprinting into the room. He yanked out a chair from the kitchen table and plopped himself there.

"You want cinnamon on it?"

"I guess. We need lunch money."

"How much is lunch?" Desiree asked while sprinkling cinnamon on top of his cereal. She placed the bowl and a glass of juice in front of him.

"Mama always made out a check for the whole month," Justin informed her, digging in.

"I'll write the check while you eat breakfast. How much is your lunch?" she repeated. "And why didn't you tell me last night?"

"Forgot." He shrugged and told her the daily lunch fee. Desiree grabbed her purse as Sherrice charged down the steps, obviously wearing heels and jeans that were much too tight. "I need money."

The checkbook hovered in Desiree's hand. "How much is your lunch?"

"I get an allowance." She named an amount that had to be far above what she actually received. Desiree handed her a third of what she'd asked for. "How much is your lunch?" she asked, hand hovering over the checkbook.

"I buy mine every day. I don't do the monthly thing. This isn't enough."

"Honey, your aunt didn't just roll off the turnip truck." Desiree handed her enough for her allowance and lunch.

"And my allowance?"

"That's it."

She frowned at Desiree.

"That's all you're getting," Desiree repeated.

"It's not the money." Tears gathered in her eyes, her face a study of anguish.

What is it now? Desiree thought. "Well, what's wrong?"

"Are you sure you can handle Christopher alone?"

"Of course I'm sure. I've been taking care of him all week."

"Please . . . please don't hurt my brother." She was looking at the boy. His tiny arm was still in a cast. He'd gotten oatmeal on it.

Desiree's heart went out to the girl. Of course she was worried, considering what happened before.

"Honey, I wouldn't hurt him. I'll take very good care of him." Desiree wrapped her arms around the girl. For the first time, Sherrice didn't stiffen at her touch. "Don't worry about your brother. We're going to have a great time. Now, eat your breakfast. It's almost time to leave." She wrote out two checks for the boys before she quickly wiped Christopher down and everyone got into the mini-van to leave.

By the time she got back she was ready for a nap, but instead she stacked the dishwasher, made beds, dusted, vacuumed floors, and cleaned bathrooms—and half the time she was holding Christopher while she worked. The other half she was able to get him interested in toys.

She desperately needed a cleaning service. This house required ten times the effort needed to keep her tiny one-bedroom apartment clean. But she wanted the place to look decent when the Social Services representative arrived around noon. And the kids were going to have to make their own beds in the mornings.

Desiree had called Robert, Jordan's lawyer. He'd agreed to meet the social worker at the house with her.

Christopher was still up when the woman and Robert arrived.

"My goodness. What a difference a week makes," she said.

"He's doing very well, isn't he?" Desiree kissed him on the cheek. He was playing with a toy until Robert and the woman arrived. Then he began to cling to Desiree. At that moment she realized she might not be able to work, especially if he suffered from separation anxiety. She wouldn't think of adding additional emotional stress.

"I'm astonished. He looks healthier. And he even gained weight." The social worker reached out to touch him, but Christopher pulled back, burying his face in Desiree's neck. He was still leery of strangers. It was going to take time for him to trust.

Desiree rubbed his back to reassure him his world was safe. "Hey," she said, smiling at him. "It's okay." She kissed his sweet-smelling cheek again.

"He trusts you." The woman smiled.

They visited for an hour, and Desiree signed a ton of papers. In addition to the papers the lawyer had already given her to sign there were still more for her to sign, including a fingerprinting application.

"I have a credit card for you," Robert said. "I've also set up a bank account for the childrens' expenses." He named an outrageous monthly amount and gave Desiree the name of the cleaning service the Paynes had used before he left.

Desiree's days were busy with the kids and especially with Christopher, but she felt . . . lost, unfulfilled, as if she had no life that didn't include the children.

She craved adult entertainment. In New York there were always a million things to do with Paul or her friends. She and Paul often met after work. They often entertained clients, Paul more so than she. She began to think about the change in their lives once they married. They both couldn't spend half the night in Manhattan after work. Someone would have to go home to make sure homework was done, drive the children to after-school activities, and attend PTA meetings.

"Good evening, Mr. Kingsley," the doorman said the next evening at the hotel where Gerard was staying. "You have a delivery. I can send it up to your room."

Gerard handed the man a tip. He liked him. He protected Gerard's privacy. "Thank you," he said.

It was a beautiful vase of flowers. Gerard glanced at the card. It read *Congratulations, great game.* It wasn't signed.

Gerard didn't often receive flowers. He never received them from Andrea. Most women he dated expected gifts from him, not the reverse.

"Why don't you keep them? I can't travel with them," Gerard told the man.

"I'll give them to my wife. She loves flowers."

His first thought was perhaps the flowers were an apology from Desiree. He wasn't very receptive to her explanation after the cookout. He'd felt as raw as if she'd physically struck him. He'd like to think the flowers were from her, but he was certain she'd sign them. She was up front about whatever she had to say.

"Great bunch of flowers. Who're they from?" Tony asked, coming up behind him.

Gerard shrugged. "Beats me."

Tony raised an eyebrow. "Weren't they signed?"

"Nope."

"Well, she'll contact you. You think they're from Desiree? Think she's got the eye for you?"

"She's engaged."

"Wonder how long that's going to last."

"She seems pretty stable."

"Pat's pregnant."

Gerard patted him on the back. "Hey, congrats. I'm happy for you, man." Inside he felt a touch of envy. "Imagine that. Miniature Tonys scooting around."

"One at a time, thank you." But Tony was grinning like a simpleton.

"When's she due?"

"November. That's why she's getting on my back about spending so much money. We've got to think about the future. But what do I know about budgeting and all that crap? We never had much more than two nickels to rub together when I grew up."

"Talk to Scott about setting up an appointment with Desiree."

"What does she know about it?"

"She works in finance or something like that."

"Why don't we go out to dinner, or lunch or something, the four of us? Pat doesn't like crowds. But she enjoyed Desiree's company at your folks'."

"I'll ask her." Gerard smiled and shook his head, wondering how it would feel to be called Daddy. To have someone look up to you and think the sun and moon shone on you. He was more than a little jealous of Tony.

Pat thought the world of him, even though he was a sports player. She might complain about the way he spent money, but Tony had a heart of gold. Which was why it was so easy for old friends to take advantage of him. Desiree wouldn't have a problem with setting him straight on that score. That woman was a real barracuda.

"A daddy," Gerard murmured. "Has a nice ring to it, doesn't it?"

Tony grinned. "I'll be walking around like you now, toting a baby. Pretty soon Chris is gonna be calling you Daddy."

Gerard shook his head. "Chris isn't mine."

"All the women want their babies to be yours."

Except Desiree, Gerard thought. He wasn't good enough for the boys to emulate.

Once on the plane, Gerard started thinking about Chris, whether he was eating properly. If he was in pain. Sometimes the little tyke couldn't settle down, especially at night.

And he wondered about the flowers.

Gerard found himself picking up the phone and dialing Desiree. She answered immediately. Sounded like she was sitting by the phone waiting for it to ring. Probably expecting a call from her Paul.

"Great game," she said.

"It was, although I didn't pitch. How's Chris?"

"Sleeping soundly, thank goodness. He was a little restless last night."

"You're up late."

"I guess we take turns. Tonight I can't sleep. By the way, I called Mrs. Gaines, the old housekeeper. She agreed to come back on Monday, thank goodness. She seems really nice. She came by here Sunday after church."

"Beverly was very pleased with her."

Her voice soothed him.

"I got a call from Jordan's distant cousin. He wants the

children back. He says he's left his wife, that he didn't realize what was going on."

"How could he live in that house and not know his wife
was on drugs or she wasn't properly feeding the boy?"

"Obviously he wants the money. But they're going
back there over my dead body. I'm not going to let him
touch those kids. I haven't had Christopher long, but already he's gaining weight. I'm not the best cook, but all
the children are eating proper meals instead of junk."

"Don't worry, you've got a lot of people behind you,
beginning with me. Scott, Jordan's lawyer, we'll all stand
with you."

"Thanks, Gerard."

"I'll see you tomorrow. I'm getting in late tonight."

"Come over and eat breakfast with us. The kids would
love to have you."

As he closed the phone, he wished she'd love to have
him.

Desiree got the children enrolled in dance classes and
baseball. She attended conferences with the teachers.

Although Gerard was a virtual stranger, Desiree missed
the camaraderie they'd shared.

She and Paul talked infrequently and their conversations were always rushed. He was either on his way out
or in meetings. There were issues they needed to discuss.
Gerard's questions had given her reservations.

When she called Paul Friday night, he was in a bar and
she could barely hear him above the music blaring in the
background. On a normal Friday night Desiree would
have joined him or hung out with her friends. She felt the
sharp sting of nostalgia.

"How do you really feel about the children? Do you
have a problem with them?"

"I haven't really thought much about it. What can you

do? Listen, it's pretty loud in here. I'll call you tomorrow, okay?" he finally said.

Desiree hung up and picked up the remote and channel-surfed. None of the shows captured her interest. She turned off the TV. The house was quiet. She'd sent the kids to bed. Even Christopher was fast asleep without fussing. And she was at loose ends.

Sighing, she called her friend Deana, who sounded like she was riding in a car.

"Where are you on your way to?" Desiree asked, picturing her dressed to party.

"Just driving to Midtown to a club. I'm meeting Joy there."

"Have fun."

"You sound lonely."

Desiree shrugged, forgetting for a moment that her friend couldn't see her. "Somewhat. I've had a full week between school and after-school activities. These walls are closing in on me. Justin and Steven have games tomorrow. I've sent them to bed already, although I doubt they're asleep."

"Of course they aren't. It's Friday night. What kid goes to sleep early on Friday?" She stopped at what sounded like a toll booth.

"If you're going to Midtown, what are you doing at a toll?" Desiree asked.

"We're breaking up. It's getting crazy. I'll call you tomorrow." Everybody was calling tomorrow, Desiree thought as she slowly hung up the phone.

She gave up. With nothing more to do, she went to the den and started searching through file drawers. She shouldn't miss Gerard. But she did. She missed his easy smile. She missed their conversations. She'd never have taken him for the sensitive type.

She lifted out the first folder. As her mother would say, there was always work.

* * *

The doorbell rang at seven. The only person stirring was Christopher. Desiree sleepwalked through heating milk for his Cream of Wheat while he crawled around with the energy of a locomotive in full steam. Picking him up, Desiree went to the door, opened it, and gawked in shock.

"You have two choices. Either move aside or give us a hug. Otherwise, I'm going to hurt you. Where's the bathroom?" Deana said with an exhausted smile.

Joy stood beside her beaming. "Got you."

It took another two seconds before Desiree was enveloped in a three-way hold. She felt like crying. She did cry. Warm tears seeped down her face. "How did you get in?"

"We have trusting faces," Joy said.

Christopher shrieked playfully and smacked Desiree's cheek with his oatmeal-smeared hands.

"You all are crazy. You know that?" Desiree said. "Absolutely crazy."

"You're just finding that out? Who have we got here? You gonna let me sign my name on that cast? Looks like the stars have already signed. Ummm. Gerard Kingsley." She tasted the name like sweet nectar. "Must be the next-door neighbor."

Joy shook her head. "You're looking too much like an old mama. Is that Tony drawn in a catcher's mitt?"

"He's very creative." Desiree could only give them a teary grin. Parked in her front yard was a green minivan packed to the ceiling, including the roof rack. "What did you do, pack up my entire apartment?"

"Just about. We knew you weren't coming back any time soon."

Having friends like these women touched her heart. She felt sad and giddy all at once. "What am I going to do with you?"

"Show us the bathroom and feed us." Joy always made light of emotional moments.

Deana glanced around the great room as she entered

the house. "You've moved up in the world. You can fit your whole apartment in this room."

"Think you have enough beds in this place to put us up?" Joy asked. "We told crazy Paul we were coming."

"I told him if he told you, we were going to string him up," Deana said, and she wasn't smiling. "Saw him hanging out at the bar the other night. He looked lonely. He usually has you to help entertain the clients."

"He's so wrapped up in work, he barely has time to think about me."

"Hmmph."

"So where're the rest of the crew?" Deana asked.

"Christopher and I are the only ones up. The others are sleeping in."

Desiree prepared breakfast while her friends showered. After eating they went to bed and Desiree took the boys to their game. When they returned, her friends were still sleeping. The children pitched in to help Desiree unload the van. Then suddenly Chad materialized with two guys and helped them.

"Where did all this come from?" Chad asked.

"My friends packed some things from my apartment. They drove all night, so they're sleeping now."

With three men helping, the van was unloaded quickly. Desiree fixed them tall glasses of iced tea, liberally drenched with fresh-squeezed lemons, before they left.

When Gerard was on his way to the game, he stopped by. It felt as though a month had passed since she last saw him. Her friends were up and she introduced them. They kept cutting their eyes between Desiree and Gerard, and she began to feel self-conscious.

"I have extra tickets if you'd like to attend the game."

"We wouldn't miss it," Deana said, with her eyebrows raised. Desiree wanted to smack her.

Gerard smiled. He was holding Christopher. Desiree had wondered if the child would even remember Gerard after a week, but he went into Gerard's arms as if the older man had never left. When he lifted Christopher into the air, the child screamed with delight, while Desiree's heart nearly stopped. She had to forcibly stop herself from yanking him away from Gerard.

Gerard's grin told her he knew exactly what she was thinking. He thought she was overprotective. Maybe she was.

In the end, all of them rode with Chad to the ballpark.

The stadium was full. Anticipation was in the air and Gerard was the starting pitcher again. When he came out on the field, Desiree's heart turned over. His hat was pulled low over his eyes. If the window to the soul was through the eyes, you couldn't tell a thing about Gerard. His were hidden. After a few powerful throws to the catcher, he jogged toward the stand where they were sitting and tossed two autographed balls to Deana and Joy.

Deana thumped Desiree on the shoulder. "He's a keeper."

Desiree lifted her hand, providing a clear view of her engagement ring. Deana put her hand over the ring, effectively blocking it from sight, and gazed at Gerard.

"Like I said, he's a keeper."

If Desiree thought this game would be any different from the others, she was clearly mistaken. She was just as tense. In the first six innings the opposing team only scored one run. But in the seventh inning, Gerard's throwing arm was clearly tiring, and a relief pitcher took over.

The audience cheered him for innings well done. Desiree took her first relaxing breath when he walked away from the pitcher's mound. By then Chad was holding Christopher, leaving her free to stand and clap.

Her friend touched her shoulder. "What did I say earlier? Paul is out of the picture."

"We're only neighbors and friends," she repeated, as she sat down.

"Do you think if you say that enough times, you'll believe it?"

She didn't make an effort to respond further.

It was true she was very uncomfortable with the way she was feeling about Gerard. The feelings just seemed to be growing into something far too dangerous. Gerard was a sports player. They seldom took relationships seriously. And even if they did settle down, the temptation of groupies following them every time they were in public was so prevalent, extramarital affairs were commonplace. Most wives turned a blind eye to it. But it wasn't something Desiree could live with. Not that he'd asked her.

She'd better get her mind off Gerard and on Paul. She loved Paul. She needed to be with Paul to reinforce their closeness and how special their relationship was.

In the next inning two players got on base, but only one scored. The crowd was tense. Christopher started to get restless. The Eclipses were leading, but the score was two, zip. Now it was two to one. It was still anybody's game. Desiree was no longer thinking of her engagement. For the people sitting in the audience, it was only a game. But it was more than that to Gerard. Much more.

There she went again, thinking of Gerard. Her thoughts returned to the cookout and she wondered at the secret that plagued Gerard.

Gerard. Gerard. Gerard. Her mind played a repeating melody of him. This couldn't continue.

"Hey, Andrea," Chad called out.

"I'm sorry I missed so much of the game. Gerard is going to be so angry."

"He understands you had to work."

"I see we're winning."

"They just replaced him."

"Way to go. What're you doing with Chris?"

Andrea spoke to Desiree, but she was checking her out as if Desiree was competition.

"We missed you at the cookout the other night."

"Yeah. Gerard and I had a little tiff. I didn't feel like being around people."

"I hope you patched it up."

"We'll see." The woman's eyes flew to Desiree again. But Desiree concentrated on the game. A sour feeling clamped her stomach and twisted it into knots. Was she jealous of this woman and her attachment to Gerard? She was engaged. Gerard was only a neighbor. Andrea was his girlfriend. She had to keep telling herself that.

By the time the game was over, Desiree had heard so much about Andrea's special relationship with Gerard she wanted to scream. The jealousy that roared through her was frightening. She didn't understand herself. There was no doubt she was in love with Paul. But these feelings were so foreign—they just didn't make sense.

The Eclipses won and Desiree applauded with the rest of the locals. She was ready to go, though. Christopher had fallen asleep on Chad's shoulder. She offered to take him, but he refused.

"That was great," Deana said. "I've never personally known a baseball player before. Makes the game more interesting."

Joy moved closer to Desiree. "Who is that chick?" She motioned to Andrea.

"Gerard's girlfriend. I told you he was taken."

"I don't like her," Deana said.

"Well, that's just too bad." Desiree didn't like her either, but she knew the root of her antipathy. "In a few minutes we'll go to the hallway outside the locker room and you can meet other players, maybe even the coach."

"Wow."

"After their press interviews and showers."

Desiree glanced at Chad. His gaze lingered on Deana. Was something going on there? Deana shyly glanced away. She was not shy. *Get out of here.*

Desiree elbowed her friend in the side and glanced at Chad with raised eyebrows. She looked away with a grin on her face.

"I might just come back for summer vacation. I might even see a game while I'm here. You're going to be here that long, aren't you, Desiree? I'm definitely going to attend the Eclipses' games in New York."

"Since when did you take an interest in baseball?" Desiree asked.

"Tonight," Deana responded.

By the time they started to the locker room, Christopher had awakened. Desiree stopped by the restroom to change his diaper. He sucked hard on his bottle as they joined Gerard.

Andrea launched herself into Gerard's arms. Startled, he closed one arm around her. "Great game!" she said, kissing him. He turned just in time for her lips to meet his cheek.

"You missed most of it," Chad joked. "You didn't see him pitch at all."

"Shame on you," Gerard said jokingly while untangling himself.

Andrea shrugged with a pretty come-hither smile. "I did my best. There was a four-car pileup and I couldn't leave the hospital."

Gerard reached for Christopher, and Desiree found herself by his side. "How did Slugger make out?"

"He was a champ," Chad said.

"I know he was. You wouldn't disgrace yourself, would you?"

"You were amazing," Desiree said quietly as the others greeted the other players Chad introduced them to.

"Think so?"

"Definitely."

He looked tired, really tired.

"I can carry Christopher. Chad held him most of the time."

"I'm fine. He relaxes me." He moved so close their

arms brushed. "I had my cook fix a spread for us. I thought about taking everyone out, but I'm not up to a crowd tonight. I need to unwind."

"If you want to be alone, I'll understand. We can take care of ourselves."

He shook his head. "It's still cool enough for us to eat in the backyard. Everything should be ready at the house."

They gathered the kids and started walking to the car. Andrea caught up with them.

"Why don't I stop by later on tonight, Gerard?"

"Not tonight," he said.

Andrea looked disappointed, but she didn't give up. "Call me."

Gerard hooked a hand on Desiree's elbow and steered them on.

"She is your girlfriend. Why aren't you spending the evening with her? My friends and I can cook."

"Andrea and I aren't dating any longer. I don't believe in hanging on if it's over. She's playing a game and I'm tired of it."

"I'm sorry."

He shrugged.

"When did it end?"

"The night before you arrived."

"Your parents think you're still dating."

"Andrea has told them it's temporary."

"Maybe you can patch things up."

"No."

The attraction Desiree felt for Gerard frightened her. But he had been her brother's very good friend. It was expected that he would take her under his wing. But what she felt was much more than that. And she didn't want to evaluate it. Yet.

In the middle of dinner a florist's truck arrived in Gerard's yard. Five minutes later, the housekeeper brought out a huge vase of flowers and handed it to Gerard.

"These came for you."

Chad teased him. "What's going on?"

With a frown, Gerard glanced at the card. The note read *Congratulations*. There was no name to indicate who'd mailed it.

"Who're they from?" Chad asked. He'd eased into a seat beside Deana.

Gerard shrugged. "It isn't signed."

"You got a secret admirer?"

"They're probably from Andrea," Chad said. "Wonder why she isn't here."

"She would have signed it," Gerard said.

Chad frowned. "Whoever sent them knows where you live."

And that was a worry. The flowers were cloaked in secrecy. Anyone he knew would have signed the card.

"There are advantages to gated communities," Chad said.

Gerard indicated for the housekeeper to take the flowers back inside.

Desiree was restless and couldn't sleep. Everyone was in bed. Her friends were leaving at five in the morning. After a long soak in her hot tub, she put soft music on and dialed Paul's number.

"Hi," she said when he picked up. She heard him sitting up in bed. "Did I wake you?"

"No, no. I just got in."

"I don't know if I like you spending so many nights out without me."

"I get lonely looking at the four walls." He always complained that he had tons of work to do when she was there.

"I have a great solution to that. Visit me next weekend."

"Hmm."

"It seems like forever since I last saw you. I miss you."

"Hasn't been that long."

"Will you come? You've never checked out Atlanta."

He thought a second. "Yeah."

"How did your mother take the news that we'll have to delay the wedding?"

"She and Dad went to the Bahamas."

"How nice."

"I'll make reservations and let you know when to expect me."

They disconnected and Desiree was still restless. She went to the den and started going through Jordan's papers. She kept coming back to the note she had found there earlier and wondered what it meant.

Finally leaving the den, she made herself a cup of tea and went out to the patio to enjoy the cool spring breeze and the solitude. She had curled her feet up on the chair when she heard someone approach.

"Couldn't sleep either, I see."

She could barely see Gerard in the darkness. He wore jeans, a T-shirt, and sneakers.

"I'm surprised you're still up."

"After I pitch, I'm so wound up I have trouble sleeping." He sat on the couch. His arm brushed hers, sending an electrical charge up her arm. "Everybody in bed?"

"Yeah."

"Thanks for coming to my game. It meant a lot having you there."

"Your joy couldn't have been more than mine. You were spectacular."

He fell quiet.

"I think we need to discuss what I said at the cookout. I sensed that I . . . I hurt you and I didn't mean to do that."

"We don't have to discuss it."

"I want to. I don't watch games on television, but I see a lot of bad press about players and their relationships. The boys are right in the middle of it. I understand that what we see on television doesn't reflect on all the players, and that any wrongdoing on their part is magnified," she said. "I also see the public service announcements you do. I see firsthand what you do around here. And I think you're more than the sport you play."

"Not really. Desiree, I enjoy my work. My parents wanted me to be a physician, but becoming a doctor wasn't my dream. I don't know what I'm going to do after my playing days are over, only that right now, I'm doing the job I want to do with the team I want to play with. I couldn't ask for a better life. And if that isn't good en—"

"It *is* good enough. More than that. Do you know how rare it is for a person to land a job that's a passion and not just a paycheck? I respect what you do. I just want Justin and the children to look beyond the glamour. To choose a career, not because it looks good or because he thinks he's going to make several million, but because it is truly his passion.

"Justin looks at you and you're every boy's dream. Atlanta loves you, and to a kid, when you're standing in the spotlight, it looks like the happening place to be. But I know it's work, it's stressful. The weight of the entire team is on your shoulders. It's enormous pressure and I don't know how you do it."

"One pitch at a time." He gathered Desiree's hand in his. He wanted a confidante—someone he trusted with his deepest desires and fears. She seemed to understand him more than most. But she wasn't his. He caressed her ring. "I like you, Desiree. And if you weren't engaged—"

"But I am. Paul's visiting next weekend."

"I see. I wonder about you and Paul."

She slipped her hand from his. "Why?"

"Because I sense you feel something for me, deeper than surface friendship. I wonder if you love Paul, I mean are you really in love with him if you have feelings for me?"

Desiree had to fight the overwhelming need to be close to him. "You're deluding yourself," she said, but those words were as much for her as for him.

He captured her hand again and pressed her finger over his pulse. His gaze was as soft as a caress. "You see my heartbeat accelerate when I'm around you? I want to take you in my arms and hold you close. I want to kiss you. I want the key to your heart and soul."

Desiree hopped out of the seat so fast she nearly tripped. "It's been a long day. I'm going in."

"You can't run away from what you feel any more than I can. And believe me, I've tried. I've tried to respect your engagement. But it isn't working for me. And I considered it might not be working for you, either."

Desiree slammed the door shut on his words, closed the curtains, and sat on the edge of her bed, trembling. This couldn't be happening. She loved Paul.

Levi listened to the sounds of evening as he tended the coals. He heard a rustle in the ground cover. For a moment he froze and listened. Then silently he moved away from the fire to hide in the cover of the trees—and listened. His meat and vegetables sat untended waiting for the fire that was now ready. He was a patient man. He waited for the sound to occur again. He lay flat on his stomach, and waited—

He was in Hong Kong and he hailed a rickshaw, the taxi carts pulled by men. He and Rebecca toured temples and museums. Guards and police were everywhere. They had security like nothing he'd ever encountered in the U.S. It didn't bother the locals. It was how they lived. Security didn't bother Americans, their cash cow.

After the tours he took Rebecca to a restaurant and they sat on pillows and talked. The food was cooked right at the table. He and Becca ate slowly. He tasted her food and she tasted his.

He wished he could stay there forever, that he'd never have to go back to war.

"After this week, we'll never see each other again," Becca said.

"I know."

She licked her lips nervously. Then she elevated her chin. "I want to spend the night with you."

He realized it took tremendous strength for a black woman to leave her home and go to some unknown place where there were few black women. Her strength was as attractive as her beautiful face, her flawless skin, her intelligence. She wore her hair in a short Afro. He smoothed a hand down her face and touched the dimple in her cheek. Her pretty round face was dotted with a dimple in each cheek. She smelled of perfume that complemented her.

He signaled for the bill, and kept his eyes focused on Becca.

Rebecca took him to her place that night. It was hot and the windows were open. The noise from the busy streets below drifted up. But as he slowly peeled the clothes from Becca's body, revealing one delightful curve after the other, the surroundings, the noise, faded to black.

He was certain she was attractive in her own right—his very sight attested to that fact. His desire for her had nothing to do with the fact that he hadn't seen an American sister in the last five months. It had everything to do with the fact that she might very well be the last woman he made love with.

And that night, thousands of miles from his beloved Macon, he paid reverence to Becca's body, he stroked her soft breasts, he kissed her from head to toe, he loved her thoroughly, intimately, he made love with her as if it might be his last time—ever.

When morning light rose, he and Becca had snatched

no more than an hour's sleep. Yet he'd felt like a million bucks. Like he'd gone to heaven and died.

A skunk slinked out of the bushes. No way was Levi scaring that animal. He stayed right where he was, flat on his stomach, as quiet as a whisper, until the animal went off into the night. Only then did he come out of his hiding place and finish cooking his supper.

The stars hid behind a cloud cover. But it wouldn't rain, he knew. He didn't smell rain tonight.

5

At five the next morning, Desiree and her friends shared a teary good-bye. She'd barely slept a wink the night before and even her face felt exhausted.

She was still upset by her exchange with Gerard. So many changes had occurred in the last two weeks. She yearned to hold on to something tangible. She knew Paul. His likes, his dislikes. Bringing over coffee and bagels from her favorite deli on Sunday mornings and snuggling together on her living room couch while they read the *New York Times* might seem tame and boring. But loving someone wasn't about a steady diet of fire and lust. Fire burned down to cinders and cooled to ashes. Love included the quiet times. She'd had the fire once, and it had been the most disastrous venture of her life. It had been a living nightmare.

The one thing she was sure of was she could count on Paul. And she hadn't many men in her life whom she could actually count on.

"I know you're committed to Paul," Deana said, "but you aren't married until the preacher says 'you're now husband and wife.' Think long and hard about Gerard, sweetie. I see the blaze you've closed your eyes to." It was as if she was reading Desiree's mind.

It was so eerie, Desiree shivered. "Get out of here. You're right. I take my engagement seriously."

"Gerard can only settle down with one woman. Anyway, a little competition never frightened you off before."

"It's not competition that concerns me. It's so many women coming after them and men like him aren't ready to settle for one. But that's neither here nor there. Paul is my fiancé and he's coming next weekend."

Deana shook her head. "I never thought that match was made in heaven. But I won't complain. It's your decision. You have to live with him."

"Can you picture Paul settling down with four children?" Joy asked. "Can you imagine him changing a diaper?"

"Come on. Men do it all the time," Desiree defended. "Besides, if we had children I wouldn't be the only one to change a diaper."

"Women change several times the number of diapers men change. You need a reality check."

"Well, if he loves me, he'll accept the children. It's not like they'll be with us forever."

"Honey, children are always your children even when they move out."

"They've had a rough time. I'm not going to throw them to the wolves. I owe them love and stability. They're my family."

Deana's smile faded. "Desiree, I see how you've fallen in love with Chris. He has replaced the child you lost."

"I can never replace my baby." Desiree swallowed the tears threatening to fall. After five years, she still felt the loss spreading through her.

"I know. Paul was willing to accept the fact that you may not be able to have children. That doesn't obligate you to settle for him."

"I'm not settling. I love Paul. I really do. Trust me."

"Okay. Okay."

"That prime piece of masculinity next door won't be

frightened off by a couple of kids," Joy said, trying to lighten the mood.

"Girl, get out of here. You have a long drive. And thank you. Not just for my things but for being here. I was missing my friends when you arrived. I needed to see you."

They hugged. "Take care of yourself, girlfriend."

"I will. And thank you, thank you, thank you. Call me when you get home."

When Deana and Joy pulled out of her driveway, Desiree waved. A sudden feeling of despair overwhelmed her. Aunt Nadine would say it was a sign. Desiree got the feeling that a permanent change had just taken place. And she wasn't ready. She just wasn't ready.

Desiree went inside and grabbed a quick nap until it was time to wake the kids for church.

Monday morning Christopher kept up a continuous banging on his tray with his juice cup. A headache grew in the back of Desiree's skull.

"Stop that, Christopher. Drink your juice."

He grinned at her and continued to bang the cup.

He was a mess when she put him on the floor. He scooted off to his toys, but the noise only increased. Desiree picked him up and gave him a hug.

"You are trying my patience this morning, aren't you?" She set him back on the floor.

The boys skidded to a halt in the kitchen, dropping backpacks on the floor. By the time Desiree was ready to drive them to school, the baby was drenched with juice. She had to change his clothes before they left. When they settled in the car she already felt like she'd put in a full day. How did mothers manage? How was she going to handle a full-time job when she returned to New York? It wasn't unusual for her to work twelve-hour days.

Her meeting with Scott was scheduled for three o'clock. Ruby Gaines wouldn't arrive before noon. At least Mrs.

Gaines was picking up the kids from school. Desiree was still concerned about Christopher accepting the woman, but she'd kept him when he was a baby. Of course he wouldn't remember that.

When Desiree returned home she made beds, washed dishes, and tidied between taking time to play with Christopher. At eleven, she fed him, then put him in the stroller and walked him around the block.

Two ladies who looked as if they were in their seventies, one white and one black, were walking in their jogging suits carrying umbrellas over their heads even though the day was sunny and bright. The wind was blowing, keeping the temperature manageable.

"Oh, he's wide awake. But a turn around the block should have him sleeping in no time," the white woman said. "I'm Harriet and this is Eleanor."

Desiree extended a hand. "It's a pleasure to meet you. I'm Desiree."

"You're the aunt."

She nodded.

"So sorry about your brother and his wife. They were a lovely couple."

"Thank you."

"Beverly used to walk the baby around this time. She pushed him in the stroller just as you are."

Desiree smiled. "It's good to know I'm keeping up the traditions."

"Well, you have to do things your own way. As long as you love a child, it doesn't matter how you do things," Harriet said.

"We stroll every day if it's not raining or too hot," Eleanor said. "If you ever need a sitter, just call us. We used to sit for the Paynes now and again. The children were always well behaved."

"Thank you."

"And if I'm not available, my granddaughter is seventeen. She babysits as well. Very responsible."

"I'll keep that in mind."

"Beverly was so looking forward to that trip."

"Yes, indeed, Eleanor. She was so stressed she was falling apart. She truly needed it."

Harriet shook her head. She backed into some shade and lowered her umbrella. "We caught her actually crying one day. She quickly dried her eyes when we approached her. It was almost like we snuck up on her. She didn't know we were there until we spoke."

"Did she mention what was troubling her?"

"Not a word. She wasn't one to complain."

"Never heard a complaint from her about anybody."

"You should cultivate a freindship with that nice ballplayer," Eleanor said. "He's so different from what we hear about them on the news."

"One day I was taking groceries out of the car and he carried them in for me. You don't see that anymore. He'll make some young woman a wonderful husband."

"We aren't dating. He was my brother's friend," Desiree said.

"Such a nice young man. Good manners. Friendly and helpful."

"Is that an engagement ring, dear?"

"Yes."

"You'll be getting married soon."

"Within the year."

"Is he from around here?"

"He's from New York."

"Oh. That might be a problem with the children."

Christopher started to fret.

"Don't let us hold you, dear."

"It was a pleasure meeting you. Have a nice stroll," Desiree said and began to push the stroller.

With their umbrellas firmly over their heads, the women continued their stroll down the sidewalk. Desiree wondered if their arms got tired of holding the things.

Everyone had said her brother's marriage was solid.

What could possibly have been troubling Beverly? The children seemed healthy. Was she ill?

Leaving Christopher wasn't easy. Desiree battled back tears and swallowed the lump in her throat as she drove away. Mrs. Gaines had become friends with him before she left.

Scott's offices took up the entire top floor of a complex on Peach Tree Drive. It was reminiscent of the South with huge windows that overlooked the street and beautiful moldings. Framed photos of prominent sports players and newscasters covered the walls.

"Scott is on a phone call," his assistant said. She looked no more than twenty and was dressed in a figure-hugging green dress and wore spike heels. "May I get you something to drink or a snack? We have coffee, tea, soda, water."

"Water, please."

Desiree sat on a navy blue leather couch and picked up *Sports Illustrated*. A striking photo of Gerard was on the cover. She searched in the table of contents, found the page number, then flipped to his story. She was well into it when the assistant arrived with the water.

Desiree glanced up and smiled her thanks. She was only halfway through the article when the assistant escorted her to Scott's office. She carried the magazine with her.

"Oh. I see you're reading the article of our latest star. You can take it if you wish. We have several copies."

"Thank you."

He took his headphone off and placed it on the desk, then rounded the desk and sat in the chair beside her.

He reminded her of an Energizer bunny, perpetually in motion. Desiree guessed him to be in his fifties. His sky-blue shirtsleeves were pushed up.

"Most of my clients came from humble backgrounds.

They were never trained in money management," he began. "Suddenly they're making anywhere from a few hundred thousand to a few million. And they spend the money as if there's no limit. I want to be a full-service agency for them. I want it known that we aren't just looking to get them the huge contracts, but also to help them manage their money. In this business you never know what's going to happen. Just the other week one of our clients was injured during football practice. He's a midlist player. He started out making four hundred grand. In four years we've worked him up to two million. But he spent it as fast as he made it. Now he doesn't have a dime. We're hoping he'll be able to return to football once he heals, but if he doesn't . . . well, you know the score."

"Are your clients open to advice?"

"It's going to take some work to convince them. I can lead them to you, but it's up to you to convince them they need you. Is this something you're interested in?" he asked.

"Very much. You asked me to draw up guidelines and I have." She took her portfolio out of her briefcase. "I also have a resume."

He took both and quickly flipped through them. He kept the resume and handed the guidelines back.

"We have a reputable accounting firm that pays their bills and makes investments. But you'll have access to their records to help you with suggesting budgeting plans."

"Wonderful."

"I've already spoken to a few players. They're willing to meet with you. I have to warn you that some of them don't like the idea of anybody telling them how to spend their money, but at least we'll get them here long enough to listen for a few minutes."

"I can work with that."

"My assistant has chosen a secretary to work with you. She has the names and dates the clients are available. She can set up appointments and get their financial information for you. Anything you need, tell her." Scott stood. That man worked like a locomotive speeding down the tracks. "I'll give you the ten-cent tour of the office and show you your office."

They sped through the offices. Even after living in New York, Desiree never saw anyone who moved at the speed of that man—as if he already was a day late and had to play catch-up.

There were photographs of players on every wall. There were even pictures of commercials. Scott and Desiree only made it through half the tour before he was called to his office for a phone call. His assistant showed her through the rest of the place.

Finally, Desiree arrived in Jordan's office. It was located in a quieter section. Pictures of his family were still on the desk. Desiree sat behind the desk. She opened the top drawer. He was neat. At home as well as at work. All his things were organized. A box of cigars was in the upper right desk drawer.

Beverly was smiling in the photo. A secret, mysterious smile. One made to keep a man on his toes. Beverly held Christopher on her lap. He was no more than three months old. The two children stood on each side of her. It was a lovely family photo.

Desiree turned on the computer and printed out her schedule. No appointments were scheduled for that week. They started on Wednesday the following week, giving her time to study the financial history of her clients.

Beside each name was the prospective date the financial information would arrive. The staff was very efficient.

Desiree was happy to get back to the working world, but she couldn't get back to Christopher quickly enough.

Gerard couldn't stop thinking about Desiree. He wanted to meet this Paul she was so in love with. What was so special about him? Gerard couldn't fathom that she could love another man when he ached for her. It didn't make sense.

All his life, Gerard had never met a woman he couldn't leave. When Andrea threatened him with her physician, he'd felt a catch in his throat. They were a couple. They spent a lot of time together. The sex had been great. He liked her—but he didn't love her. And therein lay the difference. He could walk away from someone he didn't love. He wasn't admitting that he loved Desiree, just that they shared something worth exploring.

But was it enough for her to walk away from a man who'd pledged to marry her? He flopped back in his seat. He'd missed the last play of the game. His team was clapping and he clapped with them.

Sighing, he pulled off his cap and rubbed his hand over his head. Good thing he wasn't pitching. Desiree was driving him crazy. He never thought there was a woman alive who could draw his attention from his game. He couldn't name his constant need, his desire for Desiree. He only knew that he'd never felt this sharp need gnawing at his insides.

He was always fond of the idea of a woman like Desiree. And the real woman took his breath away. He couldn't avoid her even if he wanted to. If he did, she'd have Chris growing up afraid of the world, instead of being a rambunctious boy. She babied him too much. Carried him around half the day when he needed to be exploring his surroundings. The boy needed male influence. If for no other reason, he had to hang in there for Chris's sake.

Emily Boyd, the dance teacher, clapped twice. "You're doing wonderfully, Sherrice. I'm giving you two solos in the recital. Your father would have been so proud of you. As proud as I am."

Embarrassed, Sherrice ducked her head. "Thank you."

"Up, up. Chin up. Always." With a slim index finger she tapped beneath Sherrice's chin.

Emily smoothed the hair back from the girl's face. "How are you doing, really?"

"Okay."

"And the aunt. How is it working out with her?"

"Okay."

"Well, I suppose she'll be staying here for a while. Try that stretch once more. Reach, reach, reach."

Sherrice concentrated on her move. "Will she take you back to New York?" Emily asked.

"I don't think so. Gerard spends a lot of time at our house. I think he's going to convince her to stay. I don't want to move."

"I see. Well, that shouldn't take much effort. Your family is wealthy. I'm sure your father left enough money for your aunt to run through."

Sherrice stumbled. "She doesn't care about the money. She's nice to us. Especially to Chris."

"You thought your cousin cared about you too, but look how that turned out. Your aunt is a clever woman, Sherrice. I know you *want* to trust her, but you can't afford to be too careful. Not when Chris's welfare is at stake. You're the oldest. You have to protect your brothers. All of them." She gave Sherrice a quick hug.

Fear roiled in Sherrice's stomach. If Aunt Desiree didn't take care of them, what would happen to them? Would they be separated and sent to different homes like the stories she saw on TV? What would happen to Christopher? What if someone mistreated him? Aunt Desiree was kind to him. She was kind to all of them.

"Come on, dear. Let's try the next routine. Point, step, point, step. On your toes. You're a natural. But practice makes perfect. Do you think your aunt will let you sign on for an extra hour? We want these routines perfect for the recital."

"I guess so."

* * *

Desiree met with a couple of the childrens' teachers that week, took the boys to two soccer practices, and the baby to a doctor's appointment. One week felt more crowded than a month in New York. She was hoping to get a manicure by Thursday, but that didn't happen. She couldn't get tips anyway with the way she dug things out of Christopher's mouth. For the first time since she could remember, her nails were unpolished and she had dishpan hands.

Desiree was at the ball park. Practice had just ended. A couple of parents called saying there was an accident on the highway and they were stuck in traffic. All the parents had some place to be, including the coach, and he asked if she could stay until the other parents arrived. Thinking she would only be gone a few minutes, she didn't pack a diaper bag and Christopher soiled his diaper. Then he started complaining, accustomed as he was to her changing his diaper almost as quickly as he wet himself. He might be her first experience at changing diapers, but she'd become a pro in the time she'd been there. When the families finally arrived and they could leave, the car was ripe. She drove home with the windows rolled down.

Needless to say, she gained new respect for mothers, and she was never, ever leaving the house again without the diaper bag.

"Sherrice, would you like to go shopping with me tomorrow?"

Sherrice's head bobbed up. Their eyes met through the rearview mirror.

Desiree gazed at the girl. Her attitude was different the last couple of days. More remote. Desiree wondered what troubled her. She had tried to talk to her last night at bedtime, but she wasn't forthcoming. That worried Desiree.

Between hormones and the difficulty of just being a teenager, life could be trying during high school.

Desiree glanced at Sherrice again. The girl was staring out the window. Desiree would try to talk to her one on one during their outing.

Paul arrived during Thursday rush hour. He chose to rent a car from the airport. Desiree was grateful because Sherrice had ballet and the boys had baseball practice. She still hadn't gotten the hang of having to be at two places at once.

Sherrice hadn't been forthcoming during their shopping spree. She assured Desiree everything was okay in school. Desiree made a point of visiting with each child alone at bedtime.

When she finally arrived home, a rental car was in the driveway. Her heart leaped. Paul was finally there.

Desiree had left New York three weeks ago, but when Paul gathered her into his arms, it felt as if they had been separated for months or even years. His scent, his clean-shaven chin, and . . . "You shaved your mustache."

He rubbed the smooth skin. "You miss it?"

"It's . . . different."

"It'll grow back. I wanted a change."

"Hmm. What else have you changed since I left?" He looked better with the mustache, but she held her tongue. She was willing to accept him exactly the way he was, even if he did slide over to the ridiculous sometimes. But that was only her opinion.

And the deep desire she'd hoped for was missing. It frightened her. She expected the intense emotional outpouring. Her heart should be beating her chest to death. She glanced at the kids, who were all but lined up at the door watching them.

"Paul, let me introduce you to Sherrice, Justin, Steven,

and precious little Christopher. This is my fiancé, Mr.
Paul Tremain."

"Just call me Paul," he said.

Desiree was shocked and hurt by the childrens' mumbled
halfhearted response. They were polite, but unfriendly.

Obviously the kids disliked Paul on sight. By Paul's
frown, she could tell he wasn't exactly charmed with them
either. She felt a headache coming on, and she was angry
with the kids for their rudeness, but she'd deal with that later.

"What's wrong?" she asked.

"We're tired. Emily worked me extra hard for my
recital solo," Sherrice mumbled.

"Well, go on in the house and start on your homework.
I'll have supper on the table in a few minutes."

"I'll take Chris," Justin offered.

Since the guest cottage was in back of the house and Desiree wanted to give Paul a proper welcome, she handed
the baby over. Paul grabbed his suitcase and followed her.

"This is quite an estate," he said. "Do you have help
with the work?"

"The cleaning crew comes once a week."

"You definitely need it here."

They rounded the pool and Desiree unlocked the door.
It was a one-floor, two-bedroom dwelling with a great
room.

Paul dropped his duffel bag on the floor and gathered
her in his arms, held her close, and kissed her. She felt
the comforting beat of his heart against his warm chest.
After they kissed, she laid her face against his chest and
held him tightly around the waist.

"I missed you," she whispered.

"Yeah, me too."

But she didn't have the tingling in her stomach she'd
felt for Gerard a few nights ago. As much as she wanted
to rip the memory of Gerard's closeness from her mind,
she couldn't. As much as she wanted to forget the strength
of his shoulders, she compared them to the office softness

of Paul's. Why was she comparing the two? Paul was a wonderful man. He was her fiancé. They had a wonderful life ahead of them—if she didn't try to compare him and analyze everything in minute detail.

What she felt for Gerard was simply a passing phase. She knew that. It was only the newness. He was around and Paul wasn't. That would soon change when she moved the children to New York.

Paul played catch with the boys while Desiree was setting the table. Mrs. Gaines had prepared a wonderful dinner in honor of Paul's visit. Desiree was just getting ready to call everyone in when Paul came in holding his hand.

"What happened?" Desiree said, approaching him.

"Think I sprained my finger."

She felt the area, tried to move it. He winced. "Are you sure it isn't broken?"

"Yeah."

"I'll get ice." Desiree filled a bag with crushed ice. Good thing it was his left hand. "You weren't wearing a glove?"

"No."

"I don't understand," Justin said. "Gerard plays all the time and he never breaks his fingers."

"Baseball is Gerard's profession," Desiree said, angry at the pleased expression on the boy's face.

"But—"

"Go get cleaned up. Dinner will be on the table in five minutes. And tell your sister."

Dinner was a strained affair. Christopher played with, more than ate, his food. And he was fussy. Desiree put it to having a new person in the house or that he just wasn't feeling well. Maybe she had left the soiled diaper on him too long. But that was silly. What did she know about babies and their temperaments?

She gave Christopher his bath and rocked him with a

bottle. When he finally fell asleep, she looked in on the other children.

Sherrice was staring pensively at nothing.

"Knock, knock," Desiree called out and entered the room.

Sherrice jumped.

Desiree sat beside her on the bed. "Honey, you've seemed troubled the last few days. Are you having a problem you need to discuss?" she asked.

Sherrice shook her head vigorously. "No. I was just thinking about what I'm going to wear tomorrow."

"You do know you can talk to me about anything."

Sherrice nodded.

She was getting nowhere. "Did you get all your homework done?"

She nodded again.

"Need any help?"

"I did it all."

"I notice none of your friends ever visit. Wouldn't you like to have some of them over? You've been back three weeks now."

"Some of us were thinking about going to the movies tomorrow after practice."

"I'd like to meet their parents first. But it sounds like a good idea."

"Why do you have to meet the parents?"

"You're fourteen. I want to know the people you hang out with."

"I'm not a baby. I'm in high school."

"I know, but you're not an adult either. Those are the rules."

Desiree looked in on the boys before Paul joined her in the family room. It was a warm night and they sat on the patio.

She leaned back in the crook of his arm. This was the first time she'd had a chance to relax all day.

"Your day is pretty full with the kids, isn't it?" he asked.

"Yes. I have a part-time job now teaching budgeting to professional sports players, thank goodness. I didn't know how I was going to pay the rent on my apartment without dipping into my savings. And I didn't want to do that. It took so long to build it up."

"I don't know why you're holding on to it. You can't fit four children in there. You plan to keep them, don't you?"

"Of course. You're right. I have to find another place before the end of the summer."

"Do you think the kids are really going to settle in New York? They aren't used to the city. Look at this place. They have land around them. They're accustomed to being out in the open."

He'd repeated some of Gerard's arguments, and it concerned her. "As long as they're together, they'll adjust. Just like other children," she said.

"If you say so."

Desiree leaned forward and looked into Paul's eyes. "What's wrong?"

"I don't think it's going to be as smooth as you think or want it to be. The kids don't like me. They want you to be with this Gerard person." He removed his arm from behind Desiree and leaned forward. "They're attached to that ballplayer. It seems he spends a lot of time over here."

"That isn't going to happen. It's true Gerard kept them for a little while before I arrived. And he was their parents' very close friend. So he's a connection to their parents. And he feels a sense of responsibility for them. But nothing's going on between us. He's been a good friend, nothing more." She rubbed his back in long light strokes. "Once they get to know you, they'll love you as much as I do. I'm not saying there won't be adjustments."

He sat up and smiled down at her. "You were always one to take the bull by the horns."

"I can't have children, Paul. And I want them. Sometimes life has a way of tossing us what we need."

He started to say something, but reached for her instead.

6

Christopher's loud cries cut the necking short. Desiree rushed upstairs and gathered him into her arms, trying to get him to settle down, but it didn't work. Finally she brought him downstairs. She brushed a hand over his forehead. Kissed his cheek.

"He feels a little warm. Hold him while I get the thermometer."

You would have thought she'd handed him a pit bull. Desiree was halfway to her room when Paul shouted. She ran back.

Christopher had thrown up on his shirtfront. He held Christopher away from him. The poor baby's face was scrunched up and Paul had him dangling in the air.

She took her baby from him. "I'm sorry, Paul." Desiree soothed Christopher on her way to the kitchen for paper towels. She cleaned him up and handed some towels to Paul. "You may as well go to sleep. I don't know why he's so upset. He's been cranky all day."

"It's been a long day. I'll see you tomorrow. Hope he feels better."

Desiree went to the bathroom, washed Christopher up, and changed his clothes. Then she got the thermometer and sat on the chair to take his temp.

"I hate this as much as you do, sweetie. Here goes." When she stuck the thermometer in his ear, he tried to swat her hand away.

Sherrice came to the door. Christopher cried out his displeasure. Gratefully the reading was quick.

"What's wrong?" Sherrice looked concerned.

Desiree peered at the reading. "He has a slight temperature, but not enough to panic."

"Mom gave him Tylenol or Baby Advil when he had a cold." Sherrice yawned.

"Maybe he is coming down with something. Can you get it for me?"

"Sure." While Sherrice went to fetch the medicine, Desiree walked the floor with Christopher, trying to get him to calm down. Perhaps she should call the Kingsleys. They were doctors. She had their number somewhere. They'd know what to do.

"Here's the Tylenol."

Desiree read the instructions and gave him the allotted amount. "You go back to bed. I'll take care of him."

"I can stay up with you. I'll walk him."

"Honey, I have him."

Concerned, Sherrice bit her bottom lip. "If you need me, wake me."

Desiree nodded. She carried Christopher downstairs so he wouldn't wake the boys. She sat in a rocker. Next, she walked the floor, but a half hour later, Christopher was still fussy.

When he calmed for a little while, Desiree sat in the rocker. If he stayed calm, she'd put him in the bed with her. But he didn't calm down long enough for her to put him to bed. At least the fever left.

Finally, it was two in the morning. Desiree was exhausted and Christopher was still fussy. Desiree was nearly in tears. She didn't know what to do for him. She gave him pain medication and that didn't seem to calm him down. She considered calling the doctor. But he wasn't howling, he was more restless and miserable. Poor thing, his arm was probably troubling him.

This was worse than his first night from the hospital, Desiree thought.

"What's wrong, sweetie?" She wiped his tears with a soft tissue, kissed his soft cheek, and snuggled him close. But he still wouldn't settle. Finally she took him to the screened-in porch, hoping the warm night breeze would help calm him the way a push in the stroller did. She considered taking him for a drive, but she didn't want to leave the kids alone.

The air was barely stirring, making it comfortable. Desiree sat on the soft cushion in the rocker, laid Christopher's head against her shoulder, and started rocking, hoping it would lull him to sleep. He settled only a little. He'd close his eyes for a couple of minutes, and then he'd start up again. She got up to pace.

"Hello there."

Desiree's head whipped to the side. She barely contained a screech by the time she recognized the voice. "You scared the daylights out of me." Jerked out of his comfortable position, Christopher started fussing once more.

She unlocked the door and Gerard climbed the steps. He wore gray sweats and a gray short-sleeved knit shirt. And her heart jolted the way it had no business doing— the way it should have for Paul.

"What are you doing here?"

"I flew back tonight and saw the light in your room. I heard Chris complaining when I started walking over. "What's going on, Slugger?" He gently rubbed the child's back. His arm touched Desiree's, sending a charge through her body.

"Christopher, poor darling, can't settle down. I gave him medicine, but that didn't calm him either."

He ran a hand up and down her arm. "You're as tense as he is. Both of you are stressed out."

"I guess so." Desiree was so tired and felt so ineffective, she felt like crying.

Gerard reached for the baby. "Come here, Slugger. Let's give Desiree a rest." He glanced at Desiree. "You're exhausted." Their eyes met and held. He kissed Christopher on the cheek. Then he turned and kissed Desiree. It was so unexpected and so warm, it seemed to warm her entire body. Why on Earth was she feeling these things for this man? What was wrong with her?

Desiree cleared her throat. "You need to rest. You have a game tomorrow."

"Tomorrow is my day off. You still don't have my schedule, do you?"

"But it's your only day off for a while. I—"

"Go drink a glass of wine. Read a book. Sleep. Relax. Slugger and I are just fine. You aren't. Go unwind. You're tense and he senses it."

It was so true. She felt the tension bunch in her neck and shoulders. A low-grade headache didn't help matters. His offer was too welcome to give up.

"Where's Paul?" Gerard asked. He'd almost spat the words.

"In the cottage."

"Go to bed."

"Thank you," she finally said.

As she strolled from the room, Gerard watched her backside and the expanse of gorgeous legs beneath. She wore white delicate slippers with the feathery fur on the top. Her nightclothes were skimpy and his blood heated to boiling. Did she wear that outfit for the wimp? "You kept them apart, didn't you, sport?"

What a scumbag to leave Desiree with the baby while he slept the night away? Gerard knew right then and there, Paul wasn't the man for Desiree. If he accepted the children, they were going to be hers to deal with alone. In a crisis, he wasn't going to lift a hand to help her. She could do better by herself. At least here she had a support group. At least when he was home, he was available.

Chris rested peacefully on his shoulder.

"So what's all the ruckus about, sport? You don't like him any more than I do, do you? You're my man."

Gerard stretched out on the chaise. He placed Chris so he wouldn't fall off. Since Chris was quiet, Gerard closed his eyes—only for a moment.

As Desiree went into her bedroom, she realized she only wore a skimpy nightgown. She was too tired to berate herself about it. Her heart had lit up the moment she saw Gerard in a way it hadn't for Paul. But she and Paul barely had any time together since he arrived. Tomorrow would be different. If she could get enough sleep to be coherent.

In the kitchen she poured two glasses of wine. Then she padded to her bedroom and turned the music on low. She set Gerard's drink on the table. She'd give it to him in a few minutes. She sat on the chair, took a sip of wine, and laid her head against the seat back. She'd rest for just a moment.

Suddenly she jerked awake and remembered Christopher. She was relaxed. And she didn't hear a whimper from outside her door. How long had she been out of it?

Desiree hated to move, but she did. She grasped Gerard's glass from the table and took it to the patio with her.

Gerard was stretched out on the chaise, and Christopher was fast asleep on his chest. It was such a touching scene it brought tears to her eyes. Her breath hitched in her throat. He'd make a wonderful father.

Why wasn't he chasing groupies who ran after him the way NASCAR drivers ran after the finish line? Yet every spare moment he spent with her.

Putting the glass down, gingerly she picked Christopher up. The baby didn't stir and Gerard merely turned on his side and continued to sleep. He must be exhausted, yet he'd come over to help her.

She carried the baby to his room and tucked him in the crib. He didn't stir. His sleep was deep and peaceful. She padded back downstairs and unearthed a spare blanket from the linen closet. On the patio, Gerard continued to sleep when she covered him with the blanket, making sure to shelter his pitching arm.

He was so out of it, he continued to sleep as she watched him a full minute before she went inside to her own bed. In minutes, Desiree fell asleep.

When Desiree woke up the next morning and glanced at the clock it was time for the kids to leave. They were going to be late for school, darn it. Every morning that week she had to hustle them out of bed. She shot out of bed, surprised Christopher hadn't screamed the house down.

Running down the hallway, she smelled . . . food. Puzzled, she darted into the kitchen. The kids were getting up from the table. Gerard was at the stove. Christopher had already eaten and was grinning while hitting the spoon on the high chair, a mess of grits smeared on his face, arms, hands, and shirtfront.

Paul was sitting at the head of the table with a plate of food he'd barely touched in front of him.

"Why didn't someone wake me?" Desiree said, wiping the sleep from her eyes.

"Gerard said you all had a late night," Sherrice said with a look of intense innocence.

That little scamp. Trying to start trouble. "Christopher had a bad night. Poor thing couldn't settle down."

"We know why now. Come here and take a look," Gerard said with a grin.

"What's wrong?" Desiree asked, strolling over to the high chair.

Gerard tickled Christopher in the side and the baby opened his mouth in a wide grin.

"You've got a new tooth." Desiree pressed a hand to

her chest. She felt like he'd done something grand. "Will you look at that, you little sweetheart." She kissed him and he grinned at her, lifting his arms for her to take him. She plucked him up and danced him around the room.

"I'm surprised he's up so early. He was up half the night fussing."

"He's going to be out like a light before you know it," Gerard said. "Okay, let's load up. Time to go. I'll take care of chauffeur duties this morning. And since I have tonight off, I'll babysit so you and Paul can have a night out. Have some time alone."

"But it's your only night off." She felt like a tape recorder, but she didn't want to take advantage of him.

"Don't look a gift horse in the mouth. Nice meeting you, Paul. Take it easy, man."

"Can we still go to your game tomorrow?" Justin asked, glancing at Paul.

"I have the tickets, but it's Desiree's decision."

Four pair of eyes looked up at Desiree. "Okay, sure. Now go."

The house cleared in seconds. Total silence emerged. Christopher yawned.

"You're sleepy, aren't you?" Desiree cleaned him up with a warm washcloth.

"Want to tell me what's going on?" Paul asked, his hands steepled beneath his chin.

"What?"

"Between you and the jock."

"He was my brother's friend. And he's a neighbor. He's been very helpful with helping the kids adjust. There's nothing more to it, Paul."

"And you."

"Yes. He made the transition easier for me. The kids and I are still adjusting. You can see that for yourself."

"I see more between you and the jock than the kids." His food was all but forgotten.

"It's your imagination, Paul. We have just a couple of

days together. Let's not spend it fighting about Gerard. Trust me. He's just a friend."

"Hmm."

"Aren't you going to eat your breakfast?" She put Christopher on the floor and he scampered off to his toys. "Can you keep an eye on him while I wash my face?"

"Sure."

Desiree washed her face and cleaned her teeth, but she didn't bother taking a shower. She thought about Paul's jealousy. He had no reason to be jealous. She'd been faithful to him from the beginning. She didn't play messing around.

She rushed back to the kitchen. Christopher was so sleepy he was getting fussy again. She prepared a bottle and took him to bed. He nodded off immediately.

Downstairs, she heated her breakfast in the microwave and sat down to eat. She'd skipped dinner the night before and she was starving.

The tension in the air was thick enough to slice. She had planned for Paul and her to spend their time cementing their love, but he had an attitude she just didn't have the energy to deal with after only four hours of sleep and an empty stomach. So she ate her breakfast, hoping that by the time she was through he would be over his sulk.

Mrs. Gaines arrived, and it was apparent she didn't think too highly of Paul either. Of course, the woman was prejudiced. She loved Gerard.

"Andrea has been asking about you, man," Chad said when Gerard made it home. "What's up with you two? She's not hanging out here the way she used to."

"We broke up."

"You're kidding."

"Nope."

Chad shook his head. "You dumped her?"

"She dumped me."

"That's hard to believe. I thought she was in love with you."

"Don't think so."

"Anyway, she wants to talk to you."

"Hmm."

"Don't you think you should tell Mama? She's picking out the china."

"I don't know why. It wouldn't be her wedding."

"It's going to be tough for another woman to follow in her footsteps. Mom and Dad have fallen in love with Andrea. They think of her as their daughter-in-law. Parents get attached to your dates. Especially when they really like them the way they took to Andrea."

Gerard shrugged, knowing very well his brother was correct. Their parents were very attached to Andrea, but there was nothing he could do about that.

"So what are your plans for today?"

"A couple of meetings with my agent."

"Where were you last night? I thought you were with Andrea."

"I know you aren't asking me that." His brother was out of his mind.

"Right."

"Next door. Chris was having a hard time. Desiree couldn't handle him. She was exhausted."

"You're becoming a regular family man, aren't you?"

Gerard shrugged. "No big thing."

"I thought Desiree was engaged."

"She is. I'm babysitting for her tonight so she and Paul can get together."

Chad roared with laughter. "You? Babysit? Get off it." Chad laughed so hard he held his stomach.

"What's wrong with that?"

"You and kids?"

Chad chuckled on his way to the door. Gerard hit him in the back with the dish towel. When the door closed, he picked the towel up and put it in the laundry. What was so funny about him and kids? Not that he wanted any right now.

Gerard dressed and drove to Scott's office. Scott was working out a commercial deal with a soft drink company. He spent a couple of hours there, and when he made it home, Andrea was waiting for him. He was not looking forward to a confrontation.

He beckoned her inside.

"You haven't called," she said. She wore hip-hugging jeans with a red top.

He slid out of his suit jacket and draped it on the chair. "Why should I? It's over. You have your physician."

She crimped her lips. "You could have at least asked me to reconsider."

"If he's the man you want, why would I stand in your way?"

"If you loved me—"

"Look, obviously I'm not offering you what you want. You want marriage. He's offering it to you. Take him up on it."

"You know, you can be so uncaring."

"In all the time we've been together, how have I been uncaring? I haven't cheated on you. I've given as much of myself as I could."

"You could have at least acted like you cared."

"I cared."

"But not enough."

Gerard remained silent. He'd said his piece. He didn't believe in beating a dead horse.

"This whole relationship has been about you. About what you wanted. About what you needed. It has never been about us. Yes. There is a physician who wants to date me. He cares about me. He asks how I'm feeling, what I need." Tears filled her eyes. Gerard had never expected it to go there, or that she felt that way. He'd never given the breakup that much thought.

"It was a test to see if, for once, you would fight for me. I guess I have my answer."

"I'm sorry, Andrea. I never meant to hurt you."

"I know. You jocks are all alike. I should have known going in what it would be like, but I expected more from you. I guess I was looking for what Amanda and Nolan shared. My parents fought like cats and dogs. They didn't love each other. I don't want to be part of a loveless marriage. I looked at your parents and I said to myself that marriage to their son had to be a marriage made in heaven. I guess I was looking at the wrong people."

"I don't know what to say. I could have told you I'm nothing like my parents. You never should have dated me if you were looking for what they shared."

"I wonder how you can spend so much time with Jordan's children. You're holding Chris all the time. You're driving, what's her name, *Desiree,* and the children all over the place and treating Chris like he's yours, yet you can't marry me and have a baby."

"You're blowing this out of proportion."

"I don't think so." Andrea gathered her purse and walked out, leaving Gerard heart-heavy, not because they weren't a couple any longer, but because he'd hurt her. He'd never meant to do that. He'd never loved her the way she should be loved. And he felt bad for it.

Desiree and Paul had seen the King Center, they'd gone to the Underground, and they were halfway through the Coke tour. Paul was tasting a beverage marketed for a foreign country when her cell phone rang.

"I have a client who wants to see you Monday morning with his mother," Scott started without preamble.

"Who is it?"

"Daryl. He wasn't on your list, but his mother heard about you and wants to meet you. She wants you to see him immediately. You can use Jordan's computer to pull up the info you need. Use your account password."

"What time is our appointment?" Desiree asked.

"Sorry, but it's at eight," Scott said. "He's only in town a short time, and only to see you. Your assistant will be leaving in a couple of hours, so look things over and call if you need additional info. Think you can make it?"

"Sure." Desiree glanced at her watch. They had to leave now or chance being stuck in rush-hour traffic.

"Got to leave?" Paul asked.

"Yes." They were quiet on their way out of town. It just wasn't working and she didn't know what to do to make it work. Paul was still ticked off about Gerard. And maybe if the shoe was on the other foot, she'd feel the same way. But the situation between Gerard and her was completely platonic. Maybe not completely in her heart, but at least she was committed.

Fear raced through Desiree because she couldn't make it right. They didn't necessarily have to be in each other's back pockets, but at least what they shared had worked before and she couldn't think of any way to make things work now.

Desiree dressed carefully for the date. They ate dinner at one of Atlanta's exclusive restaurants.

"I really miss you at dinner meetings," Paul said. "You know how to put clients at ease."

"I've missed New York. How was your parents' trip?"

"Wonderful. Mama found a hall in Connecticut she wants us to look at for the reception. She said it was large enough to hold comfortably all the people we'll invite. A friend of hers had her 40th anniversary there."

"I'll be back in New York the end of June."

He nodded. Conversation was stilted. There was no handholding. No touching. No dragging her foot up his legs. No reaching over to slide his hand along her thigh.

After dinner, they lingered over drinks and desserts. Paul was tense. Deep in thought, he looked off into space. Desiree reached across the table and touched his hand. When he glanced at her, she smiled.

"Hey," she said. "Penny for your thoughts."

He inhaled sharply and almost squeezed her hand. "So when do you think you'll be back in New York?" he asked.

He wasn't listening to her. "The beginning of the summer," she said. "After the kids finish out the school year."

"What's going to happen with them—eventually?"

Desiree placed her fork on the table. "What do you mean?"

"Are you going to keep all four?"

"I can't separate them."

"They have wonderful boarding schools in New York and Connecticut."

"I hadn't thought about sending the kids off. I want to keep them together." There was the problem with Sherrice. "It'll be too traumatic to send them away right now. The boys are still in elementary school. They're too young for boarding school."

"They have boarding schools for young kids. I have clients with kids that age who go to boarding school. And it's not like they'll be alone. Justin and Steven will be together."

"Boarding school is all right if the child wants to go. There are some really good ones. But I'll only send them if that's what *they* want. They have some wonderful private day schools in New York."

He wiped his mouth with the napkin.

"If you're worried about money, don't. My brother left the kids well provided for. We can afford a live-in for Christopher."

"Can you imagine my house with four kids?"

"But it's a nice size. You have enough bedrooms. The place is huge."

"I know, but I couldn't stand the noise." He took a deep breath.

"Paul, I don't know if I can have children. These may very well be the only kids we ever have."

"The fact that you weren't rushing out to have children was one of the things that attracted me to you. I don't necessarily want them."

Not want children? "Why didn't you tell me that before?"

"Even if we did have children, I only wanted one, and later on. Not right away. We're trying to build our careers. I'm climbing quickly. We work twelve-hour days. I don't have time for them and quite frankly neither do you. I mean, you're taking a real risk in being away from your job as it is."

Desiree stared at him in shock.

His gaze wouldn't meet hers. "I'm sorry, Desiree. I'm not ready to take on all that responsibility."

Desiree's throat ached with defeat. At first she was stunned. Then, the crushing pain in her heart was a familiar thing. She'd been right here several times before. She opened and closed her mouth, but words didn't emerge. She took a moment to gather her thoughts, for her brain to function again before she spoke.

"I understand. I won't force the children on you. They're my responsibility, not yours."

"I don't want to be selfish—"

"You have a right to live the kind of life you want. You don't have to take on my family. I'm not asking you to." She squared her shoulders. "I'm perfectly capable of caring for them alone."

He offered a sad smile. "We've changed, haven't we? I mean, one week we're ready to marry. Everything's perfect. And then, bam."

"Yeah." Desiree could have said the bam was much worse for the children, losing two parents at once, then being sent to an abusive relative's home.

She should have learned her lesson by now. She had

never been able to count on a man—not one—when the going got tough. What made her think Paul would be different?

Looking back, it was she who gave the most. She helped entertain his clients. She planned dinners at his home. She gave and gave and gave. And she was sick of it.

"It's not going to work, is it?" he said.

"No."

"I love you, Desiree."

"I hate long good-byes." She tugged the engagement ring off and handed it to him.

He rolled it around in his hand and glanced at her. Desiree lifted her chin. "Time to go."

Paul signaled for the waiter. In minutes they were in the car on their way home. "I'm going to try to catch a flight out tonight. I wish you the best, Desiree. I'm sorry."

"Don't be." She tilted her chin. When she lost her baby five years ago, she was alone until her mother arrived. "It's better to find things weren't going to work out now, even if the kids weren't in the picture," she said and got out of the car. He drove around back to the cottage.

She inhaled a long breath, hoping the kids were in bed and she could do a great acting job for Gerard. She stuck the key in the lock and opened the door. It was quiet.

Gerard was on the porch with the kids, who were dressed in their pajamas and playing some game. Even Christopher was up, eyes bright and lively, pulling on the table to stand before he flopped on his butt. For a moment he looked stunned, and then he grinned up at her. Of course he was up. He'd slept half the day.

Gerard glanced up from the table. "We didn't expect you so early."

"Christopher is usually in bed by now," she said.

"He wanted to stay up with us."

Desiree nodded. "I'm going to change." As she left, she heard Gerard tell the children it was time for bed.

They responded with a lot of grumbling, but he had them moving. Feet pounded on the steps.

Desiree hung up her clothes by rote, and dressed in velour sweats and a T-shirt. Tears slipped down her cheeks as she washed the makeup off her face. She washed them away.

She would not cry, darn it. Not one tear. Paul wasn't worth it. No man was.

Pulling herself together, Desiree strolled to the porch. Gerard was alone, and straightening pillows. He'd already put away the game.

"Where's Christopher?" Desiree asked.

"When I put him in the crib, he fell asleep immediately." They heard Paul's rental drive away.

"What happened?" he asked quietly.

"It's over. He doesn't want the responsibility of four children. I don't blame him. Really, I don't."

"I do. What a loser. You don't need him. You're not alone, you know. I'm right here." He closed the space between them and pulled her against his strong chest. Kissing her on the cheek, he held her securely in his warm embrace.

"We're friends first. Always. Always remember that," he whispered, his breath warm against her ear.

"For now. One day you're going to find someone special and she's going to be jealous of the time you spend with us. Then you'll have to cut back. I'm willing to go it alone. I'm prepared."

"I'm here now and that's what matters." Gerard led Desiree to the sofa. He pulled her close to him and put an arm around her shoulders.

As much as Gerard wanted to kiss Desiree until she forgot Paul ever existed, until she was senseless for only him, it wasn't what she needed right now. But their time was close. And as much as he wanted her for himself, he didn't want her unhappy.

7

Desiree called her aunt Nadine the next day. "I want to drive out to see Dad. He's been in the forest for three weeks. More than enough time for him to get himself together."

"Girl, you best leave him alone till he's ready to come back on his own. You'll stir up a mess of trouble if you try to deal with him before he's ready."

"Aunt Nadine, how can I just leave him out there?"

"What you think you're gonna do? You won't find him. He'll hide out." She sighed. "I know he's usually back by now, but sometimes when he's really upset it takes longer. This is nothing new, child. Happens all the time. Just pray for him."

"I always do."

"I was getting ready for church. Already cooked supper. You taking those kids to church?"

"Yes, I am." Desiree had been to church more lately than she'd been in months in New York. She readily admitted she'd been lax in that department.

"As bad as things are these days, we need the Lord's hand in raising children."

"I know."

"Your mama's coming back today. Guess you'll call her about the news."

"I'll wait until later. Give her a chance to settle in first."

"Don't wait too long. She doesn't like to be kept in the dark."

When Desiree hung up, Justin and Steven came into her room.

"We're sorry Paul left. Did he leave because of us?" Steven asked.

"Oh no. Why would you think that?"

"He was supposed to stay until tonight, but he left last night," Justin said. "Is he coming back?"

Desiree blew out a long breath. "No."

"Was it because he didn't like us? Are you going to leave us too?" Justin asked.

"You aren't wearing your ring anymore," said Steven.

"Paul and I decided we weren't right for each other. It had nothing to do with you. Don't worry about it."

"Are you okay?" Steven asked.

Desiree smiled. "I'm just fine. And after church I think we'll go shopping for clothes and have dinner out." She wasn't up to spending half the day in the kitchen like Aunt Nadine preparing Sunday dinner.

"I could use some new shoes," Justin said. "Mine are getting too small."

"Eat your breakfast. I'll be out in a few minutes."

Desiree couldn't fathom that she'd been so out of it last night. It had turned cool outside and Gerard had come inside with her. They'd sat on the family room couch until she fell asleep. And that was where she'd awakened the next morning. Gerard had placed a blanket over her before he left.

He'd come over to prepare breakfast that morning. She'd awakened to the pungent smell of coffee and bacon.

She couldn't afford to wallow in self-pity. She had four children to raise. After Desiree showered she went to the kitchen for breakfast.

Gerard glanced up from the Sunday paper. "You're looking good this morning."

"Thanks. For everything."

"Any time." He closed the paper. "What are your plans for the day?"

"First I'm going to give Christopher a bath. Then we're going to church."

"And she's going to take us shopping, and then we're going to eat out," Steven said.

"It's a good thing I'm not pitching."

"We wouldn't miss your game," Justin said anxiously.

Gerard rubbed his head. "Don't worry about it."

Monday was Desiree's first session with a client. She'd spent every day for the last few weeks with Christopher. She felt a catch in her throat leaving him the entire morning. But at least she felt confident he was okay with Mrs. Gaines. It didn't stop the guilt.

Since she was working part-time, with only two appointments she should be home before he missed her. In the office her gaze kept going to the children's picture. She couldn't stand it. She picked up the phone and dialed home.

"He's okay," Mrs. Gaines said. "We're going into the backyard so he can get some fresh air and play."

"He'll love that. I should be home by noon."

"He'll be down for his nap by then and you can put your feet up and eat a nice lunch before he awakens," the kind woman said. Desiree must be getting on her nerves with the constant worry. "Anything you want in particular?"

"Something light." She didn't have much of an appetite.

The intercom rang, announcing her first appointment. Daryl Bailey was tall and . . . huge. Definitely a football star. Both he and his mother wore identical frowns. Daryl was at least six four, and his mother appeared to be around six feet herself. Although she was a thick-boned woman, she was lean.

Desiree stood. "It's a pleasure to meet you."

"I'm glad Scott hired someone like you," Mrs. Bailey said.

"Would you like something to drink?" Desiree went through the selections. The assistant brought in coffee and they wasted no time getting down to business. Mrs. Bailey was a no-nonsense woman.

"You know, Daryl's father and I never really had a lot of money. But we had enough to raise our children, comfortably. I found out he's been handing out money all around town like gold foil chocolate disks. It's not like he's doing good with it. He's wasting it. I didn't raise you to waste money. It's going to stop right now."

Daryl sighed, slumped back in his seat. "Mama, when are you going to let me take care of my business? I'm a man now. I don't need you watching over me like I'm some kid."

"When you start standing up like you're a man, that's when." She faced Desiree. "You see, his father died three years ago, and Daryl felt he had to become the man of the house. I had one husband. I don't need my son taking his place."

"What's wrong with me buying you a house and making sure you and my sisters and brothers are okay?"

"You're making them no account. That's what's wrong," she snapped, then faced Desiree. "My youngest son decided to drop out of college and live the high life with no job. Knucklehead here has been sending him money, paying for his apartment, clothes, everything. Taking care of him so he doesn't have to work."

"He's my brother. I can't let him live on the street."

"He can get a job. If he doesn't want to attend school, then he works to support himself. You're making it too easy. You can't take care of him for the rest of his life.

Son, you're making him irresponsible. Your dad and I didn't raise you boys to be that way."

"Mama, how can I turn my brothers down? How can I not be there for them? They need me."

"They need you to be a role model on how to be a man, not a leech." Mrs. Bailey faced Desiree. "Okay, let's get down to business."

"I have copies of his expenses for the last year. A lot of money is going out. I think we need to explore some budgeting techniques and see where we can cut back."

"You got a copy for me?" his mother asked.

"I need Daryl's permission."

Daryl gazed toward the ceiling and threw up his hands. "Just hand it over."

Desiree felt sorry for Daryl. He had many expenses that far exceeded what anyone should spend, and Mrs. Bailey was going to have a lot to say about that.

Desiree handed Daryl's copy of the folder to her. She took her glasses out of her purse and perched them on her nose. Then she began to read through the pages with a fine-toothed comb.

When she glanced up, her lips were tight, her eyes piercing. "You know if you were younger, I'd wear your tail out for wasting money like this. Three thousand in a bar? A twenty-thousand-dollar shopping spree? What the heck did you buy? What were you thinking? I know what you were thinking *with* to spend that kind of money in a department store." She sighed long and hard. "There were many years we didn't make twenty thousand in a whole year and you spend that kind of money in one day?"

"Mama, when you're living this life, women expect it."

"You get yourself a woman who cares about you, and not one trying to break the bank. The ones you date aren't worth a twenty-dollar shopping spree. The way your daddy nearly broke his back to pull that in in one year and you burn money like that."

Desiree cut in or she'd scold the young man the entire session.

"Let's set up some spending strategies. We have to decide what's important to you. We have to establish reasonable savings while at the same time leaving enough petty cash for you to be comfortable."

Two hours later, Desiree found herself thinking that if all her cases were this agreeable, her job was going to be a piece of cake. Except she hoped the next time, Mrs. Bailey would stay home. Desiree respected the woman. She loved her son. She wanted his money to work for him.

"Knock, knock. Coming in," Gerard said.

"We're in the kitchen," Mrs. Gaines called out. "I was trying to decide what to prepare for Desiree's lunch. She wants something light."

"Mind fixing enough for me?" Gerard asked. Chris had gotten quiet. He watched him crawl toward the hallway.

"You need something to stick to your ribs."

"I'll eat whatever you fix. I'm easy to please."

"You pitching tonight?"

"Yes." He followed Chris around the corner.

"Chris?" Mrs. Gaines called out. "Where is that boy off to?"

"I'm watching him." Gerard watched him approach the stairs and climb the first step. Usually Mrs. Gaines put up the baby gate. She kept such a close eye on him that he rarely reached the stairs.

Having negotiated the first stair, Chris crawled up the next. Gerard stood behind him as he crawled up. He got halfway up before he tried to turn around.

"No. No, buddy." Gerard demonstrated how to crawl back down. When Chris made it to the bottom, the child grinned up at him as if he'd performed a heroic feat.

Desiree would have a fit if she knew, but the boy lived in a house with stairs. He was old enough to learn how to navigate them. He'd watched other parents teach their children how to climb up and down when they were around Chris's age.

"Don't tell Desiree. This is our little secret." Gerard picked the boy up and lifted him in the air, before he put him back on the floor.

Chris crawled back into the kitchen to his toys.

"He's going to want a snack soon," Mrs. Gaines said, shredding zucchini.

"He's going to love those zucchini muffins."

Desiree was going to think he was making a pest of himself, but he was pitching tonight. The kids helped him relax. Besides, he wanted to spend time with Desiree. So much time that they'd ease into a relationship. Before she knew what hit her, they were going to appear to be an old married couple.

Marriage? Step back, buddy. You want to date the lady, not marry her, not immediately anyway. He could imagine himself with Desiree a few years down the road.

Levi put away his breakfast dishes and warmed up some water from the lake to shave. He saw the reflection of his face in the mirror. He hadn't shaved for weeks. It was time to move on, he knew, but he wasn't quite ready yet.

One night he and Becca had seen Sydney Portier's *To Sir with Love*. The end of his R and R was closing in and he wanted to get as much living as he could out of the last couple of days. He spent the night in Becca's bed. But all too soon the week was up. They spent his last night together and didn't come up for air until it was time for him to leave.

Levi went back to battle in a war where there was no solution.

The next summer he met Jacqueline. She turned him on an axis. He and Becca were great together. He needed her that week in Hong Kong. And she needed him, too. But she didn't love him and he didn't love her. When they parted, Levi thought he needed to say something prophetic— something to sum up what that week had meant to him. Rebecca beat him to the punch when she said, "I hate long good-byes. What happened in Hong Kong stays in Hong Kong." It was an old military saying. "We'll never see each other again," she said, and Levi only nodded. So they said good-bye to each other and moved on without regrets.

But Jacqueline was different. He was jaded and weary to her softness and purity. He craved her gentleness like a starving man craved food. So he'd married her before he returned to Vietnam.

Her husband did not return from the war.

Levi had been torn apart mentally and spiritually. He had grown up in a Christian household. But when he saw the pillage, the devastation, bodies torn apart, and the destruction of the human soul, he questioned for the first time if there was a God. How could He let something happen like that on His watch—if He loved them?

It had taken decades for him to believe again.

And there was Jacqueline. She deserved more than he could give her. She was a strong woman. She stood by his side. His respect for black women couldn't be higher. They were the rocks. Even when he was ready to give up, she wouldn't. Then two years after he came home for good, she got pregnant with Desiree.

Jacqueline had been both mother and father. He knew that. He made sure she got his check to pay for expenses. He didn't need much. For years, he worked odd jobs to purchase the little he needed until he landed a permanent job. The owner of the company was a vet. He understood Levi's emotional episodes.

So Levi had bought the home place. His brothers told him he was crazy. The only good thing for the place was a torch. Levi closed his ears to them. He built that old house up with his bare hands.

With all his problems, he needed Desiree to know that he loved her. He'd always loved her. He made sure he told her that often. He wasn't much of a father, but he could give her that much.

But Jordan never heard those words from him. He never knew he had a father who loved him. If only Rebecca had told him, but he understood why she hadn't. She was a strong woman. Once the door was closed, as far as she was concerned, she'd never reopen it. She never considered that a man had the right to know about his children. Certain things a woman had no right to keep from a man. His children were the most important thing.

But now he had grandchildren who had no father. He couldn't linger in the woods any longer. He had to go to Atlanta to tell them that he loved them.

Levi began to pack his things and store them in the cottage. He needed to shave and take a bath. He couldn't go to them looking like some wild man and frighten them half to death.

He grabbed a bar of soap and a towel. Running to the lake, he submerged himself completely. The frigid water snatched his breath. He shook off the cold and soaped himself from his head to his feet until he was squeaky clean. Stepping out of the water, he smiled.

He was going to see his grandchildren.

He was ready.

He just hoped he didn't embarrass them.

Desiree had a half hour between her first client and the second. She made notes on the computer about her first session. She smiled, remembering the feisty Mrs. Bailey. Now, that was a strong woman. She was keeping those boys/men in line. Desiree hoped she could be as strong for Jordan's children.

Unbidden, her mind tripped back to five years ago when she'd gotten pregnant by Howard. She had fallen so deeply in love with him she knew that he felt the same way—until she got pregnant.

When he left her, she vowed she was never going to love another man again. She cared a lot for Paul, but she didn't love him like that. She'd learned to protect her heart. Life had taught her she couldn't count on a man. She couldn't count on her father. Howard wasn't worth the tears she'd shed. And Paul was out the door as soon as a little responsibility interrupted his perfectly planned life.

Desiree knew she'd spend her life alone, that a man would never share her life. And she accepted that.

The one saving grace was the friendship growing between her and Gerard. They weren't in love, but he was a good friend. He didn't run at the first sight of trouble. Friendships like that were worth more than gold.

Keith Lewis strutted in with a proud swagger. Desiree remembered Gerard's warning about his attitude and stifled her first impulse to tell this man to get over himself.

"Good morning, Mr. Lewis."

"Keith, please. Makes me feel like an old man. Old is bad in this business. I'm just getting started." The football player beamed a smile hot enough to wilt roses. A diamond winked on his tongue when he talked. And when he turned his head she spotted a huge diamond in his earlobe. He was dark, with raven hair, and he was drop-dead handsome—and knew it.

Desiree smiled. "Keith it is. Have a seat."

"I want to be up front with you. I know you scheduled two hours, but we don't need that long. I don't need anybody telling me how to spend my money." He pulled his chair closer to the desk and folded his long frame into the seat. "I've worked a long time to get where I am and I plan to enjoy every minute and every penny of it. So I'm gonna give you a list of the big-ticket items I plan to buy this year."

This was going to be as bad as the first one was agreeable.

"Wonderful. I want you to start off by telling me your goals and how you want your money to work for you. After all, it is your money and your plans."

He was going to break many young women's hearts, Desiree thought.

"I got a whole list of goals, starting with this bangin' pad I checked out over the weekend, not to mention the ride I'm about to get."

Desiree stifled a sigh and cleared her throat. "How much is the house?"

"Just under a couple mil. But my mama picked out a little place she wants. She lives in Houston. She sacrificed a lot for me. I gotta take care of her first."

"I see. And the car?"

"Only eighty-five grand, but I need to add another fifty worth of bling to make it rock."

"Hmm. All this on an eight-hundred-grand-a-year contract?" Desiree jotted all that down on paper.

"Only temporary, ma'am. I expect to hit a phat couple mil by the end of the season. With a few promotions, the sky is the limit."

"Oh, you're starting this season?"

"All I need is to get on the field. The rest will be history. Leo's great at negotiating. If I do the job, he's gonna get me the bucks."

This was going to be a heck of a lot tougher than dealing with Daryl. "Right now, let's deal with the eight hundred grand in your contract."

He shifted back his shirtsleeve, revealing his Rolex. "Gotta start somewhere."

Desiree wrote down his goals, and then they discussed a savings plan for that year.

"Wait, wait, wait. I got to have the gear and break off

all the females with a lil' bit. I can't do that off of that tiny bit. And what about my pad?"

"But you haven't made the five million yet. You can't spend what you don't have. This is a reasonable budget."

"Hell no!" He jumped out of his seat and leaned over her. If she weren't made of strong stuff, this six-five, out-raged male would have intimidated the heck out of her. "What do I need to save all that for when I'm gonna make more each year, starting with next year?"

"I understand you replaced another player? Didn't he have a lucrative contract until he injured his back?"

"Ain't going to happen to me."

"I'm sure he said the same thing. Why don't you sit down so we can discuss this logically?"

"You're messing with my Karma."

The last thing she wanted to do was destroy his Karma. "I'm trying to get you to look at your finances and job re-alistically. In just this year you'll make more money than the average person will make in fifteen years."

"Damn straight." Frowning at Desiree, he slid into his seat. "I worked my tail off to get here. And I'm aimin' to get a few rewards for the effort."

"I know. And you need to use good budgeting mea-sures in the beginning so that you won't be one of the players who end up with nothing in the end. It can happen easier than you think. Even you know of players who've made many millions but ended up in poverty. The entertainment shows report it all the time."

Some of the heat in Keith deflated. "Anybody ever tell you you sound like my math teacher?"

"Excuse me?"

"I'm not liking a thing you're saying. I can't live off that." He stabbed a finger at her pad. "The females would leave me at the starting line if I don't show 'em a good time. They ain't cheap. You oughta know that." He looked her over critically. "Ah, maybe you don't."

"The females are going to be there whether you spend

a fortune on them or not because of who you are. And you look . . . good."

He flashed a brilliant smile. "Cost a lot for you to say that, didn't it?"

Desiree barely stopped herself from rolling her eyes.

"You got a man?"

"I don't see where—"

"See, that's just it. You don't understand where I'm coming from 'cause you probably count the pennies and dimes when your man tries to treat you special. Man can't show you a good time without little cash registers ringing in your head. I mean, look at your gear. Can't see the curves in that suit."

"This is my job. I'm not out clubbing."

"You're a woman no matter where you're at. Man's always looking. When I see a babe looking like you I'm hopping the other way, else I'm trying to reform her."

"Thank you very much for your critique."

His chuckle got on Desiree's nerves. "See? You're too uptight."

Desiree gritted her teeth. "Do you think we can get back to your budget?"

He snatched the cell phone from his pocket. "Getting you to be reasonable is gonna take longer than I thought. Give me a minute."

Desiree was never this whipped when she left her office in New York. She should ask for a raise. She way undercharged for her services. You'd think *she* was spending Keith's money instead of trying to get *him* to make prudent decisions about *his* own money. Keith stalked out of her office still balking. At least he promised to return next week for a second consultation, Desiree thought as she opened the front door to her house.

In the kitchen Gerard munched on a muffin while he talked to Mrs. Gaines. His presence was totally unexpected.

"Where's Christopher?" she asked.

"Taking a nap. He was plum tuckered out. Gerard had him running around the place so. You're going to spoil that boy." She glanced at Desiree. "Lunch's ready."

Desiree sniffed the air. "With the aromas in this kitchen, I know it's delicious."

"I've started on dinner. I made my zucchini muffins. Hope you like it." She moved to the oven and peeped inside.

Gerard glanced at her. A crumb lingered on his chin. She wiped it off with her thumb. He captured her thumb in his mouth, totally shocking her.

"Hi," he said, in a very sexy voice.

Desiree snatched her finger back. Feeling singed, she rubbed the spot where his mouth had been. "Don't even go there."

"Whatever you desire," he said, then glanced at Mrs. Gaines. "I think we'll have a picnic outside. Why don't you change into comfortable clothes?" he said to Desiree.

"Such a pretty day out. I like the sound of that. You can eat before Chris awakens." Mrs. Gaines smiled at Desiree. "I fixed a light lunch for you and a heartier one for Gerard. You need your energy to get through that game. Are you going, Desiree?"

"The kids have practice."

"I'll spend the night and pick them up for you," Mrs. Gaines said. "Gerard needs his cheering squad."

"I've been away from Christopher all day."

"Ah, don't worry about him. He'll be fine. The kids will play with him. And I'll give him a warm bath and put him to bed. He'll sleep the night through," Mrs. Gaines said.

"Do you have clients in the morning?" Gerard asked.

"Not tomorrow, but the day after I have three."

"You can leave with me," Gerard said. "I'll get there early, but would you mind?"

He looked as if he really wanted her to go. "Not at all."

Gerard pointed her to the hallway. "I'll help Mrs. Gaines with the picnic while you change."

Desiree left the room wondering how she fell into his plan so easily.

She dressed in jeans and a short-sleeved blue top. She didn't need to be in his company. She wasn't going to date him, not for a moment. She wasn't over Paul yet. And Gerard was already starting in.

By the time she went outside, Gerard had spread the quilt and set it with the food.

"You're drinking wine before a game?"

"No, but you can, since I'm driving."

Desiree wasn't one for wine in the middle of the day, but a glass would relax her.

"This is some spread."

"Wait until you taste." He broke off a piece of muffin and fed it to her.

Desiree closed her eyes. "Absolutely to die for."

"She fixed chicken salad for you."

They piled their plates with food. Gerard kept up a constant chatter until they were through with the meal.

"Desiree, I know you've had some hard knocks and it's hard for you to trust. I just wish you'd give me a chance."

Desiree plucked a blade of grass. "I'm not ready. I have the children to think of. Right now I can't deal with this emotional roller coaster relationships put you through. And I don't want to invest my time in something that isn't going to last."

"You can't determine that in the beginning of a relationship." He captured her hand in his. "All I know is, from the moment I saw you, something clicked like it never has with any other woman."

"All relationships are like that in the beginning. It's the newness."

"Not for me."

"Then why were you with Andrea?"

"We understood each other. It's too dangerous to fool around. I didn't want that."

"So you and Andrea had some . . . agreement? Sexual agreement?" Desiree asked.

"For the most part."

"And now that she's gone, you want to take up with me. After all, I don't have anyone either."

"You're making it cheap and it isn't like that at all."

"You're in love with me? You want to marry me?"

"We're not at that stage at this point."

"Is that what you told Andrea?"

Gerard sighed. Desiree was making this difficult. "I knew I was never going to marry Andrea. I told her that from the beginning."

"Just like you told me."

"I'm not saying that. My life isn't conducive to marriage right now. I'm on the road all the time. Husbands should be home."

"Is that what you told Andrea?"

"Why do you have to keep harping on that? Andrea broke up with me."

"Why?"

He knew the moment he told her, she'd never date him. He leaned back on his elbows while she sat Indian style.

"What happened with you and Andrea? You've dated for two years. So why?"

"Is it important?"

"Yes."

"She wanted to get married."

Desiree flopped back on the quilt. "I rest my case."

Gerard glared at her. "No. I didn't love Andrea. I never have."

"You don't love me either."

"I know that we have something potent."

Desiree leaned toward him. "It's called sex. You're a randy man, Gerard. You kept Andrea around for the sex. You want me for the same reason."

"You're really pissing me off."

Desiree turned away. "I have never been able to count on a man in my entire life. I don't want to get my expectations up again because I already know the outcome."

"What happened?"

Desiree didn't want to talk about it. She shook her head.

He rubbed her back. "We're friends if nothing else. Talk to me," he said softly.

Suddenly she felt the need to unburden. "Five years ago, I got pregnant. I loved the man. I mean really loved him. I knew we weren't ready for a child, but I thought he'd stand by me."

"What happened?"

"He didn't want the baby. He made it clear that if I had the baby I was on my own. He wasn't going to participate in the child's life—at all. I told him good-bye. I didn't need him. Three weeks later I had a miscarriage, while he was in Las Vegas getting married." Desiree shook her head. "I should have learned my lesson then. It took years for me to trust again."

"What an ass. And then Paul came along."

"Yeah."

"But, Desiree, I don't think you really loved him. And you have to know all men aren't like them."

"I don't know if it was love, or even what love is. People get married all the time in the name of love, and look how it turns out."

"Come here. I promise you, I will never let you down."

"Don't make promises you can't keep. Listen to me. I am not going to date you."

"I thought you were one of the bravest women I've met. I never considered you a coward. Or the type who makes every man pay the price for the digressions of one or two."

"I'm not a coward. Neither am I a fool. What I have to give will be for the children. Not some on-again, off-again fling with men who don't give a damn." She sighed. "What am I doing lying in your arms?"

Gerard could have replied because it was where he wanted her, or where she wanted to be, but he didn't respond, he merely held her in his arms while the warm breeze blew over them. He could talk until he turned blue and she wouldn't believe he'd be there. He'd have to prove himself. And with all her setbacks, that was going to be tough. He squeezed her gently.

He was up for the task.

8

Several times a year Desiree's mother taught classes in various areas of the country. She'd begun to travel soon after Desiree finished high school. This time Desiree gave her enough time to unpack and do laundry before she called.

Jacqueline Prescott was out of breath when she answered Desiree's call.

"How was your trip, Mama?"

"Tiring as always. The classes went well, but I'm always glad to get back home. I tried to call you last night and finally left a message on your answering machine."

"I'm in Atlanta. Are you sitting down?"

"I am now. Is Levi—"

"He's fine. He has a son, Mama. He was born while he was in Vietnam. Before he met you."

"He never told me about him."

"He just discovered it himself four weeks ago—four months after Jordan died."

"Are you telling me the boy's dead?"

"He and his wife died in an accident." She told her mother about what had happened and the children and her weeks in Atlanta. "I'm trying to get custody."

"Do you need me?" her mother finally asked. "I swear if we didn't get bad news we wouldn't get any news."

"I pretty much have the routine together now."

"How is Paul taking the news? Is he supportive?"

"We called the engagement off."

"That—"

"Don't even say it. I don't need him. I can do this alone."

"But you shouldn't have to. I had to raise you alone, but I wanted better for you."

"Life didn't work out that way."

"I don't understand how you can be so philosophical."

"What else can I do?"

"What about your job?"

"They're holding it for me. But now I'm trying to decide if I'm even going back to New York. I'd have to move so far out, it's going to be tough handling all the kids' school affairs and activities. I'm just working part-time here and I'm running ragged. Raising kids is more difficult than work."

"It's nice you finally figured that out."

"I was a good kid." Desiree didn't remember being too bad. There were worse kids than she, weren't there?

"You have a very short memory," her mother murmured. "How is your daddy taking the news?"

"He's hiding out again. I'm debating whether I should go look for him."

"I have some vacation time left. I'll try to get down there to help out soon."

"You don't have to, Mama. But thanks."

"Is my little girl growing up?"

"It's not like I've been hanging on your skirt tail all these years."

"Desiree, I'm so proud you. But don't close your heart to love, okay, darling?"

"Is that what you did?"

"I was focused on you and a career. I just . . . didn't

have the time . . . well, to be honest I didn't take the time for anything else."

"Closed your heart."

"I loved your daddy, honey. You never knew the man he was. Only the aftereffects of the war. I guess I closed my heart to anything good that could come into my life. And that's not a good thing. We've been divorced for more than twenty years. He's got a new girlfriend."

"Daddy?"

"He's a man, honey. He's always had a girlfriend."

"That's not fair. I mean for you to hold on to him when he's moved on." Desiree couldn't fathom a more bleak existence.

"I'm not holding on to him. I've dated. But you know it's a lot easier for men than for women. Besides, I still do the things I enjoy. I travel and I date."

"Daddy certainly dates. But you know what? I don't remember him dating before I graduated from high school. I thought he'd never move on."

"He exists the best way he knows how."

The next morning before Gerard sat down to breakfast his mother entered his house like a woman on a mission.

"So to what do I owe the honor of your visit?" Gerard asked. "Join me for breakfast."

She ignored the offer. "Andrea told me the most disturbing news," she said, setting her purse on the foyer table and following him into the kitchen.

"You mind if I eat a snack while you get it off your chest?"

"You may be able to make fun of this, but I can't. What in the world is going on with you? That girl is absolutely in love with you."

"Obviously not. She broke it off, not me."

"You gave her no choice. It's past time you settled

down. You know that. You can't expect her to wait for-ever. This life you're leading isn't healthy."

"I've got my own schedule for things, Mama. And I'm not ready to marry now. But don't worry yourself about it. I've always gone my wicked way."

"Quit the jokes. This is a serious matter."

"I'm sorry to deprive you of another physician in the family, but don't you think three is enough?"

"This isn't about your chosen career. Andrea is heart-broken."

"Obviously not as heartbroken as you."

"I'm just disappointed."

"Again."

"Your father and I have only wanted the best for you."

"Don't worry. I'm sure some of those genes will rub off on some of my offspring."

She went to the fridge and poured a glass of orange juice.

"Join me for breakfast. My housekeeper will be here in a few minutes."

"I've had breakfast. Anything that woman cooks will give you an early heart attack. I told you to get rid of her or at least make sure she prepared nutritious meals. But did you listen to me? You don't take my advice about any-thing, so why am I not surprised?"

"I don't know, Mama."

"Did you let Andrea go for some floozy? One of those women running after you at hotels and bars? It's time you grew up, young man. You're getting too old to have no di-rection in life."

"What do I have to do to grow up? I support myself. I don't ask you for money. You didn't have to pay even my college tuition. I won a sports scholarship."

"Your father and I would gladly have paid your tuition, especially if you had pursued a worthy goal."

"I saved you the trouble. I haven't asked you for a dime

since the day I left high school. Count yourself lucky." As much as his mother hated baseball, Gerard wasn't going to have to count on her to pursue his goals. Anyway, his grandfather had left him an inheritance.

She stood, leaned over Gerard. "I'll count myself lucky when you get out of this ridiculous career and make a decent life for yourself."

Gerard stood too, all six feet two, and leaned over her.

"You had it all planned out, didn't you? I date the perfect little physician. She convinces me to stop wasting my life and become a doctor, too. I just don't understand why it's so important for me to be a doctor. Why aren't my dreams good enough?"

His mother shook her head. "You've been given everything. And you wasted it all."

"You have never been satisfied with anything I've done. I could have done a lot worse. Have I ever been in jail? Have I ruined the family name, other than by being a baseball player? Do I go begging you for rent every other month?"

"Let me tell you something. I had to scratch and claw to get to where I am. I didn't waste my blessings. I didn't waste the few advantages that came my way. Not the way you did. I think that's the problem about being middle class. You don't have enough to work for. You've never been hungry. You've had everything handed to you on a silver platter. You've had your grandfather's inheritance—"

"That I've never spent one penny of. Not one penny. I worked my tail off for everything I've ever gotten. He didn't leave me any more than he left Chad. At least he was fair about it."

She rinsed the juice glass and set it in the sink. "I don't know why I bother with you anyway. You never listen."

"Have a good day, Mama."

"That girl isn't going to wait for you. And why should she?"

"I don't want her to. I never did. And you're wrong about one thing, Mama. I have been hungry. Starved even."

Gerard watched as she tore out of the yard, once again assured in her assessment that her oldest child was always no good and would always be no good. He wondered why she even bothered attending his games, unless it was to put up a good front.

Gerard wasn't fit for company that night after his game. He wanted to go clubbing and to the liveliest place he could find. He found himself pointing his car toward a sports bar the players frequented. Groupies by the dozens hung out there. Agents, players, loud music, pool, card games, anything a man could lose himself in. He was going to enter the world of decadence of which his mother accused him of being a part.

And Gerard wanted to get lost. Between phone calls and interruptions, he played a game of pool with Scott. He was waiting for a prospective client he was courting.

"That guy's going to go places. Another Gerard Kingsley."

"God forbid," Gerard said, knowing that was exactly what his mother would say. He knew she loved him. Or the part of him she wanted him to be. Only he couldn't live up to her expectations.

"Tell me about the kids. I haven't had time to go back over there."

"They're great."

Scott lined up his shot. "I hear you stop by there every time you come home."

"I keep a check on things."

"I also heard you and Andrea broke up."

"What did she do, take out an ad in the paper?"

"You okay with that?"

"Yeah."

"It's not going to affect your game?"

"No. Don't worry."

"You athletes think you're going to stay young forever."

"I know better. When I marry it has to be right."

Scott looked to the right. "He finally made it. Check you later."

Gerard put up his cue stick. At the bar, he spotted Emily, the woman he'd met a few weeks ago in another bar. She didn't strike him as a groupie, but you could never tell by the trappings. She was dressed discreetly, and she was sitting alone. Over to the side he saw a couple of players making bets. Then with a wide smile, someone approached her. Probably made a bet to see which one could score.

She looked in the guy's face when he spoke. Then she shook her head. He pulled up the stool and sat beside her. She shook her head again.

Why on earth did she choose a bar like this if she didn't want to play?

Gerard approached her. "She's with me," he told the third baseman.

"Sorry, man. She didn't have a sign hanging on her."

The man moved and Gerard took his seat. "So what's a nice girl like you doing in a place like this?"

"Same thing. I was in this part of town. I wanted to relax a little before I went home. I've never been here before. I usually stop at the bar where we met, but I wanted to wait out the traffic, hear some music." She sipped her club soda. At least that's what Gerard thought she was drinking.

A big whoop went up across the room. One of the players had spread a groupie on the pool table and poured a drink on her bare midriff. Then he proceeded to lap the drink up with his tongue.

When Emily looked at the scene her eyes widened. Her hand trembled. "I guess I did choose the wrong place."

"Come on. It can get pretty lively in here. I'll walk you to your car."

"Thank you." She opened her purse to pay her tab.

"I have it." Gerard left some bills on the bar and took Emily's elbow. They stepped out into the crisp night. In a port of Mercedeses and six-figure cars, she drove a modest Honda Civic. It was a cute little car and it suited her.

She looked at him as if she wanted to linger. God help him, he didn't have anything to offer her even though she seemed willing. She wasn't Desiree. They talked for ten minutes before he closed her car door and she went off into the night.

He wanted to see Desiree. Wanted to feel her softness. Her sweet perfume drew him like a moth to a flame. He felt as comfortable in her presence as a favorite blanket. He wanted to sit and talk quietly into the night. He'd just check on the kids. Spend a few minutes with her and he'd be satisfied, he told himself. He wouldn't get too close. He'd thought about her long and hard. He wasn't ready to settle down and it would be so unfair to bring her and the kids into his crazy world.

He headed his car toward home and parked in Desiree's driveway, then rang the doorbell.

When Desiree answered it she was wearing lounging pajamas. The top a slinky tank. He wanted to haul her into his arms and hold her close to his body. He wanted to slow-dance with her, feel the sway of her body against his. He wanted to make love with her all night long.

Why did he torture himself this way?

They'd made progress tonight, Emily thought. He didn't like other men talking to her. He'd come to her and warned the other player away. He was jealous. She laughed out loud. He was jealous. She'd followed him from his game. Pleased, she steered her car toward home.

It was only a matter of time before he asked her out.
She wanted to drive by his home, but he lived in a gated
community. She'd be a fixture in his house soon enough.
She was patient. She could wait.

At home, she dressed in her dance clothes and went to
the basement. It was one huge room. She'd had padding
and wood laid to make it a dance floor. She put on a CD
and began to dance to a lively tune. She was happy, happy,
happy. She danced for two hours before she stopped.

Her body was damp with sweat. She drank a bottle of
water and went upstairs to shower, blotting the sweat
from her face with the towel.

One day she would dance for Gerard. He would see the
fluid motion of her body and fall in love with it forever. No
woman in his acquaintance could entertain him the way
she could, nor love him the way she loved him. He needed
her.

Two weeks later, the guard at the gate called Desiree to
tell her her mother was there. She thought she was hearing things.

"The Georgia heat must be getting to me," she said,
when her mother arrived at the door.

"It's not that hot yet." Jacqueline Prescott's hair hung
down a couple of inches on her neck, almost like a page-
boy but not as severe. *I'm tired of dealing with it,* she'd
told Desiree. *I want a style that's easy to maintain.*

"Why didn't you tell me you were coming?"

"Why? You don't have enough room in this castle?"

"Of course I do. I'm so glad to see you."

"I don't know why you moved to New York in the first
place."

"Career advancement, Mama."

"A job you hate."

As her mother enveloped her into her arms, Desiree

smelt the familiar scent of her Chanel. This woman could prop up the world. Suddenly a great weight tumbled from Desiree's shoulders.

"Let me get your bags," she said.

"You mentioned the guesthouse. Since I'm on vacation . . ."

"I'll get the key while you drive around to the back of the house."

In three minutes Desiree met her mother at the cottage door. It was a nice place, really, with two bedrooms and a great room, including the kitchen.

"How long will you be here?" Desiree asked.

"A couple of weeks, but you may as well know, I put in for my retirement."

"So soon?"

"They offered me early retirement. I've worked thirty years."

Desiree opened the door to the cottage. She and her mother walked through. The cleaning crew dusted and vacuumed every other week.

"Oh, this is perfect. Just point me to the linen closet."

"Fresh linen is already on the bed. I changed it after Paul left."

Her mother sighed and walked over to her. "How are you with that?"

"Okay. It wasn't the love match of the year, you know, but I thought we worked. I know it takes more than love for a marriage to work. Look at how much Daddy loved you, and you loved him."

"I know, honey. Life gets so darn twisted. I wanted better for you, but it's better to find out now than later that he won't support you in troubled times."

"I know."

"Have you heard from your father yet?" her mother asked. Desiree didn't understand why her mother put her life on hold when her dad had moved on. What was she waiting for? She was only fifty-three and still beautiful.

"Not yet, but I talked to Aunt Nadine. She said she hadn't heard a word and warned me not to go looking for him."

"How are you holding up under this?"

"I'm hanging in there. I can appreciate what you went through alone with me. I wonder sometimes why you didn't move on. Men have wanted to date you. Is this what it comes down to? 'That segment of my life is over'? I'm only thirty. You were younger. Don't get me wrong. I don't resent the children. There's a reason I'm part of their lives."

"Your life isn't over." She brushed Desiree's hair behind her ear. "I believe there's some special man out there who's just waiting for a woman like you. Just make sure you don't close your heart and not recognize him."

They spent the next half hour unpacking her mother's things.

"I have to run into the office to pick up some papers before the kids get home. Why don't you come with me? See where I work? My office is four times larger than my little space in New York."

"I'd love to come."

Levi couldn't even unpack his stuff without Nadine strutting over. Must have been peeking out her window. He couldn't make a move without her knowing. Neither could the neighbors.

"I thought I saw your truck pull up."

He'd hidden it in the garage for a reason. Nadine didn't give him a chance to open the door. She just took her key and let herself in.

"Don't come with no foolishness, Nadine. I'm not up for it."

"You see this here?" She shook the bottle of pills.

"You just take those pills back with you."

"You want to see those grandchildren, you take these pills."

"Didn't I tell you I was sick of those pills? Now go on out of here. I got to see my grandchildren. Been too long already."

"You may as well stop packing those clothes right now if you don't take 'em." She shook the bottle near his face. He slapped her hand back. "'Cause Desiree isn't going to let you anywhere near 'em if you don't take 'em. You know she means business. You two have butted heads before."

Glaring at Nadine, Levi pressed his mouth together. "Why you come over here gettin' on my nerves? I didn't ask you over."

"Just to save you the trouble of going to Atlanta and having to drive right back."

"You just being nosy. You in everybody's business. You're not satisfied less you nagging and picking on somebody. Just pick, pick, pick."

When her hand came up to her hip he knew he was in for a lecture. "I don't know why I put up with you. I try to help you and you always sassing me. See where you'd be without me. Now take this pill." Stomping to the sink, she filled a glass with water. Eyes squinted, she handed him the pill and the glass and watched him like a hawk.

Well, she still couldn't get the best of him. The day he couldn't outsmart her would be a cold day in hell. He jerked his head back and swallowed hard.

"You didn't take it. It's under your tongue. You swallow that pill, Levi Prescott. Don't play games with me."

"Why don't you go home and leave me alone?"

"*After* you swallow the pill."

He swallowed just to get her off his back.

"Even though you acted the fool, I asked the pastor to pray for you."

"Don't be asking nobody nothing for me. Y'all a bunch of hypocrites. I talk to God all the time. We got an understanding. At least I speak the truth. Y'all talk all this holy stuff and do more sinning than I do. I am what I am."

"You need to stay on that medicine so you'll make sense."

"You mean so I curb my tongue. At least now I've got enough energy to speak the truth. Now go on home."

"You just don't believe—"

"There was a time I didn't believe. When you've lived through what I've lived through, you ask questions. But time has passed, and I do believe, but the way some folks use the Lord isn't Christian and you know it. They're just saying the words off of lying lips."

"You just don't understand."

"*I* don't understand! At least I'm not a deacon sinning six days out of seven, then jump up in the church like I'm a saint. He better not put another foot on my land, either, or I'll send a load of buckshot up his butt."

"Who are you talking about?"

"Your deacon Smithers."

"You're just full of stuff. You know Pastor Wilson would never put up with that."

"I've got to admit Wilson's a good man, but he don't know all the dirt around here. He's new to the area."

"I give up." House shoes flapping, she sailed out the door mumbling about unappreciative, delusional kinfolk.

Good riddance.

When Desiree and her mother arrived at the office, Scott was walking toward the secretary's desk. He glanced up when he saw her. "Oh, Desiree, I have another client I want you to talk to. I left the paperwork on your desk. Set up an—"

"Sure. I'll get it now."

"Hello," he said, rolling down his shirtsleeves. "Scott Hayes."

"Forgive me. This is my mother, Jacqueline Prescott. Mom, meet Scott Hayes."

"A pleasure to meet you, Jacqueline. And I know this is a corny line, but I just can't help myself. You don't look nearly old enough to be Desiree's mother."

"You're right. I'm way too old for that line. I am not a young chick."

Scott flashed a brilliant smile. "Will you forgive me over dinner?"

Her mother chuckled. "You move much too fast for me. Do you think I can take a breath?"

"I'm a busy man. I don't have breath to waste." He still held Jacqueline's hand.

I know he's not trying to put the moves on my mama, Desiree thought. Except that was exactly what he was doing! She started to speak up, then realized her mama was holding her own. Of course she was. Desiree was never able to run a line on her.

"Well, don't let me hold you." She glanced at Desiree. "After you."

With a quick glance at Scott's shocked expression, Desiree moved down the hall toward her office.

"You must really have a place of distinction in this company for an office like this."

"This was Jordan's office. I'm here temporarily."

"I don't know. Don't you like it here?"

"My job's in New York. And my opportunities."

"That can change."

"Wait a minute. Let's get back to the set-down you gave Scott."

Jacqueline waved a hand. "Let's not."

"I didn't know you could be so cold. Mom, I think you were turned on."

"I'm on vacation. Don't have time for some man's foolishness."

Desiree didn't miss her mother's heightened color. "We need to discuss this. You're a free woman. Daddy's dating. Why not you?"

"Let's *not* discuss it."

"Is this why you aren't dating? You won't give another man the opportunity?"

"I've dated some. But they never lasted. And when you were home, your daddy would come to stay several times a year. He was always there."

Desiree touched her mother's arm. "I moved out twelve years ago."

Her mother shrugged. "Nothing lasted."

Desiree guessed that after years of disappointments, dating was just too much work. She knew exactly how her mother felt. But what did you do with all those feelings? The absence of a good man didn't stop the hormones from working.

Desiree liked the intimacy, the feeling of being wrapped in a man's embrace, sharing secrets, sharing period. How was she to suppress those feelings? What choice did she have?

A week later, Christopher's cast was removed and the family was celebrating the occasion. Removing the cast nearly scared her baby to death. Took her a little while to calm him down. With no cast, he kept picking at his arm.

That evening when Desiree saw two extra place settings at the table, she thought the children must have invited friends to dinner. She was sure they'd asked Mrs. Gaines first. It was okay with her.

But when Gerard arrived, she wondered why he wouldn't give her a little breathing room, but he had every right. He'd been very good for Christopher and the kids. In a sense this was his celebration, too.

He handed her a floral box.

"For Christopher?" Desiree asked.

"For you." He leaned down and kissed her as if he had a right to.

"Gerard—"

He gathered her into his arms and it felt so solid and warm, it took tremendous willpower to step back from his embrace.

"I was wondering," he whispered in her ear. "Does this not-dating thing mean you're celibate?"

"None of your business," she said.

His lips had brushed her ear when he whispered that time. Deliberately, Desiree was sure. "Of course it's my business. I'm trying to figure out how to get you in bed." Quickly, he let her go and focused on Christopher, leaving Desiree staring after him.

When Desiree glanced up, Mrs. Gaines was smiling at them. "You all enjoy your dinner," she said. "Are you sure you don't want me to stay late?"

"Go home to your family. The kids and I can get the dishes. You prepared a meal to die for," she said among groans from the kids about dishwashing.

A few minutes later the doorbell rang. Desiree answered it, thinking it was one of the kids' friends.

Scott smiled at her. He was over the threshold before she spoke. "Thought I'd bring this folder by so you wouldn't have to come in tomorrow."

"How kind," Desiree said sarcastically, but he wasn't listening. He was marching toward the kitchen. He'd showered and wore a hint of cologne.

Jacqueline was helping Christopher into his high chair. She glanced up when Scott stopped beside her.

"Hello there, Mr. Baseball. Remember me? I see you've lost your bat." He lifted the child out of the chair.

Obviously the kid remembered, because he didn't fuss as he was tossed into the air, but rather laughed with delight while Desiree's heart climbed to her throat. What was it about men and tossing babies?

"Don't toss that baby like that," Jacqueline said.

"He loves it. How are you, by the way?"

"I'll be fine as soon as you put him in his seat."

"I think we started off on the wrong foot. Let me reintroduce myself." He held Christopher in his left arm and extended his right hand. "Hello. My name is Scott Hayes. It's a pleasure to meet you."

In the face of his winsome smile, Jacqueline shook her head and laughed out loud. "Hello. Jacqueline Prescott."

He slid the baby into the seat. "What a pleasure to meet you, ma'am. I would have been by earlier, except I've been out of town."

The kids laughed and teased Scott, while Desiree and the kids finished putting platters of food on the table.

"Please join us for dinner, Scott," Desiree offered. "We have more than enough."

"Why, thank you. I didn't get lunch today." Cupping Jacqueline's elbow, he steered her to the table and held the chair for her as she slid into the seat.

Gerard and Desiree glanced at each other and smiled.

The dishes and homework were done. It was ten, and Desiree and Gerard were outside. Scott had walked her mother to the cottage, and his car was still parked in Desiree's driveway.

"Scott's trying to make a move on your mother. Maybe both of you will decide to stay."

"Her life is back in D.C."

"We'll see. Glass of wine?"

"Sure." Desiree realized she'd only been in Gerard's

house once—the day of the barbecue. She hadn't taken a tour, although her friends had.

"You're so tense," he said as he handed the glass of wine to her. "If you're afraid I'm going to kiss you, why don't we get it over with? One less thing for you to worry about."

Desiree ran her tongue along her lips and swallowed. Her pulse raced as he lowered his head toward hers. She'd wondered what it would feel like to have his mouth on hers. And then his lips touched hers, a light caress that drew a ragged breath out of her. She reached up to push him away, but by the time he covered her mouth completely to deepen the kiss, she found herself running her hands up his chest and around his neck, enjoying his taste as eagerly as she would savor the richest dessert.

"If I don't leave soon, I'm not going to be able to. Good night, Desiree. Sweet dreams." With one last sweet kiss, she watched his long strides carry him away from her. She touched her fingers to her lips. *What on earth was she setting herself up for,* she wondered as she sank into the soft sofa cushions.

9

Levi returned to work as the meds worked their way to through his system. He thought they might press charges this time, but nobody bothered him when he clocked in. His new manager welcomed him back and told him where he wanted him to work. They were glad for the extra help and coworkers welcomed him back as if he'd never left. They were deep into a couple of big jobs and the company needed the manpower. His plan was to work a few weeks, then go see his grandchildren. He should be fine by then. Maybe not quite as coherent, but at least he wouldn't have flashbacks.

He wondered if Desiree had told Jacqueline and how she took the news. He might not have met them, but he already loved his grandchildren. He regretted not knowing his son, but most of all he hated hurting Jacqueline. He'd caused her untold pain in the past. He wondered if she'd visit Desiree. Would she be resentful? No. She wasn't that kind of woman.

They moved him to a private office near the factory floor. From his window he saw his old manager skirting around the edge of the room to keep from passing near Levi's door. Levi went back to his work. As long as the man left him alone, he was fine. Besides, the medicine had his head half cloudy anyway. He couldn't even think straight. Got him walking around like a zombie. If it weren't for his grandkids, he'd stop taking the damn pills.

Nadine came hopping cross the yard every morning before he left for work, standing over him like a drill sergeant until he swallowed the blasted pill, all the while talking about her prayers and such.

As much as he loved and valued her, she got on his last nerve. Some days he didn't appreciate her at all. And she always let him know how unappreciated she felt.

It was a Saturday and Desiree met with a client who was in town. The day was gorgeous and sunny, and she ate lunch in a nearby park.

By now, Desiree knew Paul hadn't been a good match for her. She learned pretty quickly that when you were single and unattached, the world around you seemed to operate in pairs. She saw couples strolling with kids, lovers walking hand in hand. A deep sense of wistful longing welled up inside her. The whole world seemed to be in love. Even when she'd been with Paul they didn't take leisurely strolls. They were always focused on their careers.

Desiree knew she wasn't the only single woman around, there were plenty in Atlanta. Everything just looked different when you were recently unattached.

As busy as her schedule was, she felt lonely.

Gerard was in the locker room getting ready for the game.

"I talked to your old lady," Germaine Wade said. "You need to tell her to lighten up some. She's a tough cookie. I'm wondering how you ever—"

"You don't want to go there," Gerard said. "She doesn't tell me how to play ball, I don't tell her how to run her business."

"It's like that."

"Yeah, it's like that." Gerard stretched out on the work-out table.

"Why did Scott come up with the crazy idea to hire a budget manager anyway? I got to get permission from her to spend over my budget. Does this look like high school?"

"Ask Scott. He just might have done it because he doesn't want his clients to end up broke." Gerard closed his eyes while his therapist massaged his shoulders. He heard Germaine mumbling about just breaking loose from the apron strings only to be tied to them again. Working his tail off for some woman to tell him how to spend his money.

Maybe he should set up an appointment with Desiree. Get her to look over his finances. Although Scott hadn't pressed him to do so. It would be one more thing to tie him and Desiree together.

A few weeks ago, the therapist had told him he was trying to get away to visit his girlfriend's family out of state.

"Did you get to Virginia yet?" Gerard asked him.

"Yeah. Got down there for a couple days. Charlotte's parents put on a great feast. Had the relatives there. Man, I ate like food was going out of style."

Gerard chuckled. "Ready to pop the question, huh?"

"Getting close. Close as I've ever been. I finally found a keeper."

Gerard felt like it was an omen for him.

Later, when Gerard went out on the diamond, he looked toward the stands. Warmth spread through him just knowing Desiree and his family were there in his corner. That they had his back whether he succeeded or failed.

* * *

Germaine had called Desiree early that morning to tell her he wanted to talk to her after the game.

Jacqueline attended the game this time, along with the family. Scott sat with them, beside Jaqueline, actually, with his cell phone pressed to his ear and his BlackBerry in his hand. He might be interested in her Jaqueline, but business still took precedence. Whenever she was in the office, he was on the phone. And his BlackBerry was always close at hand—almost like an extension of the man's arm.

Desiree introduced her mother to some of the players' wives, families, and significant others. Her mother was dressed casually, but her beige slacks and top were flattering.

Sherrice, Justin, and Steven were talking to some of the kids they knew. They all wore the Eclipses caps.

Scott hung up from a call. Desiree's mother was playing with Christopher, who was sitting on Desiree's lap.

"You're lucky that he's such a good baby," her mother said. "I can't say quite the same for you. I walked the floor many nights."

"He has his moments."

"Well. You work with the hand you're dealt. So, is Gerard pitching today?"

Scott was looking at Jacqueline now, and she had her back turned to him. Desiree smothered a smile. She wasn't getting in the middle of that mess. But her mother was definitely interested. She was tense. She was not usually tense around men.

"He's the starting pitcher," Desiree said.

"The loneliest place on earth," her mother said.

"And I won't be able to relax until the game is over. I'm so tense I'm jittery," Desiree murmured. "You know, it's almost like I'm up there on display. Even though I have clients who play for the opposing team, I'm still rooting for him."

Her mother smiled. "Of course."

Gerard's parents and brother arrived and Desiree introduced them to her mother. Chad immediately took Christopher from her arms.

"Hey, Slugger. You lost something."

"Let's not label him," his mother said. "He may very well become a physician or an engineer."

"Well, you aren't satisfied unless everyone becomes doctors. We need the peons too."

"That's silly. He has the potential to become a very respectable professional."

"Way to go, Mom."

The team finally came out onto the field, and the breath caught in Desiree's throat. Even if Gerard were a dot on the horizon, she could still pick him out. The way he carried his head and shoulders. By the way he walked. He was slowly wearing on her.

Desiree sat through all nine innings. Gerard pitched six of them.

"I'll take the baby while you go to the dugout," her mother said after the game.

A line of reporters were waiting to speak to the players, but before Desiree could reach her client a reporter thrust a mike in her face.

"I understand, Ms. Prescott, that you are prohibiting Germaine Wade from spending his money. You've placed him on a very restricted budget. Is this true?"

Where in the world had they heard that? They must have overheard a conversation. She couldn't imagine Germaine mentioning it to the press.

"I'm not at liberty to divulge a client's personal business. You must speak to Mr. Wade about his financial matters." Then she tried to turn away and the persistent reporter tried to stop her.

"One more question, please. Are you dating Gerard Kingsley?" the same reporter asked.

"My brother was Gerard's agent and friend. He has made the transition between the children and me easier and we're grateful. Excuse me, please."

At that point Scott intercepted them. She was unaware that he'd even followed her. Scott loved the camera. And he talked about the game as well as a new prized player he'd just signed on who was graduating soon. He'd given the paperwork to Desiree, wanting her to set up an appointment with him.

When the reporter asked if Gerard and Desiree were dating, Emily's heart nearly stopped. She'd watched the game and she'd passed the family's and friends' seating area. Desiree sat center stage with the Paynes and Gerard's family. Emily was getting tired of seeing that woman underfoot all the time.

She was going to have to move things along a little faster. It was time Gerard realized he needed her. Now more than ever, before he got caught up with another woman who meant nothing to him. Another woman who could never love him or give him the support he needed.

Emily snapped pictures of Gerard with her telephoto lens. What a powerful man. What a handsome man. And he was hers.

Emily had taken an entire roll of film with Gerard in each snapshot. She would make a scrapbook dedicated to him just as her mother had made scrapbooks of her father. But Emily was smarter than her mother. Her mother couldn't keep her father. He'd eventually left them both.

He never tried to contact Emily until she was eighteen and left for college. By then it was too late. Emily wanted nothing to do with him. He still sent Christmas and birthday cards which she never acknowledged. Why did he want to come back into her life now? He had a new wife and another child. He left her for his new family. He didn't love her.

Emily was nothing like her mother. She would get and

keep Gerard. He'd never leave her for another woman. He'd never leave her children.

Emily dropped the roll of film off at Wal-Mart on her way home. She'd pick up the photos tomorrow. She already had a beautiful album picked out. Unlike her father, Gerard needed her.

At home, she changed into a leotard and tights and immediately went to the basement. There were a few steps that weren't quite perfect yet. She put the CD in the player, and the music began to swell and vibrate through her body as she danced.

She practiced her musical tribute to Gerard for two hours. One move was giving her problems. She fumbled on it every time. So she practiced the move over and over. *Practice makes perfect,* her mother had drilled in her over and over and over. Emily wouldn't quit until the routine was perfect. When she was satisfied with the results, she started the CD from the beginning and danced through to the end.

Perfect.

Later that evening, a tuxedoed waiter escorted Desiree and Gerard to a table in the Vinings Inn. The lights were low and intimate. A couple of people watched them. Desiree felt as if they were in a fishbowl.Then she spotted Bobby and Whitney several tables away.

"We're with the kids so much I haven't had a chance to get to know you—to just focus on you."

"There isn't much to know, really. You already know the important stuff."

"Hmm," Gerard said.

"You know, I really am in awe of you. You're a very good ballplayer. What is it like? Pitching, that is. Do you analyze the hitters? I mean, how do you pitch that many strikeouts?"

He shrugged. "Pitchers spend a lot of time analyzing the hitters. It's more than just tossing a ball."

"I'm sure it is. How do you feel when you're out there? I mean, you tell the public that you're so focused on each pitch that you don't have time for other emotions."

"I get frustrated with myself when the inning isn't going well, just like anyone else. I'm human. But I am focused. I just want to do a good job for the team. I want to do the things my . . . my family approves of. I'm not perfect, but I think sometimes ballplayers get a bad rap. I mean, some of the things we do are pretty wild. For the first time, you're making more money in a year than you've dreamed of in a lifetime. And some of the players, they come from humble beginnings. They've never been taught certain things, so how do you expect to take them out of one environment and stick them into another without a clue of what they're dealing with?"

The server placed two glasses of water on the table and took their beverage order.

When she left, they perused the menu.

"Crab cakes are great here, so is their fish," Gerard said.

The server returned with their drinks and took their order and Desiree continued their conversation as if they hadn't been interrupted.

"I don't see negative images about you in the news," Desiree said.

"My grandfather had the greatest influence on me. He loved baseball, and men from his era were different. They were gentlemen. He taught me manners. I spent a lot of time with him and my grandmother."

"Why?"

He sipped his water.

"I was born when my parents were going through residency. Talk about a killer schedule. So I ended up spending weeks with my grandparents. Grandpa and I would attend every weekend baseball game in town. He'd sign me up for T-ball and Little League. I started throwing a ball before I was old enough to know what one was."

"But your brother isn't involved with sports."

"Mom made sure of that. I loved sports and Granddad went head-to-head with her to have me play. She made sure Chad wasn't focused in that direction. But she wasn't about to fight my grandfather. He was a very respected physician in Atlanta. His name carried a lot of weight. Thinking back on it, I don't know how he had the time to attend my games. Yet he attended every one."

"Did your parents attend them?"

"Sometimes. But not as often as my grandparents. I suppose they had more time. At least they took the time."

"Your parents attend your games now."

"Yeah. A lot of the people in their circle enjoy the sport and they can get free tickets."

"I'm sure it's not that. They want to see you."

Gerard shrugged.

Their dinner arrived. Gerard had ordered steak and she'd ordered fish.

"Would you like to try mine?" he asked before he even sampled his food. "It's always delicious."

Before she responded, he cut off a bite of meat and fed a piece to her. She opened her mouth and he slowly inserted the fork, his eyes watching her closely. She closed her mouth around the meat, but she was paying more attention to the man than to the food.

The gesture was so romantic and she knew that moment she was falling much too fast for Gerard.

Gerard had planned well for Desiree's first evening without the kids. Getting Scott's help was easy since the older man wanted to spend time with Jacqueline anyway. Scott and Jacqueline took the children to dinner at Dave and Buster's where they had games to entertain the children.

"I finally have you alone," Gerard said to Desiree. "As

much as I want to take you to bed and peel every stitch of clothing off you, we're not going to do that. We're going dancing. That okay with you?"

Desiree smiled and ordered the flutters in her stomach to settle down. "I haven't danced in ages." She realized she and Paul never danced when they went out. Gerard's voice jerked her out of her reverie.

"Because if I have you alone in the house," he continued, as if she hadn't spoken, "I don't know if I can keep my hands off you."

She was just beginning to relax a little when the flutters bounced from her stomach to her throat.

"Dancing works for me."

He drove to the Heart of Atlanta. The club was cozy and a sister with a siren's voice sang R and B.

"I don't trust myself with you, but I still need you in my arms." He scooted his chair close to hers and put his arm around her shoulders.

With his words he was making love with her and making it hard for Desiree to resist. "You're quite the charmer, you know that?" she whispered. She inhaled the subtle aroma of his cologne.

"I'm fighting for my life here. I need every weapon in my arsenal."

Her eyes met his. "You make it sound like a war."

"It is and I've drawn up my battle plans. You aren't an easy woman, but you're worth every bit of agony you give me." He pulled her onto the dance floor and held her close in his arms. They began to move to the rhthym of the music.

"Agony? You make it sound like a root canal."

"Ah, ecstasy. No, baby, not by a long shot. When we come together, it's going to be perfect." He still wore his suit, but he'd taken the tie off. Desiree slid her hands over him and felt the hard strength of his shoulders. She longed to feel the skin beneath.

His hands moved ever so slowly on her back. His legs

brushed against hers, sending pinpoints of flames licking through her. *Have mercy.*

Slow-dancing, moving slowly against this man was driving Desiree to the brink of her sanity. It felt as if the vibes between them had been building forever without release.

Desiree couldn't remember what moved them off the dance floor and to the car. Before she knew it the car was parked in Gerard's garage and she found herself in the kitchen. Her senses focused on one thing only. Him.

He stopped for a moment and closed the door. Leaning against it, he dragged Desiree into his arms.

He was definitely aroused. Her pulse raced.

"Chad?"

"Is working."

She reached up to wrap her arms around his neck, pulling him close to meet her lips, expecting a slow, leisurely exploration. But suddenly passion exploded with a kiss, hot, searching, and discovering. Desiree slipped the jacket from his shoulders, nearly ripped buttons from his shirt to get it off to feel the skin beneath.

They dragged clothing stitch by stitch from each other's bodies. Gerard danced around on one foot to dislodge his pants and shoes.

He ran his hands along the curves of her body until she focused only on pure sensation. Her knees weakened and desire spiraled out of control.

Gerard was losing it, and quickly. Her hands stroking his body had his heartbeat pounding in his chest. He stroked her, replacing his hands with his tongue.

"You're sweet and delicious," he murmured, his voice so thick he sounded like a stranger.

She moaned.

"I can't take another moment."

She broke away, leaving him forlorn by the door.

"What?"

"Condom."

"Right here." He snatched up his pants and dug one out of his pocket, scattering a few more on the floor.

"Let me."

"Be my guest," he said, barely able to speak.

They never made it to the bedroom. He lifted her against the door. She clung to his shoulders as he impaled her. He stopped just to enjoy the feel of being completely sheathed inside her. And then he moved. He tried, how he tried to go slow. But her cries, her hands on his body, urged him to move fast and deep until they climaxed in a wave so forceful he wondered if he'd ever fall to earth.

After he caught his breath, he lifted her in his arms and carried her up the curving staircase to his bedroom.

Minutes passed before Desiree came to her senses. Lying in Gerard's arms felt so delightful. She turned to her side and ran her hand down his chest, over his shoulders.

"Your shoulders are amazingly solid and strong," Desiree murmured.

"Umm."

Gerard ran a hand through her hair. "You amaze me, you know that?"

"How so?"

"I envisaged you as a cautious lover. Never this wild vixen."

"You want caution?"

"Not on your life. I wouldn't trade the vixen for all the stars above."

The scent of his light cologne aroused her senses. She pressed a kiss to his chest. He sprang little kisses along her cheek, forehead, and neck, increasing her heartbeat. Then his tongue slowly outlined her lips, pressed at their joining. Involuntarily, Desiree opened her mouth.

He rolled onto her, letting her feel the full masculine length of him.

"I'm not a groupie." She finally had enough presence of mind to speak. "Never take me for a groupie."

He held her head between his hands, forcing her to gaze directly in his eyes.

"I never mistook you for one. Do you think you wouldn't have been in my bed more than a month ago if you were merely a groupie?"

"I don't know you."

"You know more than you admit. Holding back my feelings for you nearly did me in."

"Where are we going with this? I mean, you're my friend. When this relationship busts, and they always do, I'll have lost my very good friend."

"Who says it'll end? And who said we ever have to be enemies?"

"It's just the story of my life."

He kissed her deeply. "We're more than friends, so stop trying to predict the future. Live in the here and now. Don't you know you can't plan these things? What are you afraid of?"

She stroked his cheek with the back of her hand. "The kids need you. They love you. I can't take a chance that they will lose that."

"What if I promise to be there, no matter what?"

He shifted between her legs and she felt the fullness of him. She could barely concentrate on the conversation.

"I don't have a good track record with men," she said.

"It's time for a change, don't you think?"

He tilted her chin with a long finger. "Believe in me, Desiree."

Desiree wondered if he meant more than a relationship. But he didn't give her much time to ponder because he was doing amazing things to her body and there was no room for thought, only sensations—only him.

"Grandma, can we stay up another hour?" Justin asked. "It's the weekend."

"It's already close to eleven. That's late enough."

"I had a good time tonight. Thanks for taking us to dinner."

Jacqueline rubbed the boy's head and bent to kiss him. "That's what grandmas are for." She stood and marched to the door. "Don't forget your prayers."

"I won't."

When Jacqueline went to Sherrice's room, the girl was staring at the ceiling.

"Anything wrong, dear?"

Sherrice started, then relaxed. "No."

"You seemed quiet at dinner."

A young man had gotten his food and asked if he could join their group. Of course she'd said yes. He sat beside Sherrice and the two talked and played games until it was time to leave.

"Who was your friend?"

She shrugged. "No one special. He just goes to my school."

Jacqueline laughed. "He seems interested in you."

"Not really. I'm not dating right now."

"You've got plenty of time for that. Good night, dear."

Jacqueline stopped by Steven's room. The boy was already asleep. She smoothed the covers around his shoulders. She peeked in on Christopher last.

While she put the children to bed, Scott talked on the phone. She felt like tossing that phone out the door.

She was nervous. She and Levi had made love for years after they divorced. Sure, she'd gone out a few times but there were no serious relationships after Levi left. In a way theirs was an odd relationship. When he'd visit, they would make love as if they were still married. It seemed he was still too much a part of her life to let another man enter it.

It wasn't until Desiree moved out that they truly began to live separate lives. That was when he began to get girl-friends and when she'd tried a few dates, which never seemed to work. Men seemed more successful than women in that regard.

But Scott had rocked her boat. The last time she felt this intensely for a man was when she met Levi during the war—and she was frightened. She was a fifty-three-year-old woman now and she was scared. What sense did that make?

She proceeded downstairs. She half-filled two wine-glasses and joined Scott, setting his on the table in front of him. He talked for another minute on his cell phone before he ended the conversation.

He glanced at her, a deep and penetrating look.

Jacqueline sipped her wine and set it on a coaster. She took the phone from his hand and turned it completely off.

"I won't compete with your cell phone."

Scott merely smiled. "You have no idea what I go through with my clients. Some of them get into scrapes on the weekend when they drink a little too much or party too hard."

"Everyone deserves some downtime, even you. Besides, they're men, not children."

"There's a very thin line. But I guess I just needed a reason to take the time." He stretched his long legs, as comfortable as if he were in his very own living room. That was one of the things Jacqueline liked about him. He fit into every place he went.

"Tell me about yourself," Jacqueline said.

"There's not very much to tell."

"How did you become a sports agent?"

"I practiced law for a few years after I got my degree from Howard. A friend of mine was a football player. When he busted his knee, he decided to become a sports agent, but he knew nothing about contracts or legalities, which was my expertise. I handled that end for him and got more and more involved in the business until I eventually joined the agency. And, as they say, the rest is history."

"I'm sure you left out a lot. Have you ever been married? Do you have children?"

"I've been married. For ten years. Now I'm divorced. I don't have children. I have seventeen nieces and nephews to buy birthday and Christmas gifts for."

"You remember the number? Men usually don't."

"My mother never lets us forget. And I make sure my assistant reminds me if I do. It's mandatory to attend the family reunions and she has this huge number seventeen above a million pictures on her living room wall. She's proud of every one of them. And my father goes along to keep a peaceful household. They're both seventy-three."

"Are you the oldest?"

"Yes."

"Your mother seems loving."

"Very much so. I've already told her about you. She wants to meet you."

"Excuse me? Aren't you getting ahead of yourself? It's not like we're seriously dating."

"I don't play games, Jacqueline. Are you dating anyone?"

She took a moment before she responded. "No."

"I like you. I haven't felt this way about a woman in many, many years. And when I see something I want, I go after it. I don't beat around the bushes."

"I don't live here."

He shrugged.

"I travel a lot. I guess I'll have to come to you when you can't come to me."

Jacqueline threw up her hand. "You're moving much too fast for me. I'll be leaving in a week." She didn't tell him she'd put in her retirement paperwork.

"Tell me about you. Do you have siblings?"

"I have one sister and one brother. My brother lives in Los Angeles. My sister lives in D.C. We live just a few blocks apart."

"You've never lived any place else?"

"I grew up in Macon. That's how I met Levi. We

moved to D.C. after he left the army. He returned to Macon. I stayed in D.C. My sister is younger than me. She attended Howard and stayed after she completed her degree."

"How would you feel about moving to Atlanta?" He sipped his wine and placed the glass back on the coaster. Then he put his arm around the back of the sofa.

"Who said anything about my moving anywhere?"

"Long distance will work for a while, but not forever," he said.

"Who said we were going to last forever?"

"I do."

Jacqueline chuckled. "I've never, not ever, met another man like you."

"Good. Because if you had, you'd be with him now and not with me." He tilted her chin and his lips closed the distance between them.

He tasted of wine. Seductive, alluring, captivating. She couldn't fathom for a moment why she was intrigued by this man. Unbelievable.

10

Still dressed in her clothes from the night before, Desiree felt odd arriving home at ten the next morning. She'd planned to be there by seven, but Gerard had kept her in bed until eight, and then had taken her to breakfast. When he parked his Porsche in front of her home, a pickup truck was in the yard and a man was sitting on the doorstep.

Desiree couldn't have been more surprised. Thank God her father had finally arrived. She was out of the car before Gerard cut the motor.

"Daddy, where have you been? We've been worried sick about you."

"Thinking."

"For weeks?"

"Sometimes it takes that long. Didn't Nadine tell you I went back to work a couple of weeks ago?"

"Yeah, she did. How are you?"

Gerard slowly came around the car and stood beside her. She'd completely forgotten about him. And she should have known better than to yell at her father. She looked at him closely to determine if he was actually taking his medicine.

"Who are you?" her father asked, nodding toward Gerard.

Lord, have mercy. Please don't let him start any mess.
Gerard extended a hand. "Gerard Kingsley, sir."
The older man pinched his mouth, but shook the younger man's hand. "What are you doing with my daughter? She's engaged to another man."
"We called off the engagement, Dad," Desiree said quietly.
"Looks like a lot has happened in the last month or so."
Desiree nodded.
For the children's sakes she hoped he was on his meds. Aunt Nadine complained that sometimes he faked swallowing. When he started doing well he hated to take them. But at least he was here, she thought, and the kids were going to be happy to see him. She tried to ease herself in front of Gerard, but he stepped to the side.
"You look familiar," her father said, frowning. "You're the pitcher."
Gerard nodded.
Levi Prescott was dressed in black slacks and a beige polo shirt. He was four years older than Jacqueline. His salt-and-pepper hair was short and neat. Desiree could understand why women ran after him. He was still a handsome man. If you discounted that he was a bit worn around the edges. Of course that only enhanced his mystique.
"Aren't you going to give your daddy a hug?" When he gathered her into his strong arms, she was carried back to the good times when he smelled good and comforting. When she didn't worry about him erupting or walking out unable to deal with the problems life threw him.
"How are you, Dad?" He smelled of his favorite soap.
"Great."
He sounded coherent. They linked arms and walked into the house together.
"Some place."
"Isn't it though?"
In the living room, his gaze focused on a picture on the table. Desiree felt as if she were going back in time to when she'd first seen Jordan's picture.

"Is that my son?" His voice was thick with regret.

Desiree realized the question was a mere formality. Levi Prescott was gazing at a likeness of himself. If it weren't for his wife and children in the photo with him, one could easily conclude it was a picture of Levi with his family.

"It was taken a month before he died."

Slowly he entered the room and took the frame in his work-roughened hand. His face hardened noticeably as he stared intently at it.

"I'm going to leave," Gerard said. "Walk me outside?" he said quietly to Desiree.

"I'll be right back, Dad," Desiree said.

Once she and Gerard were outside, Gerard dragged his hands through her hair. "I had a wonderful time last night. Thank you."

Desiree nodded. "I had a lovely time, too."

"Your dad going to be okay?"

"He'll be fine."

"I felt I was intruding on a personal moment."

"He never met Jordan. It'll take time for him to deal with it."

"I can understand that. I'm not going to hold you. I'm leaving tomorrow morning. If you can get away call me."

She nodded again.

Then Gerard tilted her chin and gathered her into his embrace. And his lips met hers. The kiss was brief. And before she could get her fill, Gerard was loping to his car.

Thinking of the night before, Desiree dreamily went back into the house. Levi was still looking at the photo.

Several seconds passed by before he said, "I'll never know my son."

"That's not quite true. He had friends. He has wonderful children. You'll get to know him through them. The same way I am." She rubbed his shoulders. The bunched-up muscles were tense.

"It's not the same."

Just then the back door opened and Desiree heard footsteps coming through the house. Her mother stopped
when she saw them. She was carrying Christopher in her
arms. Gently, she put the child on the floor. Jacqueline
was expecting Levi, but seeing him in the flesh after five
years was a kick in the stomach.

"Levi?"

Levi's mouth moved, but no words emerged. Nervously
he cleared his throat. "When did you get here?" he asked.

"A couple of weeks ago. I'm leaving in a couple of days."

He nodded. "You're looking well. Beautiful, in fact.
You cut your hair."

"Easier to maintain." Why did people make such inane
conversations when a thousand thoughts were flashing
through their minds? He had more gray than the last time
she saw him. He looked older and so did she, Jacqueline
thought with a wry smile.

Levi had never seen Jacqueline with another man. She
wondered at his reaction when Scott would come by later.
It was really none of his business, but their relationship
was unique. He'd always felt responsible for her. And
though he divorced her, he didn't divorce himself from
her. They maintained a bond.

"This is your youngest grandson, Dad." Christopher
was heading to the stairs and Desiree picked him up and
brought him over to her father.

Christopher looked at him from wide eyes, but in the
face of a stranger, he clung to Desiree.

"Hey there, little fellow," her father said. He didn't try
to approach him. Just talked to him from afar. Let the
child get accustomed to his voice, his face.

Desiree had been young when her father walked out of
their lives. Even with the stress of living with him, her
father's absence had shattered her heart. Living with him
was better than the absence.

For a couple of years he'd been unable to work. It took
lots of counseling and medication to get him to the place

where he could function. Still, there were times when he backtracked. Life for him wasn't normal, would never be normal.

"Are you going to stay awhile?" Desiree asked.

"Yeah. I'll rent an apartment or something for a while. I want to get to know my grandchildren."

For all his problems, he'd always shared a part of their lives. She always knew she had a father and that he loved her. Desiree knew he would do no less for his grandchildren.

"This house is huge," Desiree said. "You can stay here."

"I need my own space." He didn't like living under the same roof with another person.

"Then take the cottage out back," Jacqueline said. "There are two bedrooms and you'll have all the privacy you desire."

Desiree glanced at her mother, but she didn't look her way.

Her father frowned at her. "Are you sure it won't be an imposition?"

"Not at all," Desiree said.

"I'll leave you two to get reacquainted," her mother said.

"You don't have to leave," her father said.

"We'll have plenty of time to talk."

"It's good to see you again."

Her mother smiled fondly and approached him. He gathered her into his arms. "I'm glad you're okay," Jacqueline said.

When he released her, her mother left the room to pack.

"Come on. Sit down," Desiree said.

They sat side by side on the couch. He was looking at the photo again.

Desiree went to the family room and gathered up albums. She handed him one and he began to leaf through the pages, as if he were leafing through his son's life.

"Thanks for taking care of them."

"They're my niece and nephews. I couldn't leave them with strangers."

Just then the other three children tumbled into the house. When they saw the man sitting with Desiree, they stopped.

"Come and meet your grandfather," Desiree said.

Tentatively the kids advanced into the room. Levi was standing. Desiree could tell he was nervous.

"I've brought you presents," he said.

"You're dancing wonderfully, Sherrice," Emily said.

"I practice every day, even at home."

"Practice and great form make wonderful dancers." She blotted her skin with a towel. "How are things at home?"

"Okay. Both my grandparents are there."

"Are they kind?"

"Yes. My grandfather fought in the Vietnam War. He brought a bunch of pictures with him."

"How wonderful. They all seem to be moving in, don't they?" She placed her towel on a chair.

"He can't stay long. He has to get back to his job."

"Let's hope not. Relatives can be imposing. They interfere with the routine of the household. I can't understand why Desiree would bring them there. Some people don't mind imposing. They have a lot of nerve. Do you see Gerard often?"

"He's out of town," Sherrice said. "But we should see him when he returns."

"I'm sure you will. He'll make a wonderful father."

Sherrice frowned. "What are you talking about?"

"Oh, nothing. It's just he's so responsible. He's a good father figure for you and your brothers. That's enough for today. I'll see you tomorrow."

Emily reprimanded herself to watch what she said around people. But she was so busy thinking of Gerard, she could barely contain herself. With her beauty and his handsomeness, they'd make a striking couple.

Mrs. Emily Kingsley. What a nice ring. *Mrs. Emily Kingsley,* she repeated several times. Her plans were turning out wonderfully.

"Emily . . ." Sherrice was saying.

"Yes, dear?" She had to get her act together. Sherrice was looking at her as if she'd grown two heads. Emily frowned, hoping she hadn't uttered the words out loud.

"I need help on one of the movements in my solo."

"Show me what you're having problems with," Emily said. She was a wonderful and patient teacher. Under her tutelage, Sherrice would become an excellent dancer.

Desiree watched Gerard's game on TV, as apprehensive as if she were watching him from a stadium seat with a crowd behind her. The spotlight was on him. And he looked serious and gorgeous. Desiree had bathed Christopher early. Her mother helped the boys with homework and got them to bed that night.

Once Desiree started watching the game, she didn't move until the commercial breaks.

After Gerard returned to his room, he called Desiree every night.

"Hey, baby." Gerard's voice was a welcome balm to her spirit. He sounded tired.

"I saw the game. You were the bomb, as the kids say. It's a good thing my mother's here, because I don't get a thing done when you pitch."

"Wish you were here."

Desiree caught her breath at the sound of his whispery soft and sexy voice.

"Yeah, me too."

"I'm looking at this gorgeous bunch of flowers. What if we'd lost?"

"What flowers?"

"Come on. No one else knew where I was staying. They're different from the ones some lunatic has been sending me."

"I didn't tell anyone where you were and I didn't send flowers, although maybe I should have. I'm jealous." She wished she could recall the words, because she definitely didn't mean to say that.

"Trust me, you have no competition. I thought they were from you."

"Your secret admirer is rather persistent. How am I going to compete with that?"

"You don't have to compete with anyone. I like you exactly as you are. Come to think of it, this is the third mysterious flower arrangement I've received."

Maybe she should do something special for him, Desiree thought. Perhaps a dinner in his honor and maybe a little something special just from her afterward. Heat seared her face and spread through her body.

"I imagine it isn't unusual for sports figures to receive gifts from groupies—especially popular ones like you."

"I don't know. So how are the kids?"

"Great. I put Christopher to bed early. Daddy kept him so busy today he went out like a light. He really enjoys the children. And the children enjoy him too."

"It's good they're getting acquainted. They never had grandparents. Jordan's mother died when he was in college," Gerard said.

"I've seen pictures of her. She was a striking woman."

"From what he said, she was very outgoing too. They traveled a lot when he was a kid. She was a teacher and she taught overseas during the summers. Jordan traveled to many countries by the time he graduated from high school."

"What an experience."

"Especially since he loved to travel, too. He had friends in practically every country. Some kept in contact." Gerard drew in a long breath.

He should be sleeping, Desiree thought. "You're exhausted."

"I want to get away with you. Maybe you could hire Mrs. Gaines for the weekend and spend it with me."

"The older kids will be okay. I don't know about being away from Christopher that long. Mama's leaving tomorrow."

"You're quite the little mama. Worried about her little chicks."

"I can't help it."

"You're good for them, Desiree."

"I try."

"I'll be in town in three days. Be waiting for me?"

"With bated breath."

"By the way, I have a benefit to attend Saturday night after the game. Be my date?"

"Sure. What's the dress code?"

"Formal."

"I look for any excuse to shop."

When they hung up, Gerard left a message for Scott about the flowers. He wanted to have him check into who was delivering them. The average person would have given up by now.

Desiree waited with Christopher in the dance studio for Sherrice. She talked to a parent who was also waiting for her daughters.

"He's a cutie. They grow so fast," the woman sitting beside her said.

"They do." Her little boy set up a series of ma-ma-ma-ma-ma-ma-ma-mas. Now and then, she acknowledged him.

"Beverly and I were pregnant together. We used to compare notes on swollen ankles."

Christopher was quiet, just observing the boy and playing with the keys dangling in Desiree's hand.

"Nice meeting you," Desiree said to the woman when Sherrice appeared. "Ready?"

"Almost. I have to get something. It'll only take a minute."

"We'll be waiting for you in the car."

Desiree buckled Christopher into his seat. Then she kissed his chin.

He clapped. "Ma-ma-ma-ma-ma-ma-ma."

"Oh, sweetie." She kissed him again. "You've learned a new word."

"Ma-ma-ma-ma-ma," he repeated, as if proud of himself.

"She's not your mama," Sherrice said.

Christopher's eyes widened at the sharp retort.

"He doesn't know what it means. He's only repeating what he's heard."

"You'll never be our mother. We had one," she snapped as if she were talking to a teenager.

"I know that, Sherrice. I'm not trying to take your mother's place."

Sherrice got into the car and slammed the door. She glared out the side window.

Slowly, Desiree got into the car, too. In the beginning, her relationship with Sherrice was good. She didn't understand the abrupt change.

Desiree started the motor and pulled out of the parking space. When she was on the road, she asked, "Is everything okay, Sherrice?"

"Fine," she snapped.

"I don't like that attitude. There's no reason for it. When you speak to me you use courtesy and respect."

The only noise greeting them was the "ma-ma-ma-ma-ma" from Christopher.

"Did you hear me?" Desiree said. If she started letting Sherrice get away with back-talking, the situation would only worsen.

"Yes, ma'am."

Desiree turned the radio on low. Sherrice reached over and turned the station.

Desiree turned it back to her station.

"It's my daddy's car. I should be able to listen to anything I want to."

"I don't care whose car it is. I'm driving it. And you do what I give you permission to do. If you want to listen to another station, then you ask politely. Otherwise, keep your hands off it."

Desire didn't know what was getting into that child. She was on the verge of smacking her.

She'd had enough of smart-mouthed kids she'd taught in New York. If this was what money did to kids, it was a good thing she came from humble beginnings.

She sighed. Sherrice wasn't always this rude. Something must have changed over the weeks.

At the light she glanced at Christopher from the rearview mirror. He had stopped talking and was playing with the toy attached to his seat.

"Sherrice, if you have a problem I'm here for you."

"I don't have a problem." She continued to look out the side window.

Her father got along with the kids. She'd have a talk with him and see if he could get Sherrice to open up.

Christopher started up with the "ma-ma-ma-ma-ma" again, and Sherrice pressed her lips together, glaring straight ahead.

When they got home, Sherrice stormed out of the car, slamming the door behind her. She used to get Christopher out of the car seat since the seat was on her side. Desiree didn't say a word as the child tore into the house as if she were running from a pack of dogs.

Desiree rounded the car and gathered the child in her arms. With a cheeky grin, he patted her cheek, and she kissed him. She might not be his mother, but she felt like it. She couldn't love him any more.

She collected the diaper bag and followed Sherrice into the house.

Desiree tried to attend most of the in-town games, but she couldn't attend the weeknight ones. Gerard hadn't had a day off in two weeks, and they were in town to play for six days before he would get a day off. Sherrice was acting up again. The boys were fine, but instead of getting better, that girl was getting worse. And she refused to talk about what was troubling her.

Desiree was worried because this might cause problems in her sessions with Social Services. And if things got too acrimonious, they might take Sherrice from her. Desiree didn't want the children separated.

Besides, Gerard wasn't pitching. If he were, she would have found a way.

Desiree had tried to talk to Sherrice again, without success. She couldn't make the girl talk. She wouldn't talk with Jacqueline or Levi, although she was always respectful.

Desiree was desperate. She had to find a way. When it was time for bed, she went into Justin's room and closed the door.

"Hi, honey. Have you picked out your clothes for tomorrow?"

He looked up from his book. "Sure."

"I'd like to talk to you about something."

"What's up?"

"Do you know of any problems Sherrice is having?"

He shook his head. "Why?"

"She seems troubled. And I was wondering if there was something I could do to help her."

He shrugged. "She talks to her friends more than she talks to Steven and me."

"Okay. Just keep an eye out."

Desiree stopped by Steven's room and discussed a seminar he wanted to attend on Friday, before she looked in on Sherrice. She was in the bed pretending to be asleep. Desiree closed her door and glanced in Christopher's room. He was fast asleep, looking like a cute little angel.

Desiree usually tried to watch at least some of the games, but she went to the computer instead and sent e-mails to Sherrice's teachers. Perhaps they had noticed something in class. She wanted to make sure she was still doing okay in her class work.

When the game was over, Gerard called her, asking if he could visit.

When Desiree opened the door, an enormous arrangement of beautiful exotic flowers was the first thing she saw, until Gerard peeped around them.

"I walked past this flower shop and they had your name on them," he said.

Desiree laughed. "They're beautiful." She smelled them and the blossoms actually emitted a pleasant aroma. Most flowers were of the hothouse variety, engineered to grow quickly, more for beauty than for the blossoms' aroma. The flowers must have been terribly expensive.

Gerard shut the door behind him and leaned against it, pulling her body into his. She felt the hardness and strength through his clothes as he ran his hands up her back.

"I thought I'd never get you alone," Gerard said and led her to the family room.

Desiree set her flowers on the table, and Gerard dragged her into his arms—and gave her the sweetest, most seductive kiss she'd ever had. He smelled fresh from the shower, but he looked tired.

Still, she was glad he wanted to see her as much as she longed to be with him.

"Now that you have me, what are you going to do with me?"

"Are you saying I can have my heart's desire?"

"Depends."

He was sexy as all get out and the smile he gave her was as wicked as it could be. "I have a long list of pleasures in store."

"Oh yeah?" The sexy timbre of his voice and his touch made her flesh tingle.

"Starting with this," he responded, pulling her into his arms.

He kissed her forehead and stroked her face gently before his tongue traced the soft fullness of her lips. His electrifying touch left her burning with fire.

"Hmm, I missed you."

"Oh, baby, these trips are getting harder and harder."

Desiree gave in to her desire for Gerard with her eyes wide open. The strong emotions almost frightened her.

Gerard took out a jewelry box and handed it to her. "Got something special for you," he said with a hopeful grin on his face.

Desiree hesitated before she took it from his hand. With a lump in her throat, she opened it.

The diamond that sparkled up at her was at least three carats. And Gerard looked at her expectantly.

"The diamond is beautiful."

"But . . ."

"You don't have to buy me. Remember I asked you not to treat me like one of your floozies?"

"How can you say that? You're special to me and I wanted to show you how much you mean to me."

"You can't do that with money. Guys march into my office all the time because they feel they have to buy bling for their women to keep them. As some kind of ownership or something. I'm not like that. I can't even dream of the amount of money you have. But that's not what this relationship is about. Thank you for thinking of me, but I can't accept this." She placed the box in his hand.

Gerard peered at it as if it were some unusual specimen he had to unravel. "I don't understand you, Desiree. Any other woman—"

"I'm not any other woman. So don't treat me like that."

"I know you aren't. You're unique. I wasn't trying to buy you or insult you. I care for you. I wanted to do something special for you."

"I know. And I know I'm not doing a good job of explaining why I can't accept your gift. But it's not me. I don't want to be lumped in the same bag with a slew of meaningless affairs. Can you understand that?"

"If that's what you want. But, Desiree, I know you're unique. I accept you for who you are. I'm not lumping you with anyone. And I don't like the fact that I can't buy you a gift if I want to."

"It's not the gift, it's the meaning behind it that troubles me. You didn't love Andrea, yet she wore, at least she still wears this huge diamond you gave her. What was the meaning behind it? I mean, this ring is larger than my engagement ring."

The next morning, Sherrice ran downstairs at the last minute as usual.

"It's time to leave. Grab something to eat quickly," Desiree told her. She was not in a good mood. She'd thought about Gerard's gift late into the night. Worried that she was just another of his trophies. As usual Christopher was up early, cheerful and ready to storm into the day.

"I hate breakfast," Sherrice complained.

"You have a late lunch, you need something in your stomach. Get a container of yogurt and drink some juice at least."

Rolling her eyes, Sherrice grabbed both.

"That had better be the last time you roll those eyes at me, girl."

Sherrice merely stomped out ahead of her, with the boys tagging behind.

"I'll put Chris in the seat," Justin said.

"Thanks, honey."

"I'll grab his diaper bag," Steven offered.

Desiree put the juice back in the fridge wondering why the boys were being so helpful. By the time she made it to the car everyone was strapped in.

The boys kept up a running conversation all the way to school. Desiree had decided to suggest a few activities with Sherrice, hopefully to bring them closer.

"I have to shop for a dress for the weekend. I saw one I liked the other day. I could use a second opinion. Would you like to go with me and we can get our nails done afterward? A manicure and pedicure."

Sherrice shrugged. "Okay."

"You don't have dance tomorrow. We can go right after school."

Desiree went in to work the next morning. When Scott saw her, he jumped up from his chair and marched down the hallway with her. He sat in the chair across from her and put his hand behind his head, leaning back at a comfortable level as he regarded her.

Desiree raised an eyebrow. "I have a client coming in fifteen minutes. You want to get to the reason for this meeting?"

"How is your mother?"

"She's fine."

"Your father was there the last time I stopped by. Is that going to be a problem?"

"You have to discuss that with my mother." Men were all boys at heart, Desiree thought.

"So where is he staying?"

"In the cottage out back."

His smile faded and he straightened in the chair. "Your mother was staying in the cottage."

Desiree rolled her eyes. "She moved out to give him space. I am not going to be the messenger pigeon between you two. You want to know something about my mother, you ask her."

"I call her every day. I think I'll be dropping by D.C. soon."

Desiree sighed. No wonder he was such a great agent. He was as tenacious as a dog with a bone. "Enjoy your trip."

Pleased, he stood. "Go a little easy on Keith. I don't want to lose a client. You can't make them budget even if it's for their own good. Remember, this is an option."

"I understand."

"I know you love your job and you're great at it. But in the final analysis, you can lead the horse to the water but . . . You know the rest. I've seen him play. He's one of my most promising prospects. I intend to go far with him, so I don't want him pissed off at us and to leave for another agency that won't give him flack about spending. I'm going to talk to him before his appointment with you."

"All right."

She completed paperwork and made phone calls while she waited for Keith. Twenty minutes later, he appeared, whipping his sunshades off and clipping them on his pocket. He was huge. Looking at the man on TV was nothing like his presence up close and personal.

"Don't start on me," he snapped. "I know I said I was going to cut back, but things just didn't happen that way."

"In the beginning it takes work to stay on track," Desiree assured him, hoping she wasn't sounding like his third grade math teacher.

"Tell me about it." He plopped down in the chair.

"Why don't we go over this together? I have a list of your expenditures."

He had pages full of expenses. He had enough bracelets and bling to keep the women in a small town pleased.

Now that she wasn't jumping on his back, he relaxed a

little, was less combative. "I'm not going to spend like that every week."

"It's a funny thing about money. If you don't take a look at what's being spent, you have no idea of how much money is really going out. Let's take a close look at what you spent this last month. And look at how it compares to each month in the last year."

Desiree put several sheets side by side and pointed out each expense. Every month was almost the same. He spent way over budget.

"At this rate you'll run out of money before the end of the year."

She talked about players who had been injured and taken out of the game.

"You got to stop this 'cause every time I come here you seriously mess with my Karma."

"Far be it from me to spoil your Karma. I just don't want you to end up losing so much after climbing so high." She talked about one player in particular who was now picking up towels in the locker room. If someone had pointed out to him budgeting methods, he'd have money to live on. She started to talk about a retirement plan and finances beyond his game, but his eyes crossed over so she left that for another day.

He wiped the sweat off his brow, and leaned back in his chair as if he'd broken loose from the defense and sprinted the whole field to score a touch down,

"Is that what you're gonna to do with your old man? Dole out every cent he spends?" He shook his head. "A date with you should be interesting with all your complaining."

Desiree took exception to his statement.

He rolled his eyes.

"I'm not a fanatic."

"Yeah, right."

11

It was so much easier not having to be in two places at the same time. While Desiree picked up Sherrice from dance class, Mrs. Gaines picked up the boys from soccer practice.

Desiree had a talk with the dance teacher after practice.

"I wanted you to know Sherrice is performing very well in class," Emily said. "I've assigned two solos for her, but I wanted to get your permission first. She's a wonderful dancer and it gives her the opportunity to showcase her talents. We were working toward that before her parents died. I think it will be a rewarding experience for her."

"Does she want to do a second solo?"

"She's expressed interest, but you might want to discuss it with her. She's capable. And she can certainly perfect the steps in time."

"I'll discuss it with her, then. Thank you for thinking of her."

"We'll need a decision soon. We're finalizing the schedule now."

"I'll give you my decision by the end of the week."

"Wonderful. You are neighbors with Gerard Kingsley, aren't you? Sherrice often talks about him. About his wonderful influence in her life. Her mother mentioned him, too."

"He's been a great help."

"I hope he attends the program. Sherrice has mentioned that. You might want to whisper the bug to him, in case he's in town that afternoon."

"I will."

Desiree pulled Sherrice from her friends and they left.

"How was school today?" Desiree asked as they drove home.

"Okay."

"Your dance teacher assures me you're doing wonderfully."

"It's okay."

Desiree stifled a groan. Sherrice made the conversation tedious and difficult. She still resented Desiree taking her mother's place.

Desiree and the boys were getting along wonderfully. They had even gone skating the other day and tried to get Sherrice to join them, but she refused. The problem was Sherrice resented Desiree's presence and she didn't understand why. What did the girl think would happen to them if she left?

Desiree stopped at a red light and regarded Sherrice.

"Your teacher discussed two solos. Would you like that?" She shrugged. "Sure."

Desiree gave up—for the moment. There had to be a way to reach her.

Desiree was lying on a sheet spread out on the family room floor with Christopher, who was playing with a toy. The boys were playing Sega Genesis with Levi. Jacqueline had flown up for the weekend. She was reading a book, stretched on a chair in another corner.

Suddenly Christopher was on Desiree, kissing her forehead.

She grabbed him and lifted him in the air. He let out peals of laughter. She brought him down and made the smacking noise on his tummy. He balled up in laughter. When she put him down he came back for more.

She glanced up to see Sherrice watching them. For once she was smiling. When she noticed Desiree watching her, she turned to walk away.

"Come on and join us, Sherrice," Levi called out.

"I'm fixin' to go to my room," she responded, then climbed the stairs.

"What's wrong with Sherrice?" Levi asked. "Not good to spend too much time alone."

"I don't know," Desiree responded with a tired sigh. She wasn't getting anywhere with her. She finally realized she and Sherrice needed counseling if they were to resolve their problem. She couldn't seem to reach her alone. She'd get Gerard's parents' number from him for a recommendation.

"Ma-ma-ma-ma-ma," Christopher said, falling on Desiree again, wanting more play. She focused on the little pint.

"Here we go," she said just before she lifted him again and blew on his tummy. His peals of laughter were delightful.

"I don't like this," Levi said. "Girl never spends time with the family."

"She's a teenager," Jacqueline said. "They're impossible to please."

"Still need to be with people who love her. House is too big. Too much room to get lost in. We didn't have all that room when we grew up. Three boys tucked in one room, two girls tucked into another. Everybody got his own room here. More money just means more problems."

"They had their problems back then, too," Jacqueline said. "Lord knows everything isn't easy to fix, Levi, whether you're poor or rich. You're always trying to fix things."

"Some things needs fixing," Levi replied. "What's got into you?"

Jacqueline growled.

"Looks like I'm not the only one round here needing medicine," he mumbled beneath his voice.

"They're PMSing," Justin whispered.

"What you know about that?" Levi said, smiling.

"Saw it on TV."

Levi shook his head. "Okay, boys, I'm winning the next game."

"In your dreams, Grandpa," Steven responded.

The three males were on their stomachs in front of the TV. Christopher looked wide-eyed at them. He pushed up from Desiree and took a tentative step in their direction. She held her breath. He took six steps before he toppled to his knees.

"Did you see that? Did you see that? Christopher took six steps."

"Wow!" Justin said.

"My little man's going to be a sprinter before you know it," Levi said.

Christopher crawled the remainder of the way to the males and sat dead center in their view, leaning on his granddad's joystick.

"I won!" Justin cried out.

"You little mess," Levi said to Christopher. "Caused Grandpa to lose the game. Won't let nobody else get away with that. You've got privileges."

He lifted the little tyke into his arms. "What am I going to do with you?"

Christopher patted him on the cheeks.

Her father was doing so well now that he was back on his medication. He balked at taking it, but he was a totally different man.

The next afternoon Jacqueline kept Christopher while Desiree and Sherrice went to Phipps Plaza to shop. A store there had agreed to hold the dress for her. Traffic in the opposite direction was already heavy.

"Maybe we can do a little shopping for you while we're here. Would you like a new dress, jeans, or shoes?"

"I guess."

"What are your favorite stores?"

She named a couple of shopping centers Desiree had stopped at when she was searching for the gown.

They made it to the store. Desiree tried the gown on and modeled for Sherrice. "How do you like it?"

"It's very pretty."

"Not too tight?"

"Tight is the style."

"I don't want to look too hoochie." It was a lavender dress with a discreet V and sequins around the neck and waistband.

"You're a long way from hoochie in that dress. It's pretty on you. Where are you going to wear it?"

"Gerard invited me to attend a benefit with him Saturday night."

"Then it's perfect. My mom used to wear dresses like that to benefits with my dad." Then her eyes grew misty.

"It's okay to remember them. I bet your mother looked lovely. You favor her, you know?"

"How do you know? You never met her."

"But I've seen pictures. And I saw pictures of her when she was younger. Do you look at teenage pictures of her?"

Sherrice shook her head.

"Well, you should. You look very much like her. Just as beautiful."

Sherrice dabbed at her eyes and glanced away.

Desiree hugged her quickly. "Well, I'm sold. I'm going to get this one. Now we have to find the perfect shoes to go with it."

Sherrice was in a much better mood. Desiree only hoped their camaraderie lasted.

"Maybe we'll find something you like, Sherrice."

"My friend has a pair that's to die for."
"We'll do better for you."

After work the next day, Desiree had lunch with Pat Parker.

"I can't believe how busy these charitable functions keep me. I'm working on the one with Amanda Kingsley. She's a great lady. You should volunteer with the hospital."

"I might eventually. But between the kids and work I don't see how I'll have the time."

"I might have to stop once the baby is born."

"How are you feeling?"

"If I discount morning sickness, wonderful."

"Well, you look great," Desiree said.

"I miss Tony. I didn't realize I'd be so lonely without him." Desiree patted her hand.

"Amanda invited me over the other day to discuss the program for Saturday night. She's angry that Gerard and Andrea broke up. I don't think they're even speaking."

"She's that involved in his relationship?"

"It's a long story. She should know Gerard isn't going to settle down any time soon. He told Tony he wasn't going to get married until he retires from playing ball."

"Must be nice to have your life work according to a preset timetable."

"Ballplayers are in a world of their own. I'm just glad Tony and I dated since high school. Otherwise I'd be afraid to trust what he felt."

It was almost midnight and Gerard and Tony stopped by the bar for drinks before they went home. They had lost the game and needed to fortify themselves.

Gerard was taken aback when Desiree wouldn't accept

his ring. A woman had never turned his gifts down before. And why did she think he was trying to buy her?

"Penny for your thoughts," Tony said, ordering a Manhattan iced tea.

Gerard shook his head. "Women."

"That says it all. Andrea's still on your back? You can do a lot worse."

"I'm seeing Desiree."

"You sure you're ready for all that responsibility?"

"I like her."

"The question is, how does she feel about you?"

"I gave her a ring the other night. She wouldn't accept it. The average woman would love a three-carat ring."

"Hey, she has four kids to think about. Plus, she's older. She's not a run-of-the-mill bimbo. She isn't into playing games."

"I don't spend that kind of money on a game. I'm serious about this."

"Give me a break. You give *every* woman you date a ring. It's a consolation prize. You just give it in the beginning. Look at this, fellows, she's mine—until I get tired of her. And when it's over she gets to keep the ring. Bam! She can't complain too much, can she?"

Angry, Gerard sipped his scotch. "You don't know what you're talking about."

"You don't even think about what you're doing anymore. It's your byline."

Gerard didn't dignify that with a response.

"You're my pal, but I like Desiree. She deserves better than that. She's not like one of your women. Neither was Andrea. But she was chosen for you. You knew that wasn't going to work. She was a convenience."

"I don't like the sound of that."

"The truth isn't always pretty."

Gerard pushed his drink aside and munched on some peanuts. He did not like the flow of the conversation. Of course he didn't love Andrea. She didn't love him either.

They had been convenient for each other. It wasn't a one-sided thing. She understood from the beginning.

By the time Gerard got home from his game it was after midnight. He undressed and looked out his window for several minutes thinking of Desiree. The light was on in her room. He wondered if Chris was having a restless night.

He found himself calling her.

"Still mad at me?" He walked to his window. He should have just gone over there, but he didn't want her to think sex was the only thing he wanted. They were more than that. Maybe this time he'd have to get to know her.

"I was never angry with you."

"Your voice is sexy, do you know that?"

Desiree chuckled. "You do change the subject, don't you? It's hard to keep up with you."

"You're doing just fine. What are you wearing?"

"Umm. I'm wearing this red teddy with a thong."

"Give me two minutes. I'll be right there." Only he didn't move from the window.

"I'm actually wearing an oversized T-shirt. Nothing sexy about my outfit."

He could hear her smile across the phone.

"I'm going to give you one of mine. I like the idea of you sleeping with something of mine close to your skin."

"You have a problem with that ownership thing, don't you?"

He heard the mattress springs groan when she moved in the bed.

"Is that what the bling is all about? You want the privilege without paying the price?"

"By price you mean marriage."

"Exactly. I'm not suggesting it, so don't go running for the hills. I know you have your time schedule for that. And now doesn't fit."

"What's this? You women get together and talk about the men?"

"Of course. Don't you talk about us?"

"Oh, Desiree. You intrigue me."

"Umm."

"What color are you wearing tomorrow?"

"My dress is lavender."

He made a mental note to order her a lavender corsage in the morning. He hoped it wasn't too late. He was competing with spring proms. "Can't wait to see you in it." A sense of guilt nagged him. He didn't mistreat women. He didn't use them and leave them.

Desiree's father opened the door to Gerard and gave him a long look.

"Desiree? Your date's here," he called out. "Come in."

Her dad could be formal at times, and he seated Gerard in the living room. The kids were all oohing and aahing over Desiree's gown. They went with her to the living room. Even Sherrice joined them. She was pleased with the heels Desiree had purchased for her.

"Oh, man, you cleaned up," Justin said.

Gerard was dressed in a tux that had to have been made specifically to fit him. This was no rental. His shoes were spit-polished black. And if he looked handsome on an ordinary day, he was drop-dead gorgeous right now.

Desiree's heart skipped a beat.

"Why, thank you." Gerard approached Desiree and pinned a beautiful corsage with lavender highlights on her gown.

"It's beautiful, Gerard."

"I didn't know whether you wanted the armband or to pin it on your gown."

"This is perfect."

After he pinned it he kissed her lightly on the lips.

The boys fell out laughing, and choking, and holding their stomachs.

"It's so romantic," Sherrice said. She looked on with a dreamy expression on her face.

Jacqueline entered the room with a camera and they posed for pictures. It felt like prom night.

"Take one with the kids," Desiree said. And all the kids lined up in front of her. Gerard held Christopher so he could be in the snapshot, too.

Levi stood back with his arms crossed perusing the scene. After the photos were taken he nodded, pleased.

In minutes, Desiree and Gerard were on their way. He'd driven the Porsche.

When Desiree looked at the program, she realized Gerard was the guest speaker.

"Why didn't you tell me?" she asked.

"Wasn't important," he said just before his parents and brother were seated at their table. Andrea was with them.

"It's good to see you again, Desiree," Gerard's father said.

Desiree smiled. Gerard's mother had arranged the seating so that his ex was sitting on one side of him. What had she gotten herself into? Desiree thought. Paul's mother had disliked her. Was she going another round with mothers who wanted to choose other women for their sons? Why hadn't Gerard told his parents they were dating? And even if Gerard hadn't told her, why did Amanda think she had to bring a date for her own son?

Desiree peeked at Andrea's hand when she picked up her glass with her left hand. A huge diamond sparkled on her finger—a gift from Gerard evidently. He doled out diamonds the way other men doled out spare change.

It was immediately apparent Andrea hadn't expected Desiree to be present, or for Gerard to bring a date. Desiree felt sorry for her. Never in a million years would she put another woman in that situation. Competition or not. It was so unfair. She looked like a nice person, too.

A few minutes later, a man about Gerard's age came to their table and invited Andrea to sit with them. Desiree breathed a sigh of relief.

"Thank you, Mother. What a generous move."

"You didn't tell me your plans. How was I to know you had a date?"

"I didn't realize I needed your permission."

"Son, we were able to raise a lot of money for the children's fund," his father cut in. "I'm grateful."

Gerard nodded.

"How are the children coping, Desiree?" Amanda asked.

"Very well." Now wasn't the time to ask about the therapist.

"You haven't told your parents about us, have you? Desiree asked in the tense confines of the car.

"I haven't spoken to my parents, period."

"Was I supposed to be some kind of dirty little secret?"

"Don't be ridiculous," Gerard scoffed.

"Your parents knew about Andrea," Desiree said, feeling offended. "But you haven't seen fit to tell them about me. Or maybe what we share is nothing more than a quick sex fix when you need it."

"Don't kid yourself." Gerard stopped at a light and frowned at her. "I don't get nearly what I need. Listen, my mother hasn't spoken to me since she found out I broke up with Andrea. And we aren't on great speaking terms anyway. She disapproves of my career, so we aren't exactly close. If I was ashamed of you, I wouldn't have taken you with me tonight." He sighed. The leather creaked when he shifted toward her. "Hey, let's not fight, okay?" He gathered her tense hand in his and kissed the back of it.

Desiree glared through the window.

"You deserve a real date, instead of quickies when you

break away from the kids, or benefits with a huge crowd around," Gerard said.

Feeling slightly appeased, Desiree cleared her throat. "It's for a worthy cause. There are only so many hours in a day. And let me tell you, Scott's clients take up a lot of my time."

"You're good for them. Over time you'll make a huge difference. Do you realize you aren't just working to change their perceptions of money, but they'll teach their kids what you teach them? The kids talk to their friends. So with the trickle-down effect, you'll be teaching generations."

"I don't know if I have that kind of power, because I won't even reach all of my clients."

"I don't win all of my games. Doesn't mean I'm going to quit. If you reach one, it's enough."

"You're very inspirational."

"Did I tell you how beautiful you are tonight?"

Desiree studied his profile in the flickering light.

"You don't like praise, do you?"

"I get enough focus on the field. I have Wednesday off. I want to spend the entire day with you."

"Unfortunately, because some of the players will be here, I have some appointments. But my afternoon is free."

"How is your dad making out?"

"It's bittersweet in a way. He's enjoying the grandkids, but he's mourning the loss of his son. Even though he didn't know him, he still feels it deeply."

"He needs time to grieve."

"I think he feels it more intensely because of the war, you know? When you've lived through the worst life can throw you, you appreciate every little nibble thrown your way."

Gerard parked in front of his house, not hers.

Inside a huge bouquet was on the table. Gerard read the card, which only said *You'll win the next one.*

"I can't believe this. This person even knows where I live."

"Look. I wasn't born yesterday. I need you to be up

front with me," Desiree said. "This woman wouldn't send you expensive flowers out of the blue."

He spread his arms wide. "I'm telling you, I don't know who they're from."

"I'm going home."

He caught her arm and held her in place. "Don't go. I'm being truthful with you."

"Gerard, I'm not ready for . . . you and the other women. It's too much."

"Are you saying I can't have a normal life because of women I'm not even aware of?"

"You don't lead a normal life."

"It's normal for me."

"But not most of the world. And you need to think about what you really want. If you still want to play the field, I understand. I just won't be part of it."

"If I wanted to play the field, I would. I wouldn't court you. I'm not stupid. You're a one-man woman who requires a one-woman man. If I weren't ready for that, I wouldn't put you or myself through the wringer. Life's too short. And sounding crude, there are plenty of women who are available for that kind of relationship."

He moved closer to Desiree.

"Don't let this spoil what we have. I want some time alone with you," he said and gathered her into his arms.

"I have too much on me for games. Don't play with me."

"I'm not. I don't have the time for them, either. But you have to learn to trust me. I know it's hard. But I promise to always be up front with you."

He lowered his head to hers and kissed her deeply.

Her arms reached around his neck. Her hand held his head close as she kissed him back. She was with him all the way and her breasts pressed against his chest. She shivered as a tingle of awareness rushed along her spine. The feel of him in her arms felt like heaven. Desiree sighed. For now she'd trust him.

Gerard couldn't believe how deeply he had fallen for

Desiree. He'd battled with himself to leave her alone and he had enormous willpower. It took a lot to give up pleasures for his career, but he had, and he continued to do so.

But he couldn't give up Desiree. He needed her like the air he breathed. He didn't understand himself. Why he would put himself through this. He could settle with one woman, though. He'd played out his wild days at the beginning of his career when women ran after him as if they were free for the picking.

Gerard carried Desiree to his bed and peeled all the clothing that had been enticing him all evening from her delectable body.

Later they lay in bed. Gerard had positioned Desiree so that she lay on his left arm, not his pitching arm.

"You know, I am so happy with the way Sherrice has been acting the last two days. For a while, I thought we would have to go to counseling."

"Sherrice? Why?"

"I don't know what it was, but she was defying me at every turn. It was almost as if she hated me."

"I don't understand why she would act that way."

"Neither do I."

"Want me to talk to her?"

"Would you? She might be more forthcoming with you."

"Of course."

"I talked to her teachers to see if she was having a problem at school, but all of them said that she was okay, other than being a little subdued, and that was a normal part of the grieving process. But the way she was attacking me had nothing to do with grieving."

He stroked her arm. "You've been really worried about this."

She nodded. "I was concerned that it might cause a problem with me adopting. I feel like these kids are mine. They were my brother's and I want to do right by them. If Social Services think we're having problems it might make the process more difficult. After all, I'm a single woman."

"I don't think that's a big issue today. Have the boys given you problems?"

"No. They're adjusting well. And I forgot to tell you, Christopher is walking and he can say mama."

"He calls you mama?"

"I tell you, it just filled my heart with joy. I know he's not my son, that he's my brother's, but I feel like he's my little baby. Am I being silly or crazy?"

He caressed her face tenderly. "Of course not. It's normal."

"It's more than that, and I want to tell you before this relationship goes any further." Desiree sat up and turned the bedside light on.

"What is it?" he asked. He plumped the pillows and leaned against the headboard.

"I might not be able to have children."

"Why do you think that?"

"I was pregnant five years ago. There were complications and I lost the baby. The doctor said having more children could endanger my life."

"Desiree, don't worry about that." He caressed her brow. "You have four children already."

"They might be the only children I'll ever have."

"Come here." Gerard gathered her into his arms. "I'm not dating you because I want you for a baby maker."

"Barren women seem to be the attractive thing now. Paul told me that was what he found most attractive about me. He wanted to marry me because he really didn't want children. The idea of having four children was the last thing he wanted."

"Children don't scare me, Desiree. Don't worry about that."

He ran a hand along her face, tilted her face to him, and kissed her lightly. Then he deepened the kiss. Desiree felt wanted, warm, and comforted as she rubbed her hand across his shoulder.

* * *

Scott drove to Jacqueline's on a whim. She opened the door wearing some slinky thing.

"You know, I tried to surprise you and flew to D.C.," he said more than a little peeved. "I made a special trip there, and guess what? Your neighbor told me you'd flown to Atlanta."

"You should have asked. I would have told you I was coming here."

"Why didn't you?" Scott asked.

Jacqueline shrugged. "A last-minute decision."

"You could have told me."

"I didn't know I needed your permission. I'm fifty-three. I don't ask anyone when I decide to take a trip." She shut the door in his face.

She actually shut the door in his face. Scott leaned on the doorbell. She opened it, stood with her arms across her breasts, glaring at him.

"I can't believe you did that." He moved her to the side and walked in.

"I didn't invite you in."

"A lapse." He sighed. "I think we need to start over again. Dating you isn't going to be easy, is it?"

"We're always starting over."

"Come here."

But when she didn't come to him, he moved closer to her. He was accustomed to being the leader in every way, and she was bucking him at every turn. He gathered her into his arms and kissed her.

He held onto her tightly. "Why are you giving me such a hard time?"

"You take too much for granted. If I give you an inch, I'll become no more to you than your BlackBerry or anything else that turns on when you want it, forgotten at all other times. And I don't intend to do that."

"I never take you for granted."

"Hummph. I'm not sure about you."

He tilted her chin until she was staring in his eyes.

"I've told my family about you. They're dying to meet you. I've been ordered to bring you to visit."

"You're moving way too fast."

"Like I've told you, I don't waste time."

12

"Thank you, Mother. That was quite a little show the other night," Gerard said.

"How was I to know you were bringing a date?"

"It shouldn't have mattered. You put both Andrea and Desiree in an awkward position."

"I certainly didn't mean to upset Desiree. If you had said one word, I wouldn't have invited Andrea."

"Why should I have to tell you anything? Even if I didn't have a date, you shouldn't have interfered."

"Fine, fine. I wash my hands of the entire matter. There's no reasoning with you. You're impossible."

"I thought you'd determined that a long time ago, Mama."

"You're right. If I say right, you'll go left. I'm just going to leave it alone."

"Thank you."

"I thought I heard your voice," Gerard's father said, coming into the room with the morning paper. "I'm just amazed by what we received for the benefit. We couldn't have done it without it, son. So many children need treatment their parents can't afford. So many families are without insurance."

"Glad to help, Dad."

"You've having a great season. Sorry I can't make it to your game tonight. I have surgery early tomorrow morning."

"I understand."

"Wish the games were earlier. But I would like to have lunch with you before you leave town again."

"Yeah, thinking of games, I have to get to practice. I'll call you about lunch."

With that, Gerard left. He always felt like the fifth wheel with his parents. Chad was the lucky one. He fit right in. He could sit down to breakfast and chat the morning away with them, but not Gerard. Whatever conversation he started would eventually turn into a fight.

He just didn't fit. Sometimes he felt he didn't fit anywhere.

Until he was in Desiree's arms. Then he felt like the sun was shining on him. In her arms he fit. A perfect fit.

Speaking of lunches, he called Sherrice. He heard the noise of the other kids in the background.

"Hey, I hear you're getting older by the second. Will you have Sunday brunch with me?"

"Brunch?"

"Sure."

"Desiree, can I have brunch with Gerard today?" she asked.

"Can we go too?" Justin asked. "Can we?"

Sherrice came back on the line. "The boys want to go, too."

"The more the merrier."

When Desiree told them they could go, he heard the whoops in the background. Now he'd only have to find a place where the boys could be entertained and he could talk to Sherrice privately.

On Sunday morning, Emily prepared herself an espresso and a breakfast of fruit, yogurt, and half a bagel. She nibbled as she read the Sunday paper from front to back.

There was so much trouble in the world, she thought. She skipped the local news section and turned to the travel page. What she'd give to be able to afford to travel to some of those exotic locales. She could afford those trips as soon as she and Gerard got married. He would be a generous mate. On his off months they'd travel the world—Brazil, Africa, Europe, even China. They would enjoy many romantic ventures.

She turned to the society pages, knowing she would one day grace those pages as Gerard Kingsley's wife.

She spilled her coffee when the picture of Gerard and Desiree jumped out at her. Never mind that his mother and father were also in the photo. Desiree was hovered up under *her* man. "What in the world? That cheating bastard. How dare he?"

Emily stared at the article. It was a benefit, it said, but she didn't care what it benefited. Just the fact that it mentioned Gerard's date with Desiree. What was he doing taking that hussy to a benefit?

Emily threw the paper down and hopped out of her seat. She stomped to her bedroom and fell across the bed, shrieking with huge tears streaming down her face. "How could he? How could he?" she wailed. She pummeled the bed with her fists. She kicked her legs up and down like a two-year-old. She couldn't help it. He'd betrayed her. And she couldn't stop the tears from flowing.

Wait a minute. She sat up. He didn't betray her. It was Desiree. She tricked him. It was her doing, not Gerard's. Gerard was an angel. He loved Emily. Desiree must have put some kind of spell over him.

Emily dried her eyes. Easing herself to the edge of the mattress, she snatched a tissue from the holder and blew her nose. She picked up Gerard's picture on her bedside table. Her eyes misted as she gazed at him, so handsome in his uniform. She'd taken it from a sports magazine. Such a perfect likeness.

Emily smoothed her hand down the photo. Then she brought it to her lips and kissed his lips.

"We'll be together soon, sweetheart. I won't let her come between us. I'm sorry for thinking you would betray me. I was so wrong. *So wrong.* You'd never betray our love."

Emily blew her nose again. "I'll have to send you a letter." She went downstairs and picked up the photo on the society page. She cut that awful Desiree's picture out and tore it to shreds. She found one of her formal photos and reduced it on her color copier until it fit perfectly into the space. Once it was lined up the way she wanted it, she taped it into place. In the den, she rummaged in a drawer until she found a suitable frame and set the picture on her dresser.

"Perfect."

Desiree and the kids went to early service, but the kids were so excited about going to brunch with Gerard, they were fidgety and kept looking at their watches instead of listening to the message. The preacher preached a wonderful sermon. Out of her bunch, Desiree was the only one listening.

When they returned home, the boys changed out of their suits into neat slacks and knit shirts. Sherrice wore the slacks she wore to church. They had barely changed when Gerard rolled to a stop in their driveway.

He wore casual slacks with a polo shirt. "Do you want to come with us?" He bent and kissed Desiree.

"No. Christopher and I will spend a quiet afternoon together. He's ready for a nap anyway. Come on in. They're almost ready."

When she turned around, her heart nearly stopped. She

started for the stairs. Christopher was at the top. He stretched out and sailed down the steps in one fluid ride.

"Oh my God!"

"He's okay, Desiree."

"He could have been killed!"

Her frantic cries brought the other kids downstairs. Desiree didn't realize tears were running down her cheeks. She was trying to get to her baby, and Gerard was holding her back.

And Christopher was grinning like he'd done something fantastic, instead of scaring the life out of her.

"Look at him." Gerard's words finally penetrated her fear. "He's fine. He knows how to climb the stairs."

"But I didn't—"

"I taught him. Beverly taught all the kids how to crawl up and down the stairs."

Desiree rounded on Gerard. "How could you do that without telling me?"

Gerard turned to the kids, who were focused on them. "Take Chris to the other room. I'll be with you in a minute."

When they left, he focused on Desiree. "Because you're too afraid—too overprotective to let him grow up."

"You stepped over the line. He could have hurt himself."

"Desiree, you can't keep him under your thumbnail. You have to let him learn things, grow up."

"That's not your decision. He's my baby."

"It's not all about you. I love these kids too and I can have a difference of opinion." He took a deep breath before he strangled her. "Beverly didn't baby the kids. She didn't fill them with fear."

Angry, he went to gather the other kids and took them out to brunch. He wouldn't look at Desiree. How dare she say that he had no role in their lives?

"Are you and Desiree fighting?" Steven asked, penetrating the fog in his brain.

Gerard glanced at the boy from the rearview mirror.

"We'll be fine. She was frightened, that's all. She's not accustomed to being around little kids. And she thought Chris was going to get hurt. She loves you and wants to protect you. So when she overreacts, understand that."

Sherrice had a strange expression on her face. Gerard wondered what she was thinking.

Gerard decided to take them to Agatha Christie.

Desiree's heart still thumped as if she'd run five miles. She eased into a seat in the family room and watched Christopher play.

He was happy. She wasn't a bad mother the way Gerard tried to make her feel. Criticizing the way she raised the children. Would Social Services feel the same way? That she wasn't a good influence?

Desiree was stiff when Gerard returned from brunch. Pleased with their outing, the children ran into the house and upstairs.

Desiree and Gerard were downstairs in the kitchen alone. She was putting away the dishes from the dishwasher. Christopher was still napping.

Gerard handed a package to Desiree. "Lunch and a peace offering. I saw no reason for you to cook."

"Did she talk to you?"

"Sherrice assured me everything was fine. She seemed okay."

"She is at times and then she'll have these outbursts." Desiree wouldn't come anywhere near him.

"Stop for a minute, will you?" Gerard asked. When she leaned against the counter and stared at him he continued to talk. "I think you're wonderful for the kids. I'm sorry for the argument and that I didn't tell you I was teaching Chris how to navigate the stairs. But he's growing. He's inquisitive. If someone forgets to put the gate up, he wouldn't know how to climb down safely. I thought it important to teach him."

Desiree nodded. "I'm sure I overreacted."

He closed the distance between them, and dug his hands into his pockets to keep from touching her. "I care about you, Desiree, and the children."

"I know. I want to protect them from everything and I know I can't. If anything happened to Christopher I couldn't bear it."

"Honey, no one can protect the kids from life's scrapes. Not even Jordan and Beverly. Don't live on fear." He tugged her to him. "Come here." He lowered his head and kissed her. She was stiff at first and then gave herself up to the desire burning between them. "What am I going to do with you?" he whispered against her lips. Then he tightened his arms around her, loving the feel of her warm, soft body pressed against him, and wondered where this family, this woman in particular, was taking him.

He talked about her fear, but for the first time, Gerard was afraid too. He had his life mapped out, and she was playing havoc with his plans.

When he was away from her, he was thinking of her, worried about her and the kids. He couldn't let her go. And he hated needing anyone, even Desiree.

"Ouch, what's wrong?" Desiree asked.

"Sorry."

"I like being in your arms, but not crushed. You don't realize your own strength."

"Umm." Gerard loosened his hold and she walked to the counter. She opened the container of food he'd bought her and dished a portion into a plate.

This family, this woman, had changed his life forever.

A week later, Gerard pitched Sunday's game. When he walked out on the field for practice throws, he threw a ball to Steven. Written on it was *Happy Birthday* and it was dated and signed. Steven was out-of-this-world happy.

Unfortunately the Eclipses lost by one run. Desiree tried to make small talk on their way back to the house, but Gerard was unusually silent.

Desiree had asked Mrs. Gaines to come by to decorate the house while they were gone. As much as her father loved baseball, he stayed behind to help out. If Desiree had stayed Steven would have been suspicious.

Levi made it to the game at the bottom of the first inning.

Back at home, as always, the boys ran into the house. For a change, Sherrice took Christopher out of the car. Desiree grabbed the diaper bag while Gerard shrugged out of his coat and left it in the car.

From inside they heard squeals. When they walked in, Steven was gushing over the gifts laid out on the floor. But most of all he was pleased with the go-cart.

"That thing will go fifty miles an hour, but I've tuned it down so it won't go that fast," Levi said. "Now, when you come out to the country where I live, you'll get to drive it. We got plenty of dirt paths there and you can ride to your heart's content."

"Can I get one for my birthday, Grandpa?" Justin asked. "Can I?"

"You sure will."

"My birthday's next month."

"I know. I know everybody's birthday. They're written down in my book. You are going to spend some time with Grandpa and Aunt Nadine this summer. She's enough to drive anybody crazy. But she loves kids. She's dying to meet you. I'm going to take you to see her one weekend soon before she disowns me."

"So what are we going to do while we're there?" Justin asked.

"This summer you'll get to meet your relatives. We're going to fish in the lake. Got a river and a lake running through our property. We're going to have a great time. There's a little cabin on the water, but I like to sleep outside in a tent. The stars are so bright they light up the sky. You all ever been camping?"

"We go to summer camp."

"Not the same. Grandpa's got a lot to teach you."

With Gerard's arms wrapped around Desiree she watched her father talk to the kids. They hung on every word. It took her back to the time when she spent summers with him and Aunt Nadine. Aunt Nadine would threaten to send her back to D.C. if Levi skipped his medicine even one day. She stood over him like a guard every day to make sure he took those pills. And he took them just to make sure he kept Desiree.

There were times he didn't take them, especially when they were in D.C. Those were frightening times. Which was why Desiree wouldn't let him near the kids without them. It should be a crime to turn a good man into something like this, Desiree thought.

Hearing the kids' laughter, she focused on her father and them again.

Later Steven blew out the candles on his birthday cake, and Desiree cut slices while Gerard dipped ice cream for them.

That night Gerard tucked the kids in, along with Desiree. When they went into Steven's room, he said, "I was so sad earlier. I thought we weren't going to celebrate my birthday."

Desiree hit him with the pillow. "Never." He wiggled until he came from beneath the pillow and laughed. Desiree tickled his ribs. Did you have a good day?" she asked.

"The best since . . ."

Desiree bent over and hugged him. "There are going to be a lot more like this one."

"Thanks for the ball." It was sitting in a place of distinction on his dresser. Levi had promised to get a cousin to carve out a stand for him from a piece of wood from his very own forest.

Gerard ruffled Steve's hair, and then went downstairs with Desiree. He helped her with the last of the cleaning and they sat in the family room and watched a movie.

Before Desiree left for work the next morning, Aunt Nadine called.

"I've told your daddy we need to sell those trees on that land," she said in a commanding voice. "They'll make plenty of money, and he's holding on to them like leaves were money. I didn't tell him to sell the land, just the trees. They'll grow back. But he's stubborn. You need to talk to him. I tried to reason with him last night, but he hung up the phone on me. After all I've done for him, I get no respect."

"He won't listen to me any more than he'll listen to you," Desiree said.

"When I try to talk reasonably to him he starts threatening me. I'm not going to be scared out of my wits about my own land. They're my trees and he's got no right to stop me."

"You need money, Aunt Nadine?"

"It's not that I need money, just that it doesn't hurt to have a little tucked away in the bank for a rainy day. It's not like I'm begging for anything. I want to sell what's mine."

"Have you considered selling your part of the land?"

"I broached that subject once, and he nearly attacked me. Your daddy already bought the rest of the land from our other siblings. That was years ago and I wasn't interested in selling then, but I'm never moving back to that land. What do I need to hold on to it for? It's my land. I have the right to sell my trees if I want to."

"I'll buy the land from you, Aunt Nadine."

"You will?"

"Sure. Name your price."

Aunt Nadine named a hefty price, but Desiree knew it was worth every penny.

"I'll get back to you in a few days, okay?"

"Thanks, honey."

Desiree knew her daddy would go out of control if he didn't have that land to go to when he was troubled. So much for trying to hold on to her savings. She'd also have to give up her apartment. There was no need to hold on to it when she'd eventually have to give up the lease anyway. She'd never move back there with the kids. She took out a pad with a list of things to do and added *fax a thirty-day notice to the apartment manager.*

Maybe the kids could stay with Aunt Nadine and Dad while she went to New York to search for a house in the suburbs. On the other hand, taking them to New York would make a nice summer vacation for them. She, Sherrice, and Christopher could sleep in the queen bed in her bedroom. The boys could sleep on the pullout sofa in the living room.

After Scott's warning, Desiree was cautious about how she approached her clients. Keith was her first one of the day. He wore casual dress slacks and an Italian shirt. He was too handsome for his own good, and still spent money like it was going out of style.

"I know you're going to give me a lecture, but a man's got to live."

"And very high, as far as I can see," Desiree said.

"The chicks don't want cheap dates. They'll be talking about me for months to come. I'd be the laughingstock of the whole town."

"At the rate you're spending, that's not going to be a problem."

"You got to let a guy live a little. We need to rearrange this budget thing a little."

"Okay, how do you want it rearranged?"

"Just like that?"

"It's your money. I can only advise."

"See? I need more to entertain with."

"Okay. What if we build more discretional spending into your budget?"

They haggled over the amount.

"You're dipping into your investments. And you have to make monthly payments on the house you purchased for your mother."

"You're not helping me here."

"Well, I'm trying to work with you. You said that if anything happens, and I'm not messing with your Karma, you still wanted to live a good life. It's a shame to make eight hundred thousand and end up on the streets. But this is your money, and I'll do what you want me to do."

"You know how to kill the joy out of a situation, you know that?"

"I'm thinking about your future as well as your present. What we can do is look at these houses you want to buy and perhaps scale down until you're making more. The more you make, the more you'll be able to afford. But consider if it's logical to buy your mother a four hundred thousand dollar house, which is half of your income for the year. Where are you going to live? With your mother?"

"Heck no. Ladies can't stay overnight at my mom's place."

"Well. Parents want what's best for their children. She'll understand if you buy her a more modest home."

"If she doesn't, I'm buying her a plane ticket to visit you. That woman can be a real barracuda. How do you think she got me and my four knucklehead brothers through school?"

"Are they sports players too?"

"I have one brother older than me. He didn't listen to Mama so he didn't go to college. Things aren't that tight with him."

"And the other three?"

"One got a sports scholarship like me, the other got an

academic scholarship. One graduates next year. A couple of teams are courting him. We'll see. The other is the brain of the family. Majored in some science. Boy never played sports. Had to toughen him up a little bit. Make sure he didn't turn out to be a wimp."

Desiree shook her head. "So who's at home with your mother?"

"Nobody. Except my brothers during the summer and my cousins visit sometimes. They aren't there all the time."

"So a modest four-bedroom house should do. Your mother lives in Houston where you can still get a decent house at a respectable price."

"All right. All right. I'll go house-hunting with her soon and we'll try to find something reasonable. You play hardball, you know that? Maybe you need to negotiate contracts, the way you don't let up."

"Who, me?"

He leaned back in his seat. Narrowed his eyes. "You always get your way, don't you?"

"No."

"I bet you do. You lead your old man around by the ring in his nose."

Desiree chuckled. "Of course not."

"I know you do. I came in here fixin' to set you straight. Now here I'm like a baby puppy, following you around like I'm whipped."

"You couldn't have possibly changed your mind because what I said makes sense, right?"

"That, too. I'm bringing my investments to you 'cause after all this sacrificing, I better make some money. I better not end up broke."

"There are no guarantees in life."

"If that's the case, I should spend to my heart's content."

He got out of his seat, came around the desk, and hauled Desiree up and gave her a big bear hug.

"Thanks. I'll be checking you out soon." He set her on the floor and was out the door like a light.

Whatever Desiree was getting, she earned every cent, she thought as she straightened her clothes and prepared for her next client. She had enough time to construct notes on the computer and e-mail changes to Keith's budget to his accountant before her next client arrived.

She chuckled at the brass young man. *I really like working with them,* she thought. She absolutely hated the idea of waste. It bothered her that so much of their money wasn't utilized properly for them.

Jacqueline had gotten up and attacked the dust in her house that morning. She cleaned the bathroom fixtures until they sparkled. She scrubbed floors until you could see your own reflection in them.

Jacqueline's last day at work was in another week. Wednesday after work she vacuumed the living room floor, she debated if she should move to Atlanta to be near Desiree. Four children were a lot. She'd need help now and then. Maybe a day off to catch a breath. With Jacqueline nearby she could give Desiree a break, the way Jacqueline's sister gave her a break with Desiree when she was younger.

She was working very long hours at her job trying to tie up loose ends before she left. Her trips to Atlanta didn't help matters. So instead of trekking to Union Station for lunch, this one day, she decided to stay in and clean.

When the doorbell rang, she hoped it was her sister's daughter wanting her to sample a recipe. Her stomach growled with hunger. She peeped through the curtain of her row house. She was wearing ragged shorts and a T-shirt and she was all sweaty. She wore a band around her hair, and strands shot out in every direction but flat.

And Scott stood on the other side, dressed in a suit and tie, and looking like God's gift to women.

She could absolutely kill him.

* * *

Gerard visited Desiree and the kids every day when he was in town. Because so many of the players were in town, Desiree ended up working longer than usual. On Wednesday, she finally got a morning off.

Gerard had given his housekeeper the day off, wanting the place to himself. Maybe they'd get into the hot tub. He'd planned to start the day by watching a movie or taking Desiree boating or something. But the moment she came into the house the only thing that shot through his mind was sex with her.

So instead of hopping in his car and taking off, he dragged her to his bedroom.

"You know, if I had my way, I'd keep you in bed all day," Gerard said as he all but tore her clothes off her.

"How romantic." But she was reaching for his too.

"But because I'm a great guy, I'm going to take you to lunch. After I've had my breakfast."

He covered her mouth hungrily. His kiss sent spirals of ecstasy through her.

She caressed the strong column of the back of his neck, and his back.

His hands explored the soft lines of her back, her waist, her hips. He paused to kiss her, whispering his love for each part of her body. He feasted on her throat, her breasts, anywhere he could reach.

They touched each other until they couldn't stand the suspense any longer. Her cries of pleasure were as erotic as her touch. He donned a condom. And when he entered her, sharp pleasure exploded through her, rose, increased until she was a glowing image of fire, passion, and love.

And when they lay side by side on his bed, fear like nothing she ever felt before rendered her immobile.

She was in love with Gerard Kingsley.

* * *

Stretched out on the living room floor au naturel, Scott could only breathe. He couldn't move a muscle. Jacqueline had pumped the last rush of breath out of him. Now she was draped halfway over him in an equally undressed state.

"Woman, I haven't ever had sex like that. Not ever. You're going to kill this old man."

"If you aren't up to it . . ."

"I'm definitely up for it." He squeezed her shoulders, then lifted his head enough to peer in her eyes. "I didn't know you had it in you."

"Like you know so much about me."

"You've got to move to Atlanta, else the airlines are going to make a fortune off me. Damn, you're a hot package."

"I was just thinking about that when you arrived. Desiree needs help. And my sister's been thinking about moving after she retires."

"Seriously, you're thinking about moving?"

"I'm going to check out the real estate when I go back."

"Don't let that stop you. You can move in with me, anytime."

"No, I can't. I'm getting my own place."

Scott frowned. He'd like to have Jacqueline seated across the breakfast table from him in the mornings. With the hours he kept, things would be more convenient if she moved in with him. They'd have more time together.

"I don't know. With my schedule, it'll be more convenient to have you underfoot."

She popped him on the chest.

"Hey!"

"I'm no man's convenience." In one smooth motion she was up and strolling away, presenting him with an attractive backside. He kept forgetting Jacqueline didn't fall into his schedule the way most women would. The average woman would be happy to be at his beck and call. By the way things were going he'd have to be at Jackie's.

Scott hopped to his feet to search out Jackie to smooth

her ruffled feathers. Maybe he could talk her into a nice soft bed this time.

Later Desiree and Gerard showered and dressed. Then they played tourists. Gerard wanted to show her his Atlanta. They visited the Martin Luther King Center and the Peachtree Plaza, and rode the elevator to the top, which offered a breathtaking view of the city.

They made it back to Gerard's house at four thirty. A beautiful vase of flowers was sitting on the table.

"We need to talk," Desiree said, eying the flowers suspiciously.

Gerard sighed and read the card. It said *I know it wasn't your fault. I love you. We'll be together soon.*

"What is going on? What wasn't your fault?"

"I don't know. But it's time I talked to the police, because I don't like this."

"Are you sure you don't know who this woman is?" Desiree asked skeptically.

"I'm telling you the truth. It's bizarre. More so because she obviously knows where I live."

"Gerard, when you said you wanted to date me, I was of two minds. On the one hand I thought I was the luckiest woman alive to have someone like you attracted to someone like me. On the other hand, I knew there would be women all over you. Are you telling me you didn't encourage this woman in any way?"

"Absolutely not. You have to trust me. If you don't, we're doomed. Because of the money involved, sports players can't move without women being in the vicinity. It's part of this life. I'll be frank with you, when I was younger, my head swelled just like the next guy's. But I'm not young anymore. I'm thirty-two. I can't afford to act like a college senior. My needs have changed. I need someone more stable. Someone who wants me for myself, not for the gifts I can buy her. I can't believe I'm saying this. You may think it's easy for us, but you can tell by your clients, it's not. You can't imagine the number of women who are going to claim one of us got her pregnant, and then having that stuff splashed all over the news."

"It's not like in some cases it isn't deserved. You all don't exactly turn all those gorgeous women down who're running after you, either. It's a two-way street."

"Hey, at a certain age we don't necessarily think with our heads first. Hormones and all that kick in. Give a guy a break."

"Pu-lease."

He tugged her to him. "I don't want to spend my one day off fighting with you. I've got plans for the evening, so give a guy a break." He kissed her cheek, her forehead, her lips. "You are my one and only."

Desiree wanted to believe him. She wanted to be as special to him as he was to her. But she couldn't afford to let her heart go free with this man. Not just yet. But he was a tempting package she didn't want to let go of. Not yet.

Gerard had an early flight out the next morning. Desiree got spoiled having him around for an entire week.

She only had one appointment for that day. She went into the office at nine. After the appointment, she worked on her cases for two hours before she returned home at noon, just in time for lunch with Christopher. It was such a pleasant day that she took a blanket outside and they had lunch on the backyard lawn.

"You're a heartbreaker, you know that?"

He grinned at her and tottered on the grass. If anyone had said Desiree would even contemplate being a stay-at-home mom, she would have laughed in their faces even as recently as three months ago. Now she understood the joy of being home with children. She liked talking to the boys and would even enjoy time with Sherrice if she weren't so unpleasant much of the time. She still didn't understand the girl's problem. What happened to cause this sudden change in her personality?

At least for the last week, her disposition had gotten better. *Let's just hope it stays that way,* Desiree thought.

"You've got a phone call," Mrs. Gaines said, bringing the portable to her. She smiled her thanks. Thinking it was Gerard, she smiled as she said, "Hello."

It was her boss from New York. Regrettably he was giving her project to another manager. Her rival.

"But I'm going to return during the summer," she said. "Before the project begins."

"They moved the date up. You're going to have a lot of upheaval in your life. This is a huge project. I really need someone who's going to be available."

"I brought this project to the company."

"I'm sorry, Desiree. But we have to do what's best for the company. You can return to your same job, but I'm hoping you'll be second in command with this project. It's large enough and Roger could use your expertise. We're holding that slot for you."

"Second in command isn't the same as heading the project. I am very capable of handling it. More so than Roger."

"We've made our decision. We're looking forward to having you back soon." He hung up and Desiree pushed the Off button.

"Damn."

"Am!" Christopher screamed.

"Oh, shoot. I've got to watch what I say around you." He grinned.

But Desiree wasn't laughing at all. That weasel Roger had been just waiting for an opportunity to backstab her, and now he'd found a way.

13

Desiree was parking the car in the garage when Mrs. Gaines rushed out the door.

"Phone for you," she called out.

Desiree took the portable and walked into the house.

"This is Pat. Did I catch you at a bad time?"

"No. I just got back from dropping the kids off."

"Why don't you let them take the bus like the others?" Pat asked.

"I spoil them. And Sherrice feels she's too grown to ride the bus."

"Right, you spoil them, but that's your right. I'll probably do the same thing. I'm calling because I mentioned to one of my church members what a great job you were doing with the players at Scott's agency. She called back a few days later and asked if you would give a seminar to high school children."

"When?"

"I guess that's up to you. But I'll give you her number and the two of you can work it out."

Desiree hunted around for pen and paper and jotted down the number.

"I hope you don't mind. But you've made a huge difference for Tony and me. For a while I didn't know what we were going to do. It's so hard to talk sense to these men."

"I don't mind at all. As a matter of fact, I worked part-time on Saturdays teaching a class of kids in New York," Desiree told her. "Those kids were wealthy and didn't appreciate it nearly as much as these will, at least I hope they will. When will be a good time for me to call her?"

"She works, so evenings will be best. We're going to have to get together for lunch some time soon."

"Call me."

When they disconnected, Desiree turned the phone off. Christopher was crawling up the stairs, happy as a clam. Mrs. Gaines was urging him up, standing behind him in case he slipped. Desiree still couldn't get used to the idea of her baby crawling up and down stairs. Made her nervous. What if he tried to stand and walk down? Poor thing could . . . Desiree wouldn't even go there.

Since she came to Atlanta, she'd said more prayers asking God to keep her children safe than she'd prayed in a lifetime. Children took a lot out of you. But there was untold joy, too. She approached Mrs. Gaines.

"I'm going to spend some time with the little guy before I go to work." She plucked him off the stairs. His back arched and he wailed.

"All right." She put him back on the stairs and he crawled down as she backed down, as pleased as pie.

"Gerard has ruined you but good," she said. Once you taught them a skill, there was no turning back. Maybe she did baby him a little too much, but she wasn't going to tell Gerard that. She wanted Christopher protected and safe.

She missed Gerard, darn it. She couldn't wait until night when the house was quiet, the kids were sleeping peacefully, and he'd call to chat for an hour.

Gerard glanced at the number in his cell phone. Scott was calling him.

"Where have you been, old man?"

"Around. They checked out the flower situation. Some woman has been sending you flowers but she always pays with cash. They have a sketchy description of her. Evidently she's small in build. Pretty tall. Indistinguishable features. Not that memorable."

"How many million women do you think that fits?"

"Exactly. The problem is she never uses the same florist twice. But they're putting notices at the shops and we'll see what happens."

"Thanks, man. Her last note freaked me out."

"I can understand that, but back to business. An automobile corporation wants to work up a contract with you for commercials. We're looking at shooting when the season's over."

"Sounds good."

"Several companies are calling in. You're having a great season. They want your face on their product. We have a few public awareness engagements coming up, too. Are you up for them?"

"Sure."

"We'll talk when you return. Good luck on the game."

Gerard disconnected. He hoped they'd quickly find out who was sending him flowers. He didn't need any more grief from Desiree on that score.

He passed a jewelry store and walked in. It was a constant habit of his. Women expected expensive gifts from sports players.

They were in Houston playing the Astros for the next three days. He was at the Galleria with Tony.

"May I help you, sir?"

"I was looking for a necklace for a friend."

"We have plenty to select from. Are you looking for anything in particular?"

"Well, if I buy her diamonds, she won't accept them."

The saleswoman arched a perfectly shaped brow. "A woman who won't accept diamonds?"

"Go figure. Makes it difficult for buying gifts. How am I going to hold my head up when she says 'my man bought me plain gold'?"

"We have some lovely selections in gold. Something that will do you proud. Follow me, please," she said, walking down the long row of cases.

Twenty minutes later, Gerard walked out with a matching set: a gold necklace, bracelet, and earrings. It wasn't nearly as costly as diamonds, not by a long shot. He would have liked to buy platinum, but knew Desiree would balk again. God, women were so difficult to please.

Emily was stiff and critical during dance practice. Sherrice didn't understand what her problem was. She'd practiced her solo. She was using good form. Yet Emily couldn't be pleased. And she picked on her most of all. By the end of the session, Sherrice was near tears.

"Emily, I don't understand what I was doing wrong," Sherrice said after the other girls left.

Emily impaled her with a look. "Are you questioning my critique?"

"No, but I've been practicing hard. And I'm the best dancer in the class."

"Is being the best of these girls good enough? Or do you want perfection? Do you want to shine above all the others? Or do you want to be one of the pack?"

"I want to be the best. But I've been practicing every day."

"Obviously not enough. If you want to be the best, then you'll have to work harder. Sherrice, most of these girls are here for fun and games. They are not serious students. You're a serious student. You can go places with this. Even dance professionally."

Sherrice beamed. Emily thought that highly of her skills. "I never considered being a professional dancer."

"You should think about it."

Sherrice thought of the Alvin Ailey Dance Group or

the Dance Theater of Harlem. She considered dancing in New York, D.C., Atlanta, Los Angeles, the world.

Emily wiped the sweat from her face. "You might want a drink of water before we begin our next session."

Sherrice went into the hallway where the other girls had gathered.

"She was such a bitch today. I wonder what got into her. I don't know how you can stand her, Sherrice," one of the girls said.

"And you have another session with her. It's a good thing it wasn't me."

"I guess I have two left feet today," Sherrice said.

When Sherrice went back to class, Emily had calmed down somewhat.

"How was your weekend?" she said.

"It was fine."

"I understand your aunt attended a benefit with Gerard and his family."

Sherrice tensed. "It was for the hospital where Gerard's parents work. Gerard was the speaker. He's always doing something for the hospital. So did my parents when they were alive."

"Commendable work. You do know Desiree paid for that dress out of your father's money."

Sherrice shook her head. "She works. She pays for her own things."

"Sherrice, Sherrice, you're so naïve. She's here for the money, darling. The whole family's here for the money. Why do you think they didn't visit while your father was alive? Because he wouldn't have anything to do with them, sweetheart. Your mother mentioned that part of the family to me. She said your father didn't want you to associate with them."

"Daddy didn't know his father existed."

"Yes, he did. He knew the kind of people they were. The entire family has moved in."

"My grandmother moved back to D.C. And my grandfather is back in Macon. They don't live with us, but they visit a lot.

"Just you wait and see. Before you know it, they will move in. Your aunt will get rid of her lease on her apartment. They'll all be living off your father's money." She smoothed the confused girl's hair. "Honey, I'm sorry you have to go through this. But I think Gerard will eventually get custody of you. He loves you."

"He's away most of the time. Besides, he isn't a family member. Desiree loves us. You should see how upset she gets when anything happens. She thought Chris was hurt the other day and nearly fell apart."

"It's all an act. Don't you know that? Gerard will marry. And his wife will love you as if you were her own."

"He's dating Desiree."

"She's tricked him into thinking she's a good woman for him. I hope he doesn't marry her, because then she'll have all the money she needs. She won't need you any more, and you and your brothers will end up wards of the state. They'll separate you. Anything could happen to poor Chris and you'll never see him again."

Sherrice's eyes filled with tears. "That can't happen. What can I do? I don't know what to do."

"Things will turn out for the best. I just want you on guard. Don't believe that woman or her family. Jordan's father could have participated in his life, but he chose not to. He had another family. He didn't want Jordan. Poor thing, had to make his own way in life. And he did a spectacular job of it—for his wife and his children. I know you're proud of your daddy. Listen to me, Sherrice. I know these things."

Desiree put Christopher to bed and went downstairs.

Sherrice met her in the family room. "I want a Prada bag and shoes for a party I'm going to."

Those would cost several hundred dollars. Except for

the house expenses, Desiree was purchasing everything from the money the children received from Social Security. Besides, a child of fourteen didn't need to spend that kind of money on shoes and purses.

Desiree chose her words carefully. "Honey, you're only fourteen. They cost too much for someone your age. Besides, we don't have the money for that."

"Why not? My father was rich. He could afford to buy me nice things. What else do you have to spend it on?"

"We live on a budget," Desiree said, trying to hold on to her temper. "You're too young for a purse and bag that will cost eight hundred dollars minimum."

"What are you doing with our money, then? I bet you're stealing it. Or using it on yourself because you grew up poor. That's why your family comes here, isn't it, so you can live off my father's money? You're nothing but a thief."

"Have you lost your darn mind? Girl, if you ever speak to me that way again, you are going to be picking yourself off the floor." Desiree's anger became a scalding fury.

"I—"

"I don't need your daddy's money. I work for a living."

"So who paid for that lavender gown?"

"I did. Out of *my* money. Don't you ever come in my face asking me a dumb-assed question like that! Go to your room until you learn some manners."

"You can't—"

"Yes, I can. Go."

Desiree took several breaths to calm herself. "You know, Sherrice, having money doesn't give you permission to be disrespectful. No, I didn't grow up with these luxuries, but I wasn't poor either. My mother and father worked their butts off to make a decent living for us. But we had respect and manners, too.

"If my living in this house is a problem for you, I could sell it and save the money for you and your brothers when you're older, and we could live off what I make. As spoiled as you are, I don't think you'd like that. Don't force my hand, Sherrice. Don't mess up things for everyone because you're selfish. If you have a problem, then I'm here to listen and help you with it. But I'm not going to take any disrespect from you."

Sherrice glowered at Desiree and turned away. When she started upstairs Desiree stopped her.

"Better yet. Come into your father's office. You can go through the checkbook and receipts. I save most things in case I have to account for what I spend. Do you know anything about checkbooks?"

Sherrice shook her head.

Desiree sat with her and taught her. They went through everything before Desiree let her go.

Sherrice had finally made it to her room when Justin joined her. "What are you trying to do, Sherrice? Make Aunt Desiree leave? Why are you so mean? She's done nothing to you and you're a witch. We're going to lose our house! You know how it was at the other place. Chris is walking. He's getting his meals on time and Aunt Desiree loves us. She's good to him and us."

"She's doing it for the money."

"I don't believe you. You're just being mean the way you were to Mama before she died. You were always fighting with her. Why do you have to be that way?"

"I'm not mean. I'm telling you the truth. You don't know what you're talking about."

"You don't know anything. You better not do anything to make Aunt Desiree leave us." Justin slammed out of the room.

Sherrice fell on her bed and cried. She wasn't the enemy here. Couldn't they see the truth? If Aunt Desiree spent all their money, Sherrice and her brothers would be out in the cold. Even though everything looked okay with Aunt Desiree's books, Sherrice didn't understand it all.

She wanted her mama and daddy. None of this would have happened if they were alive. Life was so easy then. She didn't understand why she fought with her mama. She loved her with all her heart. It was just that she didn't understand her mama at times and Mama didn't understand her. But she loved her. *Mama, I didn't mean to be mean. I'm sorry. Please forgive me. Please, Mama. Why did you leave me? I need you.*

Desiree heard the brokenhearted sobs and went into the child's room. She was in tears herself. She gathered Sherrice in her arms and held her close until the tears subsided.

"Talk to me, Sherrice. I don't understand what's happening."

"It's nothing." Sherrice couldn't trust her. Emily said she didn't care about them. Emily knew things.

"I'm going to set you up for some counseling. I don't know any other way to deal with this."

"I don't need counseling. I'm not crazy."

"You don't have to be crazy to need help sorting things out. Honey, I don't know how to help you if you won't talk to me. You have to talk to someone. You can talk to your grandparents, or would you like to talk to Gerard? He'll come if you need him."

"No."

Desiree smoothed the hair back from the child's face, held her close, and kissed her cheek. "We'll get through this. We'll work it out together. We're family. I'll do anything for you, Sherrice. I'm here for you."

Sherrice merely stared into space.

Desiree knew she couldn't wait any longer. It was understandable that Sherrice was still grieving for her parents, and perhaps grief counseling would help. But she had no experience in that area. She didn't know whom to turn to. Gerard's parents would know.

Their home numbers weren't in the phone book, so Desiree called her assistant and asked her to get it from Scott.

Three minutes later, she called Desiree with the number. Desiree called the Kingsleys, but no one answered. She left a message on the answering machine.

A half hour later, Desiree was still debating what to do about Sherrice when Amanda Kingsley called.

"Amanda, thank you for returning my call. I don't think Sherrice is settling in well. I think she needs a good counselor to talk to and I'm new to this area. Could you please recommend a good child psychologist for me?"

"I'm so sorry to hear that. I know one of the best in the area. But she's at a convention. She's taking a couple days' vacation while she's away. I'll talk to her and see if she will set up an appointment immediately. At any rate, I'll call you the moment she returns."

"Thank you. I really appreciate this. Sherrice and I haven't been getting along for some time, but the stress only seems to be getting worse."

"This woman is very good with teens. It's such an awful time to lose a parent. They're changing by leaps and bounds. They know everything and actually know nothing. It's a trying age, especially for girls."

"Tell me about it."

"Good to see you at the benefit. So sorry for inviting Andrea. Hope you weren't uncomfortable, dear."

Amanda couldn't sound more insincere if she tried, but Desiree had more important concerns. "Think nothing of it," she said.

"I'll call you as soon as I contact her."

That evening Desiree tried to relax by watching some program on TV, but when she realized half the show was over and she didn't have a clue of what was going on, she turned it off and switched on music from a local station.

She was so worried about the kids. With no experience, she was flying blind. It wasn't as if she'd met Beverly or

Jordan and even knew how they would have raised their kids. Was she doing the right things?

When Gerard called Desiree at midnight, his voice was a soothing balm to her soul. She was so stressed over Sherrice that she had completely forgotten she'd lost her promotion at her job and found herself telling him about it.

"Stay here," he said.

"Here?"

"Don't you like counseling wild baseball and football players? We need you. You have carte blanche here. Why go back to New York? Everything you need is right here in Hotlanta."

"I don't know. With everything going on, I haven't given it much thought."

"Consider it, okay?"

Then she told him about Sherrice.

"I'll talk to her again as soon as I return. She's not usually like that. As a rule she's lively and outgoing. She certainly isn't rude. Don't give up on Sherrice. They need you. All the children."

"I'm not. I called your mother for the name of a good therapist. She's out of town but will call me next week. It's just, I don't understand Sherrice."

"I'll be home in a couple of days. I'll talk to her. Maybe she will explain herself to me. You know the way women butt heads during the teenage years."

"I guess you're right." Desiree had a headache. This stress was getting to her.

"So what are you wearing?" he asked, effectively changing the subject.

She was wearing his T-shirt with sweatpants, but she said, "I'm wearing a black night gown."

"You're only supposed to wear that stuff around me."

"I was thinking of you."

"How am I going to sleep thinking about you wearing that?"

"You're a trip, you know that? I'm sleeping in your shirt. The one you gave me with your number on it."

"Whew. You had me going there. I like the idea of you wearing something of mine."

His sexy voice was a silky rasp and it calmed her.

"How sexy can I get around four kids? On a serious note, have you heard anything about the flowers?"

"Just that they are ordered from different flower shops. They have a sketchy description of the woman."

"Monday is Memorial Day. I'm going to take the kids to the grave sites to place flowers. I'm concerned about how they will react, especially Sherrice. Mom and Dad are coming. I'm concerned about Dad, too."

"It's going to be okay, sweetheart. I'll be there. We'll handle it together."

"Thank you, Gerard, for everything. Your support means so much."

When he returned to town, Gerard had lunch with his father at a restaurant near the hospital.

"It's not the best, but it's healthy," his father said. "Your mama's always nagging at me about what I eat. How have you been, son?"

"Good, Dad."

"I don't see enough of you. How are Desiree and the children?"

"Adjusting."

"I'm sure it's not easy. I'm proud of you for pitching in the way you do. Are you going with us to Dad's grave site Monday?"

"Depends on what time. I told Grandma I'll go and deliver flowers, but Desiree is taking the children to Jordan and Beverly's graves and she's concerned about how they'll react."

"You have to help them." He closed his menu. "You know, Dad would have been proud of you. He loved baseball. He wanted to play, but wasn't able to. Times were different then. I'm glad you're happy with your career. You are happy, aren't you?"

Gerard smiled. "I'm very pleased."

"Because it's not as much what you do as how you do it. You're a good role model for children. You give of yourself unselfishly. Nobody could ask for more."

Gerard's throat clogged. He never expected to hear those words from his father. "Thanks, Dad. It means a lot to me, your saying that."

"How is that arm holding up?"

He flexed his fingers. "Doing well. I exercise it a lot."

"You take good care of it. At the first indication of pain, you get it dealt with. You've had a great career, but don't neglect you health for the game."

"I won't." Gerard had almost regretted the meal. He thought his father was going to bring his mother and envisioned constant complaints, nagging, and disapproval. Gerard relaxed and ordered his food. Suddenly, he was starving.

Memorial Day arrived much too soon. Desiree and the kids stopped by the florist for flowers. Gerard drove them to the cemetery. It was a peaceful and beautiful setting. Even though they were early, they weren't the first to arrive.

Her father was already there. "Nadine said she might come," he murmured. "Probably say a prayer or something."

Chad arrived just before Jacqueline appeared with Scott. For once Scott was without his BlackBerry or cell phone. And some of the firm's employees came as well. She'd mentioned she was taking the kids, but she didn't expect the show of support. Desiree felt warmed and thanked them for attending.

"Don't you all look nice? All dressed up," Jacqueline said, hugging the kids.

This was Desiree's first trip to the cemetery. Beverly and Jordan were buried side by side. Steven's parents were buried next to them. She was glad, because it made occasions such as this easier to manage. With the absence of family, Scott had made all the arrangements.

It was a solemn moment for Desiree. She urged the children forward to place the flowers. Her father had gathered a bunch of Aunt Nadine's roses and he placed them on the grave sites first.

The boys placed their flowers. Gerard held Christopher and watched them. Sherrice was hesitant. So Desiree put her arm around her and urged her forward.

The girl dropped the flowers and ran to a tree and cried.

Desiree followed her and gathered her into her arms. "It's okay to grieve, you know. One day you're going to be full of fond memories of your parents."

"Mama hates me. I know she does," Sherrice said in a broken voice.

"No, she doesn't. You're her daughter. She never hated you, honey."

She nodded. "I used to fight with her all the time."

"You need to talk to my mother. I used to fight with her all the time when I was a teenager. It's just a stage teenagers and mothers go through. You're no different."

"You don't think she hates me?"

"Of course she doesn't. Mothers are the grown-ups for a reason. They understand what's going on even when you don't. . . ."

A familiar voice started singing a spiritual. Suddenly Desiree heard a commotion and the singing stopped abruptly. She turned sharply.

"Oh my . . ." She could have fallen through the ground. Aunt Nadine was screaming and Levi had picked up a stick and was chasing Deacon Smithers. The man was sprinting toward the road and Levi was close on his heels swinging the stick.

"Wait till I catch you," he hollered.

Aunt Nadine was yelling, "Levi, he's a man of God! You stop that this minute. Come back here right now." She shook her finger as if Levi could see her. "You didn't let him pray. Y'all come back here!"

Everybody in the cemetery focused on them. Two gray-haired men sprinting down the lane of a quiet and peaceful resting place.

Aunt Nadine continued to dance in place, screeching for Levi to stop acting the fool.

Desiree's coworkers were stunned. The boys started laughing. Scott and Gerard were chuckling so hard they caught stitches in their sides. Jacqueline poked Scott, but his laughter didn't subside.

Deacon Smithers made it to his car and jumped inside, closing his jacket in the door. Before he could get the motor started, Levi caught up with him, yelling and whacking the stick against his roof, demanding he get out.

"I told you, don't you come near my family." He caught hold of the jacket as if pulling on it would pull Deacon Smithers through the tiny crack.

Finally the car started and the deacon pulled away from the curb, leaving burning rubber.

Levi yelled, "Don't you come back here, neither. I don't ever want to see your face again."

Desiree couldn't believe it. She was mortified and everybody was laughing, even Sherrice.

"Aunt Nadine, why did you bring the deacon? You know how much Daddy hates him. You knew how he was going to react."

"Somebody needs to pray over the graves. Deacon Smithers agreed to say a sweet prayer for the departed ones. Lord have mercy. I just knew Levi didn't take that pill this morning. He must have pretended." She glared at her brother, who lumbered back.

"Levi, I can't believe you'd do such a thing. How am I supposed to get back home? How can I hold my head up in church? You know he's going to tell everybody about

what you did. Can't even take you out in public without
you acting up."

"I told you don't bring that man round me. As soon as
a girl turns eighteen he chases her like a hound after a
rabbit. He's got kids spread over six counties. He's as old
as I am and I don't want him around my children. I'm not
going to have nobody like that praying over my son."

"Hush up. He's a deacon in the church, Levi. He
wouldn't do anything like that."

"You don't know anything."

Everybody was watching them.

"Let's go home," Desiree said. "We've made enough of
a spectacle of ourselves. You've taken a solemn occasion
and turned it into a travesty—as usual. I'm through with
the both of you."

Aunt Nadine straightened her church hat and the artificial fruit dangling on the brim, and clutched her black
purse close to her side. Tossing her chin in the air, she approached her brother. "You're just going to have to give
me a ride now that you ran mine away."

Desiree's dad looked sheepishly at her and nodded
toward his sister. "It's her fault."

Desiree pressed her lips together and marched ahead
of the pack. She heard footsteps behind her. She didn't
look to see who followed or didn't.

The people she worked with had all witnessed the embarrassing scene. Times like this were the very reason she
visited Macon infrequently. Always. Always Aunt Nadine
and Levi made fools of themselves.

And somebody was always laughing at them.

She'd had enough of *There goes your crazy folks again*
to last a lifetime.

She heard a chuckle behind her. Desiree turned and
glared at Gerard. "If I hear one more laugh out of you, I'm
going to . . ." Turning, she marched on ahead. When she
reached the car, she crossed her arms and waited for him

to open the door electronically; then she got in, slamming the door after her. She just wanted to have a good cry.

For the children, the ride from the graveyard was as cheerful as the ride to it had been somber. The boys talked animatedly in the backseat. Sherrice was laughing as she played with Christopher.

Gerard kept watching Desiree. He reached over and gathered her tense hand in his, stroking it gently. "Relax, honey. It's okay."

"Easy for you to say. The people you work with didn't witness your aunt and father acting . . ." Desiree closed her mouth.

"Come on. Don't take it so seriously. Nobody else does."

Desiree glared out the side window.

"Look at the kids," he murmured, squeezing her hand.

She did. They were relaxed and cheerful. Desiree sighed, and the knot in her chest eased a little.

Maybe it was true, she thought. With every rain cloud there was a rainbow.

Everyone convened at her house, even her coworkers and their children. Mrs. Gaines had prepared a feast—ham, potato salad, chicken, greens, ambrosia, macaroni and cheese, zucchini bread, lemon pepper chicken wings—and that was just the beginning. She'd set the food and china on the buffet in the dining room, and put snacks in the family room.

After changing clothes, the boys went outside to play with their friends. One of Sherrice's friends was visiting her, and they were on the computer in the family room.

Jacqueline had stripped down to barely anything. What was up with her? She wore shorts and a skimpy tank top. She'd taken a card and was fanning herself. It wasn't that hot. Leaning back with his hands behind his head, Scott was ogling Jacqueline's legs and breasts.

Gerard pulled off his suit jacket and rolled up his shirt-sleeves. He watched Christopher and talked with Scott. Desiree kept a close eye on them to make sure Gerard wasn't teaching the child any more dangerous tricks. Those stairs still gave her nightmares.

Aunt Nadine and Levi had come into the house arguing. They finally calmed down enough for him to give her a tour.

"Desiree, this is some place here. Takes a heap of work to keep it clean, I bet. You must work from sunup to sundown. Not a speck of dust on the furniture. I checked. I don't like a nasty house."

"The cleaning crew comes every week, Aunt Nadine. Can I fix you a plate?"

"Let me catch my breath first. But I will take something to drink." She peered over her glasses at Jacqueline. "What's the matter with you? Going through the change?"

"Thank you, Nadine, for telling the world."

"Doesn't bother me a bit, sweetheart," Scott said. "As a matter of fact, I like it."

Jacqueline rolled her eyes at the both of them and poured two glasses of cold punch, handing one to Desiree to give to Aunt Nadine.

"Thank you, darling." Aunt Nadine took a sip and frowned. "A bit sweet, don't you think?"

"Would you prefer water?" Desiree asked.

"No. No. I'll make do with this."

There was never a situation Aunt Nadine didn't find something to complain about. Desiree was stressed with the lot of them. She needed to clear her head and glanced out the window. The boys were zipping up and down the street on their skateboards, and Desiree longed to join them.

In two minutes, Levi and Nadine were arguing again. She'd had it. Desiree changed her clothes and found her skateboard.

When she passed by the family room, Aunt Nadine

said, "Where you going dressed up like that? And with that helmet on your head?"

"Just going to check on the kids," she said. Her mother and Scott could entertain the crowd for a little while. They could do without her for a few minutes.

Desiree joined the boys. And for thirty minutes she enjoyed the blessed freedom, zipping up and down the street with the children until her headache disappeared and her spirits lifted.

When she picked up her skateboard and started to the house, she saw Gerard's grandmother and Chad watching her. Chad had a huge grin on his face.

"Didn't know you had it in you."

"And that was just the beginning. I'm so pleased you joined us, Mrs. Kingsley. How is your cousin?" Mrs. Kingsley had left immediately after Desiree arrived to take care of her cousin who'd had a knee replacement.

"Doing better than expected. The kids look so much better, Desiree."

"You all come in and have dinner."

Chad held the door for them. As soon as Desiree entered the house, Aunt Nadine had plenty to say about her adventure, but Desiree only smiled and nodded. She felt on top of the world.

"Girl, you out there acting like a kid instead of a grown woman. You got four children to take care of and acting worse than they are."

"Aunt Nadine, I know how to take care of the children. They aren't lacking in anything. Are you ready for your plate?"

"I guess so. That ham looks good, but I'm not supposed to eat too much on account of my pressure. Give me a little piece, anyway."

No wonder the woman drove Levi crazy, especially if he had to listen to her complaining every day. Desiree piled food on a plate for Aunt Nadine and handed it to her.

She spent the rest of the time talking with each of her guests, making sure they all had plenty to eat and drink and were entertained.

Later, when Desiree was stacking dishes in the dishwasher, Scott came in with a pile of plates. He rolled up his sleeves and rinsed while she stacked.

"I heard you aren't getting the raise you'd hoped for in New York."

"The promotion fell through."

"Why go back there? You can continue to work with me. And if you want you can work full-time. It's up to you."

"I thought you only wanted someone temporarily."

"What you're doing is really useful for the players. I've gotten many positive responses from wives, and parents. Some players even admitted they need your skills. So let me know. If you want to keep the job, it's yours."

14

Gerard spent half an hour talking to Levi. He mentioned the land Nadine wanted to have stripped of trees. That Desiree promised to buy it from her. Gerard's mind went off into another tangent while Levi continued to talk. Desiree didn't want him buying diamonds, but perhaps she'd accept the gift of the land. He'd call his lawyer and have him check into it.

Gerard had a game that evening. He took flowers to his grandfather's grave before he went to the stadium.

After the game, he stopped by Desiree's house. With his arm around her waist, they walked to the family room.

"You want to tell me why you were so upset today?" he asked, easing down on the couch beside her.

"You have no idea how it was growing up with those two. My home was in D.C., but I spent summers with Aunt Nadine and Daddy. This is just one of a million episodes. And Daddy was on his medication. Can you imagine what it was like when he was off it?"

Gerard put his arm around her shoulder and snuggled her close.

"Somebody was always pointing and laughing at us. We can't have a normal family gathering."

"Children get embarrassed so easily."

"I felt so guilty, too. Daddy loves me. He's doing the

best he can. He's a great father, really, he is. What more can I ask for?"

"You know, people can be mean sometimes. But underneath, it's the family support that really counts. As eccentric as they were, they were here. They supported you."

"They always have."

"In the long run, that's what counts. Not the laughs. Sometimes laughter covers enormous heartbreaks. Just think about it. Sherrice was falling apart. The boys' hearts were crushed, yet everyone left the graveyard feeling good instead of gloomy. They spent time respecting the departed. Yet they left feeling the love of family members gathered around them. Can you ask for a better Memorial Day? Especially for the children?"

Desiree touched his cheek. "How do you always put things in perspective? You should have been a counselor. You're a natural with people."

"Think so?" He pressed a kiss to her forehead. "Where's your mom?" he asked.

"Out with Scott. Besides, she's sleeping in the cottage. Did she tell you she's retired? She's looking for a place to buy. She's moving here to be near the kids."

"Does that mean you're staying?"

She glanced at him, wanting to shake that pleased expression off his face. But she said, "Yes. It doesn't make sense to uproot the children."

"I bet Scott's as pleased as I am with that news. Otherwise, we'd both have a lot of traveling in our futures."

"I guess. It's unusual seeing my mom dating. Seeing her kissing a man who isn't my father. But she's happy. I'm so happy for her."

"Speaking of kissing . . ." His lips grazed her earlobe. "Feels like forever since I've had you in my arms," he whispered and tugged her close to his heart until his heartbeat felt like her own. He tilted her chin and pressed his lips to hers. His lips were warm and sweet. Her senses jolted to life and desire spiraled to every nerve in her body.

She snaked her hands beneath his shirt to feel the texture

of his chest. Crisp hair, rippling muscles, and hot skin met her seeking fingers, and the deep rumble of his moan caused her flesh to tingle.

With his body, he pushed her back until she was flat on the couch, and the pleasant weight of him pressed her into the cushions. He slid down her, brushed her shirt up to bare her upper body. Desiree caressed his shoulders, his back, anything she could reach.

Using his tongue and lips he made her body sing with desire. He tugged on one brown nipple with his lips until Desiree's body was screaming with pleasure.

"Aunt Desiree?" A small voice barely penetrated her sexual haze.

Gerard shot up as if a lightning bolt had struck him, pulling Desiree with him.

Disoriented, Desiree quickly righted her clothes, ran a hand across her face and hair.

"Yes?" came her weak response.

"I don't feel good."

Desiree found Steven at the foot of the stairs rubbing his tummy.

"Think you ate a little too many sweets, buddy?" Gerard asked. Desiree didn't realize he'd come up behind her.

"I don't know."

Desiree laid the back of her hand against Steven's head. He wasn't hot to the touch. If he had a temp, it was very low-grade. "Go lie down, honey. I'll bring something up."

As he trooped up the steps, Gerard pulled Desiree into his embrace for one last quick kiss. "I've got to get you away. I need you. You need help with him?"

She shook her head. "I'll give him some medicine. He should be okay."

Desiree watched him stride out and turned to see about Steven. Her nerve endings were still humming with unfulfilled desire.

* * *

"Desiree?" Aunt Nadine called before she could get Christopher out of the crib the next morning. She and Levi had left late the afternoon before. She'd sent heaping plates of food home with them.

"You never got back to me about the land."

"I'll buy it from you. I'll speak to my lawyer this week about drawing up the paperwork. And then I'll come out there. It shouldn't take long."

"Well, all right. I wasn't trying to rush you."

"I know. Is Dad taking his meds?"

"I guess. He hasn't acted the fool lately. Of course the word has spread all over town about what he did."

"I truly doubt the town is that interested. Besides, both of you had a hand in it."

"Hmmph. I've dedicated my life to that man. And he doesn't appreciate it. Not one bit."

"Of course he does."

As much as Aunt Nadine complained, for the first time Desiree realized her aunt needed her dad as much as he needed her. She and her husband didn't have children, so instead of clucking over grandkids, there was Levi. She needed someone to complain about, someone to make her feel useful. They propped each other up.

Desiree shook her head. They were both crazy. Her father could use Vietnam as the cause, but what was Aunt Nadine's excuse?

After Desiree dropped the kids off at school, she called her father's lawyer in Macon to get the paperwork moving on the property. Sherrice went to school and Desiree went into the office, but she didn't feel comfortable and couldn't concentrate on work. Sherrice weighed heavily on her mind.

"You look like Beverly and Jordan just before they died," her assistant said. "I am so sorry. I didn't mean to—"

"What do you mean?" Desiree asked.

"It's just that Beverly was upset about something—

really upset. I think she was on the verge of leaving Jordan. And he was upset, too. He was getting these flowers and Beverly was angry that he was having an affair with some woman. He swore there wasn't anyone else, and quite frankly, I don't believe there was. I mean, some of the guys who work here have women on the side, and you know it. Most of us work a lot of overtime. It's not your nine-to-five routine. It's impossible for the word not to get around. Never Jordan. Besides, he was really in love with Beverly."

Which was exactly what Gerard had said about his flowers. It wasn't that Desiree was insecure. She was uncomfortable with having a beautiful arrangement of flowers from a woman thrown constantly in her face.

On some level she knew Gerard very well. She knew how he handled the children, which showed a great sense of responsibility and loyalty. And he was always there for her.

The woman who sent flowers to Gerard wasn't necessarily the same woman who sent them to Jordan. On the other hand she *could* be. It was a situation that warranted investigating.

"I wonder if he saved any of the notes she sent."

"Most of his stuff is still in the desk. Scott wasn't in a hurry to clean his office out."

Scott was out of the office that morning. She knew he was speaking with the police about Gerard's problem. She sent him an e-mail, then started searching through Jordan's desk.

"Aunt Desiree?"

"Yes?"

"Are you going to leave us? And Grandpa and Grandma. Are they going to leave us, too?"

Steven was twisting his hands nervously.

Desiree was searching through Jordan's home office desk. She closed the drawer. "No, honey. Why do you ask?"

He shrugged. "Don't know. It's not for me. Justin's worried. 'Cause Sherrice is acting up."

"Honey, I'll deal with Sherrice. I'm not going anywhere."

"I know how much you want to get back to New York. We'll go with you, although we like it here better. We'll get used to a new place. Are the kids there into computer games?"

"Just as much as you are. I'm not going back to New York, except to clean out my apartment. I've already given my notice. I'm hoping all of us can take a family trip to New York before my lease is up. Have you been there?"

"Yeah, but I was too young to remember much."

"Now you're old enough to remember."

"Will we get to skate at Rockefeller Plaza?"

"They have a restaurant there in the summer. We'd have to take a winter trip to skate." She rubbed his head. "Want to help me set the table?"

"Sure."

"Go wash up. I have a phone call to make first." Desiree called her supervisor in New York and explained that she wasn't returning to her job. She told him she would put a formal resignation letter in the mail the next day. And she thanked him for holding her slot while she was away.

"We were counting on you to help with this big project."

"I know. But I have to do what's best for the children. Their home is here."

Desiree felt relieved once she'd made her decision. She'd have to volunteer with the PTA next year, and maybe get more involved with the teams the boys played on and the dance school.

Not to mention Christopher. He was getting bigger by the day. Before she knew it, he'd be playing T-ball.

Gerard called that night after the house fell quiet.

"I gave up the lease on my apartment," she told him. "As soon as the kids get out of school, I'm taking them to New York to pack up my things. I don't have that much. I can drive a U-Haul back."

"When will that be?"

"In June, right after school's out."

"Check my schedule and see if I have a day off. If so, I'll join you and help you."

"Oh no. I won't be responsible for damaging that multimillion-dollar arm."

"I'm always cautious."

"About everything?"

"I thought we were talking about my arm. Is Sherrice asleep?"

"Probably not."

"Let me speak to her. Then you get back on the phone so you can calm me down and I can get some sleep tonight."

Desiree pressed the intercom button for Sherrice's room. "Phone, Sherrice."

When she picked up, Desiree hung the phone up.

"How's my favorite girl?" Gerard asked.

"Okay."

Gerard sensed immediately she wasn't going to be forthcoming.

"How are you, really?"

"Okay."

"Desiree is concerned about you."

"No, she's not."

"Of course she is," Gerard said. "She loves you."

"Why can't we live with you?"

"Honey, I'm on the road practically nine months out of the year. You need someone who can be with you all the time."

"You could get married."

"You're ready for me to march down the aisle, ha." Gerard chuckled. "Desiree loves you, honey. You can't buy that."

"She just wants our money."

"Desiree works. She doesn't spend any of your money on herself."

"That's what she said, but I don't believe her."

"Will you believe me?"

"You're gone all the time. You wouldn't know."

"I'll take you to visit your father's accountant. He'll show you that she isn't using your money on herself."

"Okay."

"Honey, I don't understand why you feel this way. As far as I can see she isn't spending extravagantly on anything."

"How come Daddy never let them around us?"

"He didn't know about his relatives. His mother told him nothing. And they didn't know about him."

"That's what they said, but I don't trust them."

"Why? Have they done anything to make you distrust them?"

"I don't know." Sherrice fell silent.

"What have they done?"

"Not anything, exactly."

"So where is your distrust coming from?"

"I don't know."

"Has someone been talking to you?" Gerard asked.

"Why do you ask that?"

"Because you're evasive. Honey, you loved your parents. And I know your mother and father would be happy that you still have a family, especially an aunt who loves you with all her heart. Desiree didn't have to leave her job and come to you the moment she heard about you, but she did. And she took you in, even in the face of destroying her own career. She made a choice between her career and you. She wouldn't do that if she didn't love you."

Sherrice was quiet.

"We're going to visit your father's accountant when I get home. And I'll take you to dinner and discuss whatever is bothering you, okay?"

"Hurry back, Gerard."

"I'll be there in three days, honey. Just three days."

* * *

Gerard had pitched that day, so he wouldn't pitch for another few days. He made reservations for a flight out late that night. In the morning when Desiree came downstairs he was at the door.

She flew into his arms. "I can't believe you're here."

At that moment Gerard couldn't tell if he was in Atlanta because Sherrice needed him or because he needed to feel Desiree's warm body pressed against his. In all his years as a professional ballplayer, he'd never left a game, even when he wasn't pitching. But the feel of Desiree's warmth around him felt so reassuring, he wanted to turn to her. But he couldn't.

He didn't want to need her. He was accustomed to standing alone. He gently pulled away from her, kissing her on the lips again, for good measure.

"What are you doing here?" Desiree asked.

The moment his thoughts turned, Desiree sensed the difference, although he tried to make light of it. One moment he wanted her, needed her, the next she was just another woman in the sea of women who'd passed through his life. Only he couldn't isolate her in his mind.

"To see my ladies," he said. "You were really stressed out. Would you mind if I spent a little time with Sherrice this morning? She'll only be a couple of hours late for school."

"You think it would help?"

"We'll see."

"She'll be pleased to see you. More than anything we need whatever problem she's going through to be resolved. If you can get her to talk, I'll be forever grateful."

"Let me help with breakfast."

The kids were thrilled to see him, and when he told Sherrice they were eating breakfast together at her favorite place, the boys begged to have breakfast with him, too.

"You have tests," Desiree murmured.

"You can call in sick and the teacher will let us make it up," Steven offered.

"No way. You're not sick."

"Neither is Sherrice."

"Sherrice doesn't have tests," Desiree said.

"I don't know why she gets to have breakfast with Gerard, as bad as she's been," Justin said.

"That's enough. Eat your breakfast. You're going to school and that's my final word."

Justin pushed his bowl back. "I don't want oatmeal."

"Eat it anyway. You asked for it," Desiree said. "You'll get some time with Gerard later, okay?" Her mind was only half on the boys' complaints. She prayed that Gerard would be able to break through Sherrice's icy shield.

Marriage, Gerard thought. The expected chill didn't race through his body. Was Sherrice worried that if anything happened to Desiree, she and the boys would be on their own again? But marriage was drastic. He hadn't let the thought seriously enter his mind—not this early in the game.

He readily admitted there would be plusses. He'd get to sleep with Desiree. No sneaking around to make love. But waking up with the same person for the rest of his life? Was he ready for that?

Desiree was watching the puzzled expression on his face. He smiled and hoped it appeared real.

Gerard and Sherrice ate a hearty breakfast at IHOP, but she wouldn't open up more than she had the night before.

"I set up an appointment with your father's accountant. He'll be waiting at his office. He's going over Desiree's expenses with you."

Sherrice nodded.

"I'm still confused about why that became an issue. Desiree is generous to a fault."

"Some of my friends told me about guardians who spent their inheritances on themselves instead of on the children."

"You don't have that to worry about with Desiree."

He drove to the accountant's office. They were there for more than an hour. The man went over in detail all the expenses from her parents' accounts. Except to make some suggestions on investments, and good ones at that, Desiree hadn't touched any of the money. Just as she'd said, she took care of the children's expenses off their Social Security checks and managed to save a portion of that. Only the household expenses the accounting firm paid for came from her parents' estate.

There was a tiny park across the street. After the meeting Gerard steered Sherrice there.

"Now, are you satisfied?"

Sherrice nodded.

"So you won't be giving your aunt a hard time, Sherrice?"

She shook her head. She bit her bottom lip. "Do you love her, Gerard?"

"She's special."

"I mean love her. You're dating."

"That's true."

"Do you think she loves you?"

Gerard inhaled a long breath. He wanted to be honest with her, because he wanted honesty from her. "I don't know, Sherrice. We never talk about love. It's too early yet."

"What is love anyway?"

"Good question. I guess it's not something that can be explained. You either feel it or you don't."

"Are you having sex with Desiree?"

"Now you're dipping in my business."

"You dipped into mine."

"That's grown folks stuff. You've got no business thinking about sex."

"Oh, please. I know all about sex."

"You just make sure you stay away from it until you're forty."

"Ha!"

"Seriously, don't be giving away your jewels to these knuckleheads. You're too young. And these knuckleheads will fill your head full of love poems just to get to you and then they're on their way, leaving behind babies and God knows what else. Don't let them take advantage of you."

She ducked her head. "I'm not a baby. I'm not doing that. Besides, I don't want to talk about that with you."

"Girl, you're going to have me jacking up some fool."

She blushed and giggled.

"You sure you don't have a few things to get off your chest? I'm a great listener."

"I'm okay."

He tilted her chin until she looked directly into his eyes. "I worry about you, you know?"

"Why?"

"Because I care. You still have my cell phone number?"

"Yeah."

"A lot of people love you, Sherrice. Your brothers, grandparents, especially your aunt. And you have relatives who're dying to meet you this summer. Your granddad told me all about them."

"Grandpa said they'll come to the farm this summer and we'll spend time out on the river and the lake with them."

"Be like summer camp."

"I guess."

Gerard checked his watch. "Time to go."

Gerard dropped Sherrice off at school. By the time he made it back to Desiree's, she'd gone to work.

He'd had the jewelry wrapped and asked Mrs. Gaines if she'd give it to Desiree. Desiree might be prickly, but a man should be able to give his woman a gift if he wanted to. It was traditional for men to give gifts, regardless of their economic conditions. He was sure she didn't turn Paul's gifts away.

He made it to the airport and caught a flight that allowed him to make it to the stadium before the game began.

When Desiree arrived home, a smiling Mrs. Gaines handed her a package. "Gerard was disappointed he missed you."

"I didn't know he was stopping by."

"He must have picked out something special," she said, nodding to the package. "Even the bows and wrappings are pretty."

"I'm sure he did." Desiree went to her room. Did that man listen to anything she said? She'd specifically told him she didn't want him buying her gifts.

Chad usually slept between his parents' house and Gerard's. When Gerard was in town he stayed with his parents to give Gerard and Desiree privacy.

"Chad, will you set the table, please?" his mother asked. "Your father should be home in a few minutes and we can all have dinner together." Amanda wore an apron over the dress she had worn to her office that day. She didn't take the time to even change clothes before she began her second job of the day, preparing dinner. As whipped as he felt, Chad would have picked up something from the cafeteria.

By the time he got the plates on the table and his mother set out platters of food, his father arrived. His mom must have this down to a science.

His father said a prayer and they dug in with gusto.

"Didn't you have Memorial Day off, Chad?" his mother asked.

He glanced at her. "Yes."

"Why didn't you go to the graveyard with us?"

"I joined Gerard and the kids. They went to the kids' parents' grave sites. You should have come to the house after going to Grandpa's grave. I took Grandma to Desiree's. There were lots of people there."

"We weren't exactly invited," his father said.

"I don't think she invited anyone. People just started showing up. And they were welcomed. She had lots of food. I should have brought some home."

His mother shook her head. "Desiree is having quite a time of it with those children. Well, I don't know what to say for your brother. I'm sure he's helping his neighbors as best he can what little time he's in town. I still don't understand why he broke up with Andrea. He's determined to ruin his life."

"He never loved her," Chad informed her. "Not the way he loves Desiree."

"Love Desiree?" his mother queried. "They aren't even dating."

Chad chuckled. "Sure they are. He brought her to the benefit."

"Oh, that. He doesn't date every woman he brings to formal occasions. You know he doesn't go to those functions alone."

"Trust me, they're dating, Mom."

"In that case," Nolan said, "we should either invite them to dinner or take them out. We can even have them over when Gerard's out of town. We certainly want to make Desiree and the children feel welcome."

"I guess he'll never go back to college now," Amanda said, shaking her head.

"Why are you always harping on that?" Chad asked. "He's made a good life for himself. I'm proud of my brother. I can save lives, but I can't influence the number of people Gerard can and does."

"You should be proud of him," Nolan said. "I'm proud of him as well as you. You never hear negative things about him in the media."

"And that's saying a lot," Chad muttered.

"I think Gerard feels isolated from us," his dad continued, wiping his mouth on the napkin. "We have to show him that we love him and accept him for the man he is."

Amanda's fork clattered on the plate. "What are you trying to do, build a shrine for him? He's an intelligent young man. He could have done so much more," she stated adamantly.

"Mom, what more can he do? You want to raise money for your charities, who do you call on? He makes millions. More money in one year than I'll make in a lifetime. He gives generously. And he isn't hurting anyone. He's a good man. He's pulling away from us and I don't like that. He's my brother. I can see how hard it hits him when you're always gloating over me and you never, ever praise him even though he's done so much more."

Amanda sighed. "A mother has the right to expect great things from her children. She is expected to steer them in the proper direction."

"But children grow up to be men and women and they should have the right to choose. He could have done so much worse. He shouldn't feel that you don't accept him. He's got enough pressure on him on the mound. Having to always put up a front with the media and fans. He shouldn't have to do that with his family."

Amanda sighed tiredly. "Am I really that bad?"

"Yes," Nolan said, gazing tenderly down the table at her. "Why don't you invite him to lunch and not complain once? Why don't you tell him how proud you are of him? Deep down you have to be."

"I didn't realize I was such a terrible mother."

"This isn't about you, Amanda. It's about our son."

15

Desiree was digging through Jordan's things again. His office was neat but he saved literally everything, either in his bedroom or in his office. A neat pack rat. She'd searched for days, found all kinds of secrets, but not one note from a flower delivery.

"Aunt Desiree, if I don't go to practice, I'm going to lose my place in the recital," Sherrice said. "We're supposed to be at practice every session."

"We'll see."

"But the recital! There's no getting through to you." Sherrice threw up her hands and ran upstairs.

Desiree was considering that perhaps she should let the girl return to practice. It might be the only thing holding Sherrice together. She couldn't see the therapist yet. She might need the healing effect of an activity she loved.

Desiree just didn't know what to do. What would Jordan or Beverly do? God, she just didn't have all the answers. How did parents cope?

Desiree pulled out another drawer. She sifted through mints, paper clips, staples, tapes, odds and ends . . . and then she saw a small card. She lifted it out and opened the small envelope. It read *You've betrayed me.*

Well, the message certainly wasn't the same. But nevertheless it was worth checking out.

Desiree went into the kitchen and put the card in her purse. She'd give it to Scott later at work.

While she was at the office, Sherrice's dance teacher called, asking if Sherrice was well. Desiree assured her she was fine, that Sherrice would return the next day.

Desiree hoped she was making the correct decision. Sherrice certainly wasn't getting any better by staying at home.

The next day after the first practice session, Emily pulled Sherrice aside and crossed her arms. Her voice was so cold it frightened Sherrice.

"So tell me, why did you miss practice? And while you're at it, tell me why I shouldn't take you out of the recital when it's only two weeks away. You know the rules. You're expected to attend every practice. It's essential. You've let the class down."

"I wanted to come, but Aunt Desiree was giving me a hard time."

"Why?"

Sherrice shrugged.

"Well?"

"The things you said about Aunt Desiree aren't true. I talked to Gerard."

"And what did you tell him?"

"Just that I thought she was using our money on herself. He took me to my parents' accountant. He said Aunt Desiree hadn't used any of the money."

"You silly girl. Do you really think she's going to show her hand immediately? Don't you think she's planned this through? She planned your parents' murders, Sherrice. I tried to protect you, but you're impossible."

Tears fell down Sherrice's cheeks. "You don't know

what you're talking about. They were killed in an accident. They weren't murdered."

"The brakes were cut. Of course they were murdered. There was too much damage to the car for the authorities to get a definitive answer."

Sherrice covered her mouth to hold back a scream. She looked at Emily in horror.

"As they maneuvered up the steep hills and curves, the brake fluid slowly leaked out of their car until the brakes gave out completely, and . . . well, you know the rest. That evil woman left you and your brothers without parents."

"That can't be true! How could you know? I don't believe you."

"I didn't want to tell you this. I wanted to spare you the gory details. But I can't have you trusting that woman. She's a great actress. You and your brothers aren't safe around her."

Tears were streaming down Sherrice's face. "It can't be true. She can't have killed my parents."

"It's true. I'm only telling you this so you can protect your brothers. They are depending on you."

"They're all angry with me for causing Aunt Desiree so much trouble. I think they hate me."

"Come here," Emily said more calmly and wrapped her arms around Sherrice's shaking shoulders. "They don't know, honey. She's cunning. What do you expect? You're the smart one, Sherrice. You're the knowledgeable one. It's up to you to look out for your brothers."

Emily handed Sherrice a tissue and wrapped her arms around her again. "Come on. Let the dance take you away from your worries. There's nothing you can do about it. Gerard will fix everything. Trust him."

On the way home, Sherrice barely said a word to Desiree. She sulked on the way from school, too. What was wrong with the girl now?

Desiree had let her take the dance class. Had even talked to the teacher, who said Sherrice had caught up quickly with the rest of the class, but had asked that Sherrice not take any more days off.

Desiree shook her head. She didn't know what was going through that child's head. *Please just hold on until the therapist returns,* she thought. Desiree felt so helpless and ineffective.

"Everyone else has had supper," she told Sherrice when they returned home. "Yours is on the stove. I'll warm it up for you."

"Don't bother. I'm not hungry."

"I'll leave a plate out for you then," Desiree said. "You can eat later."

Sherrice merely ran up to her room and shut her door.

What was it now? Desiree wondered. Sherrice usually exploded when she talked to her, so she was going to give her a few minutes to calm down first. Then maybe they could talk quietly. Thank God, Gerard was due back tonight. Sherrice was closer to him. Desiree hated to depend on him so much, but she had no choice.

Desiree started to follow Sherrice up the stairs. She couldn't let this continue. The phone rang, stopping her progress.

"Amanda Kingsley here. Nolan and I would like to invite you and your family to dinner Saturday afternoon. We'll make it a cookout. Chad has promised to join us."

"Thank you, Amanda. We'd love to come. What can I bring?"

"Just yourselves. I have everything planned. The invitation is open to your parents if they are here. We're looking forward to seeing you, dear."

Well, that was strange, Desiree thought, hanging up the phone. She and Gerard had dated for a while and Amanda never acknowledged her.

"Aunt Desiree?" Steven called out.

"Yes?"

"Can you take Chris so I can finish my homework? I have a test tomorrow."

"Of course. Do you need help studying?"

"I'm okay." Desiree ran upstairs to get her baby. Jacqueline had told her Scott was coming by later, after he talked with some players who were in town.

Gerard was almost home when his cell phone rang. Desiree, he thought with a smile as he answered it.

"Gerard?" It was Sherrice, not Desiree. The child's voice was choked.

Sherrice's tearful voice scared the living daylights out of him.

Calmly he spoke to her. "It's me, honey. What's up?"

She cried as if her heart was broken, and it was a sound a man never wanted to hear. Gerard's heart pounded with fear.

"Talk to me, honey. Are you hurt? What is it?"

His only response was heartbroken crying, which tore Gerard's insides.

"I'll help you, Sherrice. Just tell me what happened. Are you hurt? Is anyone else hurt? I'm close by. I'll be right there."

"She killed my parents," she finally said. "She killed them! I can't take it anymore."

"Hold on, baby. Who killed them?"

"Aunt Desiree."

"That's impossible." Her out-of-left-field accusation couldn't have come out of the blue. Was that what she'd been holding against Desiree all this time? That she believed she'd killed her mom and dad? "Why do you think that?"

"Somebody told me."

"Who?"

"I can't tell you."

"Honey, listen to me. Somebody has been trying to

cause trouble between you and Desiree. They've been telling you things that aren't true." Deep-abiding anger bubbled up in Gerard. All this time, somebody had been torturing that poor child.

"She said it's true, though."

"Who said?"

Silence. Sniffles.

"Talk to me, honey. You can trust me. I'm here for you."

"My dance teacher. Emily. She said Aunt Desiree killed them because she wants Daddy's money. Daddy knew about her but didn't want us to have any contact with her." She burst into tears again.

Gerard had to wait before he could talk to her.

"Listen to me. Your daddy and I were good friends. He talked to me before he died. He didn't know his father was alive, much less that he had a sister. Just before he left that weekend, he asked his lawyer to hire a private investigator to search for his family. He wanted to know if he had any relatives on his father's side of the family. He thought there might be distant cousins. The investigator hadn't even begun the search by the time your parents died. Desiree didn't know your father, and he didn't know her. So that much is definitely untrue."

Sniffle, sniffle, then, "Are you sure?"

"Of course I am. Honey, Desiree has no idea what has been going on. She's worried sick about you. We have to tell her."

"But—"

"Trust me, okay? She hasn't killed anyone. Your teacher is telling you lies. The woman is crazy to do something like that. I'm pulling up in your yard. Desiree and I are going to meet in your room, okay sweetie?"

"'Kay." Her voice was teary, but at least she seemed calmer, Gerard thought as he hung up and called the cottage for Jacqueline. Thankfully, she answered immediately.

"This is Gerard. Can you come to the house right now?

Desiree and I have a problem. I need you to look after the kids."

He hung up, bounded out of the car, and sprinted to the door.

He used the key he'd never returned.

"Desiree!" he called out.

She came around the corner with the washcloth in one hand and Chris in the other. "Thank God you're here. I was just going upstairs to talk to Sherrice. She was in a bad mood when I picked her up from dance. I just don't know what's going on," she said.

"I'm here." Jacqueline was frowning when she came through the kitchen. "Here. I'll take Chris."

Gerard proceeded to tell them what Sherrice had revealed. They were livid.

"We're going to that school right now." She marched to her brother's office and uncovered the number, then called the studio's owner, telling her that she'd be there within a half hour.

"Let's talk to Sherrice first," Gerard said.

She was a mother on the warpath when she pounded up the stairs to Sherrice's room. The poor child was blowing her nose and looking at them with a frightened expression.

When Desiree saw the sad, frightened child, she tried to bring her anger under control to deal with Sherrice. That woman's manipulation had put Sherrice through hell.

Sherrice was a teenager who'd recently lost the most important people in her world. Desiree was virtually a stranger to her. She'd known Emily longer.

Desiree approached Sherrice and put her arms around her frail shoulders. She'd lost weight, she thought. And no wonder. Her life had been a living nightmare. Desiree sat beside her and took her hand in hers.

"How long has she been doing this to you?"

"For weeks."

"I need you to tell us what this woman has been saying to you."

Sherrice glanced at Gerard before she focused on Desiree. "She said that you wanted us for Daddy's money and that you didn't love us. She said you cut the brake line to the car so they'd . . ." She started crying again. ". . . so they'd pitch off the side of the mountain."

Desiree closed her eyes to stifle the rage so she could deal with Sherrice.

"Honey, I didn't know your father existed until the night before I met you. I received the call at midnight, and I took the next flight out. Your father's lawyer met me at the airport and drove me here."

"That's what Gerard said."

"I don't know why that woman is saying those awful things, but they're untrue. I don't need your father's money. I've worked hard for everything I have. As a matter of fact, I've lost a promotion because I came here. But that isn't important. You and your brothers are what's important to me. We're a family. I'm upset and I'm hurt that you felt you couldn't talk to me."

"I . . . I was scared. I didn't know what to do. I'm sorry." She pitched into tears again.

Desiree hugged her, patted her back. "I know, honey, I know. In the future, please come to me."

"Everybody hates me."

"Nobody hates you, honey. I love you. We'll work through this together. Never think that I hate you, because I don't. I will always love you, Sherrice. Always. Even when you go to college, when you get married, when you have your own children. I'll always love you."

"Justin hates me. He's mad at me because of all the trouble I gave you."

"He doesn't understand what you've been through," Gerard said. "He still loves you, even if he doesn't understand. Brothers and sisters don't stop loving each other because of a misunderstanding."

"We're going to the dance studio to talk to the manager. She needs to know. Emily could be doing this to other students. Mama is here. And she'll be here until we return."

She nodded.

Desiree hugged her again, and the three of them walked downstairs. When they reached the car, Gerard gathered her into his arms.

"Calm down, honey. We know what we're working with now. Now we can fix it."

"What can be wrong with that woman that she'd tell an impressionable child some wild story like that?"

"She's got to be unhinged. A normal person wouldn't do that."

"But why? What was her purpose? It doesn't make sense."

"Who knows?" He opened the door and handed Desiree into the seat.

"When I think about the hell she's put our family through I want to knock her out."

"Tell me about it." He could see her doing it too. He might have to keep her out of jail.

Good thing the studio wasn't far from home. When he and Desiree walked into the studio the owner, Doris Reins, was waiting for them.

"It's so good to see you. I talk to Emily frequently about Sherrice and she's one of our star students. I hope she's enjoying the program," she said, shutting the door behind them.

"I've been having problems with Sherrice lately and it all stems from the lies Emily has been telling her." Desiree detailed what Sherrice had told her.

"Those are serious charges. Give me a moment, please." Doris opened the door and called to the secretary. "Get Emily for me please, and have someone else take over her class. I want her in here immediately."

In three minutes, Emily arrived, looking dainty and regal in her tights and top. "You called?"

"Yes. Sherrice has told her aunt that you've told her she doesn't love her and that Ms. Prescott killed her parents."

"I'm glad we can bring this out in the open." She glared at Desiree. "You don't deserve those children. You killed their parents. And now you're trying to trick Gerard into believing you care for him. But I can see through your ruse. Gerard will wake up soon and see you for who you really are."

"Emily?" Doris was clearly shocked.

"Lady, you're crazy." Before Desiree knew what she was doing she was on her feet, going after Emily. Gerard jumped up and held her back, putting himself between them. "How could you torture a child that way? You aren't fit to be around children. I'm pulling Sherrice out of this school." She glared at the director. "How could you allow someone like this around our children? She's obviously crazy."

"Don't you do a background check on your teachers before you hire them?" Gerard asked.

"I'm shocked. I had no idea. Her references were above reproach."

Emily tilted her chin. "Am I the only rational one around here? Someone had to tell her the truth. I can see through you when the others can not."

"I am so sorry, Ms. Prescott. I had no idea," Doris muttered.

"And, Gerard, you know she's tricked you, that you belong with me. I'm patient. I know you'll come to your senses soon."

Doris called the secretary to escort her out.

"Emily, please wait out in the reception area. Do not return to class. Do you understand? Do not return to class." Doris got up and started for the door.

"Gerard, why don't you speak up for me? We belong

together. I know it's all her." Emily pointed a sharp finger at Desiree.

"Lady, you need to be locked up," Gerard said.

The secretary grasped Emily's arm, but she broke away from the woman.

"Why are you betraying me this way?" Emily pleaded to Gerard.

"Emily, leave this office, now," Doris demanded. "I'll be out in a few moments to speak with you."

Emily made a sharp turn, tilted her chin, and gracefully swung out of the office. Doris spoke briefly to the receptionist before she returned.

Desiree saw shades of her dad, only worse. She saw the madness when he'd been off his pills. As angry as she was, she knew something had to be done, more than just firing her.

"I am so sorry. She came with the highest recommendations," Doris said. "We do background checks. She will no longer teach children here."

"She obviously has a serious mental problem. Perhaps you should contact someone in her family. Firing her isn't going to be enough."

"Unfortunately she was an only child. She has a half brother and a father she has no contact with. Her mother died a few years ago. But I'll look into it. In the meantime, I extend my deepest regret for your family's trauma. I do hope you'll keep Sherrice in the school. I will teach her personally. I can't begin to excuse the horror Emily has put Sherrice and your family through, but I will give her free lessons to atone for this."

Desiree stood. "I'll think about it."

When they moved through the reception area, Emily was gone.

Desiree was a strong woman. For protection, she'd learned long ago to hold her emotions in. She clenched her fists until her nails bit into her hands. When she opened her fists, little crescent moons marred her skin. And still the pain tore at her insides.

Suddenly she felt Gerard's arms around her. "Let it out, else it'll kill you. You've got four children who need you. Can't keep this crap bottled up."

"God. How could people be so cruel?" She wept and felt embarrassed even as she felt better for the release. She pushed away from Gerard's chest. "Thanks, I needed that."

"Feel better?"

"Loads."

He started up the car and pulled away.

"Thanks for being here, for both of us."

"Anytime. Always wanted to be a knight in shining armor."

She smiled through her tears. "You deserve your medal tonight."

When they returned home, Scott had arrived. Desiree talked to all the kids while Scott called Jordan's lawyer. They had to take out a restraining order for the kids to keep Emily away from Sherrice and the boys. The next day Desiree was going to the schools to talk to the principals.

This called for a low-key evening where the family entertained together. What Desiree would give for a workout on her skateboard. Work out some of the tension. But Sherrice didn't skate.

They settled on a DVD movie. Desiree made popcorn and warm apple cider. That night Sherrice slept in Desiree's room. Desiree was afraid to leave her alone. Sherrice tossed and turned for more than half an hour before she finally drifted off to sleep.

Finally, Desiree eased from the bed. Scott, Gerard, and Jacqueline were in the kitchen. Christopher was sitting on Scott's knee. Scott was sipping on bourbon. Gerard handed Desiree a glass of wine. She nodded her thanks.

"Is she asleep?" Gerard asked.

"Finally. What is Christopher still doing up bright-eyed?"

He patted the seat beside him and Desiree eased into it. Christopher was as bright-eyed as if it were morning instead of after eleven.

"It's always some mess going on, isn't it?" Jacqueline said.

"It's a strange situation. What made her fixate on you?" Scott asked Gerard.

"I saw her a couple of times when I was in the bar. You know, that night I talked to you, Scott? I knew she was Sherrice's teacher, so I escorted her to her car when things started to get wild. Didn't think she was ready for how rowdy the room was about to get."

"And suddenly she decided you were in love with her?" Desiree asked.

"She's got a serious problem. She could be imagining all kinds of things. Come to think of it, she could have been following me. I saw her another night in a bar. She came in a couple of minutes after I did. That's the night I discovered she was Sherrice's teacher."

"Wonder if she could be the one sending you the flowers," Scott said.

"Oh, I just remembered something. I found a card in Jordan's desk drawer." Desiree went to her purse and retrieved it. "I was going to give it to you, but completely forgot." When she turned to hand it to Scott, he was rubbing his finger across Christopher's gum and the baby was gumming on it as if it was candy.

"What's on your finger, Scott?"

"He's teething. I put a little bourbon with honey on his gum. Calms him down."

"Give me my baby." She plucked the child from his arms. Christopher was still smacking his lips. "Feeding my baby liquor."

Scott shrugged. "That's how my mom always calmed

my brothers and sisters when they were teething. Worked for them."

"Nadine used to put whiskey on your gums when you teethed," Jacqueline added. "Didn't kill you."

"No telling what Aunt Nadine gave me. It's a wonder I turned out normal." She shook her head. Christopher was still smacking his gums and trying to get back to Scott for more honey and bourbon.

"See there? He's fine with it. Wants more. Sorry, buddy, we've been caught. Next time we have to be more careful."

"It still puzzles me that Emily would offer such details about that car accident. Is it crazy of me to think she could have tampered with the brakes?"

"What are you talking about?" Scott said.

"She said that I had cut the brakes so that the fluid leaked and finally gave out once they were in the mountains."

"That was a horrible accident. I'll pass the info along to the detective. He can get data from the jurisdiction, where the accident occurred," Scott said.

"She's just crazy enough to do it," Gerard added. "She's really off her rocker."

Desiree touched Gerard's arm. "You better be careful. She's in love with you."

"God forbid."

"I'm putting my baby to bed," Desiree said finally. When she kissed Christopher's sweet cheeks, she caught a whiff of bourbon mixed with sweetness, and took her baby upstairs to bed.

Gerard joined her.

"So what's your schedule tomorrow?" Scott asked Jacqueline.

"House-hunting. What else?"

"You know how I feel about that."

"I'm not moving in with you, and that's final." As he stared stonily at her, she tilted her chin. "You should help me. You know the area and you know what I'm looking for."

"I'm not helping you to move away from me. Besides, you're not going to spend much time there."

"Says who? I'll spend as much time there as I want to."

He tugged her chair near his and leaned close enough to kiss her lips briefly. "Because I intend to keep you with me as much as possible."

"You're assuming an awful lot."

"Why do you fight me every step of the way?"

"It's not that I'm fighting you. You just assume you have more control than you do."

He regarded her with narrowed eyes. "Okay. So how do I get you with me?"

"If I need to spell it out for you, then you have a serious problem."

Clearly at a loss, he leaned back in his chair. "Let's change the subject. We're getting more and more female athletes in the agency. Would you like to learn the business and work with me?"

"You're offering me a job?"

He nodded.

"Why would you do that?"

"Because I think you'd be good at it. And as you've complained before, we don't have enough females in higher positions there. You'll fit right in."

"I'm very interested. But my working with you won't give you any advantages in my personal life."

He pulled out his BlackBerry as if he were going to record her statement. "Duly noted."

Jacqueline couldn't deny for a second that this man turned her on. He knew his appeal to women, her in particular, and he played on that. This was war. She wasn't going to give him an inch.

His head was buried in that BlackBerry as if she didn't exist. Desiree and Gerard were still upstairs tucking Chris in. The other children were asleep. With quick steps she was in front of him and she straddled him.

His shocked gaze touched hers. The BlackBerry hung limply in his hand before he quickly dropped it on the table. Jacqueline tilted his chin and kissed him. His hands explored her hips, her back. She rocked on his lap, feeling the bulge in his slacks, the ragged moan that tore from his deepest core.

"Damn, baby. If you don't quit it, I'm gonna come right here."

Jacqueline gave him a wicked, knowing grin, and captured his mouth once more. By the time they heard footsteps on the stairs, they were both breathless with need. Jacqueline slid off his lap, strolled to the fridge, and pulled out a soda, holding the can against her forehead. Tuning toward Scott, she stood in the open door.

"You are one wicked woman, you know that?" Scott scooted his chair close to the table and ran a hand across his face, shaking his head as if he was confronted with a dilemma for which he didn't possess the answers. With unsteady hands, he picked up his BlackBerry, but he didn't have a clue of what he'd been working on.

16

Emily couldn't finish her dance the next morning without the blasted doorbell disturbing her. And the person wouldn't leave. Just kept leaning on the bell as if a finger was glued to it.

Emily had a headache. Nevertheless she climbed the stairs, with the hopes that the intruder would disappear before she got there. She opened the door expecting to see some salesman. But it was her employer. Ex-employer. Doris had come by her house the night before, but Emily had ignored the bell.

"Are you out of your damn mind?" Doris had the nerve to come barging into Emily's house—her personal sanctuary—without an invitation.

"If you don't mind, I'm doing my morning dance routine." Emily slammed the door and stood straight and tall in front of it. She wasn't going to offer Doris a chair.

"I don't give a crap about your routine. You damn near ruined my business. They could still sue me. What in the hell were you thinking to tell that child those awful things? What is wrong with you?"

Emily tilted her head. She was the best dancer at the studio and they'd let her go. Doris couldn't be too smart. See how well they'd do without her.

"I only told her the truth," Emily said. "If they didn't want to hear it, it wasn't my problem."

"But they're all lies. What's wrong with you?"

"They weren't lies. Someone needed to tell Sherrice the truth. And I was the only one to do it. Although she betrayed me."

"Emily, you begged me for this job because no one else would hire you. I gave you a chance because we were friends in high school. How could *you* betray *me* that way?"

"I was the best dancer you had, and you know it. I am an exemplary teacher. You were lucky to have me."

"Do you understand that I could lose my business over a lawsuit?" Doris shook her head. She couldn't believe what she was hearing. Emily stood ramrod straight, as if she were about to execute a dance step. Doris turned away from the door. She couldn't believe what she was seeing.

"What is this?" Pictures of Gerard Kingsley littered the living room tables and walls. Most of them were of him in baseball uniforms. He wore suits in some of them. They were all natural shots of him as he played baseball or walked to and from places.

"You're stalking him?"

"Don't be silly. Soon we will be engaged. Forgive me if I don't invite you to the wedding. You see, he needs me. But you wouldn't understand that. Not yet, anyway."

"Emily, you need help," Doris said quietly. "You heard him. He doesn't even know you."

"Yes, he does. We met at bars a couple of times."

"*He* was *at* the bar, Emily," Doris said, feeling as if she were in the twilight zone. "He didn't meet you there."

"He wanted to meet me there."

Doris was getting nowhere, and she didn't know how to handle Emily's problems. She couldn't leave her to her own devices. Like Sherrice's aunt had said, Emily needed help. "Do you know where your father is?"

Emily straightened a picture on the coffee table. "I

have no contact with that man. I'm sure whatever he's doing has nothing to do with me."

"Where is he?"

"Somewhere in Atlanta. How would I know?"

"Didn't you say he sent you Christmas and birthday cards?"

"I toss them away."

"Emily, you need help."

"I need you to go so I can practice my dance."

Doris stared at Emily a few seconds, then opened the door and walked out. She was going to find Emily's father and get her some help. No telling what she'd do in the condition she was in.

Back in the office she pulled out the phone book and searched for Joseph Boyd's name until she found it. She wrote the name on a pad and glanced at the clock. It was still early. Hopefully he was still home. If not, she'd leave a message.

Sherrice improved rapidly without Emily's poisonous influence. Desiree only kept her out of school one day. When the therapist returned, Sherrice saw her a couple of times a week.

Before Desiree knew it, the kids were out of school and they were all headed to the airport to board a plane to New York.

"I'm so excited," Steven said. "What are we going to do there, Aunt Desiree?"

"Lots of things. We'll see the Empire State Building, the location where the World Trade Center used to be. We'll visit Harlem, the Rockefeller Center. We'll see a play. We're going shopping."

"That's girl stuff," Justin said. "Who wants to waste time shopping when we can do other stuff?"

"I do," Sherrice said. She was looking healthy and happy. Desiree still worried if she was doing the right thing with the kids, if she was raising them the way Beverly and Jordan would have wanted her to.

"I chose this week because Gerard is there. We'll see him, too. And of course you get to help me pack."

Everybody groaned.

Desiree's mother was coming with them to help with the packing. Scott also promised to visit. He'd brought them to the airport, and he and Jacqueline were still saying good-bye while Desiree and the kids checked the luggage.

The older couple were in love.

In the beginning Desiree had planned to rent a U-Haul in New York and drive it back, but Gerard had convinced her to hire a moving company. She and the children would have more time to enjoy the city. And they did, from the flight to all the places they toured.

"How did you live in such a tiny place, Aunt Desiree?" Justin asked. Everybody was going crazy with only one bathroom between six people. "You can't just go outside to skateboard. Too many cars on the street."

"That's true. But there are other things you can do. Like walk and skateboard in Central Park."

"I'm glad we're staying in Atlanta."

"For your sake, so am I."

"Gerard's close by too. I'm glad you're dating him. You're going to marry him, aren't you?" Sherrice asked.

"Honey, we haven't discussed marriage. We haven't known each other that long."

"I hope you marry him. I like him," Justin said.

"Me too," said Steven.

The kids had really grown attached to him, Desiree thought. They expected her to marry him. How disappointed they'd be when they discovered they weren't going to marry.

Deana and Joy came over to take her to the bar. "We're going to miss you. I told everyone you were coming tonight, so expect a crowd."

"Go ahead. I'll keep the children," Jacqueline said.
"Have fun with your friends."

So Desire dressed and went to their favorite hangout.
She was a little apprehensive about seeing Paul. They'd
hung out there together.

It had been almost three months since Desiree left New
York, but it felt like three years when she walked into the
bar. The music was loud. Everyone was trying to outtalk
each other. And wouldn't you know, Paul was holding
court with some of his friends. Desiree wondered if the
woman sitting between him and his friend was his new
girlfriend.

She expected to feel . . . pain, but she felt nothing.

Desiree visited with old friends. It almost felt like old
times, except the news had changed and she was out of
the loop.

An hour later Paul saw her and came over.

"Are you back for good?" he asked.

"Just here to pack up my things. I'm moving to Atlanta."

"My clients still ask about you. They miss you."

What a loser she'd been to settle for the loveless match
Paul had offered. Ostensibly, she was only his entertainment hostess, who, after all, was easily replaced.

Paul quirked an eyebrow. "So all the talk is about the
game this weekend. Is Gerard in town?"

"He's playing against the Yankees."

"He and Desiree are the hottest couple in Atlanta these
days," Joy said. "They've even been showing up in the
Atlanta society pages." Joy never liked Paul and would
use any bit to irritate him.

"So you're getting married after all," Paul murmured.

"You never know," Joy responded. She looked behind
Desiree and smiled.

"Mind if I join you?" said a familiar voice.

Desiree could have died. She hoped Gerard didn't hear
that comment about marriage. It would send him running
for the hills, for sure. He looked much too handsome in

a jacket and dark slacks. She could swear her heart
skipped a beat when he leaned down and kissed her
briefly on the lips.

"How did you find me?"

"I called him," Joy said.

"Don't hog her. Let a friend get a hug," Tony said, and
gave Desiree a hug.

"How's Pat?" she asked.

"Finally stopped complaining about morning sickness.
Now she's worried I'll be away when the baby comes, but
I won't. The due date is in December."

"What perfect timing."

"I'll say."

She introduced Gerard and Tony to her old friends.
Some of the patrons recognized them and asked for his
and Tony's autographs.

"It's hard dating a star, isn't it?" Deana whispered.

"Take care, Desiree. Good seeing you," Paul said, and
joined his group.

How she'd grown in the space of three months, Desiree
thought. She had talked herself into believing that what
she shared with Paul was good enough for a lifetime, but
it wasn't.

Life was ironic. She loved Gerard, but he wasn't a settling-
down man. She didn't love Paul, but as long as she fit into his
perfect life, he was willing to marry her.

Someone left the seat next to Desiree, and Gerard sat
beside her. He put his arm around the back of her chair.
Desiree wondered if he could feel the increase in her
heartbeat.

She was happy with Gerard. She loved him, but did
he love her? Paul's question threw her. Was she marrying
Gerard? Of course not. She had settled for a going-
nowhere relationship because why? Did she feel she was
unworthy of love? First Howard, who'd married another
woman while she was having a miscarriage. Paul, who
really didn't love her, but she was a convenient hostess

for his clients. Now there was Gerard. She couldn't deny that he helped her enormously with the kids, but he still wasn't a permanent fixture in their lives. She was a convenience for him. Easy sex. No attachments. He easily doled out gold and diamonds in exchange for exclusivity.

And there were the children. They were growing more and more attached to Gerard. When he left, the blow would be huge, but it would be even worse a year or two from now.

Desiree had settled again and for exactly the identical relationship Gerard had shared with Andrea. If Desiree gave him an ultimatum of marriage or nothing, he'd leave her as easily as he'd left Andrea.

She was worth so much more than to be his temporary plaything.

The children deserved more.

Scott arrived at Desiree's apartment while Desiree was still out. He swooped Jackie into his arms and swung her around.

"Hey, you missed me that much?"

"And then some. This traveling business without you isn't working. I want you with me every second of every day."

Jacqueline chuckled and led him to the couch. She fixed him a shot of bourbon and handed him the snifter. "Guess what?"

"What?"

"I've sold my house, and I've found a place in Atlanta. I have to fly back to D.C. soon to close the deal. But I didn't think it would sell so quickly and for the price I wanted."

"I'm happy you've sold your house . . . but I don't want you to move to another house, Jackie. We won't have much time together."

"You know—"

"Marry me."

"What?" She reared back in shock. "I thought you were a confirmed bachelor."

"You have to know I love you. Marry me. Back at my parents' place. There's a small church where I grew up. My best friend is the pastor. If you don't have any objections, I'd like him to marry us."

Jackie looked down at his hand. He squeezed her fingers so hard her hand was cramping and he didn't even know it. She was touched. More touched than she'd ever been. This strong, big man loved her. "Okay."

His eyes widened. "Just like that?"

"You want me to say no?"

"Hell no." He swooped her into his arms.

Emily was tired and furious. Gerard had not contacted her. She'd stayed home for days on end waiting for him to call. She'd made sure her answering machine was turned on. Had taken the portable phone with her to the bathroom. Yet, he didn't call and he left no messages.

She was beside herself. Finally she rented a car and parked in his development—and watched him take Desiree out to dinner, the traitor. And now Desiree and Gerard were missing.

Gerard was playing the Yankees. The children were out of school. He'd taken them to New York to be with him, Emily was sure.

She took one of the picture frames and threw it against the wall as hard as she could. Fury overrode her. She grabbed another, and another, and another until her floor was littered with shards of glass and none of the frames were left intact.

Emily stood in the middle of the floor trembling. This was all Desiree's and Gerard's fault. They'd both betrayed her. And Sherrice as well. She had confided in that stupid child. She had no business going to them with her revelations. After all she did to help that child, she betrayed her.

Worst of all, Gerard betrayed her, just like her father betrayed her mother and her. He'd walked out on them when Emily was nine, and never returned, not even to visit. All those years, she'd thought he loved her, that nothing could separate them, only to find out it was all lies.

Her mother just let her father go, but Gerard was going to pay for his deceit.

When someone rang the doorbell, Emily jumped. It had better not be Doris. She'd had enough of her. She'd already fired her, so she should leave her the heck alone.

She snatched the door open. An older man. With gray hair that once had been raven. He might be years older, but she still recognized her father.

She slammed the door, but he stopped it before it shut completely.

"Hello, Emily."

Emily pinched her lips. "Please leave."

"Invite me in, Emily."

"I don't open my door to strangers."

"Invite me in."

Emily stood firm. "No. Say your purpose and please leave."

The timing couldn't be worse. He *had* to arrive right after her tantrum. The floor was littered with the broken frames. She wasn't about to let him see that and go back to his family laughing at her. They would all laugh at her.

"How have you been?" he asked.

"Wonderful."

"I wanted to talk to you about why I didn't contact you all these years. Your mother wouldn't allow—"

"Don't say one word about my mother. You deserted us. She was there. Go away." Emily slammed the door in his face.

He knocked on the door for several minutes before he gave up.

* * *

Gerard knew something was troubling Desiree. She hadn't been herself since they returned from New York. Was it Paul? Did seeing him make her realize she really was in love with him? Did she miss the guy? Worse, did she want him back?

"What's wrong, Desiree?" It was better to know the truth up front than obsess over it.

Desiree really didn't want to talk about it, because she knew the outcome beforehand. When pressed about making a commitment, Gerard would bail. She couldn't give the children false hope and she couldn't let them fall for Gerard any more than they already had. When she and Gerard separated, the children would be hurt, but if she let things go for another two years, the pain would be that much worse. If it were just she, she could hang on until their relationship died naturally. But she couldn't do this to the children.

Desiree gazed at his strong profile trying to remember so many little details, like his odd smile. She'd fallen in love with him and could not imagine her days without him. Yet, she couldn't continue a relationship that would never go anywhere. Two years down the road she saw herself in the same situation as Andrea must have discovered.

She glanced up at him, then away. "I'm not comfortable with where this relationship is going."

"What are you talking about?"

"I'm just another groupie."

Gerard bit off a curse. "That's the biggest bunch of crap I've ever heard. You're not a one-night stand and I don't treat you that way."

"I'm still just a convenient bed partner. Look, I have four children and I have to protect them. You're not going to be a permanent part of their lives. In the long run it makes it too hard on them. They're beginning to depend on you. And you're not going to be here."

"You're not Andrea. Do you think I'm going to let you keep me from the kids? *You* might not need me, but the children do. Sherrice is at that age where she needs to know that she doesn't have to prove herself to receive love—especially with males. These knuckleheads out here run a number on girls. The boys need male influence, as well as yours. You might think you can do everything, but you can't be the daddy, Desiree."

"And all that is to say what? What do you want? Visitation rights?"

"You have a low opinion of me, don't you? A convenient bed partner. Is that all I am to you?" He reacted as if he was hurt.

Desiree gazed into the distance. "No. I love you. But that's my problem. Not yours."

"That's funny. You love me, but you want to leave me. Desiree, the time isn't right for marriage. I'm gone all the time. Kids need fathers who're home."

"Children need fathers period, Gerard. You're just giving me excuses. Some ballplayers play until they're in their forties. There is no exact moment. What if you leave baseball and you choose another career where you have to travel? Will you put your life on hold again? Look at the amount of time Scott travels. His schedule is crazy. He runs around behind these ballplayers from state to state," she said. "You have a right to live the kind of life you want, but I'm not going to sit around and wait for you to decide what's going to happen to my life."

"I thought both of us were involved in this relationship. I didn't know it was so one-sided."

"I want more than to be your arm piece for the next few years. I deserve a full life and I'm not settling for less."

"Does this have anything to do with your mother's marriage?"

"Of course not. My mother doesn't have four children to consider."

* * *

Gerard wasn't in the mood for company the next morning, especially critical comments from his mother. He wondered what he'd done to warrant a visit.

"So, what did I do this time?"

She put her purse on the table and regarded him critically. He hadn't shaved yet. He hadn't ventured near a mirror.

"You look awful," she said. "Are you sick?" She placed the back of her hand against his forehead.

"I'm fine. Just didn't sleep well last night."

"Well, perhaps I chose a bad time to come by."

"Why are you here?" he asked again.

"I smell coffee. I could use a cup. By the looks of you, you could use one too." She took two cups from the kitchen cabinet, and poured coffee into them. Then she added cream and sugar before she sat at the table across from him.

Gerard wished she'd get to the point. Usually she was up front about her critical comments. What was taking her so long this time?

"I wanted to apologize if you've felt that I don't admire you for your success."

Gerard's cup was halfway to his mouth. He dropped the cup on the table sloshing some of the coffee on his hand, burning himself. But he was too wrapped in his mother's apology to notice.

"Am I hearing things?"

"No, I've given it a lot of thought. I am proud of you. As you've pointed out before, I was disappointed you and Andrea broke up. But I've come to terms with it. I understand you're dating Desiree."

Gerard didn't comment, so she continued.

"I plan to invite her and her family over for dinner soon. I'll try to work around your schedule."

"Things aren't going well with us right now."

"So soon?"

Gerard was speechless.

"Is that why you're looking like you've been hung out to dry?"

Gerard nodded.

"Well, if she's the one for you, fight for her. Don't give up. Let her know what she means to you."

"I can't believe you're saying that." This was the last comment he'd expected from his mother.

"I want you happy, son. I love you."

Gerard couldn't remember ever hearing those words from his mother and he had to clear his throat to gain control of his emotions.

"You get a nap and you'll be able to think more clearly. The right solution will come to you." Amanda gathered her purse from the table. "In the meantime, I'll plan that dinner."

"I'm not touching that worm," Sherrice said to her grandfather.

"Fisherman's got to bait her own hook," Levi said. "It's not going to hurt you."

Sherrice frowned and stepped back. "It looks horrible. All squishy."

"If you eat it you have to catch it. Fish don't come already caught and filleted. Somebody caught it, cleaned it, filleted it, then cooked it. Doesn't come already prepared. Got to learn how to survive off the land."

"But this isn't Daniel Boone's day. I can find anything I need in the store," Sherrice said.

"Don't know what the future will bring. What if you're in a situation where you have to live off the land? How would you survive if you don't know what's safe to eat and not? There's plenty of safe food in the forest. Plenty of poisonous greens, too. And if you've got a river close by, if you don't know how to fish and prepare it, what would you do?"

"I might not have a fishing pole on me, then what?" Justin asked.

"I'll teach you how to make one."

"I need gloves," Sherrice muttered. "I'm not touching it with my bare hands."

"Might not have a pair of gloves handy, but you'll still need to eat." Levi sighed and pulled a pair of latex gloves out of his pocket. "Here you go. We'll start off with this, but by the end of the summer, you'll be baiting the hook with your bare hands."

It was a bright, sunny, and hot summer day.

The kids were spending the week with Aunt Nadine and Levi. Desiree was only staying the weekend. She had to get back to work.

"Put that hat back on your head, Steven," Aunt Nadine called out. "Sun's too hot. Give you a heat stroke."

The boy did as he was told.

Desiree tuned the conversation out. She'd heard it all years ago when her dad told her the very same story of survival. She sat on the stump, contemplating.

She'd told Gerard she was leaving him to save her heart. It was already too late for that. The pain in her chest was sharp and real.

"Looks like he's growing by the day," Aunt Nadine said. She was sitting on a chair fanning herself. She'd take care of Christopher while the children were there. Desiree wasn't too keen on leaving him, but Aunt Nadine insisted. She hadn't had a baby to look after for a while and she missed having them around.

Desiree tuned her father in again. All five poles were in the water now. Her father had set out two for himself.

"All right, now wiggle it a little, gets his attention. I'll be right back."

He sipped from his Coke, then joined Desiree. He hunkered down by the stump.

"So tell me about this mess going on back home."

"Don't worry about it, Daddy. Scott has notified the police."

"I want to know what's going on with my granddaughter."

"This woman who fancies herself in love with Gerard told her that I killed her parents." She went over the details about the flowers and what Emily told Sherrice.

"This woman sounds dangerous to me. You can't just sweep something like this under the rug."

"It's very serious. I was having such a time with Sherrice for a while. Daddy, I was really frightened."

Levi rubbed her hand. "Of course you were. Raising kids is a huge responsibility. And it's not like the same thing works for every child. You just do the best you can. That's all anyone expects of you. And you're still gonna make mistakes. You're a perfectionist. You want to make everything perfect. But life isn't. You got to work with what you got. It's the best you can do."

Desiree stared at her father.

"I caught something. I got one!" Justin shouted.

Her father started loping toward the pier. "Reel 'em in, nice and slow so he won't get away. Nice and slow. That's it."

"I see it, I see it," Steven shouted.

"Y'all gonna scare all the fish away with all that shouting," Aunt Nadine said, fanning herself with a church fan.

"Ahh, that's a pretty one," Levi said. "A nice old butterfish. You're going to have some good eating tonight." Levi donned a pair of gloves and took the fish off the hook. They exclaimed over it before they tossed a man's catch into the cooler.

Desiree remembered fishing expeditions with her father. Aunt Nadine would fill a cooler and bag with sodas and snacks. And she would stop whatever she was doing to go fishing with them. Aunt Nadine's husband was alive then, but the older woman had always taken time out of her life for Levi and Desiree. In a sense, Desiree was the closest she'd come to having children of her own.

"Got another one," Levi said. "See that line wiggling?"

"Oh yeah!" Steven said.

"Got one. Reel him in before he sneaks away." Slowly Steven began to reel until the fish was lifted in the air. It wasn't quite as large as Justin's.

"Make a good-size serving. Nice and sweet," Levi said, just before Sherrice caught one.

After Sherrice reeled hers in, Levi sat back in his lawn chair and sipped on his soda. He was happiest, Desiree realized, when he was around the children. If ever a man was made for them, it was her father.

"I love y'all, you know that Grandpa loves you, right?" he said.

"We know, Grandpa," Sherrice said and hugged him around the neck.

Tears filled Desiree's eyes. As much as Aunt Nadine and her father embarrassed her with their constant public fights and craziness, Desiree wouldn't wish for another life. Even with the damage from Vietnam, her father had always been a loving and caring father. He never used an excuse to shirk his duty. Nothing. Absolutely nothing could keep him away from her when she was growing up, even though he lived hundreds of miles away. He wasn't perfect, but he was available for her.

Not only his presence, but he provided financially as well. He would go without a shirt on his back before he would let her go without the things she needed. Sometimes she thought he worked just so he could provide for her.

Desiree came up behind him and wrapped her arms around his neck. She kissed his grizzly cheek, and held him tight. "I love you, Dad."

His work-roughened hand captured hers and, forgetting about the fishing pole, he gazed up at her. "You're my shining light, doll baby."

"I'm taking the kids to church Sunday," Aunt Nadine said. "They need to be in the church."

Levi grunted.

"I mean it, Levi."

"Okay, okay."

"You mean you aren't going to argue?"

"I'm going, too."

Aunt Nadine stopped fanning and leaned forward. "You're going to church?"

"I go sometimes. Don't act like I've never been there."

"Three, four times a year. You don't go on a regular basis like you should."

"Got nothing against the church."

"So why you always fighting me about Deacon Smithers?"

"Don't want him around my children."

"You're a strange man, Levi. I'll never understand you."

"You just finding that out?"

Desiree tuned out the arguing.

17

Gerard drank a glass of juice. He had a strong urge to hit something. Had wanted to since Desiree had given him the freaking ultimatum. No, she didn't come right out and ask him to marry her, she was too smart for that. She broke it off. Just like that, as if the last three months had meant nothing.

"Leave it out," Chad said, rushing downstairs.

Gerard poured his brother a glass before he put it back into the fridge. "Kind of late to be going in to work, isn't it?"

"I'm meeting some friends for lunch. Looks quiet next door. Where is everyone?"

"Visiting Desiree's aunt and dad."

"You two haven't been together much lately. Anything wrong?"

Gerard shrugged. Despite what his mother had said, rage burned like fire in his gut. Desiree was trying to control him. The deep, relentless ache in the pit of his stomach wouldn't quit. He'd never needed a woman before. And he didn't know how to handle his obsession with her.

But he would. Baseball was his salvation. He would lose himself in the sport he loved.

His stomach muscles unclenched. Then clenched again. "She left me."

Chad's glass was halfway to his mouth when he set it back on the table. "Why?"

"She wants to get married. I can't right now, and she doesn't understand that."

"I don't understand it."

"It's simple. I'm not here."

"Sure you are. You're together all the time. That's not an excuse, is it?"

"Excuse?"

"For not getting close. The crap Mom put on you has to have affected you."

"I can handle her."

"You shouldn't have to. And I told her so."

That brought out a chuckle. "Little brother, you taking up for me?"

"Sure. You fought for me enough. Turnaround's fair play. It comes down to, do you love her or not? That's all it is. As simple as that. Are you willing to let her go the way you let Andrea go?"

"It's not simple. There are other things to consider."

"You don't want the responsibility of four children."

"I've thought about it. But I think I can deal with it."

"The question you have to answer is, do you love her enough to deal with it?"

Gerard sighed. "How did you get so smart in your young age?"

Desiree didn't feel like convincing anyone that he needed to budget his money for his own good. But her job was to guide them, and even though her spirit was low, she did her job.

"Desiree?" her assistant called over the intercom.

With a sigh Desiree depressed the button. "Yes?"

"You have another client waiting for you."

She flipped through the day's schedule. Her client was due in an hour. "This one isn't on my schedule. Is he early?"

"A last-minute addition Scott made."

"I don't have any information on him. Did he send me a file?"

"I'll bring you the folder."

Desiree straightened her short-sleeved jacket and stood.

Instead of a client, her assistant escorted Gerard into the room. He was the last person Desiree wanted to see. Her heart was still aching over him. She didn't need the fresh reminder of his presence. It was enough that the children talked about him day and night.

"What are you doing here?" she asked. Her eyes blazed at him.

"I told you I wanted a consultation with you about my finances."

Some excuse, but she could play his game. "He's mostly given me new players, not the older, more experienced ones."

"We can all use some advice."

"Gerard, let's not play games. You aren't here for me to evaluate your spending habits."

"That was only one of the reasons. My trip has a dual purpose."

"What's the other reason?"

"One. Will you marry me?"

"Why? Because it's what I want?"

"It's what you said you wanted."

"So you're marrying me under duress? What kind of marriage will we have? You'd soon resent me."

"Nothing I do pleases you, does it?"

"I just want you to follow your heart. If you don't love me, you shouldn't marry me. Because eventually a woman you love will come along. It's hard enough to keep a relationship going when two people love each other. It's nearly impossible when they don't."

"Well, let's table the marriage and go through my finances."

Desiree opened the folder. "I need time to evaluate it before I go discuss it with you. I never do it cold."

"Fine. I'll set up an appointment with your assistant." He marched out of the office.

Sighing, Desiree sat down at her desk and opened his folder. Then frowned. This wasn't an expense statement. It was the deed to her aunt's property. He'd purchased the land and had gifted it to her. She jumped up to run after him, but he was already gone. She had another appointment and couldn't leave the office.

It was hours later before she could leave. After parking the car in her driveway, she immediately marched across the lawn to his house and pounded on the door. He answered immediately. Marching into his house, she rounded on him.

"Gerard, I appreciate your generous gesture, you don't know how much. But you and I no longer date. The land is too much. Tell me how much you paid—"

"Don't insult me. The deed to the place was my gift for you. And we were dating when I purchased it. It can't be undone."

"It's too—"

"What is it? You can't believe I care about you?"

Desiree wanted to cry. "Of course you care about me," she said softly. "That was never the problem."

"Well, take it in the spirit in which it was given. I was happy to purchase the land for you. Accept it in the same light."

"Gerard, why are you doing everything in your power to bind us together? I want to sever the ties."

Suddenly he swooped down and kissed her. His strong arms came around her. She was of a mind to fight him, but with the familiar scent, and the fact that she missed him every second of the day, she found herself responding.

She realized that although his arms were around her, they were not tight. She could easily slip out. The captivity was only in her mind.

But she was tired of fighting. And she wanted him. This was it. She would not see him after tonight. She would make tonight last her a lifetime.

* * *

Emily watched Desiree cross the lawn to Gerard's house with quick, angry steps. She heard raised voices from within, then the quiet. The quiet was worse than screams. She wanted to storm in there and kill both of them, but she waited. It was much too early. It was still light out. Anyone could see her.

Levi was late leaving Macon. Nadine had the children tucked in tight for the night. Even Chris was fast asleep. The boys were tuckered out from their hike in the woods. Nadine had traveled in the golf cart with Christopher buckled in the seat Levi had fashioned for him.

The woman had sprayed everyone with insect repellent. She'd toted ice and water in the cart. It was a wonder Chris didn't suffocate with all the clothes she'd put on him to keep bugs away. She'd even put on some of that snake-away stuff to make sure snakes didn't come around the cart. Levi shook his head.

He'd kept an eye on Chris, watching for signs of dehydration. The little tyke sat in that seat as pleased as a rabbit in a vegetable patch.

The boys had enjoyed the hike. Sherrice had been a trouper.

Levi had pointed out wild plants, and taught them how to catch animals in the wild if you were starving. He believed in killing only for sustenance, not for sport.

His grandchildren were wonderful children. He enjoyed every moment spent with them, but he had to protect Desiree. So now he was driving to Atlanta, to see what Emily was up to. He'd gotten the girl's name out of Desiree before she'd left. She was worried, he could tell. But he wondered if something else had been on her mind.

* * *

Desiree hadn't meant to go to bed with Gerard. It was the single most idiotic thing she'd done in the past six months. Well, she'd done plenty of stupid things lately.

Gerard was sleeping soundly beside her. She was lying on his shoulder, his pitching arm around her waist. She snuggled comfortably in his arms.

What was she going to do? This just could not last.

Oh, why did she even come to his house? She shifted to her side to ease out of the bed, but Gerard tightened his arm around her. He had a game the next day and she didn't want to awaken him, so she stayed in bed a few more minutes before she tried to move again. This time he turned to his side, moving his arm, and she slipped out of bed. Quickly she dressed and tiptoed down the stairs. Quietly she opened the door and stepped outside.

It was a warm night. A crescent moon shone above in a clear bright sky. Desiree started walking toward her house and suddenly something hit her over the head and . . .

Levi coasted toward Desiree's house. Her car was parked in the driveway instead of the garage. He hated the idea of her staying in the huge house alone. Jacqueline was with her agent friend most of the time. A knot built in Levi's stomach. After all these years, after many women, a part of his heart would always belong to Jacqueline. It was he who had moved away, not she, so he couldn't complain.

Jacqueline had been a loyal wife. She would never have left him, even with the trouble he caused her. He could not bear having her put up with him when he was no longer the man she'd married, so he'd done the only honorable thing he could. He'd left. But he could not stay away entirely. So several times a year he'd returned. And being in Jacqueline's arms had been a space of heaven.

But when Desiree turned eighteen he gave Jacqueline her freedom. He wanted her to find a man who was whole. Someone worthy of her love. He hoped Scott was that man. He seemed to love Jacqueline and he seemed good for her.

Although Levi dated, he'd never marry again. Not ever.

He scouted his surroundings as he drove. He parked two blocks from her house, left his car, and walked.

Gerard turned, expecting to snuggle against a warm body, but encountered only cold covers.

"Desiree?" he called out softly. He looked toward the bathroom, thinking she'd gone in there, but it was dark. *I know she didn't walk home in the dark alone.*

Gerard hopped out of bed and pulled on jeans and a shirt. He glanced toward Desiree's house. It was dark and uninviting. He was getting ready to go downstairs when he thought he saw a shadow.

He dialed her number. She didn't respond. Her car was still in the driveway.

He sprinted downstairs and crashed out of doors in a run. The shadow had disappeared. He sprinted around the house.

Emily came to mind. Had the crazy woman attacked Desiree? Gerard ran to Desiree's place. Crap. He forgot the key.

"What's going on?" Levi's whispered voice was so close it startled him.

"When I looked out my window I thought I saw someone. Desiree was with me earlier, but she left while I slept."

"I didn't see anything on this side. I've been here for a few minutes."

"I checked around my house," Gerard said. "Nothing there."

"The only other place is inside," Levi said. "I would have seen any cars that passed."

With a few quick moves, Levi opened the door. They stood there listening, but they didn't see a thing—didn't hear a sound. One by one they began to quickly search the rooms, starting with the first floor and then upstairs.

They met at the door and searched outside again. Levi glanced down the street. "You know where that crazy woman lives?"

"Yeah. Scott went by there."

They hopped in Levi's truck and he tore down the street. They made it to Emily's house and the car was still rocking when they hopped out. Emily's car was not in the driveway. Her one-car garage didn't have windows.

When they burst into Emily's living room, their feet crunched on the glass on the floor.

"What the heck?" Gerard glazed around in horror. Broken frames littered the floors. He turned one over. His blood ran cold. All the pictures were of him. One by one he gazed at likenesses of himself. It was one thing being told, but quite another seeing it for himself.

"We've got to find her fast," he whispered.

It was obvious Emily had been in a fit of rage when she destroyed the room. She could very well take it out on Desiree.

They stood quietly listening for clues, quickly scanned the rooms on that floor, and proceeded to check out the entire house, room by room. But they found nothing. Gerard checked out the garage.

"Her car isn't in here," he said.

"Like I said, I didn't see a car pass me. Desiree is too heavy for her to carry alone," said Levi.

With his hands on his hips, Gerard threw a worried gaze around the room. An eerie feeling passed through him seeing so many pictures of himself. The woman possessed more pictures of him than he did. It didn't take a genius to determine that a madwoman did this and that she had Desiree. "You think she had help?"

"Who knows? My guess is she's close to home," Levi said.

"Let's go, then."

Just as they were leaving, the door opened and a tall man came through. "Who are you?" the man asked.

"Who are you?" Gerard asked.

"Emily's father, and I want to know why you're in my daughter's house."

"I believe she's kidnapped my daughter," Levi said. "And we're looking for them."

"Is your daughter the one they were having trouble with at the dance place?"

"The girl's aunt. We don't have time to waste," Levi said. "Let's get going."

"Where are you going?"

"Back to Desiree's house."

"I'm following. Maybe I can help. I'm Joseph Boyd."

"How come you haven't done anything about her before?" Gerard asked as they went to their vehicles.

"It's a long story. I don't think we have time to get into it."

Men are so stupid. Emily laughed out aloud. They thought Desiree was safe because this was a gated community. But there were ways around that. Her boss hadn't told the students why Emily was fired. The woman who usually asked her to walk the dog when the family went on vacation lived in that community. She left word at the gate that Emily had permission to come every day to take care of the animal. When there's a will, there's always a way. She chuckled at her own wit. She'd hid in the bushes, lying flat on the ground while the men searched Desiree's house. Then they left for her house, she was sure.

In his rush to save his precious Desiree, Gerard forgot to lock his door. Emily went inside and opened one of the three massive garage doors. Then she rolled Desiree into a quilt and dragged her inside before she activated the remote to close the door.

Desiree groaned.

"He can't save you, you know," Emily said. "Don't pretend you're asleep. I didn't hit you that hard."

* * *

Desiree couldn't move her arms or legs, only her feet and fingers. Her wrists and ankles were bound and she was wrapped up in something. It was as if she was bound from head to foot and something was tap-dancing in her head.

She heard footsteps, but it could be . . . She didn't know what the heck was going on. She was groggy. Her head exploded with pain and she didn't have a clue where she was. Only that she was lying on a hard and unforgiving cold surface in an overheated room. She was so hot she thought she was going to faint and she could barely breathe.

The last thing she remembered was . . . leaving Gerard in bed and slipping out of his house. What on earth happened to her? Were the children all right? Gratefully they were safely tucked away in Macon with her father and Aunt Nadine. They had to be fine.

Suddenly she heard footsteps nearby; then she found herself rolling and rolling until she was free. The bright light blinded her. Emily slapped her in the face.

"Sit up." She dragged Desiree until she was sitting upright. "I bet you're wondering what this is all about. Both of you will pay for betraying me. He was in love with me, but you tricked him. You used your wiles to turn him completely away from me. You'll both be sorry."

Desiree rubbed her hands across her eyes to clear them. Emily didn't look like herself. The woman wiped a hand across her face, leaving a streak of dirt. Her hair was wild. Dirt streaked her clothes. The garden dirt.

"Emily, please tell me what's going on."

"As if you didn't know. This entire mess is all your fault. If you hadn't moved here, Gerard would never have left me for you."

Desiree had to try to control her voice and speak in a reasonable manner. Maybe then Emily would let her go.

"I didn't know he was dating you. Had I known, I would have respected your wishes."

"You kept him much too busy with the kids and you.

We didn't have the time to develop our relationship. But that's going to change. You'll be out of the way. Unfortunately, I can't trust him, either."

"Why don't you explain it to me?"

"You're a smart one. You think I'm too dumb to know what you're up to? Let me enlighten you. As soon as he comes home, I'll kill you in front of him. Then I'll kill him. Perfect justice."

"Emily, if Gerard had known how you felt about him—"

"I know what happened in that office. He betrayed me in front of everyone . . . everyone. And I lost my job. So don't tell me about Gerard."

"You never told him you loved him. How was he to know?"

She nodded her head up and down several times. "He knows how perfect I am for him." She straightened her shoulders. "He needs someone who understands him, who will be an asset to him and his career. I can do all that. I can take care of his needs, but he won't let me. He just won't let me. Just like Jordan."

"What about Jordan?" Desiree asked.

"Jordan's kids will have to go, too. They'll have to be punished."

Fear streaked through Desiree. "Emily. They have nothing to do with this."

Emily pulled Desiree to the shelves and tied her to them. Gerard would see her as soon as he entered from the door leading to the house.

Emily was winded and struggled for breath. "You're here because of them. If they weren't here, you would never have come." She narrowed her eyes, looked critically between Desiree and the door. "That should do it."

"What are you going to do?" Desiree asked.

The shrill ring of Emily's laugh sent goose bumps through Desiree. "Kill you, of course."

"You're sick. You need help."

"I don't need any help. You need help. People just don't understand my brilliance."

Desiree knew there was only so much reasoning you could do with a delusional person. When she'd tried to reason with her father when he was off his medication, the conversations ultimately made no sense.

She heard noises outside and hoped Gerard would realize she wasn't in bed and come searching for her. But the quicker he came, the more danger they would encounter.

Why should he search in the first place? He probably thought she went home to her own bed. Everything would have been all right if she'd stayed in bed with him. After all, like a fool she'd slept with him. Now she'd endangered both their lives.

Gerard watched the streets closely as Levi drove to Desiree's.

"Slow down," Gerard said suddenly.

"What is it?" Levi asked.

"Back up. Back up."

"What's going on?" Levi asked as he backed up the car. Joseph had stopped several paces behind him.

"That looks like Emily's car."

Gerard hopped out the door and glanced around. It *was* her car. He scouted the area carefully, but saw nothing.

"She's hiding near here."

Levi burned rubber getting to Desiree's house.

They went through her house from top to bottom. They checked every closet. The garage. The guesthouse. Around every shrub and bush. Everything. Still no Desiree or Emily. Only Desiree's car parked in the driveway.

Gerard stood in the yard looking toward his house when Levi approached him, Joseph at his side. "There's your place. You lock the door?"

"I tore out of the house so quickly, I don't remember," he said, jogging toward his own house.

The door was unlocked. He immediately went to his bedroom. It looked as it did when he'd left. With Emily's father's help, they checked each room. Again, nothing.

Emily's father opened the garage door.

"Light's to the right," Gerard said. He popped on the light.

"What the . . ." the older man started, and Gerard shoved him aside. He bumped into something. Straight ahead was Desiree, tied to the built-in wooden storage shelves.

To the right Joseph was fighting with Emily for a gun.

And then she had the gun in her hand. "Back up."

"I can't let you kill anybody," he said, using the SUV and his body to block her view.

She sneered. "You're nothing to me."

"I love you, girl."

"Oh no, you don't. You weren't there. You left me for your other family. Your other wife and kid. We didn't mean anything to you."

"I wanted to be there, believe me I wanted to. Your mother kept me away. And I've tried to reach you since you were eighteen. But you wouldn't have anything to do with me. I've visited. You wouldn't open the door. I've sent letters. I've called. I've tried everything."

"You left us. And I didn't need you anymore."

"I left your mother. I never left you."

"You've ruined everything. I don't need you now. Move, or I'll shoot you."

"You're gonna have to shoot me. I'm not letting you shoot that girl. There's still a chance for you. You haven't killed anyone."

While they argued, Gerard eased back to untie Desiree, then pulled her safely behind the vehicles while Levi moved stealthily around the other side to get in back of Emily. He felt certain she was going to shoot her father.

Levi reached Emily and yanked her arm upward. A shot fired into the ceiling. In a second, he had the gun out of her hand and shoved her to the floor, putting his knee in the center of her back.

"Don't hurt her," Joseph said.

Levi wouldn't dignify that with a response. Emily was

going to kill his daughter. But when he looked into the man's haunted eyes, Joseph gazed back with a father's heart, love, and disappointment. Levi was a father, too. He eased up a little, but not enough for her to escape. Never that.

"Everything under control over there?" Gerard asked.

"Yeah," Levi said. Then his daughter came around the corner. He wanted to hold her in his arms, but he didn't. He kept Emily where she was. And he continued to do so until the police arrived.

Gerard had gone into the house to call them.

After the police left, Levi finally left for Macon. They'd discovered that Jordan, Beverly, and Steven's parents had actually been in an accident. Emily had not killed them.

It had been really late when they settled down. Desiree didn't feel like being alone in that huge house and she'd spent the night wrapped in Gerard's arms.

They were both up early the next morning and prepared breakfast together. Desiree was a little shaky, a little nervous. Gerard kept watching her. Every time she turned around he was watching her.

"What is it?" she finally snapped.

"I could have lost you last night."

"It's over." She rubbed her brow. "I don't even want to think about it."

"I need to talk about it."

"Gerard—"

"Just hear me out, okay? You were right. I've never said this to a woman, Desiree, but I love you."

"What we went through with Emily was traumatic. This is just the aftereffects of that. Trust me, in a couple of weeks, you'll wish you'd never said that."

"Just listen to me, okay?"

"Gerard, I can't go through with this. We are still going

our separate ways. I needed you last night. I know it's selfish, but I didn't want to be alone."

"If that was the case, you would have gone to Macon with your father, but you didn't. He asked you to. In Macon your family would have surrounded you. But you chose me."

She all but tossed the filled plate on the table. "Okay, so I wanted to be with you, so sue me."

"It's more than that." He massaged her tense shoulders, then tugged her gently in his arms. "I love you, Desiree. I guess I was afraid of failure."

"That's a laugh. You're so successful." She tried to ease out of his embrace, but his arms felt so comforting it was painful.

"Stop struggling for a moment and sit down." He took the utensils out of her hand and led her to a chair. He pulled his own chair out and sat facing her.

"I'm not talking about work, I'm talking about failure as a man. I was always afraid of not being good enough. That as long as I kept women at a distance, I didn't have to worry about failing them or myself—of not being able to live up to their expectations. And in this business it's easy because it's all about the athlete."

"I know that."

"What you don't know is that strategy works just fine when you don't love the women. But, Desiree, I fell in love with you and it all changed. Scared the pants off me. For once I had to measure up. And that night at my parents' barbecue when you were talking to Justin, I realized your opinion of athletes wasn't too high. All my life I've battled with my family about my choice of career. My mother hated it most of all. I thought she never accepted the fact that I play ball and I didn't pursue medical school. I couldn't give you up, but I couldn't live with being viewed as someone less because of it."

"I don't think less of you, Gerard. Nor do I think less of the players, especially my clients. What's important is that you choose a career you love and you're the best you can be at it. And I see that in you. I'm not snobbish. You're good at sports. You're better with people. But if you needed to do something else you have skills, you have an education that will let you take other paths. My problem comes with someone feeling that this is it, and when they don't consider a backup plan."

"Desiree, that's true with any career."

She nodded. "You're right. Look at me. I never thought I'd teach budgeting skills."

"The other problem is I'm away so often."

"You're here when we need you."

He leaned back in his chair. "I guess there are no more arguments. I love you, Desiree. Will you marry me?"

"There are a lot of us. Are you ready for it?"

"Yes."

"Then I'll marry you," she whispered, and found herself gathered in his strong arms. He held on to her as if he'd never let her go. After becoming a mother of four children, she never believed something this wonderful could happen to her. With a whoop he lifted her into the air and swirled her around. Desiree laughed freely, a heavy weight falling from her shoulders. She wrapped her legs tightly around him.

Gerard groaned, buried his face in her neck. "Let's go celebrate, and then we'll go to Macon and tell the children."

Dear Reader,

I hope you enjoyed your time with Desiree and Gerard. In *Bittersweet,* I chose a more urban setting than my usual tales of small town life, but it is still centered around family life and its complexities. Atlanta is a fascinating city and offers so many opportunities for African Americans.

I know many people feel that a relationship with a sports figure is doomed to failure, but I think people make choices whatever their career. In this case, the sport doesn't make the man. Even stars have their bitter moments. So I hope you feel Desiree and Gerard will live a full and meaningful life together.

Please travel with me to a fictitious island near Virginia Beach, Virginia, and go treasure hunting in my next novel, *Out of the Past,* which is part of a three-book "Quest for the Golden Bowl" series. It promises to bring you lots of intrigue and fascinating twists and turns, and it turns up the volume on sultry, sizzling heat.

Readers like you give me confidence to try new things. Please accept my heartfelt thanks for your support and for so many kind and uplifting letters and e-mails.

I love hearing from readers. Please visit my new web page at: members.cox.net/candicepoarch

My new e-mail address: candicepoarch@cox.net

You may write to me at: P.O. Box 291, Springfield, VA 22150.

> With warm regards,
> Candice Poarch

Discussion Questions

1. Which character did you feel the most sympathy for? Why did that character affect you?

2. Sacrifice is one theme of *Bittersweet*. What did each of the primary characters sacrifice for someone or something else?

3. How does falling in love with a celebrity affect a relationship? What is it about Desiree that will help her cope with her husband when he isn't thought of as a regular person but as a notch on someone's belt?

4. Desiree made choices that totally interrupted her life. She has given up all her dreams. Instead of hiring extremely competent people to take care of these children, she does it herself. She's using skills she didn't know she possessed and has gotten into a situation totally foreign to her. Is this expected of women? Why not men?

5. Why not let her aunt take care of the children? Under many circumstances, the aunt is someone who would be expected to do so. Who's more important, Levi or his grandchildren?

6. Everyone in *Bittersweet* is on the verge of some kind of change. What changes does each of the characters go through, and how do all these changes affect the other characters?

7. The hero in *Bittersweet* has a different set of changes. Other than the fact that he's falling in love with Desiree, what do you think drives him to be so close to that family?

8. How does Steven fit in with the extended family? Is this part of a tradition of taking people in? A way of handling things in a community? How do you think

he feels thrust in this family situation since he was an only child?

9. Everyone in *Bittersweet* is thrust into a situation they never thought they would be a part of. How do you think each person feels about it? How do the different attitudes affect the way each reacts to the situation?

10. Discuss Desiree's unresolved issues regarding her family. Is she trying to make a family different from the one she had? She didn't have the perfect family growing up. Is she trying to recreate that?

11. Jacqueline is the farthest from this situation. The children are a product of a relationship her ex-husband had before he met her. What does this have to do with her except that it disrupts her daughter's life?

12. Does the life Levi chose work for him? Could his relationship with Jacqueline have ever survived?

13. What kind of bond is there between Levi and his sister? Why is this bond so close?

14. How would you react to a relationship with someone who is rich and famous? How would it affect your life? What would you be willing to do to keep that relationship? What might make you abandon it?